By the Red Glare

STORY RIVER BOOKS

PAT CONROY, EDITOR AT LARGE

BY THE
RED GLARE

| **A NOVEL** |

John Mark Sibley-Jones

FOREWORD BY MARION LUCAS

The University of South Carolina Press

© 2014 University of South Carolina

Published by the University of South Carolina Press
Columbia, South Carolina 29208

www.sc.edu/uscpress

Manufactured in the United States of America

23 22 21 20 19 18 17 16 15 14
10 9 8 7 6 5 4 3 2 1

Library of Congress Cataloging-in-Publication Data
Sibley-Jones, John Mark.
By the red glare : a novel / John Mark Sibley-Jones.
pages cm. — (Story River Books)
ISBN 978-1-61117-399-4 (hardbound : alk. paper) —
ISBN 978-1-61117-400-7 (ebook)   1. United States—
History—Civil War, 1861-1865—Fiction. I. Title.
PS3619.I254B9 2014
813'.6—c23
2013041126

This book was printed on a recycled paper with
30 percent postconsumer waste content.

For Julia

On one side the sky was illuminated by the burning of Gen. Hampton's residence a few miles off in the country, on the other side by some blazing buildings near the river. . . . Sumter Street was brightly lighted by a burning house so near our piazza that we could feel the heat. By the red glare we could watch the wretches walking—generally staggering—back and forth from the camp to the town—shouting—hurrahing—cursing South Carolina—swearing —blaspheming—singing ribald songs and using such obscene language that we were forced to go indoors.

When the World Ended: The Diary of Emma LeConte

CONTENTS

PART III

January 1865

PART IV

February 1865

FOREWORD

Long before Union general William Tecumseh Sherman left Atlanta, Georgia, in November 1864 on his famous march to the sea, the reports reaching the South Carolina capital were that Sherman intended to torch Columbia. Refugees fleeing Sherman's army in Georgia poured into the Palmetto State, recounting stories of savagery and destruction. Sherman, they assured frightened Columbians, was on his way—determined to burn "the cradle of secession," the place where all of this began.

Against this backdrop of widespread fear and sectional animosity, John Mark Sibley-Jones transports us into the thick of his vision of Columbia on the eve of destruction in this craftily written and thoroughly researched historical novel, *By the Red Glare*. In a seamless blending of art and history, Sibley-Jones combines a handful of Columbia's famous residents during the closing days of the Civil War with inventive fictional characters who carry the moving narrative of love, ambition, and ideals overshadowed by the looming power of historical events larger than any individual can truly fathom.

Much of *By the Red Glare* is set at the temporary Confederate hospitals on South Carolina College's campus, the site of the modern-day University of South Carolina. It is no surprise that the facilities are desperately short of medical supplies and overcrowded with injured Confederate soldiers and Union prisoners. Two of the novel's principal protagonists—devoted surgeon Dr. Thompson and tireless administrator Joseph Crawford, both fictional—labor in hospitals on the campus's iconic historic Horseshoe. Louisa Cheves McCord—a real-life strong-minded widow who has already given her only son to the Confederate cause—serves as the hospital's head nurse. Born into one of South Carolina's wealthier families, Louisa is a brilliant intellectual who successfully built a reputation as a classical economist in a state long dominated by males. Meanwhile, the fictional Meredith

Simpson—a sympathetic, dedicated, common-sense nurse—refuses to be intimidated by her aristocratic supervisor who wishes to define her station in life. Through the eyes and personalities of these major characters, Sibley-Jones skillfully guides readers through the South Carolina College campus, carefully describing every building as well as a handful of professors who remained on campus.

Here readers also encounter professor of belles-lettres Maximilian LaBorde, who views the disruption of his beloved campus by the Confederate cause with displeasure; highly respected chemistry professor, Joseph LeConte, director of the Confederate Niter and Mining Bureau at the college's laboratory; and LeConte's precocious teenage daughter Emma, who strolls daily through campus, always with a book in hand.

Sibley-Jones also provides a vivid picture of Columbia during the three weeks before Sherman and the Union army arrives. Thompson and Crawford tour downtown Columbia in a carriage shared with Benjamin F. Perry, one of the state's few reluctant secessionists. Eventually siding with his home state, Perry remains uneasy—aware, as his fellow citizens seem not to be, that it is easier to start a war than to end it. The tour terminates at the home of South Carolina's famous diarist, Mary Boykin Chesnut, where the three gentlemen join Mrs. Chesnut, her husband General James Chesnut, Jr., Louisa McCord, and several others in spirited conversation and debate.

Once Sherman enters South Carolina, his army moves inexorably, virtually unopposed, toward Columbia. Meanwhile city leaders wonder why no preparations are underway to defend the capital. Repeated demands that Confederate officials in Richmond, Virginia, send reinforcements bring only General Wade Hampton, General P. T. G. Beauregard, and a token cavalry force. Even so, just three days before the Union army enters Columbia, Mayor Thomas Jefferson Goodwyn, as instructed by Confederate military authorities, assures Columbians that the city is safe.

Sibley-Jones vividly describes the chaos that reigns in Columbia as civil and military authority crumbles during the next three days. Artillery blasts heard in the distance signal a mad rush to evacuate the city. An unruly mob descends upon the railroad station as panic-stricken passengers fight for seats. Last-minute efforts to pack and remove Confederate and state military and commissary stores are largely unsuccessful. But surprisingly the evacuation of Union prisoners is successful, with only a handful escaping to greet Sherman's arrival.

The disorder and confusion in Columbia leads authorities to declare martial law on February 15. That same night the situation deteriorates when Confederate troops enter Columbia, break into stores, and grab whatever they want. Soldiers and townspeople soon discover large quantities of whiskey and wine stored throughout the city. During the next two nights of February 16 and 17, Confederate stragglers and the town's rabble plunder the city and the first cries of fire are heard. Such is the confusion when Mayor Goodwyn and the aldermen, carrying a white flag, ride to the edge of town and surrender Columbia at ten o'clock on the morning of February 17, 1865.

As Federal soldiers enter Columbia that chilly, windy day, inhabitants greet them with bottles of wine and whiskey. In the late afternoon, increasing numbers of soldiers become intoxicated, and by nightfall a riot breaks out on the streets as drunken Union soldiers enter homes, intimidate citizens, and steal whatever is handy. Sometime around eight o'clock that night, a blazing fire, initially driven by strong winds, races across the center of town. Some soldiers spread the flames; others fight the fire. It is a night of unforgettable tragedy for most Columbians. By daybreak, one-third of South Carolina's capital is in ashes.

In one of the novel's most poignant scenes, Sibley-Jones captures Louisa McCord's resolute belief and unshakeable faith in the superiority of southern civilization even while her home is being ransacked by unruly Union troops. In sharp contrast to her harsh reaction is the obvious kindness of Union general Oliver Otis Howard. Sibley-Jones's description of Dr. Robert W. Gibbes's tragedy is equally graphic. His home, burned to the ground by Yankee soldiers, contained a host of irreplaceable manuscripts and local historical documents, an impressive library, and valuable collections of fossils and rare coins.

Finally, juxtaposed against the violence and destruction, readers will encounter a series of romances as characters struggle to establish connections with one another for the future as the past and present go up in flames around them. *By the Red Glare* is, at its heart, a very human story of representative lives lost and remade against a sweeping historical backdrop of a city ablaze and a divided nation facing an uncertain transformative future.

Marion B. Lucas

ACKNOWLEDGMENTS

For this book I owe a great debt to many people who can be sorted into three groups: the dead, the living I don't know personally, the living I cherish. I'll start with the dead, as they are least likely to take offense (at least none I'd be made aware of) at the contents of the story. The great Confederate surgeon J. J. Chisolm had not only a great medical mind but also an elegant pen. His *A manual of military surgery for the use of surgeons in the Confederate States Army* is a fascinating account of Civil War medical knowledge, diagnoses, treatments, and rather gruesome reports of surgical procedures. I could not have written any of the surgical or doctor/nurse-patient bedside scenes without the aid of his book. The following works offer valuable insights into the character of life for many Columbia citizens during the war and especially throughout the terrifying ordeal of the city's burning: Mrs. Campbell Bryce's *Reminiscences of the hospitals of Columbia, SC during the four years of the Civil War* and her *Personal experiences . . . during the burning of Columbia, SC by General WT Sherman's army February 17, 1865; The Autobiography of Joseph LeConte* and LeConte's *'Ware Sherman: A Journal of three Month's Personal Experience in the Last Days of the Confederacy.* LeConte was exceptional: superb athlete, brilliant scientist, playful adventurer, Renaissance man. If I'd lived back then, I might have majored in chemistry for the sole purpose of being his student. Maximilian LaBorde's *History of the South Carolina College* offers an intriguing account of the personalities that shaped the college from its inception. Of course, Mary Boykin Chesnut's monumental chronicle and Emma LeConte's brief but impassioned diary are indispensable.

Contemporary scholars whose works have been helpful include Peter McCandless, Charles Royster, Jessie Melville Fraser, Tom Elmore, and Mark Smith. McCandless's *Moonlight, Magnolias, & Madness: Insanity in South Carolina from the Colonial Period to the Progressive Era* helped me to understand the interplay between racism and medical diagnosis in the ante-bellum era and gave me both the idea and the historical credibility for Jim's character. Royster's *The Destructive War: William Tecumseh Sherman, Stonewall Jackson, and the Americans* offers a gripping narrative of the events leading up to and including the burning of Columbia. Fraser's thesis on Louisa Cheves McCord is a beautifully written piece that details McCord's home life from birth to death and her remarkable intellectual achievements. Fraser's work led me to several of McCord's articles published in various journals between 1849 and 1857. It's hard to believe that a book on a city's historical landmarks can be riveting, but Tom Elmore pulls it off in his *Columbia Civil War Landmarks*. He opened my eyes to the haunting history of a city I've lived in for thirty years. Mark Smith's *Debating Slavery: Economy and Society in the Antebellum American South* and *Sensing the Past: Seeing, Hearing, Smelling, Tasting, and Touching in History* fired my imagination from the get-go. Smith's ability to re-create a landscape and to place his readers there is magical. The man can write.

Finally, thanks to the wonderfully kind and generous librarians at South Caroliniana Library; to Linda Fogle at USC Press for her encouragement and guidance; to Mom for demonstrating over the course of her thirty-year career as a writer a hallowed respect for the wonder of words; to my father-in-law for getting me hooked on Civil War history more than a decade ago; to Don Greiner for his brilliance with that damnable red editing pen of his (on a previous unpublished novel) that helped me hone the craft; to my brother, Eric Jones, for reading and improving the quality of the work; to my buddy George Singleton for telling me time and again that writing fiction is a ten-year gamble with yourself, and for his thirty-eight-year friendship through thick, thin, and murky; to Spencer, Jack, and Emma, my great joys; and to Julia, without whom nothing.

| PART I |
November 1864

| 1 |
The Lunatic

The tree to which Jim Wells was chained stood dead-center in the front yard of his father's sprawling plantation in Greenville. For nine years the declivities of earth surrounding the tree had provided shelter for young Wells. His father had put him there. Mr. Wells told his wife it was the safest place for their deranged son.

Each winter, Jim clawed with his fingers deep recesses around the base of the towering oak, giving the habitat the appearance of a fortress with moats on all sides. His mother gave him two thick, coarse blankets. He burrowed like a mole into the earth and formed with the dirt-encrusted coverings a seamless wedge with the ground. The oak stood fast against the wind when it blew in a more or less angular direction. When it swirled and twisted like a snake around branches and trunk, the wind bit into his flesh. Then he curled into his body.

The temperature of the soil remained at a near constant throughout the harsh months. With other natural provisions—twigs, bark, leaves fresh in autumn, decayed by late November—and his mother's care with the blankets (she scrubbed them once a week), Jim made a home for himself. When rain or snow fell, Jim's father unhinged him from the tree and, tugging with both hands on the far end of the chain, dragged his howling son some twenty-five yards through mud and slush, and then kicked the boy's legs and buttocks until he squirmed under the house. Release from the dark place came when the sun emerged from hiding. Mr. Wells unlocked the hovel he'd built with his own hands and pulled Jim back over the same terrain to his abode.

Jim liked the smell of earth. He liked its taste. Not in mouthfuls, but with gentle laps of his tongue he savored the fecundity of dirt. With his molars he cracked nuts. He studied the chiseling jaws of squirrels.

The only creature on the plantation that showed Jim any human kindness was Rachel, a half-wit slave born on the plantation eighteen years earlier. She dipped water from the well and brought him the ladle every night after Jim's father and mother went to bed. It was risky, she knew, for she had seen what happened to slaves who disobeyed their master. Mr. Wells had made it clear that he alone would feed the boy. That meant that Jim might miss a meal and go thirsty if his mutterings agitated his father. But on those nights when Jim went hungry and he stabbed at his parched lips with a dry tongue, Rachel sneaked under cover of darkness to the tree and pulled scraps of bread from a pocket of her dress and tilted the ladle to his mouth. They sat facing each other, each wondering in dumb silence at the similarity of their features. Except for the difference in the color of their skin they might have passed for siblings. And even that difference was slight: her complexion was light; his was tawny and leathery, the result of perpetual exposure to the elements. Both were of medium height, thin but muscular. The marvel of their being in physical proximity was that Rachel's features—the sheen of her dark eyes, the sleekness of her neck, the hue and texture of her skin, even the scar that his father's foreman had carved with the whip years earlier and that ran from her left shoulder to just below the scapula—had a calming effect on Jim. In her presence, he was content.

On spring evenings when Mr. and Mrs. Wells sat in their rockers on the veranda of their spacious home, Rachel crouched behind a row of shrubs and watched. When Jim's moans interrupted his parents' conversation, his father went into the house and returned with a short leather strap. Mrs. Wells pleaded with him not to be too rough. Brutality made her squeamish. He assured her that the strap served only as a corrective measure.

From her place of hiding, Rachel cringed and whimpered each time the leather strap scored Jim's flesh.

Yet no matter how painful the strap might be, it was nothing in comparison to the long and tasseled whip with which Mr. Wells's foreman taught rebellious slaves their Christian duty of submission. How devilish Negroes could be, how inured to the punishment required to enforce obedience. Too often, Mr. Wells thought, he'd had to stand by his foreman straining his voice to declaim Scripture above the lash of cord and striping of flesh.

When the beatings occurred, Jim sat like a toad at the base of the tree and watched impassively. Until Rachel was caught. That evening, Jim provoked his father. "Stop grunting like a pig," Mr. Wells said. He hit Jim four times with the strap, then told the cowering boy he would go without food and water until morning. Later, when the couple retired for the evening, Rachel came with her pocket of crusty bread and ladle of water. Before she lifted the ladle to Jim's lips, Mr. Wells jerked open the front door. He raced to the tree and backhanded her. She fell unconscious into one of the holes Jim had dug. Jim howled. The strap cut into his back.

The next morning at sunrise Mr. Wells stood beside the whipping post with his Bible in hand while his foreman strung Rachel up and stripped her blouse from her shoulders. Her body trembled. Mr. Wells began the reading—"Slaves, be obedient to them"—as the whip fell and opened a gash beneath her neck—"that are your masters according to the flesh"—another stripe, then dripping rivulets of blood—"with fear and trembling in single-ness of your heart"—the third lash gaped the wound and Rachel yelped as blood pooled at the waistline of her skirt—"as unto Christ; not with eye service, as men-pleasers"—the whip struck her neck and her head jerked backward—"but as slaves of Christ, doing the will of God from the heart."

Jim could not watch any longer. He stuck his head in one of the holes and clawed until his head was covered with dirt. He imagined sinking his teeth into his father's neck, as he'd seen wild dogs do to each other.

Mr. Wells raised his hand for the whipping to stop not long after Rachel fainted. The foreman expressed his fear that other slaves would learn nothing from such merciful treatment of the girl. Mr. Wells ignored him. He was grateful that Rachel had not wailed as much as others under the whip. Caustic sounds made by the beaten irritated him. Their exaggerated cries accosted his ears with a ringing sensation that caused him headaches and exhausted him before nightfall. Would these dark creatures but heed the sacred word, Wells lamented, he would be free of such troublesome duties.

Except for his son's redemption, Wells desired most that his slaves would attain a purity of heart that compelled them to do the will of God day in and day out. He dreamed of a world in which there were no whips, no need of corrective procedures, or of the divine call to enforce discipline. Sometimes he wondered whether his failure to be a more devout master was at once the cause of his slaves' recalcitrance and of his son's lunacy: God's punishment for the sins of the father. Indeed, was it not the duty of the master to be a father to all subordinates on the plantation?

| 2 |

The Steward

Joseph Crawford needed opium. His amputees pleaded for it. Chloroform served well enough for surgery, but it was no match for prolonged pain and the putrefaction of dead flesh. The overflow of wounded sent from hospitals in Richmond, Petersburg, and Augusta to the Columbia hospital taxed the pharmacy's supplies as well as the resolve of the wounded. Joseph prayed for a delivery of the narcotic as he entered the ward in Rutledge.

In spite of all the blood spilled on these floors since he had arrived nearly two years ago, the place still had the feel of a college campus. Not even a governor's orders could wholly convert halls of learning to wards of healing any more than a surgeon could reattach severed limbs or implant the will to live in soldiers haunted by the cries of the dead.

Joseph removed his coat and shook off the chill of the November morning as he listened to a nurse recount the night's activities. "Blevins is worse," the young woman said. He couldn't remember her name. He thought she was one of many who volunteered at the hospital the day after Jefferson Davis spoke to the city from the front porch of the Chesnut home nearly six weeks ago. That October morning, several hundred people filled every room and hallway of the house, stood three abreast on the stairwell, and spilled out onto the front lawn. Even now Joseph could see the president grip the rail of the front porch with one hand and shake the other fist in the air as he thundered: "I say to my young friends here, if you want the right man for a husband, take him whose armless sleeve and noble heart betoken the duties that he has rendered to his country, rather than he who has never shared the toils, or borne the dangers of the field."

The next day, more than thirty women appeared at the hospital. Joseph wondered how many were there to find husbands. Whether they came for love or duty, he did not care. He was grateful for their service either way. More grateful yet that they worked under the strict supervision of Louisa Cheves McCord. Hers was the only name he recalled day after day, hers the only face—other than those of his dead wife and child—imprinted on the canvas of his memory.

Joseph said, "Blevins was fine last night. What happened?"

The woman's shoulders drew inward and she lowered her head like a turtle seeking the protection of her shell. She couldn't be more than eighteen, Joseph thought.

"I'm not accusing you of negligence," he said. "An increase in the severity of pain during the night is not unusual."

"Mrs. McCord says I do well with the soldiers." Her voice suggested an even younger age than Joseph had guessed.

"Of course you do. Now tell me what happened."

The nurse explained that Blevins became restless late in the night. She checked on him. He made no particular complaint, only of general discomfort. But two hours before dawn he began to rant mindlessly. He wrapped himself in his sheets, then struggled to extricate himself, and repeated the procedure. His pulse quickened. To the touch, his flesh was clammy.

"And the arm?" Joseph asked.

"I changed the bandage. He complained about that, so I checked to make sure it was not wrapped too tightly."

Joseph looked at the woman's thin face, resisted the impulse to ask her why she hadn't removed the bandage again to examine the stump. He knew how difficult it was for some of the women to look at these mangled bodies. That they even made the effort was, in some measure, meritorious. He thanked the woman for her help and walked down the corridor.

In the room Blevins and three other soldiers lay on their respective cots. One of them, a man with a grizzled beard, stared vacantly at the ceiling. His left leg had been amputated above the knee two weeks earlier. He had not spoken since the operation.

Two others faced each other, propped on elbows, playing cards. A cigarette dangled from the mouth of the younger one.

Blevins looked through pallid eyes at Joseph.

"How are you, son?" Joseph asked.

"Hurts," he croaked, and with his right hand reached across his body to stroke the phantom arm.

Blevins had told his story to Joseph more than once, as if the retelling itself might enable him to make sense of all the horror he'd seen. He'd joined a regiment in Tennessee a month before his seventeenth birthday so that he could march with his older brother. They fought together under General Bragg at Chickamauga, where the elder took a bullet in the neck and died looking into his brother's mud-caked face and gurgling his name.

Fourteen months later, a bullet shattered Blevins's forearm as he fought under Lee at Petersburg. A field surgeon sawed off the arm at the elbow. The following evening, Blevins slept in the Richmond Hospital. It was the first night in two years he'd not slept on the ground.

Initially the procedure appeared a success. Blevins was among those healthy enough to endure transport to Columbia. With the few convalescents who were able, he hobbled the half-mile from the depot to the hospital.

Blevins held his hand above the stump. "Feels heavy. And hot, like fire shooting through."

Joseph removed his coat and examined the wrap for seepage. Lately, he'd done more than his share of bandaging wounds. In the early months of his appointment, his primary responsibility was to administer the running of the hospital. With the exception of the surgeons, all other personnel answered to him. He made purchases for the facility, took care of the hospital stores and of the dispensary, put up prescriptions, saw to the burial of the dead, made sure their graves were marked. Only occasionally did he assist in the dressing of wounds. In the latter months of 1864, however, the demand for patient care had overwhelmed his administrative duties.

With care Joseph unwound the bandage. He winced when Blevins sucked air through his teeth. Joseph had never been able to adopt the surgeon's calm detachment in the face of human suffering. At each grimace from the patient, the steward felt the need to apologize.

The stump looked awful. Hard and swollen, it discharged a thin, gleety liquid colored with blood and little masses that looked like clumps of grits. Over the course of the night, the limb had swollen to twice its normal size. The skin was tense and almost translucent, purpled veins prominent on the surface. Sweat dripped from Blevins's body. His pulse was weak. He struggled to breathe.

"Stay with me, son," Joseph said. "I must go for Dr. Thompson."

Blevins's voice shook. "I'm dying, ain't I, sir?"

"You're not dying," Joseph said. "I'll return shortly."

In the hallway, he asked another nurse whether she'd seen Dr. Thompson.

"He was called to Hospital Three before dawn," she said.

"Tend to Blevins," he said. "The arm needs repair."

Joseph ran from Rutledge Building two blocks southward to College Hall, where Dr. Thompson spent most of his time. The hall had been converted to the third campus hospital in August of 1862, under orders from the medical director of the Confederacy to increase accommodations by 300. Buildings on the south side of campus—Rutledge, Legare, Pinckney—had their own surgeons-in-charge and division surgeons, as did those on the north side—DeSaussure, Harper, and Elliott.

Like Joseph, Thompson initially was an administrator, assigning daily operations to division surgeons, and then only at his own post. Exigencies of war augmented his duties and his frenetic movement from one hospital to the next.

Joseph hoped Thompson would not be in the middle of another surgery when he arrived. Blevins's slim hope of survival depended on immediate care.

Minutes later, Joseph found the doctor. Elbows propped on his desk, head resting in the palms of his hands, he appeared to be asleep. Blood stains covered his white coat.

"Sir?" As if by some trick of ventriloquism, Joseph conveyed in a quiet and soothing voice a sense of urgency.

Thompson's shoulders jerked. His head slipped from the perch of his hands. He rubbed his eyes and brought Joseph into focus.

"Forgive me, sir. It's Blevins."

"The arm?" Thompson's voice was dull with fatigue.

"Gangrene has set in."

Thompson shook his head. "How many times have we seen this, Joseph? I've come to expect it of our amputees."

"Yes, sir." Joseph moved forward to help the elder man out of his chair. Of all the surgeons he'd met and worked with the past two years, he preferred Thompson. They worked well together. When Thompson gave orders, he never spoke with condescension or a tone of impatience. The surgeon's manner quickly earned Joseph's loyalty. Staff members and volunteers learned never to question Thompson's decisions or methodology in Joseph's presence. A pharmacist had done so in May of 1863—behind the doctor's back—in an attempt to impress a nurse. Joseph overheard the conversation and summarily dismissed the man from his position.

The men walked briskly toward Rutledge. Side-by-side, their physical differences were accentuated. At just over six feet tall and with a long stride and erect posture, Joseph dwarfed his companion. Thompson was of average height, but with shoulders hunched as if he were contending against a stiff wind, his gaze directly on the ground before him, he seemed much smaller. While Joseph's thin frame was well-proportioned, suggesting wiry strength and agility, Thompson looked frail. Joseph's thick brown hair provided such a stark contrast to Thompson's gray head that the difference between their ages seemed greater than the twenty years that separated them.

Thompson lifted his head and looked at Joseph. "Is it your impression that we shall have to take the arm at the shoulder?" he asked.

"I believe so, sir." Joseph knew the doctor had made his decision already. Not that Thompson, like many Confederate surgeons—particularly those in the field—preferred amputation as the most expedient measure, but he trusted and had listened carefully to the results of Joseph's examination. Joseph appreciated the doctor's confidence.

"Our supply of chloroform?" Thompson asked.

"We need more."

"Opium?"

"I hope for another shipment today."

They turned into Rutledge and raced up the stairs. With a precision that Joseph admired, Thompson examined the arm, then told the soldier what had to be done.

"Reckon this stump wouldn't have done me much good, no ways," Blevins said. Only his agnostic eyes betrayed the attempt at bravery.

Joseph applied the rag of chloroform. When Blevins was unconscious, the surgeon took his scalpel in hand and began to cut through flesh and tissue. For the bone, he would need the saw.

| 3 |

Sawbones

Dr. Thompson braced himself with a foot on the edge of the table and thrust a finger into the open artery. Joseph marveled at the speed and efficiency with which Thompson had amputated the upper arm. All other space in the room occupied, Joseph placed in the window sill the nine-inch stump, then once more pressed the rag of chloroform to Blevins's nose.

Thompson jerked his head in a vain effort to divert runnels of perspiration that clouded his vision. His finger slipped. Blood spurted like a fountain and painted the doctor's shirt.

The lower torso bucked. Joseph had seen enough convulsions to know that these were involuntary. He knew also that later that night he would be visited by dreams. Intermittent at first—often a reprieve of many weeks between disturbances—lately they'd begun to recur with savage regularity. Severed limbs. Blood-pooled floors. Befouled sheets. Disembodied voices, as though emissaries from beyond the grave were seeking to convert Joseph, make him an apostle of dark visions.

From the doorway came the voice that Joseph had come to detest: "Man, how dare you open that wound alone, and without the necessary preparations."

Dare, indeed. The only unwarranted dare in the room was LaBorde's challenge to a superior surgeon. *Take off your dandy coat, roll up your sleeves, and help,* Joseph wanted to say. He wondered whether Louisa McCord had sent for the professor. Emergency procedures had become so routine that it was not uncommon for all the surgeons to be simultaneously engaged. LaBorde would have to do.

"Enough," said Thompson, with a nod toward Joseph's hand.

Joseph lifted the rag and looked at LaBorde. The professor still had on his long coat. Could he not be bothered with blood and viscera? Could these effete professors do nothing more than pontificate in a classroom?

LaBorde approached the table. "What may I do?" he asked.

Thompson struggled to stanch the flow of blood. He shook his head wearily. Joseph watched as the surgeon's hands trembled. Fatigue had worn him down. He was not fit to operate.

"Can you sew him up?" asked Thompson.

"If you guide me," said LaBorde. "I've not done this since medical school."

LaBorde shed his coat as Joseph pulled from a nearby drawer the necessary instruments: clamps, needle, ligatures. He laid them out, grabbed towels from a wooden bin, dropped to his knees, and began to clean the floor.

As he mopped up the blood, Joseph silently berated himself. LaBorde was no villain. He had done as much for the Confederacy as any man. And he was no dilettante. Thompson had told Joseph the professor's story. By means of a capacious intellect, Maximilian LaBorde had achieved much.

Graduated from the South Carolina College at the age of sixteen; thereafter studied law; soon turned his attention to the study of medicine and took his degree from the Medical College of Charleston at the age of twenty-two; literary tastes prevailing, established and edited a weekly paper, *The Edgefield Advertiser*, and at the same time opened and attended to the oversight of a drug store. The man's energy and industry were boundless.

When Joseph first arrived in Columbia, he'd admired LaBorde. His reputation as Professor of Belles-lettres at the South Carolina College could hardly be exceeded. Yet what had come to irritate Joseph was the professor's proprietary regard for the college. He'd never wanted it closed, not even in March of 1862, when only nine students under the age of conscription were left. Twice LaBorde refused the request of General Beauregard to use the college as a hospital. The general went to Governor Pickens, who ruled in the Confederacy's favor. LaBorde never ceased to show his displeasure. He complained to anyone who would listen that the army allowed horses, cows, hogs, goats, and sheep to roam the campus, destroying grass and trees, marking the turf with their dung, defiling the air with their odor. Joseph didn't care to see cow paddies and other animal excrement on the lawn either—he detested the stench—but he believed that no man should stand in the way of the Confederacy's needs.

Thompson had encouraged him to be sympathetic to LaBorde's devotion to the college. Since the departure of the students, the man had been deprived not merely of his vocation, but of his living. No professor at the college had received a salary since the summer of 1862. The legislature's assurance that salaries would be paid retroactively in full at the conclusion of the war now seemed as uncertain as the Confederate economy itself. LaBorde had reason to be disgruntled.

Joseph shook his head, told himself the professor was not the cause of his vexation. It was the war he hated. The war and these mutilated bodies. And the most insidious effect of all: the endless reach of war's tentacles. It wasn't just soldiers, but fathers, mothers, brothers, sisters, wives, friends, horses, cows, sheep, dogs, rabbits, all creatures—even the earth itself—that withered in its clutch.

When he finished cleaning the floor, he stood and watched the doctors. LaBorde worked smoothly. His dark eyes gleamed. Whatever he lacked in experience, he made up for with compassion and scientific fascination.

As the professor closed the main artery with more than a dozen ligatures, Joseph recalled his own numerous readings of J. J. Chisholm's *A manual of military surgery for the use of surgeons in the Confederate Army.* The book was holy writ for practitioners. Joseph had read various sections so many times that he could practically quote long portions of text. In fearful anticipation of having to operate in an emergency, he'd committed to memory Chisholm's remarks on certain surgical procedures. Between the ideal prescribed and the reality of LaBorde's skill there was no discord. Each movement of the surgeon's hand brought to the forefront of Joseph's memory the precision of instruction: *In ligating the vessels, tie every artery which bleeds, or is likely to bleed. It is not derogatory for a surgeon to apply ten, fifteen, or even twenty ligatures to a stump; it shows that he understands his profession; experience has taught him the great trouble and annoyance of reopening a stump to find a bleeding vessel, when he has but little time to attend to the urgent demands of the wounded. The rule is, neglect no small artery.*

Neglect was the cause of Blevins's dilemma. Not Thompson's neglect, or LaBorde's, but that of the field surgeon who first treated the wounded man, and later that of Richmond physicians. Yet even they could not be blamed entirely. Triage was necessary in hard times. Surgeons and staff worked night and day to care for the wounded in a regressive order that began with the most severely wounded who still held a dim hope of survival. Those beyond the pale were left to die, small doses of opium their sole comfort. Joseph had heard reports of a Richmond nurse who used a pillow to smother a patient who had no hope of recovery. His bed was needed for another who might survive. There was a time when rumors of the nurse's action would have enraged Joseph. Not now. Such were the brutal demands of war.

Thompson and LaBorde continued their work. In spite of their expertise, Joseph knew the outlook was grim. Few survived a second amputation.

"More chloroform," said Thompson.

Joseph reapplied the rag. Thompson held the limb and supported the skin flaps while LaBorde sewed them together, careful to keep the stringy segments of flesh in apposition.

Opium, Joseph thought. Blevins would be begging for it by nightfall.

The stitching completed, both surgeons assisted Joseph in bandaging the wound. Using strips of isinglass-plaster they covered the length of the stump to leave exposed the angle where the ligatures escaped in order to allow for drainage.

Joseph would change bandages frequently over the next several days. Fuming nitric acid was the most effective cleansing agent. Painful, to be sure, but of greatest benefit to the convalescent in the long run. How strange it seemed to Joseph that the mineral pulled from the earth to make explosives for the Confederacy was also used to heal.

"You gentlemen have saved another young man's life," Thompson said.

"We did what we could," said LaBorde. "What happens now is providential."

Of course, thought Joseph. *Let the Almighty decide which of these young men to kill. How convenient this theology of warfare. Men march blithely into battle believing the choice of life or death rests with God alone.*

Thompson said to Joseph, "Perhaps a shipment of opium has arrived on the morning train."

"I'll check, sir." Joseph left the room. He was grateful for Thompson's interjection. It gave him time to fume privately. Besides, there was no arguing with someone who assigned every human event—catastrophic or otherwise—to God's design. Such a man surely believed his every bowel movement was controlled by the prestidigitating finger of God. He had grown sick of the piety that spilled like venom from the tongues of the devout. Was such devotion, he wondered, true to the hearts of these people? Or was it simply a means of absolving themselves of the terrible burden of human error?

How would such people finally resolve the conflict between the justness of their cause and providential design if God led them to their doom?

| 4 |
Drapetomania

Two nights after Rachel's whipping, Mr. and Mrs. Wells rocked quietly on the porch. Mrs. Wells laid her knitting needles and yarn in her lap and looked at her husband. "I saw on your desk a letter from Dr. Parker."

Wells pulled a Meerschaum pipe from his mouth and brought the rocker to rest. "You read it?"

"Of course not, dear. I recognized his signature. You have shown me earlier correspondence. His hand is distinctive, is it not?"

Wells returned the pipe to his mouth. Through down-turned lips and the narrow cavities of his nostrils, tendrils of smoke escaped, encircled his head, and wafted upward. Presently, he said, "Dr. Parker says there is a place for Jim."

She looked at her husband, then at the forlorn creature who sat on his haunches staring at them, mouth open, feet splayed. "I worry that he will be mistreated," she said.

"Dr. Parker is an honorable man. The asylum is better suited to Jim's needs than what we can provide." Wells tapped the arm of the rocker with his fingers. "Besides, he and Rachel should be separated. There is something unnatural about their affection."

Mrs. Wells dared not question her husband's assessment, even if she had her own suspicions about the cause of her son's attachment to the light-skinned girl.

Wells raised the pipe again. After a few moments, his head jerked as if in reflex to the irritation of a fly. He glanced at the knitting materials in his wife's lap. "You have finished your work?"

"My fingers are tired. I sent six pairs of socks to the Wayside Hospital yesterday."

"Our soldiers are grateful," he said. "This war effort would have collapsed long ago without the aid of our women."

"I fear it may yet."

Wells pulled at his beard. "Our cause is just, dear. God will defend us."

"I wish He would show His preference for us more than He has of late." Mrs. Wells ignored her husband's reproving glare.

Jim lunged at a roach that scuttled out of the dirt. The chain rattled. He crushed the insect and with a swift and powerful movement of his forearm, popped the morsel into his mouth. Mrs. Wells shook her head. Her eyes were heavy with twenty-seven years of sorrow since the birth of her only child. Her husband's grief, she knew, was no less severe. She understood also that, alongside the terror of an unnamable guilt he bore toward God, he felt at once an aversion to the living reminder of his sin and a fierce duty to it.

They had tried every remedy available to them. When Jim was a boy of five, his mother would hug him to her chest, pinning his arms to his side to prevent him from gouging himself with sticks, knives, stones, any sharp implement he could find. She smothered his savage groans in the crease of her neck and caressed the back of his head and whispered, "It's all right, Jim. You're going to be all right."

But as Jim got older, his behavior became more injurious. Redness in the face often announced the coming of a fit. He grabbed his head with both hands and with feverish eyes stared at his parents, at his father's slaves, at anyone within range of sight. Only Rachel seemed able to calm him, but Mr. Wells would not allow her to approach him. Sometimes Jim's vision clouded and his eyes rolled. He gnashed his teeth, shouted obscenities, overturned furniture, heaved chairs and dishware across the room. Once, at the age of eighteen, he struck his father, and might have beaten the man to death had not the foreman and four large slaves managed to subdue him. That night he slept for the first time chained to the oak. There without probation he'd bedded every night since.

Mr. Wells smoked his pipe and meditated in his rocker. He'd thought often of taking Jim to the Lunatic Asylum in Columbia, more frequently of late after discussing his son's condition with his longtime Columbia friend, Dr. William Gibbes, who provided the lengthiest diagnosis of Jim's aberration. Gibbes introduced Wells to the work of Samuel Cartwright, an authority on mental disorders. Cartwright detailed the physiological effects of madness and prescribed immediate measures to subdue the lunatic.

Wells was equally fascinated and disturbed by Cartwright's work. Fascinated by the doctor's pinpoint accuracy of the manifestations of madness. Disturbed by the similarities between the descriptions of bedeviled Negroes and the antics of his son. Perhaps he was reading too much into the literature, or too much into his son's behavior. Better to trust Cartwright's opinion that some forms of lunacy were unique to the Negro. His diagnoses were certainly intriguing.

Particularly interesting was his analysis of *drapetomania*, which he defined as "the disease causing Negroes to run away." Wells had observed the effects of the disease in a slave he'd long since sold to a business associate in Laurens. Their relations soured when the buyer later had to dispose of his purchase. He felt that Wells had cheated him by withholding information about the slave's rebelliousness. But Big David (as Wells called the strapping Negro, both to acknowledge the man's stature and to distinguish him from the mulatto he thought to be his son, Little David) had been obedient to Wells. He did not expect the man to run away from the plantation in Laurens to return to his wife and son, whom Wells had refused to sell.

Wells had no objection to Big David's hanging. The slave had run away three times to return to his wife and child. Insubordination could not be tolerated. So of course Wells had Big David seized each time he returned to his family. Wells was a man of honor. He was legally and ethically bound as a gentleman to turn Big David over to his rightful owner.

What most concerned Wells was how Jim reacted each time Big David reappeared, only to be captured and returned. Jim was excited by the flurry of activity: the foreman's sighting of Big David, the fugitive's flight to the woods, the immediate call for patrollers nearby, the chase, capture, beating, Big David's wife and son crying, Big David's lacerated body, pouring of salt into the wounds, his limp and shackled body hauled back to its rightful owner. Viewing all this activity from his tree-home, Jim yanked at his chains and grunted like a feral boar. Following the third capture, Jim himself attempted escape. It happened as his father was dragging him out of the rain to stow him under the house. With a jerk, Jim pulled the chain from his father's grasp and ran toward the woods where Big David had sought refuge. Had the boy been infected? Was Jim, like Big David, a drapetomaniac?

His attempts at escape increased. Wells had to get two other men to assist him when he dragged Jim to the cellar. The burden of duty was more than any man should have to shoulder. But as for the master, so for the father, the most effective means of cure was to teach the duty of submission decreed by Scripture. When accompanied with the traditional remedy of "whipping them out of it," as Cartwright encouraged, health was often restored quickly. Yet the measure never cured Big David. Nor did the less severe beatings subdue Jim, whose flesh remained intact even if it showed marks of deep bruising. Perhaps the treatment in its more abrasive form would work for Little David, in whom the early marks of *drapetomania*—sulkiness and dissatisfaction—were becoming increasingly obvious.

Once more, Cartwright's medical genius offered understanding. Wells saw in Little David's behavior the signs not only of *drapetomania*, but of *dyaethesia aethiopica*, commonly termed *rascality*. Cartwright advocated treatment based on "sound physiological principles." Those who suffered the demoralizing illness required stimulation of the skin. As the skin of blacks was known to be "dry, thick, and harsh to the touch"—more like the hide of cattle than the flesh of human beings—what was needed was harsh scrubbing with warm water and soap, followed by an application of oil "slapped in with a broad leather strap." Then the patient should be required to do hard work in the fresh air and sunshine, as physical exertion expanded the lungs and forced out the vaporous airs of the disease. After a brief rest from labor, the patient should be fed wholesome food "well-seasoned with spices and mixed with vegetables." The meal finished, the slave would be sent to the field for more work, followed by another bathing and rest in a warm bed. Daily repetition of the treatment would soon "effect a cure in all cases which are not complicated by chronic visceral derangement."

Yes, this treatment soon would have to be applied to Little David. If by the age of nine he did not show signs of improvement, something would have to be done. The child suffered dangerous abnormalities. He did not play with his mates. He sat in the dirt and moved his mouth incessantly, as if speaking, yet without sound. The boy was not mute. Wells had heard him make sounds in response to his mother's calls, and even earlier in his life to the voice of his father, whom he now seemed not to remember. The boy certainly had the symptoms of disease. Better to correct the child early than to ignore idiosyncrasies that one day could manifest themselves in rebellion like that of his father. Spare the rod, spoil the child. The same rule he applied to his son.

Oh, the heartache caused by equating the behavior of Negroes to that of his own flesh and blood.

But if meditation on Cartwright's medical remedies provided solace, the theories themselves did not always meet as happily with the demands of practice. Yet Wells often returned to the annals of medicine. How elegant were the proofs of science. Earlier in their marriage, when their son was a boy, Wells on occasion would read to his wife a lengthy passage that described with exacting detail Jim's condition or the strange behavior of one slave or another. Recitation of the procedures of treatment stirred in them both no small measure of hope. But that time had passed.

Now, his eyes tracing the path from the bottom step of the porch to the base of the tree, Wells looked not at his filthy son but at the rim of one of the deep holes Jim had carved out of the earth. As if looking for the deep dark earth itself to give answer, Wells stared at the impression until, minutes later, he acknowledged with a grim-faced nod that his decision was right: They could not make adequate provisions for their son's care. No effort to find a cure had worked. No flurry of prayers offered to heaven had appeased God.

Wells had to admit defeat. And with news of Sherman's advance into South Carolina, perhaps the Lunatic Asylum was the safest place for Jim. Surely the Union general would not burn an asylum to the ground. Buildings of commerce? Yes. The capitol? Yes. Institutions of learning? Yes. But asylums, hospitals, other places where the wounded and decrepit were housed? Not even Sherman could be that depraved.

| 5 |
The Company of the Dead

Joseph sat by Blevins's bed and watched the stump contract. His stomach pitched. He'd seen it dozens of times, yet hadn't grown accustomed to the disturbance excited by the division of muscles. He'd stayed with the patient through the night. Something about the boy reminded him of someone he could not name. A memory without substance, ephemeral as a dream.

Blevins mumbled something incoherent. A call for a loved one, perhaps. A protest against the avalanche of bullets falling upon him and his fellow soldiers as they charged across a field, tripping over corpses, the pleas of the dying echoing in their ears. A cry to his brother, whose bulleted neck gaped before him.

Thank God a new supply of opium had arrived. Blevins would be raving were it not for the palliative. Better the arm than a leg. The voiceless man who lost his leg weeks ago had nearly been lifted off his bed several times by a tumult of twitching, as though the stump was elevated not only by means of its own disturbance, but also by the phantom limb. Maimed bodies had ghosts.

And what of Blevins? Hardly a man. More like the boy Joseph felt he knew. If only he could attach a name to the memory. Too much of the past was a dark maze.

If the boy lived, would he be whole again? And what did it mean to be whole once the body had lost its original form? Doctors, nurses, volunteers, the wounded themselves spoke of *recovery*. But once a limb was gone—a leg, an arm, even a digit like a toe or a finger—what could be recovered? Not the flesh.

Re-cover: To find that which was lost. To regain. To cover again what has been exposed. To restore to a normal state. To heal.

Strange terms all. Euphemisms. An avowal of the untrue, as though the avowal itself brings to life that which has been named. *In the beginning was the word.*

In the end, no word, no body.

Joseph detested the way his mind roamed through the night and into the early hours of the morning. During such senseless meanderings, he questioned his legitimacy as head steward of the hospital. It was not the first time he'd suffered this crisis of confidence. Certainly, he was qualified. Few men in the Confederate Army could claim a college degree, or facility with the financial accounting and oversight of staff duties that the position demanded. Since being declared unfit for field service in February of 1863 by the Medical Board of Richmond, Virginia, he'd sought another way to serve his country. That a man of his condition should be appointed head steward was, he thought, ironic.

The first seizure struck in the fall of 1862 on a march through the mountains of Tennessee. He'd just turned forty-two. He attributed the fit not to his physical state, but to emotional strain. The loss of his wife and nine-year-old daughter three years earlier to typhoid had nearly killed him. On the day he laid their bodies in the graves he'd dug with his own hands, he decided with the conviction of a man who penned his signature to a deed that no matter how long he lived, he would die of grief. The battlefield would have suited him. If not that, some other place of carnage. Following the medical release, Joseph was relieved when Secretary of War Seddon assigned him to the hospital at South Carolina College.

He had not admitted then or since—not even to Dr. Thompson—that his sole compulsion was to be among the dead.

And yet he detested the sight of human suffering. His own he could bear; that of others brought to mind his wife and daughter's agonized withering.

Blevins quivered under the sheet. He had told Joseph before the surgery that many times since Chickamauga, he'd seen his brother Malachi in his dreams, had seen the bullet enter his neck, the blood come, his brother's eyes widen suddenly, then dim.

"Nathaniel, it's Joseph Crawford." He leaned forward and stroked the boy's shoulder.

Blevins's eyelids fluttered. He struggled to focus. He would be in and out of dim consciousness for several days, as long as the drug supply held out and demand did not increase drastically.

"I need to check on some of the other soldiers," Joseph said. He knew Blevins could not comprehend even if he heard the words. Still, it was important to Joseph that he speak. Often it seemed to him that sound alone was the last stay against death.

He left the boy and walked two doors down to a room where a nurse offered a plate of food to a Union soldier. Thick gauze encompassed the man's head, shrouding his eyes. It was a wonder the bullet had not pierced his brain. He would never see again.

"The plate is by your bed," said the nurse, a tall woman with brown hair. Meredith Simpson was her name. A rumor circulated that she had been for a short time a prostitute in one of the brothels on Gervais Street. But whoever started the rumor—perhaps a man who had enjoyed her services or a jealous woman—had been lost or forgotten in the flood of gossip. Two years earlier such a scurrilous report would have persuaded Louisa McCord not to put the woman on her staff of volunteers. Now she had little choice but to give every able-bodied woman the chance to serve. When Meredith came to the hospital looking for work, Louisa reluctantly assigned her duties, and assured her that she would tolerate no disreputable behavior. She spoke to Joseph of the matter. Ever since, he had expected to hear any day of Miss Simpson's dismissal. Louisa McCord was not a woman to tolerate nonsense. Moreover, she did not trust Meredith Simpson, not only because of the lewd stories, but also because the woman was common. Louisa McCord, for all her skill with the patients and her staff, had little regard for working-class nurses or, for that matter, enlisted men. The former group was to be put to any good use they could serve, while the latter, in spite of their low class, had been wounded in the service of the Confederacy, and therefore deserved medical care.

From the doorway, Joseph watched the nurse. Although she faced the patient, she appeared to be inattentive to his needs. He groped with his left hand for the food. Miss Simpson stepped away from the bed and turned toward the door. She started at Joseph's presence.

"You might assist him," Joseph said, and nodded toward the plate.

The woman's eyes narrowed. If she'd had a sword, Joseph thought, she would have lunged at him with it. He'd seen this before: some Southern women unwilling or unable to help a wounded Union officer. Joseph knew better than to order the woman to a task she could not perform. Perhaps she had lost a father or a brother in battle. Perhaps in this blind man grubbing for food, she saw the cause of her grief.

Joseph walked over to the bedside, lifted the plate, and placed it in the man's hands. The soldier said nothing, but smirked. Joseph had an impulse to strike him. He turned away and motioned Miss Simpson to follow him into the hallway.

"I know there is nothing easy about this, Miss Simpson, particularly when some of the men are rude. And yet I must insist—"

"He is more than rude, Mr. Crawford. The man is a brute. Last night he swore at me, and said he wished he could find the Johnny Reb who had done this to him." She pointed two fingers at her eyes. "He said he would carve his eyes out with a knife."

"I am sorry you had to hear that, Miss Simpson. I daresay most of the soldiers, however, are grateful for your care."

"Most of them, yes."

"And I am grateful, as is Mrs. McCord."

Miss Simpson's face flushed. The mention of her superior's name had the effect that Joseph intended. He couldn't risk having a sullen nurse on staff. A foul mood was a contagion that threatened everyone.

"I will do better," she said. "I would be grateful if you would not report me to Mrs. McCord."

"I've no intention of doing that, Miss Simpson."

She lowered her head and entered the next room.

Joseph continued his tour of the floor. Occasionally he spotted Miss Simpson making her way from one room to the next. She avoided his gaze. She appeared now to be attentive to her duties. Joseph appreciated her efficiency. It was the single attribute he most needed in the staff. Hospital policy required the assignment of one nurse to every ten patients, but this was now impossible. He was lucky to have one nurse for every eighteen patients, a ratio that exhausted the women and compromised the quality of care they could provide.

He thought little more of the encounter with Miss Simpson, having been satisfied with its resolution. What now occupied his thoughts was having stood face to face with the woman for the first time. He was impressed not only by her size, but by the way it augmented rather than diminished her beauty. She was almost as tall as he, just under six feet, and sturdy. He could tell from the fit of her blouse that her long arms were muscular. Dark brown eyes accentuated high cheekbones. Her complexion was not fair like that of ladies accustomed to spending their days in the parlor or refining their musical talents with hours of practice, but tawny, suggestive of early years spent laboring on farmland or playing in fields. He thought for a moment of his own youth, his father's poor farmland in Tennessee, the two-room house that always seemed crowded, his constant desire to escape to the woods where he was free of his father's harsh oversight, the glee he felt when in seclusion he sat in the shade of a tree and read a book—any book—his high school teacher, the only advocate of Joseph's intellectual prowess, had given him. It was a habit his uneducated father detested, and for which he would punish Joseph if he caught him, each strap of the belt accompanied by a curse of all disobedient sons, from Cain to his own, who scoffed at the duties God and their fathers assigned them. Joseph was glad that his father died before Joseph finished high school, itself a remarkable achievement in light of the old man's disdain for learning. Had he lived beyond Joseph's sixteenth year, he never would have allowed his son to leave the farm to advance his education.

Joseph completed his rounds and returned to Blevins's room, where once more he found himself in the company of Miss Simpson. This time she heard him enter the room. She acknowledged his presence with a look that indicated empathy with the bed-ridden fellow. The contrast to her earlier demeanor was remarkable. With her right hand she moved a forelock of Blevins's hair from his brow and combed it into place with her fingers. Her expression was like that of a child comforting a pet. Joseph approved the gesture. Surely the reports of her waywardness were exaggerated, if not altogether false.

| 6 |
Head Nurse

Joseph stood before the stolid woman unable to quell his edginess. He hated that a widow eleven years his senior had such an effect on him. More troubling than their age difference, however, was the discomfort he felt in the presence of one well above his station. Louisa McCord was born to privilege. Books that Joseph had to borrow from teachers and hide from his father would have been readily available to her, a multitude of volumes shelved neatly in her father's library, and later her husband's. She outranked Joseph in learning, property, inheritance, and class. Still, he couldn't deny the ardor of his affection. Not since the early days of courting the woman he would later marry had he felt like this. That an older woman of such refinement could move him was preposterous. And in such a morbid setting. Surrounded by suffering and death, war's advance now threatening their very lives, how could he make sense of this madness? It almost undermined his longing for death, made him feel like a betrayer to both the haunted past and his present conviction.

"Mr. Crawford, are you well?"

He looked away from her, gathered his wits. "Yes, Mrs. McCord. I apologize if I seem inattentive. Perhaps I am more weary than I have allowed."

"You must see to your own health, sir, not just to that of the sick. This hospital depends on you. We all do."

Yes, that was the way she flustered him. What did *we all* mean? Did she view herself as preeminent in that community of needy people? Did she depend on him more than others did? On him more than on others, including her own staff of nurses? Did he dare to tell her that he wanted her to depend on him? That he desired her confidence, her trust, her willingness to see themselves as partners in this futile effort to preserve life? Or that since working alongside her and revealing to each other in private moments the agony of their losses—she a husband ten years earlier, her only son, and a nephew at Manassas—he'd come to appreciate her friendship?

Louisa Cheves McCord was tall and regal. Strands of gray marked her dark hair, a contrast that added luster to her obsidian eyes. Her skin was pale, but not sickly. At the age of fifty-five, she had more strength than many men half her age. Joseph agreed with the assessment of Mary Boykin Chesnut, who told him one evening at a dinner party that she believed Mrs. McCord had the brain and energy of a man. Chesnut also observed that Mrs. McCord found in service to the wounded soldiers a means of sanctifying her grief over the loss of her son. Joseph understood.

Mrs. McCord shook her head. "The patient is unmanageable, I'm afraid. Neither I nor any of the nurses can reason with him. Twice this morning we had to change his bed sheets. He has dysentery."

"His name?" Joseph asked.

"Hagstette."

"Not the Hagstette from the Lunatic Asylum, surely."

"Yes."

Joseph scratched his forehead. "Dr. Thompson performed surgery on him four months ago. The man didn't listen to anyone the first time he was here."

Bill Hagstette was first admitted to the hospital after carving a fourteen-inch gash in his belly with a knife. He told Dr. Thompson then that he meant to kill himself.

"You nearly did a fine job of it," Thompson said. "What in the name of reason would persuade you to injure yourself in such a manner?"

Hagstette's eyes bulged. "Caught my wife with a nigger! Would've kilt him if I'd of got hold of him. He cut out through the woods 'fore I could fetch my gun. Don't know whose nigger he is, neither. Ain't seen him since."

The difficulty with Hagstette's story was that no one could corroborate it. His wife had left him earlier in the year, and no one in Columbia had seen or heard from her since. Hagstette lived by himself in a shack near the Congaree River. He would have died if a fisherman hadn't found him in the woods staring at his intestines, which lay in his lap. The man and his son carried him out of the woods, laid him on a mule-drawn cart, and hauled him to the College Hospital.

After stitching Hagstette up, Dr. Thompson asked Dr. Parker to admit him to the Insane Asylum and keep watch over him. Parker acknowledged Hagstette's need for help, but soon enough complained that the man could not get along with anyone. He started a fight with another ward at the asylum. He stole pound cake from a woman whose family had the means to secure for her a private room with her own nurse.

"Who brought him here?"

"Three attendants from the asylum. Dr. Parker sent a note."

Mrs. McCord handed Joseph a piece of paper. He recognized Parker's handwriting. Hagstette had told Parker the evening before that he

"honed for candy." He refused to believe me when I told him that sweets would exacerbate his dysentery. Last night he escaped from the asylum, made his way into town, bought candy, and ate every piece. I do not know how he obtained money for his purchase. Knowing the strains under which the hospital functions, I am sorry to turn

him over to your care. Mr. Hagstette may, however, require surgery. We haven't the
means to accommodate him here. We shall receive him here when you think that his
health permits release.

Your obd't ser'vt,
John W. Parker.

Joseph folded the letter and put it in his shirt pocket. "I will go for Dr. Thompson," he said, "although I hate to bother him with this matter. He is overworked as it is."

Mrs. McCord nodded and gave Joseph a look that suggested he ought to have as much concern for himself as for Thompson.

When Joseph returned with the doctor twenty minutes later, Mrs. McCord was making her way from room to room checking on the patients. She stepped into the hallway and asked if she could assist the men.

"I am not sure we can perform surgery on this man again," Thompson said. "The risk may be too great."

In the room, Thompson asked the patient to describe his symptoms.

"I got the quickstep," Hagstette said. "My bowels won't settle on me."

Thompson looked at the seepage from Hagstette's breeches and waved a hand across his nose. "How severe is the pain?"

"The pain don't matter, doctor. It's no use you doing surgery, neither. I will die tomorrow at twelve-o'clock."

"What makes you think so?'

"I seen my coffin last night. It come right down through the roof."

"What have you done?" asked Thompson.

"Well, doctor, I just et all the candy I wanted."

"And have killed yourself," said Thompson.

"I suppose that's just about exactly it. I'd like to see Mrs. McCord again."

Joseph said, "What have you to do with Mrs. McCord?"

Hagstette offered no response. Thompson nodded at Joseph, who went for Louisa. He found her three rooms away attending a soldier whose sight had been lost to a bullet that pierced the optical nerve. When she finished feeding the man, Joseph said to her, "Hagstette has asked for you. He says he is going to die tomorrow. I can't imagine what he wishes to say to you."

"Something about his wife, I should think," said Louisa. "He spoke of her after you left."

Thompson moved away from the bed as Louisa approached. Hagstette propped himself up as best he could, the strain of movement showing on his face. She adjusted a pillow for his comfort.

"Mrs. McCord, I'm going to die tomorrow, and I know my wife Mandy will marry again. I want you to promise me you will have my gun and blankets and clothes put in my coffin. I don't want number two to get them."

"I hardly think you can appoint the hour of your death. And given what you have told me about your wife, I do not believe she will remarry. The law does not permit a white woman to marry a Negro."

"No, ma'am. She won't marry the nigger. It'll be a white man who takes her to wife. But he'll soon wish he hadn't. She'll run on him just like she done on me."

Louisa made one more attempt to reason with him, but it was useless. He folded his arms against his chest and set his chin. She looked over her shoulder at Joseph and Thompson, then turned again to Hagstette. "All right, then. I shall see that your request is honored. But now you must do as Dr. Thompson tells you."

In the hallway, Thompson said to Louisa, "Hagstette must be treated with strong tea made from dogwood bark. He must drink as much as possible today and through the night. It is the only purgative that may save him at this point."

"I will see to it," she said, and left the men to resume her visits.

Joseph watched her until she turned into a room. Did the woman ever grow weary? She coordinated the nurses' schedules. She passed out food to patients, wrote letters for them, did what she could to relieve their anguish. When she was not roaming the corridors of the hospital, she was at home with her daughters supervising the preparation of meals in her kitchen for these convalescents. The able-bodied often went to her home on the corner of Bull and Pendleton Streets, less than a block from the hospital. They ate meals on her piazza.

He thought it a cruel twist of fate that war and death had brought them together. Crueler yet that one or the other would sunder them.

| 7 |
The Asylum

Jim liked to ride in his father's carriage. Except for searing pain in his wrists every time he jerked at the manacles attached to a ball and chain that lay between his feet, he was happy. He looked out the carriage window at the trees, thin branches of the leafless ones swaying like the skeletons of hanged men. When a breath of wind swept through the aperture and touched his face, Jim closed his eyes and flared his nostrils to take in the scent of dust. The sensation made him delirious.

Wells hated the stirring of the wind. The older he got, the more vicious this land seemed. Trees and grass and swirling dust and even the budding flowers of spring seemed to close off his lungs. He labored for breath.

They passed a herd of cattle grazing at the east end of the plantation. Jim stuck his head as far out the window as his chain allowed. "MO-O-O-O-O," he bellowed.

"Jim!" Wells shook his head and slapped the back of the seat with his right hand. Jim's mouth widened into what might have passed for a smile had not his brown teeth and confused expression been so sinister. Wiry dark eyebrows came together. A wide jaw, grizzled beard, and brown hair thick and unruly as thatch accentuated his frightful bearing.

At least he'd been bathed. Wells oversaw the operation by his foreman and three strong slaves as they wrestled Jim into the large basin of water and scoured his body with brushes. Rachel stood fifty feet away wailing and pulling her hair. Wells ignored her for the moment; he'd attend to her when he returned.

His son's filth had always been an embarrassment to Wells, for whom cleanliness was a sign of moral sobriety as well as social position. Although the land was the source of his living, Wells believed that no gentleman should appear in public with dirt under his fingernails. Proper hygiene suggested a man's control of himself and of the world he inhabited, not to mention his spiritual refinement. The unclean were an abomination to God. Many sleepless nights he tossed in his bed angered by the appearance and odor of his son, who expressed his contempt for forced washings by clawing fiercely at his earthen pits and showering himself with dirt the moment he was returned to his lair. Today Wells's men had managed to dress and secure the lunatic in the carriage before he fouled himself again.

Dr. Parker had assured Wells that bathing was a regular procedure at the asylum. It was encouraged not only to promote cleanliness but in the belief that warm water and gentle scrubbing aided the regeneration of mental faculties. Many a frenzied patient had been calmed by the gentle ministrations of nurses who bathed them.

Wells trusted Parker. He'd met the man in 1856, shortly after Parker was appointed superintendent and chief medical officer of the South Carolina Lunatic Asylum. Wells's friend Dr. Gibbes had made the introduction.

A man of medium height and slim build, Parker looked the part of a chief medical officer. He neither smiled nor frowned but wore a serious expression, thin lips pursed, green eyes fixed in concentration as he engaged others in conversation. Every question he listened to attentively; every answer he inflected with a tone of gravity. Wells looked forward to seeing the man again. Parker had promised to meet him at the train station in Columbia.

Transport from the carriage to the train was easier than Wells or his men anticipated. Jim marveled at the great black vessel. He'd never ridden a train. As it pulled out of the station, he pressed his nose to the window and drooled. Presently, the world moved at blinding speed. Fields, animals, buildings receded into the distance. He blinked once, twice, and they were gone.

True to his word, Parker was standing on the platform when the train pulled into Columbia. Wells waited while Jim struggled with the ball and chain, then stepped down to the platform and looked through bovine eyes at Parker, who glared at the restraining device. He motioned for a large attendant to assist with the ball and chain. When the man reached for the chain, Jim slapped his hand away. "Niggers don't heft my load."

"Settle down, Jim," said his father. "This man is no different from our servants at home."

Jim bowed his neck and bared his teeth at the man.

"Accept my apologies, please," said Dr. Parker. "As a rule, we have the white staff take care of our white patients, but at present I am understaffed. This man is all I had at my disposal." With a wave of his hand he ordered the large man to move away from Jim. The man's head bobbed and he shuffled into place two feet behind Parker.

Jim lugged himself and his shackles to Dr. Parker's coach and lifted the ball into place and took his seat. Wells was relieved that he hadn't had to pull from his bag the leather strap. What a scene might have ensued.

Parker's man drove the carriage slowly through the wide streets of the city. The gentlemen talked about recent developments in the war and its effects on the asylum.

"I cannot keep an adequate staff," said Parker. "I cannot pay them. Our funds have diminished considerably since the beginning of the war. I now have more paupers than paying patients, and from the latter I cannot depend on regularity of payment. The regents cannot attend monthly board meetings, which makes it difficult to conduct the business of the asylum. Patients beg for better food and clothing. You know how the cost of both has risen in the last three years. The employees I have left are despondent. And for the past two years we have breathed noxious odors emanating from the Nitre and Mining Bureau. I have spoken to Dr. LeConte about the problem. There is nothing he can do. I applaud the professor for providing the Confederacy with explosives, but my staff and patients suffer."

"I have seen my own fortune drop," said Wells. "And that of others throughout the state. Because of this damned federal blockade, I can't export my cotton. I've a cousin in Charleston who can't export his rice. The war has ruined us."

"It has. I am sorry to complain so bitterly of my own predicament."

Wells inquired about Dr. Gibbes. Parker said he'd seen him recently and he looked well.

"I was concerned when I saw him last," said Wells. "He appeared to be overwhelmed with duties."

"This war has demanded much of us all. I fear that Dr. Gibbes has shouldered a greater burden than most, save those in the field."

"I've never seen him despondent as he was in the weeks after Jackson's death."

"He is not the only one," said Parker. "Since the general's death, our only gain has been Chickamauga. The women in Columbia were more demoralized than the men. Mrs. Chesnut and Mrs. McCord have often wished for Jackson's return. They claim that convalescing soldiers at one hospital or another cry that if Stonewall were alive, this war would have ended long ago."

"Are there enough women to make rounds daily?" asked Wells.

"They manage. Some days they go to one of the wayside hospitals, other days to the hospital at the college. If they are not bandaging wounds, they are feeding the wounded, praying for them, singing hymns, knitting socks. They are tireless."

"My wife also continues to make socks for the soldiers. Her spirit seems to fall every time she sits to work. I fear that with each thread she pulls, she counts the loss of yet another man."

"Perhaps the sacrifice of our women is greater than that of our men," said Parker. "It is one thing to die for one's country, quite another to give up fathers, husbands, and, most grievous to their hearts, sons." Parker looked at Jim, studied his chafed wrists, the heavy restraints. Wells looked out the window.

The carriage rolled into a gated compound. At the end of a great expanse of field stood a massive brick building, three stories in the center with wings of two stories on either side. Parker's man opened the door of the carriage. He held out a hand to each gentleman, then kept a safe distance as Jim struggled with his ball and chains.

Parker dusted his long coat, said to Wells, "We prefer not to manacle our patients within the confines of the asylum unless they pose a threat to themselves or to others."

"I have spoken to you frankly, Dr. Parker, about my son's condition."

"Yes, sir, you have. I am grateful for your confidence. But our policy is to follow the rules set for all patients insofar as the behavior of each permits. It has been my observation these many years that a warm bath and a kind word will generally do more to subdue the furious maniac than either solitary confinement or any restraining apparatus that has yet been invented."

Wells scratched his beard before pulling from his coat pocket a key with which he unlocked the manacles. Jim walked toward a large tree at the west end of the building. Parker's servant hoisted the ball and chains with difficulty to the floor of the carriage, and bowed to the gentlemen. He took the reins of the lead horse and circled the team and left through the gate.

Parker pointed at Jim, who had sidled up to an elm tree some eighty yards away. "He has a fondness for trees, I see."

Wells grimaced. "More than for the human community. My son is wild, sir. His constitution is more suited to nature than to the confines of a building."

"He will have many opportunities to be out of doors here. I cannot promise that he will breathe fresh air in these environs, but his body will enjoy the rigors of exercise."

"I thank you for your assistance, Dr. Parker. And now I must bid you farewell."

"Will you not stay for a meal with my wife and me? We are modest in our provisions, but would be honored to share with you what we have."

"Thank you. I have accepted an invitation to dine with Dr. and Mrs. Gibbes this evening. He has known for several days of my coming. We regale each other with stories of our days at the college. We fancy ourselves younger men when we reminisce. It makes the heart less heavy for the return trip."

"I understand. Perhaps you would like a moment with your son?"

Wells raised a hand to his brow and glinted at Jim, who was talking to the tree. "We have said our goodbyes. It would be best for me to leave without disruption." He turned and passed through the gate.

Parker trudged toward his newest patient, whose arms stretched wide to measure the circumference of his new home.

| **PART II** |

December 1864

| 8 |
Rations of Crows

Dr. Parker chafed at the mayor's announcement that more than 1200 Federal officers would be moved to the grounds of the lunatic asylum. Thomas Jefferson Goodwyn, a short, thin-lipped man with an aquiline nose and deep-set gray eyes that seemed to recede into his skull, insisted that allowing the asylum to serve as a temporary prison would provide a noble service for the Confederacy. "We have nowhere else to place them, John. Too many have escaped from Camp Sorghum. Close to four hundred at last count."

Goodwyn explained to Parker that Camp Sorghum, a five-acre open field overlooking a stream not far from the confluence of the Saluda and Congaree Rivers, initially had seemed a good place to detain enemy soldiers. In this harsh and rainy winter, the rivers nearby were so cold and treacherous that swimming across them seemed foolhardy if not altogether impossible. The guards were not trained soldiers—most of them either too young and scrawny or too old and feeble to join a battalion—but they were able enough to hold and point rifles and to keep watch over their captives.

Besides, most of the prisoners had traveled far afoot already, many of them wounded in various battles or suffering the effects of various illnesses—typhoid, measles, pneumonia. Moved by train from Georgia to Charleston as Sherman advanced, and later to Columbia when an outbreak of yellow fever threatened the coastal city, the men were sick and cold and hungry. Attempts to flee were not likely. Or so it seemed.

"But many did escape," said Parker.

"They sneaked away at night," said Goodwyn. "They made their way through woods and swamps and across the narrowest branches of one river or another. I fear they are attempting now to find and join Sherman's advancing troops."

"I suspect many are hiding from Sherman, seeking a way home to avoid more bloodshed," said Parker.

"The asylum is the only sensible place to secure the captives, John. At least here we can restrict their movement." Goodwyn pointed toward the brick wall at the far end of the grounds. He said, "This is not a permanent solution. We intend to find a more suitable location. At present, this place is the best we have."

"This could be a disaster, Thomas. What am I to do with my patients? They need their daily exercise. If prisoners occupy these grounds, I can make no provision for the care of those I am entrusted to serve."

"We have a greater duty to our country, John. I am sorry to impose this on you, but we are desperate."

Parker looked around the grounds of the asylum. He envisioned tents sprawled across the campus, ill and dirty soldiers clumped together, guards with their bayonets and rifles—yet another danger to patients who might react fearfully or, worse, fractiously. The two with whom he'd had the most difficulty, Wells and Hayes, would surely take advantage of the opportunity to sow more discord. Two days earlier Wells had attacked Hayes with a sharp-edged stone. Parker said to Goodwyn, "You must know how difficult it is to control some of my inmates. One man lies in a ward now, recuperating from an attack by a fellow patient. The man tried to defend himself. He struck his assailant with his fists several times in the head. The blows would have knocked most men out, but so crazed was the assailant that his victim would have had to kill him in order to stop the assault. More likely, he would have been bludgeoned to death had not three attendants, at risk of injury to themselves, grabbed the assailant from behind and wrestled him to the ground."

"What have you done with these men?"

"The victim received twenty-seven stitches stretching from forehead to the bridge of his nose. For the other, still yelling obscenities and kicking at the attendants as they dragged him into the building, there was no alternative but the restraining chair. It is a device I loathe, but occasionally it is necessary. After pulling and jerking against the straps for most of the day, the man wore himself out and calmed down. He slept through the night. Now we have attendants watching vigilantly to keep the adversaries separated. They will not be allowed outside to exercise at the same time. Nor will they enter the refectory at the same time. They will dine on opposite sides of the room. Under no circumstances will they be housed in the same wing of the asylum. Enforcing such discipline is difficult enough, Thomas. Now, with the imminent impressment of Union soldiers on the grounds, there is no telling what ruckus either patient might try to create." Parker paused, then said, "Thomas, this war has to end soon. We cannot last much longer."

"We cannot lose heart," said Goodwyn. "Not when so many are coming into our city in search of refuge. Providing for their safety and that of our citizens is yet another reason to keep the prisoners behind these walls. Remember, too, what Jefferson Davis told us two months ago."

Parker looked out across the expanse of the asylum's enclosure and recalled that first Wednesday of October when Davis addressed the townspeople from the porch of the Chesnut home. He and Goodwyn had often recalled to each other that momentous day. They remembered how wildly people cheered when Davis announced that General Hood's army of Tennessee had gotten stronger since the fall of Atlanta, and that Hood soon planned to encounter Sherman in the heart of the Confederacy.

They recalled how Davis praised South Carolina for being the first state to secede, for having the courage to lead the way in the struggle for freedom. Both Parker and Goodwyn had saved copies of *The Charleston Courier,* whose October 6th issue printed the speech in its entirety. On the evening of October 8th, when Dr. and Mrs. Parker dined with Mayor Goodwyn and his wife in their home, Goodwyn read aloud various parts of the speech. Now, as the men faced each other on a frigid December morning, each of them seemed to hear once more the echo of Davis's declamation:

"If there be any who feel that our cause is in danger; that final success may not crown our efforts; that we are not stronger today than when we began this struggle; that we are not able to continue the supplies to our armies and to our people, let all such read a contradiction in the smiling face of our land, and the teeming evidences of plenty which everywhere greet the eye; let them go to places where brave men are standing in front of the foe, and there receive the assurance that we shall have final success, and that every man who does not live to see his country free, will see a freeman's grave."

On that October afternoon, Parker felt that he did believe the president's words. So what that the availability of medical supplies had dwindled and their costs risen dramatically in the past four years. So what that adequate food for patients was in increasingly short supply. So what that the economy of the South had been crippled by the war. Davis was nonetheless right to point to "evidences of plenty which everywhere greet the eye." Were not the wealthy from Savannah and Charleston and other great cities bringing their goods—household belongings, wines and liquors from their cellars, troves of clothing, and not least of all their most valuable property, their slaves, both the sign of former economic stability and the promise of recovery—into the capital city? Yes, Davis had done well to remind Columbians of prosperous times and to point to signs of renewal. He had spoken truly.

And yet it was more than belief in the integrity of Davis the orator that bolstered Parker's faith. Trust in the integrity of their cause strengthened his and every loyal Confederate's devotion. They fought not only in defense of land and life, but of their God-given right to independence. Their cause was more than just; it was holy.

No wonder, then, that people attended to Davis's speech with reverence. The assembly cheered and wept in remembrance of the sons and fathers and brothers they had lost to the war when, with fists clinched and raised in the air, Davis said:

"Your brave sons are battling for the cause of the country everywhere; your Fort Sumter, where was first given to the breeze the flag of the Confederacy, still stands. The honor of the State has not been dimmed in the struggle, and her soldiers will be sustained by the thought that when they are no more, South Carolina will still retain that honor with which she commenced the war, and have accumulated that greatness and glory which will make her an exemplar of all that is chivalric and manly in a nation struggling for existence."

Parker remembered how those words inspired him that day. They moved him in a way that little else had in a long time. But much had happened to dampen his enthusiasm in the weeks following Davis's departure from Columbia. Sherman's advance through the South was relentless. Neither Hood nor any other Confederate general had been able to turn him back. Who could guess where Sherman would lead his army after the sack of Atlanta? Rumors abounded that not even Grant always knew the whereabouts of his best general in the field. Secrecy was the key to his strategy.

There was nothing mysterious, however, about the devastation he caused. One of his own staff was said to have written that Sherman's march could be traced only by the glare of fire by night and columns of smoke by day. Burning houses and barns and fields in every direction. Cattle, sheep, hogs slaughtered by marauding soldiers who cared nothing about the women, children, and slaves left to starve. People commonly lamented that a crow flying over the devastated land would have had to carry its rations with it. And was it not proof of the godlessness of Union forces that many of Sherman's men were known to have claimed, "Billy could flank God Almighty out of heaven"?

Parker hated the apostasy. The idolatry. The diabolical evil. All of it was too much to bear. Worse yet was the lurking fear that the South's mounting losses called into question the sanctity of their cause. What else could explain God's allowing the wicked to prevail? For what terrible sin was the South being punished? Hadn't God's judgment—if such were the cause of the South's irremediable losses—been severe enough already? What of the more egregious sins of the North? How could crazed and violent abolitionists not see that the fate of John Brown awaited them all, if not in this life, then surely in the next? How much longer would the exile of Babylon endure for the South?

Goodwyn placed a hand on Parker's shoulder. The old friends acknowledged with a single silent nod the burden of leadership. Theirs was more than a duty to their people; it was a calling from the throne of heaven, and therefore had to be obeyed. Of course the prisoners should be quartered here. Goodwyn was merely the emissary of divine counsel, Parker the vehicle of dutiful enactment. Both would fulfill the demands of their calling. What else were men of God to do in defense of homeland and honor?

| 9 |
A Cousin's Love

George McClinton saw the imprint of the hand of God on every calamity. He accounted the loss of his left hand neither principally to an enemy soldier's bullet nor to the surgeon's knife, but to God's just punishment of the lustful ways of his youth when he stroked himself night after night in his straw-tick bed in the three-room house in Kentucky. He'd helped his father and uncles build the structure when he was thirteen years old. God took their first home when He hurled out of his purple-fisted hand a bolt of lightning that turned the shell to cinders. Perhaps it was his father's whiskey drinking that called forth divine wrath that day. Or perhaps his father's sin was more terrible than that. God had killed the child of David and Bath-sheba for their sin. Did the burning in that swift inferno of the McClinton baby, George's only sister, have a similar cause?

Now, nine years later, as George sat on the edge of the hospital bed in Columbia and looked at the wrap on his stump, he thought once more of his cousin, Laura Wilson, the catalyst of his spiritual degeneration in the months that followed the burial of his sister. Laura's soft voice and gentle touches soothed him as prayer could not. Two years older than George, she had a maturity that he thought he would never achieve. He trusted her. He adored her. When Laura took him to a secret place in the woods behind her parents' cabin, less than a hundred yards from where his own stood, and lifted her frock above her shoulders, George shivered. He thought to run, but his legs would not move. She pulled his left hand between her legs and showed him what to do with his fingers. On a pallet of pine straw she lay him down and placed her knees on either side of his hips. George's seed gushed out of him before she could fully mount. Within minutes she had him ready again. This time she rode him harder than a Pony Express mail carrier out-running bandits.

The next day she pulled her frock only to her waist. George wanted to see more, but she said they needed to hurry, her father would leave the field soon and they dare not be caught.

"Come here," she rasped, looking at him over her shoulder as she kneeled and nestled her elbows into the ground. He grew reverent in his groin. He'd seen how their bull did it to the cows. Dogs, too. *Dipping from the backside of the well*, he and Laura called it as they practiced the wonders of their craft. It became his favorite position that spring and summer of 1855.

In the fall Laura's belly swelled. George was heartsick when she married Randall Craft from the next hollow east of them. Randall was the father, she assured her parents. Randall agreed. George learned later that it might have been Randall or any of several other boys in the area. Still, he loved her. At night, when he lay alone and suffered the torture of visions of Randall Craft usurping his place at the backside of the well, George could not prevent his left hand from its downward movement. His desperation turned to horror as he recalled the tremulous voice of his mother, herself of a harsh Calvinistic upbringing, reading Scripture to him. Yet he could not let himself go until he found relief. Guilt gnawed his bowels.

How terrible, he thought, to have a sin named for you. If his mother knew, would she say she should have named him *Onan*? But in spite of the ugliness of his sin, he could no more prevent the degeneration of his mind with thoughts of Laura than he could move the towering blue mountain above their home with a prayer.

Just as God directed the Union soldier's bullet through George's wrist, his own bayonet into his assailant's skull through the right eye, so God guided the teeth of the surgeon's saw. Every sinew sacrificed, every vessel stitched a reminder of God's severe mercy. *And if thy hand offend thee, cut it off, and cast if from thee: for it is profitable for thee that one of thy members should perish, and not that thy whole body should be cast into hell.*

George knew also that God commanded the unrelenting rains of this cold winter. Had not God destroyed the earth in the days of Noah? Was not this present war another sign of the perpetual wickedness of man? George was living in the last days.

He knew that he should return to his home in that depressed Kentucky valley and wait for the Lord to come. With less than three weeks remaining on his thirty-day furlough, his heart was for home. Best to be raptured with his people.

Dr. Thompson assured him that he would be fit to travel by then. George was able now, if his escape the previous evening from the college campus with two other convalescents was a reliable indicator. It was after midnight when they sneaked across the college green and made a jaunt to the lower side of the city, toward the river, where brothels dotted the landscape. From the gated entrance to the college green, they walked two blocks north along Sumter Street, then west at Gervais where stood Mayor Goodwyn's home and the State Ordnance Warehouse. They passed five commissary stores and Evans and Cogswell Company, where Confederate money was printed, before they reached Huger Street, one block from their destination. Joseph told his companions he was tired and had to stop.

"Hell, you'd think you ain't never marched," said one of his co-conspirators.

"It's this arm," George said, and held up the bandaged stump. "It's paining me."

In the gloom of night, George sat in the dirt at the corner of Gervais and Huger, and looked up at the imposing Confederate Armory. All the weaponry contained there might as well have been aimed at his heart. For

George was marching toward his own destruction; of that he was certain. Yet thoughts of Laura inflamed him, consuming his hope of salvation.

That his companions hailed from opposite sides of the rift was yet another sign of the coming of the end. *Brother shall betray brother to death, and the father the son; and children shall rise up against parents, and shall cause them to be put to death.*

Tobias Frederick came from New Jersey. He told George that he prayed he would never see his cousin from North Carolina on the other side of the battlefield. Stewart McHenry of Georgia said he had an uncle he'd never met who lived in New York. Could Tobias or Stewart be Satan in disguise? George wondered. Which of them had suggested a visit to the brothel? He couldn't remember. It might have been any of them, himself included, as eagerly as he agreed to the escapade.

"Come on," said McHenry. "It's cold out here, liable to start pouring rain again any minute. We got to go."

"Here then, help me up." George stuck out his hand and McHenry pulled him to his feet.

"You'll be all right once you get there," McHenry said. "Won't he, Tobias?"

Tobias nodded. "About as all right as we'll be, I reckon."

And he was all right once he entered the building and adjusted his vision to the dimly lit, smoke-filled room. He had three choices. He chose Becky. She had a nice smile. She was about Laura's size, too. Wide in the hips. Large breasts, soft and pendulous. She took him upstairs and they wasted no time.

"You like it this way?" he asked when he positioned himself to mount her from behind.

"It's two ways you can go in from there, you know. Take the one what suits you." She arched her pelvis so that her hips lifted.

George tried it both ways. He liked to hear their grunts mingle in the dank air that encased their hard passion. Once he thrust hard, as deep as he could go, and whispered to her, "Laura."

"What'd you call me?" asked Becky, starting to pull away.

With his one hand he grabbed her right hip and pulled her back. "Lovely. I called you lovely."

When they finished, and George pulled his shirt over the shadow that had once been his hand, he felt the dark spirit descend. He sat on the edge of the bed. Moonlight filtered through the second-story window and cast elongated shadows on the floor. Becky asked if he would come to see her again. He nodded, but did not look at her.

"Well, you got to leave now," she said. "I got other customers'll be wanting their time."

He rose from the bed and passed into the hallway, down the stairs, and waited in the parlor for his companions to join him. Tobias came out first, a grin plastered on his face. Stewart followed moments later. He fumbled with the buttons on his shirt as a woman stood behind him and said, "You go on, now. You got it twice and ain't paid but once."

"And good the second time as it was the first," Stewart said.

On the way back to the hospital, George was silent while the others talked of their conquests. Their words blended into a jocund, senseless hum. What George heard distinctly was his mother's voice, a strident ring that started in his ears and reverberated all the way down his chest, her recitation a presage of the final imminence. *Heaven and earth shall pass away, but my words shall not pass away. . . . For as in the days that were before the flood, they were eating, and drinking, marrying and giving in marriage, until the day that Noah entered into the ark, and knew not until the flood came, and took them all away: so shall also the coming of the Son of man be.*

He saw visions: eagles feeding on human carcasses; the sun turning to blood, stars falling from heaven. The cold air pierced his skin and bit into his bones.

They were less than a block from the college green when rain began to fall.

"Hellfire," said Stewart. "If my lungs wasn't so tore up, I'd run for it." He coughed. George looked up and saw in the man's pale complexion the sign of his death. He won't make it home, George thought.

All was quiet on the ward. The men took off their boots and waited for a nurse to turn a corner, then tiptoed to their respective rooms.

For the final act of their ruse, Stewart and Tobias said they would pretend to be asleep when the nurse came to check on them. George remembered that as he lay in his bed and wept.

| 10 |
Nothing but Trouble

Jim adjusted to the asylum. He liked it more than his father's home. All he missed there was his tree and Rachel. Especially Rachel. His heart ached for her. But he didn't long for anything else at home. Not the cellar. Anything but that. He hated the cellar. Total darkness. Here, there was always light.

There was only one problem at the asylum: the new fellow. Well, that other one, too—Hagstette, or something or other—but he was gone. This new one was worse. Jim disliked him before he ever laid eyes on him. He'd overheard two attendants talking about the fellow. Hayes, they called him. Brought over from the Camden Jail where he'd been locked up for preaching sedition among the niggers. Goddamn abolitioner. End up like that fellow they hung at Harpers Ferry. Sons too. Or maybe they was shot. Jim scratched his head. He'd heard his father talk about it years earlier. Might have been last year, might have been ten years ago. Didn't matter. Whole lot of them—father, wife, sons, daughters, cousins, friends—should've been torched. People like that, you can't trust.

Same with this Hayes, Jim told himself. What's a white man want to stir up niggers for? Nothing in it but trouble. Reason this war's being fought. Crazy man in Washington wanting to free them. Emastication what Pa called it. Nothing but trouble. All wrong. Niggers acting white. Thinking they can own land. Who'll work it for them? Whites? Make niggers of the whites?

Pa'll teach them. Take the whip to them. Get old Frazer to. Pa standing right by him and reading the Scripture over their yips. That Frazer can do it. Good with a whip as any man. Jerk a chicken's head right off with one lash. Glad Pa never put him on me. Strap bad enough. Not like the whip. Hate him for the way he done Rachel. Kill him if I could. Don't nobody touch my Rachel. Brown cord black hide red blood. Yip like a dog.

Time to go out. Don't like a pent-up room. Not warm like back home. Earth dirt leaves blanket. Dr. Parker's rules. Bed to a patient, bed to a patient. Outside better.

Yonder he goes, walking by his self. Hands crossed behind his back like he's overlooking the land. Must think it's his. Likely sees cotton in the field. White niggers picking, bringing their sacks for the weigh-in. Better be right. Bring out the whip if it's too light. Brown cord white skin red blood. Yip.

Nothing but trouble, that one. Tell it the way he holds his nose up to the sky.

Well, well, I'll lay by for him. Get him when he ain't looking. Do him like they done that fellow at Harpers Ferry. Sons too, he has any. All of them. Sons wives daughters cousins friends parents. Pa. Mama. Nothing but trouble.

| 11 |
Falling Sickness

Joseph's body jerked as if struck by lightning. He'd recognized the signs of the attack—agitation of the left leg, blurring of vision, mounting pressure behind the left eye—just before he arrived at Louisa McCord's home. He'd overheard her tell one of the nurses that afternoon that her daughters Hannah and Lou were visiting relatives at the McCord plantation near Abbeville.

He walked through the rain in twilight on the pretense of having forgotten to tell her earlier in the day of not receiving a shipment of supplies, and of the dual hardships that would impose on the patients and her nursing staff.

He would not remember the purpling of his lips, the way his mouth formed bubbles that looked like fish breath on the surface of water, the soiling of his breeches, the roughness of Louisa's manservant's hands as he bathed and redressed him in clothes that her son used to wear. She had left his room and all its articles as they were before Cheves's death.

"I heard a thump at the foot of the steps," Louisa said later that evening. She sat in a chair opposite the couch where Joseph slumped. He faced the fire that the manservant had banked after attending to him. "When I found you lying in the mud, I was afraid someone had shot you."

Joseph was embarrassed by his condition. He hated the word that defined him. The sound of it suggested effeminacy at best, cowardice at worst. The soft *e* at the beginning followed by the soft *p*. All the vowels and consonants had the delicacy of a rose petal, until the very end, the harsh *c* voiced like a *k*, as if to emphasize the sudden shock to the body and the pathetic loss of control, which rendered a man mute, unable to call for help, incapable of preventing the release of his bowels.

"This is the third time it has happened," he said. To his own ear, his voice seemed to drag, to fall behind the words as they came to his scattered mind. "I would appreciate your not telling Dr. Thompson."

"I should think he would want to know. He is your friend, Joseph, as well as a doctor of considerable renown."

It was the first time she had called him by his Christian name. An act of intimacy or of pity? He was afraid to ask. If she gave the answer he feared, he would loathe himself more than he did at present.

"I am afraid he will ask me to resign my post."

"I cannot imagine." Her voice warmed him more than the fire itself. "He has told me that you are the finest steward a hospital could have. Surely you know he intends to recommend you for any position you desire when this war ends. He would keep you here, I am sure, but he feels you will want to return to your home."

Joseph stared at the flame as it danced between one log and another. He swallowed hard. He did not remember his throat being so raw after the first two episodes. Of course then the weather had not been so harsh. Would these rains never cease? Or was it sleet that fell upon him when he writhed in the ground at the base of her steps? "I have no home, Louisa." He paused, let the sounding of her name either force her away or invite her to sustain the intimacy. After a moment, he said, "None that I would return to."

"I understand."

He knew that she did. No husband to return to her at war's end, her only son lost to the conflict, what remained for her? Surely Mary Chesnut was right about her friend: Louisa McCord found in her care for the sick and wounded the only means of assuaging her grief. This was her home: the hospital, the war, the place of the dead.

"He is confident in my abilities as steward," said Joseph. "But what if this should happen when I assist him in surgery?"

"You are not an assistant surgeon. He expects you to fulfill the duties you are assigned, not those given to others."

"We haven't the luxury of maintaining an easy separation of duties. With soldiers coming to us from Richmond and Petersburg and Augusta, each of us must perform many tasks. Less than a week ago, I was with Dr. Thompson when he amputated Blevins's arm. Had Dr. LaBorde not appeared, I might have been required to assist in the stitching."

"It was fortunate he was there."

"And had he not been? What then?" Joseph asked.

"There is no better place for you to be than here," she said. "Dr. Thompson knows how valuable you are to him and the hospital, and I daresay that you should recognize his value to you. Each of you offers in your own way the best care that the other needs."

"I am his steward, not his patient, Louisa." The vehemence of his protest surprised him, as did the expense of energy it required. He wrapped the blanket more tightly around his shoulders and sank into his gloom.

Louisa walked to the door of the sitting room and called for a servant. She told the woman to prepare hot tea for them, then returned to her chair. "You must forgive Nathan," she said.

"Who is Nathan?"

"The man who assisted you with your bath."

"Forgive him? I believe I should thank him."

"You were not aware of his behavior when he assisted you?"

Joseph struggled to recall the large man's mannerisms, his words, the feel of his hands on his body, even his scent—anything that would connect his present condition of being clean and clothed with the person who had performed the service. "I'm sorry," he muttered. "I don't remember."

"I was afraid his moaning might have offended you. He believes that your condition is either a sign of God's blessing or of demon possession."

Joseph shook his head. "And how many others think the same?"

"Oh, come now, Mr. Crawford. Nathan is primitive. No person whose opinion you should regard holds such a view."

He recoiled at the formality of address. His spirit felt the blow as had his body the convulsions. *Stupid,* he told himself. *Cannot make it work. Cannot find the words.* He wanted to tell her that he had read about the pathology and treatment of epilepsy in books that Dr. Thompson offered him. He knew the ancients, like her man Nathan, regarded epileptics as either blessed by the gods or inhabited by evil spirits.

He wanted to tell her what he'd discovered in the works of Galen and Celcus. Impress this learned woman with his knowledge. Tell her that in Celcus he found warrant for his belief that the disease emasculated him. There was more than an evocation of effeminacy in the word itself; Celcus compared epilepsy to women's hysteria, the disease arising from the uterus and leaving them in such a weakened state that they were prostrated, as after an epileptic fit. He did, however, note differences between the ailments. If the hysterical woman was enervated by her condition, at least she did not foam at the mouth. Nor did her nerves convulse, her eyes distend, her bowels discharge.

Galen claimed to have cured a child of epilepsy by hanging the root of peony around the child's neck. For the sake of experiment, he removed the root and stood by as the child was seized by convulsions. Reapplication of the root, he said, once more effected the cure. Not so for Joseph, who in spite of Dr. Thompson's scoffing at the ancient practice, procured a root of peony and used it as an amulet under his shirt. Thompson must have discovered it when he examined Joseph after his second attack, but the good doctor was merciful enough not to mention it when Joseph regained consciousness.

Haltingly, he spoke: "Dr. Thompson believes that my condition is idiopathic." It seemed to Joseph to have taken several minutes to utter the sentence, the last word causing confusion. Was it the right term? His mind too easily failed him in the hours after a seizure. "I wasn't born with it, he says. It was caused by my war injury."

Louisa helped him through his account. She supplied words when he couldn't find them, waited through his long pauses, encouraged him with nods and compassion that emanated from her eyes. He talked of James Longstreet, of the general's quiet courage, of the confidence he inspired in his men. He talked of the way cannon blasts and gunpowder created such a haze that morning at Bull Run that earth and sky melded together and it seemed to him in the moment just before he was shot that he might walk to the ends of the earth and never pass through the fog. And then, the moment of impact: the bullet entering and exiting his arm from back to front and upward. To this day he wondered about the projectile's course and trajectory. They were yet within fifty yards of the enemy. Had he been shot by a fellow Confederate whose gun discharged as he fell to his death? And who or what had struck him in the back of the head? A boot? The butt of a rifle? Twice he felt the crushing blow. If others came, he did not remember. Nor did he know what happened to the assailant. Had he left Joseph for dead and moved on to others with his attack? Had a friend rescued Joseph with a fatal shot or with a bayonet to the man's chest or head?

Joseph took solace in Thompson's belief that the head injury caused the seizures. The diagnosis at least offered the possibility of full recovery if that part of the brain repaired itself. There was in the doctor's assessment an avowal of Joseph's manly virtue. Better to sustain an injury in battle than to be born with the effete disease.

They talked late into the evening. A few minutes after ten o'clock, Louisa said, "You must be starved. I'll have Harriet bring food."

"No, thank you," Joseph said. "I've no appetite, and I have overstayed my welcome." He leaned forward to gain purchase on the arm of the couch. Louisa called Nathan, who appeared moments later.

"Bring the coach, Nathan," she said. "You will drive Mr. Crawford to his quarters on the campus, and help him to his room."

"Yes, ma'am." Nathan bowed his head and turned toward the door, still holding Joseph's left arm.

"I can walk," said Joseph. He nodded his gratitude at Nathan, gently pulled his arm away, and turned to face Louisa. "I am ever in your debt."

"No more than I am in yours," she said.

The carriage protected his head, but rain swept in from the right side, soaking his trousers. He did not care. His weary mind groped for the meaning of each nuance of her speech, the significance of a tilt of her head, the force of her intelligent gaze. *Not since my wife,* he thought, and closed his eyes in an attempt to recall her features. All he saw, however, was the face of his daughter. His wife had always said it was the replica of her father's.

| 12 |

Follow the Star

Rachel squatted in a row of shrubs and drew blood from her forearm with the jagged edge of a stone. She bit down on her tongue to stifle a cry. The squeak of the porch rockers twenty feet away made her see visions. She turned her glassy eyes up to the dark sky and imagined Bill, the strongest man on the plantation, doing as she'd asked, his big hands wrapped, as if around the neck of a chicken, twisting until Wells's snapped. "I'll let you if you do it," she'd said, and pulled her dress up to her navel.

Bill shook his head and backed away. "Don't want no part of that man," he said. "He done killed my daddy. Kill Mama too, if I turn on him. Jim, too, if I touch you. Put a hex on me."

Rachel lowered her dress and wept. She didn't want Bill. Or any other man, save Jim. It was for him that she wanted Wells killed. The way he used the strap on Jim. Way he dragged him across the ground. Jim had been gone too long. Sometimes she couldn't breathe for thinking of him.

She'd heard the word *Columbia*. From the shrubs she had to strain to hear the master and his wife, but she was sure they'd said the word several times over the last few weeks. Jim was there. Where was it? What was it? A place for people like Jim and her? Was a big tree there? Big enough for Jim to dig holes around? She wanted to find him, help him dig holes, bring nuts and berries to him. Biscuits when she could steal them.

Bill know, she told herself. *He know everything. Bill smart.* She scuttled backward out of the shrubs, then turned and crawled on her belly so the master could not hear her or see her shadow by the light of the moon. Minutes later, she stood and faced Bill.

"Don't ask me that again," Bill said. "Done told you I ain't doing nothing to that man. He the devil."

"Where Columbia?"

"What? What you care about Columbia?"

"Where it at?" She drew her hand back. Bill saw blood drip from her arm, the sheer point of a stone in her fist.

He pointed toward a star. "You crazy, girl. You can't get to Columbia. Too far. All this cold and rain. You die 'fore you get there."

"Don't you say nothing. You say where I gone, I bring Jim back for to put a hex on you."

Bill took two steps back. He'd seen that look in Rachel's eyes before. Every time the master whipped Jim, Rachel's eyes turned mean. She clawed at the dirt, yanked at her hair, scratched her skin or stabbed at it with stones until she bled. "I ain't gone say nothing," he said. "But you come here." He motioned with his hand toward the dirt-floor cabin twenty feet away. There, he pulled from a corner a coat, thin and torn in several places, but more substantial than the faded calico dress she wore. "Take your dress off," he said.

"What?"

"Take it off."

She did as he said. Bill took the dress and rubbed it vigorously in the dirt, then handed it back to her. "Now you put on the coat. It got my scent. They'll send the dogs for you. They be sniffing for you. Every chance you get, you wash in a creek. You best hope that coat keep my scent."

Rachel's eyes softened. She looked at the dirt floor and whispered, "Thank you."

"No need to thank me if them dogs catch you. You be cussing me then. Now, you do what I tell you." Bill pointed the way to Laurens, gave her landmarks to look for, told her some of his people were on the Bailey plantation there. "Ask for James Porter. Him first. He not there, ask for Isabella. They give you food, point you the rest of the way. Don't let anybody see you on the road. Keep to the woods in daylight, edge of the road—but not too close—at night."

Rachel turned to go. Bill put a hand on her shoulder. She turned to him and accepted his embrace. Then she left the cabin, made her way around the back side of the plantation, and followed the star to which Bill had pointed.

| 13 |
Order in the Asylum

Life in the asylum was governed by routine. Dr. Parker saw to that. Order was reasonable. To live the ordered life was to pay homage to God in whose image all rational creatures were created. As God ordered the day and the night, separating each from the other, appointed the seasons, and established the hierarchy of creatures, giving man dominion over them all, so those who followed the dictates of a daily order honored the designs of Providence.

In faithful obligation to those designs, Dr. Parker daily announced with a shrill ringing of the bell the tides of morning—five o'clock in summer, six in winter. Summoned from their beds, patients washed themselves under the scrutiny of attendants. Then they were marched to the refectory for breakfast. Afterward most patients were escorted to the courtyards where they exercised. A sound body houses a sound mind, Dr. Parker told them.

Patients who achieved emotional stability by benefit of rigorous daily exercise were rewarded. They were invited to help the staff clean the building. Labor alongside attendants in the execution of household duties marked one's progress toward reform. Those tasks completed, attendants spent the rest of the morning engaging patients in various amusements and labors—weeding the garden, shoeing horses, feeding cattle, attempting to calm those agitated by the noxious odors coming from Professor LeConte's Nitre and Mining facility nearby.

Promptly at noon, patients returned to the building and waited while the staff prepared lunch. Prescribed afternoon activities included walking, reading, or resting. The bell called everyone to supper at six o'clock. Patients retired by ten o'clock in summer, nine o'clock in winter. When Dr. Parker caught attendants sending their charges to bed earlier, sometimes immediately at nightfall, so as to enjoy an evening to themselves, he complained. A more severe reprimand he could not afford to issue. He was short-staffed already, and if a disgruntled employee left, it was nearly impossible to persuade people on the outside to consider work in the Lunatic Asylum at abysmal wages as an opportunity for gainful employment.

Order prevailed in the assignment of patients to their respective quarters. Men and women from families of means were separated from paupers. The docile were shielded from the deranged. That Mrs. Austell, a sixty-five-year-old patient who'd been in the asylum for six years, should enjoy a private apartment and her own nurse was as it should be. Her wealthy family had made ample provision for her care. So ample, in fact, that the contempt she heaped on her caretakers was largely ignored. If she demanded pound cake at every meal, as she had for more days in succession than any of her nurses could count, she would have it. Not to be mollified, however, Mrs. Austell raved against the incompetence of her nurses and the indignity of being housed with bedlamites. She hated the noises they made, their cursing and swearing and incessant babble. What order can there be, she complained to Dr. Parker, when a woman such as she was confined to a madhouse?

Dr. Parker maintained his equanimity in the storm of her tirades. He tried to reason with her. In a soothing voice, he advocated his belief that her son and daughter-in-law knew best what she needed, and that returning to the family plantation in Charleston was not it. He assured her that he and his able staff would make every effort to secure her comfort.

The rotund woman's eyes darted wildly as she spat through lips dry with the residue of her morning cake: "I cannot bear it, you imbecile! It is not right. Your holding me here is criminal. I should have gone mad already, were it not for the care of my blessed Savior!"

"And your Savior continues to care for you in this sacred place," said Dr. Parker. "He calls to you every Sabbath to join us for services led by Reverend Hort."

Mrs. Austell's cheeks reddened. "I cannot listen to that fool."

"Please, Mrs. Austell, he is a man of God whose sermons do me the most good."

"He is a Lutheran! What does he know of the ways of Providence?"

Although Dr. Parker could not prevail upon the fat Calvinist to broaden her theological perspective, he nevertheless continued to invite her to the service held in the large room on the first floor every Sunday. She refused. Still, the order of Sunday services bore no interruption. The obedient servant of the Lord, good Reverend Hort, who also ministered to the small congregation at Ebenezer Lutheran Church, preached Sunday in and Sunday out to the happy faithful and to the grudgingly compelled alike.

Jim was one of the compelled.

So too was Hayes.

Their mutual antagonism toward attending under compulsion might have enabled the men to come to an understanding, a sharing of common ground. For what these men loathed with equal intensity was order. Jim, however, failed to see that Hayes's stoic posture throughout the service was yet another form of rebellion. Unable to remain calm for the duration of the ritual, Jim chewed his fingers until they bled. Or he farted loudly in the middle of a prayer. Or fell to the floor during the singing of a hymn and feigned a paroxysm of spiritual intoxication. Always, it took several attendants to remove him. All the while, Hayes remained in a trance.

Lay by for him, Jim told himself. *He won't know what's coming till the day of judgment.*

And Jim did lay by for Hayes. They had fought once already, and Jim had gotten the better of him. But it wasn't enough. Jim wanted more. More blood. More satisfaction. Day after day he made his way out to the field, to the tall elm to which he whispered the details of his awful plan, and around which he wrapped his arms like a child clinging to its mother.

One day in late December, chance favored Jim's design. The wind blew hard that morning. Very few wandered outside. Jim was the first to test the bitter cold. Dr. Parker took his brisk stroll around the yard. Nothing challenged the man's constitution. Exercise, prayer, good diet, supervision of the staff to ensure consistent care of patients: To all of these rules he adhered zealously. His vigorous walk completed, Dr. Parker returned to his office to oversee the affairs of the morning. Jim had the field to himself. Until Hayes came.

At first Hayes ambled on the far side of the expanse away from Jim's elm. But after a while, he changed direction. He walked straight toward Jim.

Jim's heart pounded. He stepped behind the tree, kneeled, and pulled from a hole he had dug a stone the size of his fist. He'd buried several others —an arsenal he was storing. But this one was the best. Its heft and weight just right. On one end a jagged edge protruded. A perfect arrowhead.

Hayes moved deliberately. His gait quickened the closer he got. Jim pressed the point of the stone into his palm.

Then, within twenty yards of the tree, Hayes veered west. He returned to the building and entered, one last glance over his shoulder before pulling the door shut behind him.

Goddamn him, Jim muttered. *He knowed what was coming. Somebody told him.*

Jim did not reason that his silence on the matter would have prevented anyone's knowing his design. It only made sense that someone betrayed him, for nothing else could explain Hayes's abrupt detour. Someone had to be blamed.

Jim blamed Mrs. Austell.

He had never actually seen the woman. He'd only heard her. He heard her berate her nurses. He heard her demand more pound cake at each meal. He heard her condemn *those bedlamites* who made too much noise. He did not know the meaning of the word, but understood that it had something to do with noise. Although she made a lot of noise, she was not herself a bedlamite. Mrs. Austell was an important woman. She had servants. She got cake on demand. She was fat. Jim knew that from the remarks he'd overheard her nurses make when they thought no one else was close enough to hear them. Jim got close. He hid in corners. Like a cat he prowled. Jim knew secrets.

That fat woman told Hayes to watch out, Jim Wells was laying by for him. Well, he'd lay by, all right. Not just for Hayes, now. He'd lay by for that fat woman. The one who betrayed him.

Jim Wells would put to rights the order of revenge.

| **PART III** |
January 1865

| 14 |
A Tour of the City

Joseph felt himself fortunate to receive an invitation to a dinner party at the Chesnut home the last Friday in January. He dressed in his finest: gray trousers strapped beneath the instep; pleated dress shirt; cravat knotted to create an impression of indifference; single-breasted shawl collar vest; black single-breasted tailcoat. Including his attendance when President Davis addressed the city from the front porch of the house on Plain Street, this was his second visit to the Chesnut home. He knew the meal would be splendid and the conversation stimulating. Most enticing of all, Louisa would be there.

He was to be at the front gate of the campus at six o'clock. Thompson had offered to pick him up. The doctor was bringing along a friend from Greenville, well known to the Chesnuts.

Joseph stepped out to the college green half an hour before Thompson's carriage was to arrive. He had admired the green and its walkway, shaped like a horseshoe, since he'd first looked out on it the morning of his arrival. Tonight seemed ideal for a stroll. It had rained earlier in the day; he could hardly remember a day over the last five weeks when it had not. A moderate breeze blew westerly. Joseph wrapped his arms together and walked up the south side of campus away from Sumter Street. As always, he was struck by the size and solidity of the buildings.

There were ten structures in all, five on either side of the green. Each stood three stories tall. Six dormitory and classroom buildings—Rutledge, Pinckney, and Legare on the south side, DeSaussure, Harper, and Elliot on the north—were divided into three sections. On either side of the central structures, wings extended some eighty feet in length. He arrived at the last building on the north side, Rutledge, the first unit erected on the campus in 1802. He could not count the number of times he'd been in its chapel in the last two and a half years. Situated in the center of the building, it occupied two stories. Thompson had told him that originally the floor above the chapel housed the library, later converted to a dormitory when the new library was built. Now, Joseph thought sadly, in place of the repository of learning were hospital beds and blood-stained floors. He entered the chapel and looked at the pulpit surrounded by a semi-octagonal stage. On either side of the pulpit, steps led to seats that would be occupied on the Sabbath by church officers, another set of steps to the pulpit itself. Windows rose very nearly to the high ceiling, intricate ornamental work around each one.

He left the chapel and continued his walk around the top of the horseshoe. On the north side of the campus stood DeSaussure some three hundred feet from Rutledge. The buildings, nearly identical in appearance, faced each other, as did the two other dormitory and classroom buildings on the north side and their counterparts on the south. Thompson had told him that before the campus was converted to a hospital, Harper housed the Euphradian Society, and Legare the Clariosophic Society.

Joseph passed the McCutcheon House, a faculty residence. As did the dormitory and classroom units, this faculty house faced its complement on the south side. When he arrived at Harper, Joseph stood with his back to the building and looked across the green. Stately elm trees appointed the grounds. He could only imagine how beautiful the college green was before the war. Now the place was trafficked by horse- and mule-drawn carriages which tore up the sod, especially since so much rain had drenched the ground over the last several weeks.

In the center of the green stood a solid granite base from which rose a beautiful marble obelisk almost nine feet tall. The Maxcy Monument honored the college's first president. Thompson had told Joseph that Robert Mills designed the monument, that it was built in 1827, and that it represented the initial stages of an architectural design that reached its artistic peak in Mills's masterpiece, the Washington Monument, erected nine years later.

He resumed his walk, came to the end of the pathway, and stood in front of the library, an expansive brick edifice with four massive white columns appointing the entrance. On the opposite side of the green sat Lieber College, now occupied by Professor LeConte's family. The library and Lieber College were the only buildings on campus that faced and did not resemble each other. Even so, each structure was magnificent in its own right. Joseph recalled that when he'd first arrived, he was given a tour of the campus by

LaBorde. The professor told him that prior to the war, the South Carolina College library had been one of the best in the nation. Built in 1840, it was the first free-standing college library in the United States. Harvard followed a year later with a library independent of any other building on its campus. When LaBorde had been a student in the 1830s, the facility was larger even than Princeton's or Columbia's, and by 1850 it held more than 18,000 volumes. Joseph imagined the pleasure he would derive from spending hour after hour in such a place, poring over books of philosophy, history, literature. Days spent as a youth in the fields, stealing time away from his father's mean oversight to read the books his teacher had given him, would be as nothing to the opportunity a great library would afford him.

A few minutes before the hour, Joseph arrived at the wall that fronted Sumter Street. Nearly seven feet in height, the brick structure, if LaBorde were to be believed, was built initially to keep in unruly students who often escaped the confines of campus to carouse in town and frequent taverns and houses of prostitution. Ah, he thought, the vagaries of youth. How many of those young men would now exchange lewd behavior and warring alike for the opportunity to seclude themselves in the library, or to participate in a debate or a literary discussion sponsored by one of the learned societies, or to worship in the chapel.

He meditated at the gate until the carriage arrived. As he made his way toward the street, he caught the edge of a cow paddy, and anxiously cleaned the boot by dragging it several times through the wet grass. He completed his ministrations just as the driver hopped down from his seat and opened the door.

Before Joseph adjusted his vision to the inside of the carriage, Thompson greeted him: "Good evening, young friend."

"To you as well, sir." Joseph sat across from the two men.

"Joseph, it is my honor to introduce you to Mr. Benjamin Perry."

Joseph shook Perry's hand. He was impressed with the firm grip. The carriage started. By the slant of moonlight through the windows, Joseph could make out the man's features. Of medium height, Perry's most prominent attributes were an aquiline nose, a rigid jaw, and small spectacles. Joseph had heard much of him since coming to South Carolina. Perry's Union sympathies were no secret to anyone who resided in the heart of secession. Yet when South Carolina finally broke with the Union, he stood in support of his state.

As the carriage passed Trinity Episcopal Church, Perry pointed to the Gothic structure, its two citadels on either side towering above the sanctuary, and on each citadel eight pinnacles topped with a fleur de lis pointing skyward, thus augmenting the appearance of height. On the left side of the building, a wrought iron fence surrounded the famous graveyard where lay buried a number of South Carolina's Revolutionary War heroes. Joseph wondered how many bodies of Confederate soldiers would soon be entombed in that hallowed ground.

"I have always admired that building," said Perry. "The original church was built in 1812, Mr. Crawford. What you see now was remodeled twenty years ago by the renowned architect Edward White. It is majestic, is it not?"

"It is," said Joseph.

"Have you ever been inside?"

"No, sir. I am not an Episcopalian."

"Which is your church, Mr. Crawford?"

"I was raised a Presbyterian. I must admit, however, that of late I have not been a regular attender."

"Your duties at the hospital have demanded much of you, I know. All of you." He nodded at Thompson. "When you have occasion, you might enjoy a look inside Trinity. Its stained-glass windows were shipped from Munich just a few years ago, and are as stunning as any I have seen in America."

The coach turned onto Gervais Street. Joseph said to Thompson, "I believe your coachman has made a mistake."

"No," said Thompson. "I promised Mr. Perry a quick tour."

They passed Mayor Goodwyn's home. Perry said, "I have not seen Thomas in a long while. How is the good mayor these days?"

"Nervous for his city," said Thompson. "I think he will be happy to relinquish his post."

Perry looked at Joseph. "As many times as I have visited this city, Mr. Crawford, I never tire of seeing places that are familiar to me. I took a brief walk earlier from the Congaree Hotel to the campus. Dr. Thompson is kind to indulge my whims. These buildings bring to mind momentous events in our state's history. Sometimes I look at them and it seems I can hear from brick and timber the voices of friends long gone."

On Richardson Street they passed the Congaree Hotel, the Independent Fire Company of John McKenzie, the Town Hall Market, the State

Ordnance Warehouse, a Confederate Government Office, three commissary stores, the Naval Agent Office, the Commandant of Prisoners Office, Confederate State Military Offices, and two Treasury Department Offices.

Thompson swept a hand right and left. "The industry of war."

Perry nodded. "How the city has changed these past four years."

They passed two more Confederate Government Offices and approached the First Baptist Church on Plain Street. "May we stop here for a moment?" Perry asked.

Thompson leaned out the carriage window and called to the coachman: "Pull over, Henry."

The men stepped down and stood with their backs to the church. Perry pointed across the street to a large brick house with high arched windows. "There lives a great man, Mr. Crawford. Do you know Dr. Gibbes?"

"I've not had the pleasure of making his acquaintance."

"Have you not, Joseph?" asked Thompson. "I am surprised. He has often been in my office."

"I have seen him on the campus, but we have never been introduced."

"I will see that you are," said Thompson.

Perry said, "I hope one day you will have that privilege, Mr. Crawford. Dr. Gibbes is a man of extraordinary achievement. You will find in his home more volumes than you can count—science, history, literature, art. He has shown me quite a number of eighteenth-century manuscripts that concern South Carolina's involvement in the Revolutionary War. I hesitate to estimate the number of fossils and other specimens in that house. Thousands, I am certain. We have not always seen eye to eye on political matters, the doctor and I, but always I have respected his intellect. Do you know his work, *The Present Earth the Remains of a Former World?*"

"I read it some years ago. As I recall, the major argument has to do with the age of the earth."

"That is correct. Dr. Gibbes maintains on the basis of his study of fossils that the earth is millions of years older than is traditionally believed." He paused, then said, "As beautiful as his house is on the outside, its contents are more impressive, and the man himself even more."

"I look forward to meeting him," said Joseph.

Perry turned his head toward the church. "What a contrast we have here." With a finger he tapped his chin a few times, as though contemplating the structure. Then he lowered his hand and said, "I do not like the Greek

Revival Style. This—" he pointed at the four thick columns supporting the roof—"looks more imposing than inviting to me."

Thompson said to Joseph, "This is prelude to a more scathing appraisal. His quarrel is more with the place itself than with the architecture of the building."

Perry smiled, as if to acknowledge the truth of Thompson's remark. He looked at Joseph and said, "My friend refers, of course, to my objection to secession. This is where the delegates gathered five years ago to cast their unanimous vote. But there is more to my regard for this institution than a quarrel over political leanings, Mr. Crawford. How many within those hallowed walls do you think would scorn Dr. Gibbes if they read his work?"

"Many, I am sure."

"I daresay all of them would. It is a great pity that an institution we need for the cultivation of morality seems to require of its adherents a closing of the mind. Would we be foolish to imagine a time when science and religion may be compatible?"

"Are they not already?" asked Joseph.

"How do you mean, sir?"

"The church embraces the advances of science when doing so is convenient. When the delegates to the Secession Convention entered those doors in 1860, they were fully prepared to vote for us to go to war. Not one of them would have hesitated then or now to use the engines of war that science has afforded us."

"And yet they who call themselves Christian would crucify a man for arguing a scientific hypothesis that contravenes their reading of Scripture."

"Yes," said Joseph.

"An irony that confounds me," said Perry. "I sometimes wonder whether the breach between science and religion will grow to such proportions that one or the other will have to concede the fight."

"Either extreme would cause us great harm."

"Damned on the one hand, ignorant on the other."

"To be one is to be the other," said Thompson.

"Yes," said Perry, and looked again at Joseph. "Let us hope that wisdom prevails, Mr. Crawford."

"I cannot imagine that a hundred years from now the church will rail against the achievements of science. Surely the pulpit will not be the mouth-piece of ignorance."

The men stood side by side reposed in thought. After a few moments, Perry shivered. "It grows colder by the minute. I cannot remember a harsher winter than this one. Let us go and enjoy the hospitality of friends."

Rain began to fall just before they arrived at the Chesnut home. The men dashed from the coach to the front porch. Before they entered, Joseph's stomach pitched. He was nervous about being in the company of people well above his station. As much as he wished to be considered their equal, he knew that he was not.

| 15 |
Hunger

She had learned from Jim how to fend off the cold. The deeper she dug, the more she could burrow into the hole and be shielded from the wind. She pulled broken limbs and dead leaves over her, welcomed the dirt as it settled on her body and in her hair.

How far she had traveled, she couldn't guess, but she'd slept many nights in different places, each one farther removed from home. Dogs bayed in the distance, but she knew they weren't chasing her. Their barks receded moment by moment. After somebody important, she imagined. Somebody the master want. Master don't want me. Never did. See the way he look at me, shame and hate in his eyes. He ain't gone send no dogs for me. Patrollers neither. Still, have to watch for them. Patrollers worse than dogs. Dogs kill you fast. Patrollers make it take long. Way they done Big David. Way they do Little David one day, he not careful. Not me, though. Master don't want me. Want me gone.

Deeper and deeper she clawed into the earth. Hungry. She felt it crawl over her arm. Knew by the way it inched across her flesh that it couldn't be anything but a harmless worm. Good when you're hungry. What Jim said. He showed her. Lifted the slithery morsel to his mouth, dropped it in. Keep me alive, she thought, and curled her fingers to her mouth, sucked first, then crunched the thin body between her front teeth.

| 16 |
In the Company of the Great

Inside the Chesnut home, James Chesnut conversed with Campbell Bryce and Reverend William Martin, the good Methodist, in a corner of the parlor, while Mary Chesnut, Mrs. Bryce, Mrs. Martin, her daughter Isabella, and Louisa McCord talked in the other corner. Conversation halted as everyone greeted the newcomers.

Joseph was intimidated by the Chesnuts. He'd heard that Mrs. Chesnut could be either gay or glum. When her spirits were good, she was as delightful as any hostess in the city. But she could just as easily turn a dark eye on the whole gathering. Her mood was said to be as variable as the wind. The general, on the other hand, was solid. He was a quiet man, reserved, befitting his rank. Chesnut motioned all the men back toward the fireplace, where he and Bryce resumed their dialogue.

"Hampton believes Sherman has no interest in Columbia," said Chesnut.

"Surely he will not neglect the capital city," said Bryce.

"Sherman will not want to engage Hampton's troops. Beauregard is also prepared to send reinforcements."

"There is much here that will interest Sherman," said Dr. Thompson. All the men turned to him. "The federal officers imprisoned at the asylum, for example. More than twelve hundred, I am given to understand. Not to mention Federal soldiers at the hospital. Our military depots. Professor LeConte's mining operation. Sherman must know of the recent influx of people into Columbia, and of the storing of jewels, title deeds, bonds, and other valuables in our banks. This city has much to offer him, I fear."

"And many obstacles, as well," said Chesnut. "He might have come here in 1861, when the city's population was one-third what it is now. If Sherman enters Columbia at this point, he knows he will have thousands of slaves to contend with. Many of our good Negroes will oppose him, while a few rebels will want to attach themselves to his company, which places upon him the burden of feeding them along with his army. Either way, he will be greatly inconvenienced."

Joseph wanted to believe that Chesnut's information was reliable, that the general had been apprised of Confederate reconnaissance that he could not divulge to citizens. It was common knowledge throughout the city that the Chesnut home had been for several weeks the gathering place of Generals Johnston, Wheeler, Lovell, Beauregard, and Hampton. Here they studied maps and guessed at points of Sherman's advance. Chesnut had to know better than any man present what he was talking about. But Thompson's analysis seemed reasonable. And of course the point that no one had yet mentioned: Sherman must surely covet the prospect of burning the city where secession began.

Shortly after eight o'clock the group moved to the table. Joseph was pleased to be seated between Louisa and Isabella Martin. To Isabella's right sat Thompson, and beside him Mrs. Bryce. Across the table were Perry, Campbell Bryce, and the Martins. The Chesnuts presided at either end of the table.

Midway through the meal, Mary Chesnut asked Perry whether he might ever again consider editing a newspaper.

"I harbor no illusions of returning to that mad business," Perry said. "There is no more contentious work than that of putting into print the opinions one holds on the important matters of his time."

Joseph wondered whether Perry had foremost in mind his duel with a rival editor who had vilified Perry for his support of the Tariff Acts some thirty years earlier. Thompson had told him the story. Perry shot his antagonist through the hip. Hours later, the man died.

"A friend of my father's wrote for the *Southern Recorder* more than forty years ago that freedom was as important to the Negro as to the white man. He challenged his readers to consider whether they would not prefer freedom with poverty to the best condition of the slave. The man heard no end of slanders to his name. To this day he is scorned by his adversaries."

"As well he should be," said Louisa. "What a preposterous idea. Such a man has lost his wits in silly notions propounded by the likes of Mrs. Stowe."

Perry looked at her. "And how would you propose to disabuse Mrs. Stowe and her legions of sympathizers of such notions?"

"By having them visit our state, Mr. Perry, and observing firsthand the condition of our Negroes. I doubt very much whether Mrs. Stowe ever bothered to cross the line of a slave state. The abuses she describes in her little romance may occur in a border state, but not in the heart of the Confederacy. And those abuses would not occur in border states were it not for the meddling of fanatical abolitionists who would deprive every man of his property. The slavery of these Southern United States has done more to improve the lot of the Negro than any other institution under which he has labored."

"Come now, Mrs. McCord," said Perry. "You cannot be serious. Do you wish to argue that slavery has done more for the Negro than the institution of religion?"

"Let us not draw a facile distinction between the one and the other, Mr. Perry. God established the system of slavery."

As if cued by Louisa, Reverend Martin pointed a finger heavenward and said, "Both thy bondmen, and thy bondmaids, which thou shalt have, shall be of the heathen that are round about; of them shall ye buy bondmen and bondmaids. And ye shall take them as an inheritance for your children after you, to inherit them for a possession; they shall be your bondmen forever."

Joseph noted that Isabella Martin's head drooped slightly and she closed her eyes, whether in gesture of prayer or embarrassment at her father's interjection, he could not say. In any event, she had the attention of Mrs. Chesnut, who watched her solicitously.

"I could cite many others, chapter and verse," said the minister. "Nowhere in the bible is there a prohibition against slavery, despite the wayward testimony of abolitionists."

Poor Mrs. Martin, nearly deaf, bobbled her head between her husband and daughter, and squinted as though to will the jingle of words to appear on a script.

"Ah, yes," said Perry. "The Calhoun position. Slavery and Christianity are bound together in the fabric of humaneness. The Negro improves morally, physically, and intellectually in servitude to his master."

"Do you doubt it, sir?" said Louisa. "If the country had listened to Mr. Calhoun forty years ago, we might not be in this mess today. Dare you posit a logic by which the Negro, given the squalor and ignorance from which he came in Africa, might humanize himself?"

"A point well made," said Mrs. Bryce. "Negroes were savages when brought to this land. They knew nothing of decency, of civilization, of Christianity."

She spoke with a confidence that Joseph understood to be the property of those whose views were rarely challenged. Nevertheless, Mrs. Campbell Bryce did not seem overbearing, any more than her husband, whose demeanor in no way suggested that he was a man of violence. Yet Campbell Bryce was said to have killed a man with a dagger in his youth when they quarreled. Perhaps his reserve hid his true nature. What was it about such people that gave them to believe so wholeheartedly in their convictions that they could as easily slay an adversary as compliment a friend? Joseph had once heard Mrs. Bryce herself claim that her husband taught their daughter to mold bullets and make cartridges for the Confederate Army. When a hot bullet scorched the girl's wrist, she was said to have boasted that she was the first soldier wounded for the cause. And if reports Joseph heard were true, on the morning the Bryces' son rode out of Columbia with the Congaree Cavaliers, it was his mother, not his father, who buckled his sword. Yet if hot blood ran through the veins of this family, they were also known for their tireless generosity. Save Louisa McCord, no woman in Columbia worked harder to relieve the suffering of soldiers than Mrs. Bryce. Since the beginning of the war, she had not ceased to work on behalf of the sick and wounded.

"And in bondage," said Perry, turning to Mrs. Bryce, "they are afforded the advantages, as you say, of decency, civilization, and Christianity?"

"Of course they are," she said. "Here, thank God, in our great land, they have been Christianized. Do they not owe us gratitude for rescuing their souls from the flames of perdition?"

"So we have saved them!" said Perry.

"We have been the emissaries of the gospel," said Mrs. Bryce. "It is God alone who saves."

Perry tented his fingers and rested his chin on the apex.

Reverend Martin cleared his throat, an act of invocation. When everyone looked at him, the minister smiled and said, "God, in his all-wise providence, permitted the enslavement of the Negro to bring him to the saving knowledge of Christ our Lord." He then leaned toward his wife and repeated himself.

Louisa said, "There is more to this matter than religious principle. We could as well examine the idiocy of Mrs. Stowe's economic theory. Would any sane master whip to death his property, and thus lose what he has invested for his own well-being and that of his family? Why not go out and shoot all your cattle for sport, or slay the mule for not pulling the plow fast enough? The logic of commerce alone prevents a slave-owner from disposing of his property. Mrs. Stowe forgets that even the vices of men are so arranged by an omniscient Providence that they are frequently found to balance one another. Even if the slave-owner were the devil she imagines him to be, his malignity must be checked by his avarice."

"A convenient argument for the slave-owner, if not for the slave," said Perry. "Are we not to assume that the Negro, in daily observance of the freedoms his master enjoys, will not therefore become jealous of those freedoms, and of the master himself?"

"Jealousy exists only among rivals, Mr. Perry. Brother may rise against brother, friend against friend. Competition and conflict exist in any relationship where there is equality of intellect. But between master and slave no such rivalry exists. Shall we encourage the infant to judge himself the rival of his father?"

"What do you say to those who insist that the inequality of which you speak has nothing to do with innate ability, but rather with the social station, or in this case, the race into which one is born?"

"No one of any scholarly repute would argue such foolishness. Science has proven that the Negro is intellectually inferior to the white man. Surely you know the work of Josiah Nott."

"Josiah's wife, Sarah, is James's cousin," said Mary Chesnut. "You must be referring either to his *Types of Mankind* or *Indigenous Races of the Earth*."

"Both," said Louisa.

"What did she say?" asked Mrs. Martin.

Her husband growled into her ear.

"Yes, yes, I am familiar with the work," said Perry. "And with the thrust of both: the Negro and the white man are separately created species."

"Not only science, but experience confirms it," said Louisa. "Were it not for us, the Negro would remain forever in bondage to ignorance and superstition. God made the white man to teach and to lead. To forsake that duty is to deny our sacred calling. Slavery is God's dispensation, a providential caring for the weak, a refuge for the portionless. We have made and shall continue to make Christians of this heathen race."

"But liberty, Mrs. McCord." Perry's eyes brightened. He leaned into the table. "Liberty cries out from every breast. What are we to say to the slave who struggles to break his bonds?"

"It is not the Negro who dreams of liberty. Never has there been a better cared for or happier innocent than the Negro slave of the South."

Joseph recalled the dark, sullen face of a woman who entered the parlor of the McCord home the night of his seizure, deposited a tray of tea and refreshment, then left the room when told to attend to other duties. He was about to say he had seen Harriet faithfully perform her duties, though he could make no claim to knowing her. But before he could speak, Louisa turned once more to Perry and said, "Vile abolitionists like John Brown and silly women like Mrs. Stowe may speak of the Negro's desire for liberty, but the Negro cannot grasp a conception which belongs so naturally to the white man. In his natural condition, the Negro may be, by turns, slave or tyrant, but never the free man."

"Certainly not in the same land inhabited by whites," said Mary Chesnut. All eyes turned to her. "Anarchy would follow abolition. Every Negro would turn on every white person. It would be worse than any slave rebellion we have seen thus far. We have all seen that terror, and surely we have learned its lesson. The kinder and more tolerant the master, the more terrible the Negro's vengeance. Left to themselves, they are brutes."

The party was silent. Everyone there knew the story of the murder of Mary Chesnut's cousin by her slaves in Society Hill. Her cousin was too lenient with her Negroes, Mary said. She could not bear to let her husband punish them when they needed correction. That they turned on gentle Mary Witherspoon was proof that at heart, Negroes were monsters.

"Thank heavens my father-in-law knew how to quell a rebellion," Mary Chesnut said. She looked at her husband.

"That was nearly fifty years ago," said James Chesnut. "Let us not dredge up those wretched events of long ago."

"Not so long ago as we may wish to think, dear husband. Has this war not excited troublesome Negroes throughout the South?"

Joseph saw in Louisa's grim expression a compulsion to respond. He could hear her challenging Mary Chesnut's claim, conceding only that while a few rebellious slaves might cause strife, most were content with their condition. Where else, she would insist, would slaves receive the Christian love and care that their masters provided? But she restrained herself. Decorum would be preserved at all costs. Mary Chesnut's remembrance of her murdered cousin trumped all argument.

Mrs. Martin interrupted the conversation by cupping a hand to her ear, leaning toward her husband, and muttering, "Wha—?" The minister, ever dutiful, shouted a few words into her ear. She grimaced and nodded.

Joseph felt a tingling sensation in his left leg. He looked at Thompson and indicated with a downward glance that he needed to leave. Thompson announced that he was sorry to have to excuse himself. "We are expecting a train from Richmond tomorrow. Another forty patients. I don't know where we shall put them."

Outside, Thompson helped Joseph up into the carriage, and sat beside him. Perry took the seat facing them.

"How is it now, Joseph?" Thompson asked.

"I'm all right, I think."

"The leg?"

"Better now. I smelled a noxious odor just before we left. I feared it was the sign of an approaching seizure."

"You need rest. We stayed too late this evening. Much too late, given the demands of our work." He looked at Perry and said, "Forgive my abrupt departure. I have pushed my young friend beyond the limits of human endurance, and I am sorry for it."

"No need to apologize," said Perry. "I am weary myself."

They rode in silence to the campus, where Thompson and Joseph bade Perry farewell. Thompson then told his coachman to return Perry to the Congaree Hotel.

The men walked up the promenade. Thompson proffered an arm when Joseph halted before the first door of Pinckney. "What?" said Joseph.

"One door up, Joseph."

"Oh yes, of course."

At the second entrance, Thompson said, "Shall I stay with you a while?"

"No. I am fine. I will see you at dawn."

"Not so early, Joseph. The train will not arrive before eleven o'clock. Rest until then. We'll have plenty to do once the wounded are here."

Joseph reached for the door, then pulled his hand back, and turned once more to Thompson. "I am sorry to have made you leave earlier than you may have wished."

Thompson looked surprised. "You are jesting, surely. I hope my desires were not so obvious."

"To stay?"

"To leave. I cannot bear such company for too long."

"But I thought you liked—"

With a wave of the hand, Thompson interrupted him. "They are fine people, all, Joseph. But a bit rich for my blood. I was not born to such privilege. I am happy to dine with them on occasion. But after a short time, I grow weary of the airs of the high and mighty."

The admission stunned Joseph. He'd always assumed that Thompson came from a prominent family in the region. More surprising yet was the fervor of the doctor's declaration. Joseph could not recall a moment when Thompson looked as though he felt so out of place at the party as Joseph had. That Thompson genuinely liked Benjamin Perry was obvious in the way he introduced his friend when they picked Joseph up at the college gate. And Perry was every bit the landed gentleman that any other man at the table could claim to be. What, then? Was it class or manner to which he objected? Had the vehemence of Louisa's argument with Perry offended Thompson? Had he regarded her manner as haughty? Or was it that he simply disagreed with the woman?

Could Joseph blame his friend if in fact he had found Louisa rude, her position untenable? Joseph thought her argument naïve, but he never would have said as much. He certainly had never met a slave who appeared to be grateful for the opportunity to be Christianized. But of course he did not actually know that many slaves. He'd *seen* them, yes, many of them, but that was no substitute for owning them, or for overseeing their work in the house and on the land every day, or for being so close to them day in and day out as to know them by name. Louisa had surely spoken as if she knew them, understood them better than they understood themselves, could discern their deepest desires, their truest needs, when they themselves could not. Perhaps that was what riled Thompson: the smugness of her position, the self-assurance of her piety.

Joseph had no idea how to respond. He merely nodded, thanked Thompson, and entered the building occupied by convalescing soldiers in every room save one, his own. Joseph's room was eight feet square, and included a bed, a small bureau, a chair, and a table with a reading lamp. He sat in the chair and, eyes closed, envisioned the faces and voices of those gathered at the Chesnut home. Louisa, as always, saber-sharp of mind, unwilling to concede an inch in argument. As tough in battle as Lee or Longstreet, and every bit as ready to defend her country and its principles. Perry, either goading or challenging her, as eager to take ground as she was to defend it. Mary Chesnut chilling the crowd with mention of her cousin's murder. The others making brief and intermittent contributions to the exchange.

All except Thompson, that is, whose silence Joseph understood now not to be the sign of fatigue or docile agreement, but rather an acknowledgment of what Joseph himself felt: that the more insistent one's defense of a cause, the more inevitable its defeat. The exact opposite, perhaps, of the soldier's widow whose grief is so immense that she cannot cry, can hardly utter a word, and when the first sound finally issues, it comes as a calm and gentle respiration, nearly as still as the body in its grave.

What, then, was all the fuss about at dinner? A desperate attempt to defend one's position in the face of all that threatened to destroy it? A declaration of the nobility of an idea, or a cry against the sweep of history that crushes every human monument to its own ingenuity?

Joseph opened his eyes and lifted from the table his copy of Chisholm's *Manual of Military Surgery*. He turned to a familiar passage:

Malingering, or the feigning of disease, has ever been, and will continue to be, popular with soldiers, irrespective of the material of which an army is composed. Honesty of purpose and patriotic motives are not the only incentives to enlistment, even against such an invasion as our enemies are now carrying on for the destruction of all our most sacred and cherished rights.

Included in the list of feigned illnesses was epilepsy.

Joseph closed the book and blew out the lamp. For a few minutes he sat slumped, rubbing his temples. He cursed his weakness, then lugged himself to bed.

| 17 |
The Whipping Post

Joseph woke to the noise of a steady downpour a few minutes before eight o'clock. He couldn't remember having slept so late, or for so long, since the weeks following the death of his wife and daughter. Even then, he didn't sleep so much as refuse to leave his bed.

His leg felt strong again, absent the tingling sensation of the night before. He looked through the window at the gray-black sky, grabbed his coat, and set off for the City Hall and Market on the corner of Washington and Richardson Streets. He liked to spend a half hour or so at the market on Saturday mornings, not to buy goods or trade gossip, but to watch people. It was a pleasant diversion to move from the confines of the hospital with its moribund patients to the bustle of life in the city square.

Half a block from his destination he came upon a large crowd of people gazing at a wooden platform on which two slaves were shackled. One of them was strapped to a whipping post. The man's bare back was exposed to the cold. The other slave, bound hand and foot, stood ten feet away from the post. He would be next.

On the platform stood a white man dressed elegantly. He faced the crowd and called out, "These men must be punished for rebellious activity. I found them behind my barn laughing and carrying on about Sherman." The man pointed at the slave bound to the post. "This one said, 'Uncle Billy what his soldiers call him.' He pointed to the other. This one said, 'Soon be *Master* Billy to these whites.' I won't tolerate such talk from saucy niggers." He waved a fist in the air. Cheers erupted from the crowd.

A burly man more than six feet tall held a bullwhip. Joseph recognized him as Robert Towns, the owner of a pack of bloodhounds that he rented to plantation owners or to municipal officers to hunt down escaped slaves and Federal soldiers. Tales circulated throughout Columbia about the way the dogs mauled their prey.

Towns scanned the faces in the crowd and settled on the freckled visage of a small boy who stood next to his mother. Rain dripped from his brow. Towns smiled. Ugly teeth—some yellow, some black—showed through a grizzled beard. The boy wrapped both arms around his mother's leg and buried his face in her dress. He did not look up until the first crack of the whip. Then he watched in awe as each lash made the black flesh quiver. A man in the crowd yelled, "That'll teach them niggers. Give it to him hard, Towns."

Joseph lost count of the lashes, but was sure he'd seen upwards of forty. Rivulets of blood poured from the man's back. Pieces of flesh tore away and were hurled liked fish bait on the reptilian tail of the whip. If the beaten man cried out, Joseph could not hear him for the noise of the crowd. Some cheered Towns on; others grunted as though they felt the sting of the lash on their own bodies.

Excited by the clamor of the crowd, Towns inhaled deeply, and with all his strength brought the lash down once more across the man's back. The force of the blow made the man's body shake. His head jerked upward. This time, Joseph heard him scream. The sound, however, did not seem to issue involuntarily. Nor was it a cry for mercy. The voice was filled with more rage than pain, and seemed to be directed primarily neither at Towns nor at the man's master, but at heaven itself.

Before the next lash fell, the man opened his eyes, glazed with anger and pain. They settled on Joseph. Joseph could not move. He could not look away. Something in those eyes arrested him in one moment, and in the next caused a searing sensation throughout his body, as if burning coals had been heaped on him. The man appeared not only to see him, but to know him. The eyes held a fierce and penetrating intelligence. It was as if the beaten man saw not only into Joseph's heart, but into the very heart of the world. Why, in that brutal moment, had he chosen to share only with Joseph the wealth of his grim and terrible knowledge?

Joseph leaned forward. He reached a hand toward the man, a gesture ridiculous in its aim, for they were separated by more than fifty feet. He was on the verge of speaking, demanding that the whipping cease, when down came the lash again, and the man's head fell forward. Joseph felt he had been released from a spell more powerful than any he'd ever known, save that of the dark one that settled on him and threatened to destroy him in the months following the loss of his wife and child. He lowered his head. As he began to back away, he bumped a man behind him. Before he could turn and apologize, he felt the jab of an elbow in his back. "Watch where you're going."

Joseph balled his fist and turned. The man was old and feeble. His body bent leftward over a cane. In the man's face Joseph saw the reflection of his own rage. He shoved past the withered gawker, nearly toppling him, and moved beyond the frenzied crowd. The crackle of the whip faded as he reached the far side of Market Square. He was afraid of being spoken to, afraid he would stumble over his words, speak gibberish. People might think him a bedlamite escaped from the asylum. He needed to escape, find a haven that would keep him safe, isolated, free from human contact.

Head lowered, he walked as fast as he could down Washington Street. He passed the Methodist Church before he realized he'd gone too far, then turned back toward the college green.

In his room, he doffed his coat and sat on the edge of the bed. He could not dismiss the image of Robert Towns, face red and wild with the ecstasy of power. His neck bulged. His long and muscled arm moved backward and forward, backward and forward, the mechanics of movement refined to inflict pain. He played to the crowd's awe, exerted all his energy to perform for them, as though in hope that reports of his skill with the whip would be told with the reverence he attached to the savagery of his hunting dogs. He could do to a man's body what the hounds could do, yet with surgical precision, stretching out the pain until the victim fainted, administering more pain when he revived. The dogs mauled; Towns cut, sliced, tore. They were beasts gorging themselves on human flesh, he a sculptor chiseling with his instrument until he achieved what he desired: a body deformed by torture, a creature reduced to abject submission.

Joseph hated the man. He hated the way Towns paraded himself before the people, posturing as a man of admirable repute, someone they should revere. Or rather, fear. Robert Towns was an imbecile drunk on notions of self-importance. He was common. Dirty. His teeth were rotten, his odor rancid. He was no better than a pig wallowing in his own filth. How could others stand by and cheer on such a wretch, as if he himself were of the rank and voice of authority? He was nothing of the sort. Robert Towns was the instrument of his superiors, nothing more. Appointed to administer punishment, not to decide the rule of law, but to execute it at the order of his betters.

More powerful than his contempt for Towns, however, was his empathy for the beaten man. Surely he chose Joseph out of all people gathered to settle his gaze on, for the eyes themselves seemed to say, *I know you. I know this world and its ways, and I know what this world does to people like you and me.* Yes, that was it: The man's look was penetrating precisely because it was prescient, prophetic. He saw not only into Joseph's heart in that moment, but into the heart of the world as it was and as it was coming to be. And that gaze, in all its demanding intensity, staked a claim on Joseph: *what this world does to people like you and me.* As if they shared an understanding, a bond that neither of them had with any other in that mad crowd.

But that's crazy, Joseph told himself. He doesn't know me. He can't know me. And he can't really have seen me. The severity of the pain would not have allowed him to focus his vision well enough to identify anyone in the crowd, much less a person he'd never seen.

Yet no matter how much he tried to reason his way out of discomfort and to restore his mood, Joseph could not rid himself of the vision of the brutal lashing, or of the empathy he felt with the man who looked at him. Looked *into* him. It was the being looked into, being understood, being known that most disturbed him. And known in such depth that Joseph could not even claim to know himself as well. The man had unlocked something in Joseph, and if the man saw clearly what had been released, Joseph did not. Not yet. It would take time for him to see it. How long, he could not say. As long, perhaps, as it takes any man to know himself.

| 18 |
Change of Allegiance

Jim longed to put his hands into the dirt. He had been good in the days following his altercation with Hayes. Perhaps he had killed the man after all; he couldn't remember. But Hayes was nowhere to be seen. Not in the yard. Not in the building. Not in the refectory. Jim had not caused any more trouble since that day—six, seven, eight past; he'd lost count of the passage of time—when Hayes taunted him and Jim set out to make him pay. Why, then, hadn't Dr. Parker given him permission to roam the grounds with those other people out there? What had they done to deserve the privilege of sitting in dirt? If Dr. Parker didn't soon grant permission, why then Jim would plan his escape. He could outwit those mean attendants who were always spying on him. Those men out in the field were his friends. He'd seen them looking at him as he stood at the barred window of his room. They wanted him to join them.

Confinement in his room had made him sick. His bowels ached. Diarrhea. What the doctor fed him made him sicker. He'd heard the doctor's words: *opiate enema, burnt brandy, blue mass, camphor.* All poison to Jim. His stomach cramped and his hole burned. Had to get out, go to his friends.

He waited for the dark. In the dark he could move like an earthworm through dirt. Unseen. Quiet. Worms were his friends. He saw into their souls. He understood them so well that he saw through them, their bodies translucent to his gaze. They liked Jim, wanted him to thrive. Why else would they squirm with delight when he lifted them and allowed them to enter the dark cave of his mouth? They made his gums happy. Sometimes they crawled between his upper and lower teeth and made a soft crunching sound. Sometimes they crawled out of his mouth. He knew the ways of worms. He'd find passage to them.

That fat woman might have to be taken care of. A good rock to her head would do it. She was loud. Calling for her pound cake all hours of the night. Yelling at nurses. Jim still hadn't seen her but he knew she was getting fatter by the day. He could hear it in her slobbery voice. If she kept the nurses up all through the night, running up and down the hall, then Jim would have to become as small as a worm to make his escape. He could do it if he had to. He knew the ways of worms. But getting small like that made his body hurt. Better to stay in his own body and just move like them, twisting through dirt.

Sloop, sloop, sloop. The only sound made by the opening of his door. Good. Quiet. Fat woman Austell stuffing her mouth with cake. Sloop sloop sloop. If anyone came into the hall, he'd change color, make his skin translucent, not pink but colorless. No one see him. Sloop.

Big room where the attendants beat him up so long ago. Careful. Cling to the wall like a worm to a small root. Sloop sloop. Big door creaks. Shhh. Sloop sloop sloop.

Outside. Dark. Smell of dirt. Nasty odor in the air. But the earth smelled good. Sloop.

Where were his friends? Hiding in the tents. Jim knew the game. Like worms that hid from him in the dirt, then squirmed with joy when he found them and moved them to the cave.

He'd play. But not just yet. Not in the dark. Wait for the sun. Time to rejoin the dirt. Sloop sloop. The dirt. Good smell. Rich loamy feel. Warmth. Home.

| 19 |

Mama's Boy

Dear Mother:

You will see that this letter is not written in my hand, which God in His infinite wisdom saw fit to sacrifice to the war. Do not weep for me, for you must know that I am well. Many others have lost far more than a hand. I have seen legs, arms, and some heads scattered across blood-filled land, and none of us left standing able to find the bodies to which they belonged.

I must tell you that the person who pens these words is Mrs. Louisa McCord. She writes mostly what I say, but helps me with the wording so as to make my meaning clear. I allow her that, as her words are prettier than mine. But I tell her to keep my meaning, for in that way you will know that it is your son who is speaking to you. She asked me whether I thought it fit to report to my Christian mother such horrors as I have just described. But I thought you should know. You have always taught me to tell the truth, as God is my witness, and that is all I know to tell.

I am grateful to Mrs. McCord, as are many in this hospital. She writes letters for us who cannot, reads Scripture to us, makes sure that we are well fed, and every day at noon you may see on her porch just beyond the hospital many soldiers gathered and talking and eating their fill of food prepared by her and her lovely daughters and her niggers. Next to you, she is the most God-fearing woman I know. It will please you to know that she shook her head at me, and said she should not write those words, but I pointed at the paper and told her I could make out words well enough, and if she did not write what I said, why then I would have a boy from Georgia write for me. He is not a Christian. He is a heathen. I tried to bear witness of Jesus to him one evening as we walked in the city, but he would not hear it. You would think him better suited to service in the Union Army. I do not approve of his ways, but I know he will write for me if I ask him to, and that is why Mrs. McCord agreed to write as I said, and I am grateful to her.

How is Laura? Has she had any more children? When has Randall last been home to be with her? If you hear news of his death, please write to me, as I will want to know. Tell Laura that I remember her with reverence, and hold her close to my heart as I pray for her every night, as I do for you all.

Mr. Crawford is the hospital steward. He is a good Christian man. He makes sure that we all get our medicine as we need it.

I must close now, as Mrs. McCord has many more letters to write, but I will write to you again—or she will, but it will be my meaning, along with some of her pretty words.

Tell Pa to keep the field in good condition for when I return. Give my love to Laura and to yourself and to all others as well.

Your loving son,
George

Louisa asked George whether he was sure he'd said all he wanted to say to his mother. He nodded. He looked like a child. An infant. Like her own son many years ago, when he looked contentedly into his mother's eyes after nursing at her breast.

She turned her face away, laid the pen and pad on the bedside table, and told George that other patients needed her attention. She would check in on him later.

When she advanced to the door, George called to her: "Mrs. McCord?"

"Yes?" She glanced once more at the young man's beatific face.

"Thank you, ma'am. For writing for me." And then, in little more than a whisper: "You'd like my mama. She's a fine Christian woman, like you."

"Thank you, George." She left the room, and in the hallway chastised herself for the fragility of her emotional state. Fatigue, she told herself. No other reasonable explanation. Morbid fatigue.

| 20 |

God's Mark

"Girl, you ain't gone make Columbia. Look at you now, and you ain't made no more than Laurens." The large woman held Rachel by the shoulders. Her hands were massive against Rachel's thin frame.

"I stronger than I look," said Rachel.

The woman pursed her lips and studied Rachel's face. After a moment, she said, "I 'spect you are. Columbia, say? What, they sell your man down that way?"

Rachel nodded. "I aim to find him."

"God bless you, child. I tried the same thing twelve years ago when they took my man from me and my babies. You see here what they done to me." The woman unbuttoned her shabby dress and let it fall to her waist. She twisted her back toward Rachel. Long, wide purple welts bunched together at the top of the woman's shoulders and slithered midway down her back.

"Where James Porter?" Rachel asked.

The woman shook her head. Her sad eyes revealed all.

"Isabella," said Rachel.

"You looking at her."

"Bill sent me."

Isabella clutched Rachel to her bosom. "Lord Jesus," she whispered. "Tell me he safe."

"Bill safe," said Rachel. "Strongest man I know. How you know him?"

"He my sister's first child. Like my own. That child marked by God. Marked, I tell you."

Rachel told Isabella everything, leaving out only Jim's full identity. She said the master had chained him to a tree and left him there season after season. That was enough to tell. Let Isabella reason that Jim was like any other slave to the master.

Isabella made good on Bill's word. She fed Rachel sweet potatoes and sorghum, bitter coffee. Then she stuffed Rachel's coat pockets with dry biscuits. When Rachel was ready to leave, Isabella said, "You lucky you made it this far. Maybe you got God's mark on you like Bill. I pray for you, child. Pray for you every day, you get to Columbia."

Rachel pointed to the sky. "That the star I follow?"

"That's it," said Isabella. "Here now, you take these." Isabella handed her two pairs of socks, holes in each of them.

Rachel squirreled the socks away in one of the bulging coat pockets.

"No, child, you wear them socks. Keep your feet warm."

"Wear them when I stop walking. That's when my feet gets cold." She let Isabella press her once more to her bosom, then she left. The sky was clear, and her star shone brightly. But she smelled rain in the air. If it didn't come tonight, it would be here by morning.

| **PART IV** |

February 1865

| 21 |
Provinces of the Heart

Meredith Simpson had worked a minimum of twelve hours a day without interruption for the past two weeks. Except to grab a quick meal, she refused to sit and rest for fear that fatigue would overwhelm her the moment she gave in. Such was the workload for everyone on staff—doctors, nurses, maids, cooks—at the end of the first week of February 1865. Sherman had advanced from Savannah through Pocotaligo, Branchville, and Hardeeville, burning railroads, farms, and homes along the way. In spite of General Hampton's attempts to reassure Columbians that Sherman would not march to the capital city, talk on the streets and in homes was that the ill-tempered Union general would want to burn the place where secession began. Citizens attempted to secure household goods in hidden cellars or to send them to places far removed on the train. More than a few people had left Columbia —some on train, some on horseback, others on foot—and the number of evacuees increased daily.

Meredith entered George McClinton's room. Asleep, he did not move until she pulled back the bed sheet to examine his arm. Instinctively he reached for the covering, but Meredith held it away from him. She glared at McClinton. "Have you told Dr. Thompson about this?"

The soldier had managed for the past three days to hide from her view the chancres that had formed around the abscess of his stump. But they had grown larger and were now inflamed, impossible to conceal. He held his forearm up to his face. "I ain't paid it no attention. It don't hurt. If I say something, he's liable to start cutting me again, and it's no cause for that."

"Dr. Thompson will decide what is necessary."

"I reckon I know what's best for me."

"You're a fool if you believe that," Meredith said.

McClinton thought to respond, but halted when he looked into her fierce green eyes. Meredith Simpson was prettier than any woman he'd ever seen, his cousin included. The gravity of her expression only added to her beauty. He was smitten.

"I'll bring this to the doctor's attention," she said, and left the room in search of Joseph. She found him making his way toward the stairwell, jotting notes on a pad as he leaned into the door. "Mr. Crawford, may I have a moment?"

Even at the doorway, Joseph seemed to be in motion. Every brain impulse told him to stay on the move in spite of his concern that the burden to his body would induce another epileptic fit. His left leg was perpetually warm and heavy, and he felt as if he were lugging a weight, which made his back ache. He wondered as he looked at Miss Simpson whether his eyeballs twitched in their sockets. It took all his effort to decipher her every word, to fit each one together into a recognizable pattern of meaning.

"It's McClinton," she said. "Ulcers have formed around the abscess."

"Have you applied a new wrap yet?"

"I thought it best to wait in case Dr. Thompson should wish to examine him."

"Very well, Miss Simpson. I will discuss this with the doctor within the hour." He knew without looking that in all probability McClinton had contracted syphilis. Miss Simpson's description of the sores might have been applied to any number of cases he'd seen since coming to the hospital. Some of the men had visited brothels long before coming to Columbia, and of those, he remembered one in the final stage of the disease. His head and nose were bulbous, as if he'd been beaten with a blunt instrument until his features swelled to gargantuan proportions. Thompson treated the man with many penile injections of silver nitrate and cauterization of the sores, but the disease was too far advanced. Joseph recalled the man's shaking violently and yelling obscenities on the night of his death. Perhaps young McClinton's disease had been caught early enough so that injections and other forms of treatment would cure him.

Joseph decided to see for himself. Best to make a well-informed report to Thompson. He reversed his tracks and was about to enter McClinton's room when he heard him and another man talking in loud whispers.

"I could hog-tie and plug that nurse any time I wanted to," McClinton said. "You seen the way she looked at me."

"I wasn't watching how she looked at you. I was watching them tits bob in her dress when she leaned over your bed. You so sure about plugging her, you oughta pressed your face in them tits when you had the chance."

"Maybe next time I will."

"No, hell, you won't."

"Watch and see what I will or won't."

Joseph cleared his throat and stepped into the room. The men stopped talking. Perhaps they'd merely egged each other on, needing no provocation from Meredith Simpson or any other nurse to get them going. Nevertheless, he would report—minus the men's coarse language—the substance of their conversation to Louisa. If indeed Meredith Simpson were playing up to these men, Louisa would want to know it.

He stood bedside and lifted McClinton's arm to examine the chancres. Pus oozed out of them. "I should think you'd be in some pain," he said, and laid the arm back on the bed sheet.

"I've felt pain worse than this. I got kicked by a mule once. Got me right here." He pointed with his good arm to his left shin. "Near 'bout took my leg off. You think I let something like that keep me from my work? Naw. Little thing like this"—he held up the damaged arm—"it ain't nothing."

"You're a brave young man. Let us hope this amounts to nothing. Dr. Thompson will want to examine you."

"I don't want that old sawbones poking at me."

"Then you'd better plan your funeral now, son." Two years earlier he might have dealt more tenderly with McClinton, but this endless war and its uncounted casualties had made Joseph brittle. Nor would he brook any insult of Thompson. "Have you kept to your room at night?"

"'Course I have. What you getting at?"

"You have all the signs of the early stages of syphilis, McClinton. I've seen it kill better men than you. Dr. Thompson may be your only hope now."

McClinton's eyes dimmed. He turned his face away from Joseph's gaze. After a moment, he mumbled something.

"What did you say?" asked Joseph.

"Said it don't matter what happens to me. This is the end times. Brother against brother. Jesus is coming."

"He's had more than enough chances to set the world right or destroy it before now, McClinton. I wouldn't count on a miraculous intervention. If I were you, I'd put my trust in the doctor."

"Yeah, well you might. But for me, it's none better than the Lord."

Joseph left the room. On his way to College Hall, he saw Professor LaBorde crossing the college green toward him. Joseph wished to avoid him, but couldn't do so without being obvious. He thought, *I leave one crazed zealot only to be met by another who will speculate about the designs of Providence.*

LaBorde walked with his hands behind his back, shoulders hunched. A thick mane of black hair fell over the collar of his long coat. His stride was deliberate. Joseph could not imagine him taking a leisurely stroll anywhere, no matter the time of day. Every step had to have purpose, an aim toward some intent that demanded immediate address.

"Good morning, Mr. Crawford." LaBorde nodded.

"Dr. LaBorde. I hope you are well."

"I am, thank you. You are headed for College Hall?"

"Yes. A patient requires Dr. Thompson's assistance."

"May I join you?"

"Of course," said Joseph, and began to walk at a pace slower than LaBorde's. If the tactic flustered the professor, he did not show it.

They passed beneath tall elms that lined the campus east to west. Joseph had admired the trees from the day he set foot on the college green. The yard, too, had been lovely once, until Confederate troops and the local citizenry abused it by bringing their horses, mules, cows, sheep, and dogs within the gate. With all the rain of the two previous months, the ground was pockmarked with mud, manure, and fetid cesspools that the men had to be careful to avoid.

They approached the three-story building where Joseph LeConte and his family lived. "Dr. LeConte, you must know, is at pains to decide what to do with his chemicals. So, too, Dr. Rivers with his books." LaBorde pointed across the quad to the library.

"You must forgive me for thinking our patients and the medical staff of greater importance than the materials of one professor or another."

"I mean you no offense, Mr. Crawford. My point is simply that all of us have borne in one way or another the hardships of this war."

Joseph stopped walking, LaBorde with him. They faced each other. They were nearly equal in height and weight, though LaBorde's prominent jaw and thick dark hair made him appear the larger man.

Out of the faculty house came a young woman wrapped in a long coat. She read a book as she walked.

"Good morning, Miss Emma," said LaBorde.

The woman halted and looked up. As he had on several occasions, Joseph admired the intelligent bearing of the sloe-eyed Emma LeConte. In gravity of purpose and intellectual strength, she seemed to him a younger version of Louisa McCord. He thought his own daughter, had she lived to such an age, might have found in Emma LeConte a compatible spirit.

"Good morning, Professor LaBorde, Mr. Crawford."

"What occupies your thoughts?" asked LaBorde, with a gesture toward the book.

"Hesiod," she said. "Father suggested it. I find much to admire in his esteem of land and labor."

"Your father's child, to be sure," said LaBorde.

"I thank you for the compliment, sir." She curtsied and walked toward the library, resuming her reading when she passed them.

"Such a serious young woman," said Joseph when she was out of earshot.

"As are all the LeConte children. Do you know the skeleton in our museum?"

"I have seen it."

"Professor LeConte's youngest daughter, Caroline, calls the specimen her doll."

"What a strange remark for a child to make," said Joseph.

"Perhaps not so strange in light of her father's devotion to science. He studied natural history with Agassiz at Harvard, you know."

"Perhaps all his children will be drawn to the sciences."

"Not Emma, I think," said LaBorde. "Her father says she has a predilection for the pen. Always scribbling furiously in some diary, he says."

"Let us hope she can entertain happy thoughts in these morbid days," said Joseph.

"Even in time of war, a young woman must entertain notions of love and romance. I should think her writing filled with the ardor of expectation."

"Dreams of some dashing soldier who may return to her, perhaps, sick of bloodshed and eager for the nurture of a family," said Joseph.

They walked on. LaBorde said, "I wish you had known this college before the war, Mr. Crawford. We have a noble history. Many distinguished scholars have walked these halls." He described a circle with his hand to take in all the buildings surrounding them. Did you know that our first president, Jonathan Maxcy, was elected to the presidency of Brown, his alma mater, when he was but twenty-four years old? A man of remarkable brilliance."

Joseph shook his head. "I did not know that."

"The man who succeeded him, Thomas Cooper, achieved international renown as a scientist. He was a fierce supporter of Thomas Jefferson, and an adamant secessionist. Dr. Cooper did more than any man in South Carolina to formulate cogent arguments in support of states' rights, slavery, and opposition to the federal tariff. Perhaps it will not surprise you, therefore, that more than twenty of his former students were delegates to the Secession Convention five years ago. Our last four governors—Gist, Pickens, Bonham, and now McGrath—studied under Dr. Cooper."

"I know of Cooper," said Joseph. "Not of his work, but of the man."

"You know of the scurrilous reports, I am sure, for there is still talk in Columbia of his heretical religious views." LaBorde frowned. "Unfortunately, his views did considerable damage to the college's enrollment. During each of the last ten years of President Maxcy's tenure, we had more than one hundred students on campus. By the end of Dr. Cooper's tenure, we had half that number. Many blame his virulent agnosticism for the decrease. There were other reasons, of course. Dr. Cooper enforced the strictest academic standards for admission. Many young men were turned away for want of adequate preparation."

"I am told that Dr. Cooper did not believe in the existence of the human soul or the eternal duration of punishment for sin."

"He also denied the doctrine of the Trinity," said LaBorde. "But there was more to the man than his strange religious views. His vision for the college and for the state was extraordinary."

"I've no quarrel with his theology, nor with any man's, Professor LaBorde. I think religion a personal matter best kept within the province of one's heart." Joseph had no desire to hear the litany of scholars who had served the college since its inception. But he did not dare to turn away from LaBorde, whose passion might have demanded satisfaction for any rebuff.

"Our third president, Robert Barnwell, graduated valedictorian from Harvard. He was a classmate of Emerson, who admired him as a bread thrower of stunning accuracy. He is said to have initiated a goodly number of food fights in the college refectory." LaBorde's eyes shimmered. He suppressed a burst of laughter, and continued: "For all his brilliance, Barnwell was a prankster whose antics drove John Adams to such a fit of rage that he recommended to the trustees that flogging be revived."

Joseph smiled at LaBorde's show of amusement. There was about the professor a quality Joseph had not seen before, a playful mischief, like that of a child caught up in the telling of a tale to a captive audience.

"We faculty members have had our disagreements, to be sure. Lieber and Thornwell, for example." LaBorde put his hands on his hips and looked at the ground. A mound of sheep dung floated in a shallow cesspool. "What a teacher Lieber was. A model of regal deportment and keen intellect. Yet he had nothing but loathing for Thornwell's theology."

"James Henley Thornwell. The college's sixth president, if I recall."

"That is he."

"I have read his justification of slavery," said Joseph. "I think it futile to argue with a man who waves his bible with one hand and pounds the pulpit with the other."

"Thornwell accused abolitionists of being atheists, socialists, communists, Jacobins. For him, the battle for the preservation and order of the world hinged on this single issue. Those who opposed slavery, he said, were the enemies of Christ."

"I take it that was the source of Lieber's quarrel with him."

"It was. I think he could not give the minister a fair hearing on that account. Lieber was a nationalist. He never felt at home in the south. One Sabbath we left the chapel together. I was delighted to see him that day, as he did not frequent the place. We were a suitable distance from the front door when I asked him what he thought of the sermon. His face soured. He almost spat out the words, fuming that he had no tolerance for that brand of preaching that cries out against the sins of man and threatens torture in the hands of an angry God. 'Thornwell seems to forget,' he said, 'that *Savior* means *healer,* and that religion ought to be a source of hope and comfort to all.' I recall the words as if he were speaking to us this moment. He turned his face up to mine and said, 'For my soul, there is nothing more sublime and pure in all of religion than Christ's sermon on the mount.'"

"A compelling argument," said Joseph.

"Even so, it would not have mattered to Lieber what Thornwell said from the pulpit. Their opposition on the slavery question was so virulent that neither compromise nor understanding was possible. Had Thornwell preached the love of Christ, Lieber would have felt the fires of hell at his feet."

Joseph pointed toward Sumter Street and invited LaBorde to resume the walk with him. They passed a young soldier on crutches hobbling up the promenade toward Rutledge. Joseph recognized him as the boy from Georgia whose face had been badly disfigured by a minie ball that passed through one cheek, along the angle of the jaw, taking out most of his teeth and the left eyeball. When they were out of the soldier's earshot, Joseph recounted for LaBorde what the boy had told Dr. Thompson when he looked at himself postsurgery in a mirror. "His greatest fear was that when he returned home, his fiancée would spurn him out of fright at his appearance."

LaBorde said, "I am troubled by thoughts of what our young men have faced since they left the college and joined the army. It is dreadful to have the memory of those young men's bright hopes and eager minds as they sat before me in class."

Joseph looked askance at his companion. LaBorde's thick jaw seemed to droop, making him appear less stalwart, less confident. His shoulders arched forward as if to protect his body from the chill. *His children,* Joseph thought. *He sees them as his own. What must happen to him when he receives the report of a young man's death? And the others—Lieber, Thornwell, the LeConte brothers, Barnwell, Cooper—more than friends and colleagues, predecessors or successors. They are like family to him. He has to tell their story. It is the only one he values. This is his home. The campus, the library, the chapel: Everywhere he turns, everything he holds dear, he fears the war will take from him.*

A wave of emotion washed over Joseph as he saw once more the face of his daughter, still in death. He shook his head and addressed LaBorde: "What do you miss most, now that your students are gone?"

LaBorde thought for a moment. "I thought when they left that it would be the teaching itself, the opportunity to refine and clarify my thoughts as I worked through each draft of a lecture. But that is not it. I miss their voices, their bustle, the liveliness they brought to the place."

"The college will fill again when the war ends," said Joseph. "They will gladly exchange warfare for the opportunity to return to their books."

"Yes, but how different a place it will be, and how different those who return."

They reached the entrance to College Hall and bade each other farewell. "Thank you, Mr. Crawford, for your time."

Joseph made toward the door, hesitated, and turned to LaBorde again. "I have misjudged you, sir, and I am sorry for that."

"Misjudged?"

"I thought you more concerned with your college grounds than with the affairs of the hospital. I see now that I was wrong."

LaBorde said, "I did not want the college to close. Twice I refused General Beauregard's request to use these buildings as a hospital. Had Governor Pickens not ruled, we may yet have been at an impasse. It is not the case, however, that I had no concern for our wounded soldiers. One hardly knows one's mind on these difficult matters. I wanted to preserve the sanctity of this place of learning. It sounds preposterous now, even to my own ears."

"No, sir. Not preposterous in the least. Should we not all prefer the life of this place of learning to the death and carnage we have wrought?"

He turned into College Hall and, as he approached Thompson's office, attempted a mental inventory of supplies. He had enough silver nitrate to treat McClinton. He would need to order more opium. Always, there was need of opium.

| 22 |

AWOL

Jim slept in the hole he'd dug beside the elm. He dreamed of home. His mother knitting socks. He'd always wanted a pair from her hands. The blanket. His father's belt. The sound of the whip scoring the hides of troublesome slaves. Rachel. Father's deep voice reciting the words of Scripture: "be obedient to them that are your masters . . . fear and trembling . . . as unto Christ . . . slaves of Christ . . . will of God."

He might have slept until morning had he had not heard movement nearby, voices whispering. He rubbed his eyes, adjusted them to the dark. Twenty yards away two dirt men illuminated by the thin light of the moon. Friends.

Out of the earth he crawled. Sloop sloop. Can't hear the worm. His friends moved slowly, all the while keeping their eyes on the building. They were looking for him, hoping he'd come to the window and hold up a candle. *No, boys. That'd give us away. Keep moving. I'll be along directly. Careful you don't wake those mean attendants. Or the fat woman. She'll want cake. Needs a rock upside her head, is what. On down yonder. Ease forward. Long way over the gate. We'll help each other.*

Thirty yards to his left Jim spied a boy slumped over on a log. The barrel of his musket, nestled between shoulder and head, moved gently with the rhythm of his breathing. He and some other slumbering watchmen would pay hell in the morning.

His friends reached the wall ahead of him. In the shadow of the structure, hidden from moonlight, they disappeared. He saw the space they entered, knew they were either right there or creeping eastward, away from the nest of tents. Presently he entered the same dark passage, stood a few moments, then whispered: "Boys, I'm here. It's me, J—"

When he awakened, he felt a dull throb at the base of his skull. Instinctively, he reached for the pain, but his hand was slapped away. A heavy weight pressed upon his sternum, and a sharp object against his jugular. "A peep out of you, I'll cut you ear to ear."

He heard another voice: "Don't do it, Lorenzo. Might be he means to go with us. We don't know this place. Do us good to have a guide."

Jim tried to speak, but his mouth was dry, and the first speaker might make good on his threat. He waited, wondered why his shirt was getting wetter.

"All right," said the huskier voice. "I'll let you up. But you call out or try to run, I'll kill you dead."

With a tug from his assailant, Jim sat up. He felt the wetness on the back of his neck, then put his fingers to his mouth. Blood. *Got whacked good,* he thought. *Like I done what's-his-name. Fat woman, too, had my way.*

"You'll live," said the young man at his side. "It's just a bump. I could've done you worse. I held back thinking you might want to join up with us."

Jim could barely hear him, but he heard enough to make sense of the statement. "Join up for what?"

"Shhh. You hush your mouth. Keep it low."

Jim's head hurt. He tried to keep still. He asked the question again in a whisper.

"To get out of here," said the man. "We mean to get out of this place forever. We're homebound."

"Where's home?"

"Ohio."

Jim squinted, tried to make out the man's features. "That ain't near here, is it?"

"Hell, no. Are you crazy?"

"Course he is, Lorenzo." The voice of the second speaker was small, and not only because of the effort to keep quiet. Jim imagined a delicate-featured young man, thin of bone, a scruff of fine white hair on his face.

"Oh. Yeah," said Lorenzo. "Guess you are."

"Are what?" said Jim.

Lorenzo said nothing. Then, "You in with us, or not?"

"I might be if I knowed what it was I was in."

"Getting out of here."

"Sure I'm in. That's what I came to tell you. This here place is full of crazies."

Lorenzo said, "Charles, bring me that rag you got in your pocket."

Jim heard a shuffle, then felt hands behind his neck and the pull of the rag into place at the base of his skull. He bit his lower lip and breathed heavily. With Lorenzo's help, he struggled to his feet and stood on wobbly legs between the two men.

They moved toward the east end of the wall. Lorenzo stopped and turned to Jim. "What's your name?"

"Jim."

"Jim, we're going to give Charles a boost over this wall."

"He better be a good climber. This wall ain't like a tree."

"What you mean?"

"Don't have no limbs to it."

"Well, Goddamn my ignorance," said Lorenzo. "You know a better way out of here?"

"No."

"Heave to when Charles puts his foot in your hands. Wait till he's set both feet in place. I'll give you the word."

Jim felt the advantage of Charles's size right away. They could have thrown him over the wall if they'd wanted. But that would have left him and Lorenzo in the lurch. They boosted him as high as they could. Three times they failed. Charles toppled backward, but Lorenzo caught him before he struck ground. On the fourth attempt, Charles dug his fingers into a small crack in the brickwork. Lorenzo and Jim repositioned their hands, then pushed.

"Got it." From the top of the wall, Charles looked down at the others. "What now?"

"Straddle the other way," said Lorenzo. "Let your legs drape off the back and lean down to us far as you can. I'll give Jim a boost. Grab his hands and help him the rest of the way."

"He's liable to pull me back over."

"Just do what I said, Charles. You better hold on for life, because that's what this amounts to."

Finding fissures in the wall was like clawing in the dirt for Jim. He used Charles's light pull only for leverage. Soon the two men were perched beside each other. Lorenzo jumped and reached for Charles's hand. "You're too high. I need something to stand on."

Charles said, "Go back up the hill and ask one of them guards will he give you a boost."

"That ain't funny. I get caught, I'm taking you with me."

Jim assumed Charles's position and reached both hands as far down the inside of the wall as he could. "See if you can touch my hands."

On the first leap, Lorenzo grazed Jim's fingers. Jim said to Charles, "Crawl down on my back. When you get to my ankles, hold me in place."

Like a squirrel on a tree, Charles scampered down, then hung from Jim's ankles. Jim sucked in his breath and stretched. When Lorenzo jumped again, they locked hands and Lorenzo scurried up the wall.

Jim hit the ground and crumpled. His head pounded. The blood flow increased.

"Get up," said Lorenzo. "If you can't make it, we'll leave you here."

"I can make it. I just need some help. My bowels is off again." With blood on his back and loose stools dripping down his breeches, he was soaked head to foot.

"You stink," said Lorenzo.

"I don't feel good," Jim said. "Y'all gone have to help me."

"Damn if that's so."

"We need him, Lorenzo," Charles said. "Don't neither one of us know this country."

Lorenzo thought for a moment. "All right, then. Help him."

Charles placed his small body against Jim's right side, and pulled the arm of the rank man over his shoulder.

"Lorenzo was right," Charles said. "You stink something awful."

"It ain't all me. Some of that smell's coming from the nitre plant."

"All I smell is you."

Jim muttered, "I pray the Lord to heal my bowels. They got to regulate."

The three of them set off into the darkness.

| 23 |
Daughters of Thunder

"There may be nothing to it," Joseph said, almost wishing he had not brought the matter up. It was late afternoon and he was exhausted. So was Louisa, but her weariness did not diminish her anger. Joseph knew this would not go well for Meredith Simpson. For that he was sorry, and almost wished he'd said nothing to Louisa. But he could not take any chances, even with Meredith Simpson, whom he'd come to admire. The quality of her work and her endurance far surpassed those of any other nurse on staff. Still, if she were in any way playing up to soldiers' lurid fantasies, something would have to be done. Left unchecked, such behavior could have disastrous effects on the conduct of the patients and the morale of the staff.

"Were her arms exposed?" asked Louisa.

"Pardon?"

"Her arms. Had she rolled up her sleeves?"

"I did not notice that." He hesitated. "No. I think she had not."

"I am sick of these women who display their arms, shoulders, and throats. They do it secretly, and then recompose themselves before leaving the patients' rooms. I've caught two of them already. I'm certain that Meredith Simpson is the leader of this vulgar pack."

"I think not. In fact, I suspect the young men were simply goading each other with no provocation from her." His rush of anger left Joseph unbalanced. He didn't know whether he was angriest at himself for speaking to Louisa about the matter, or at her for calling Meredith Simpson vulgar.

"She is common," said Louisa, her face crimson. "I've no use for low-class women. I'll dismiss her at once."

"No," Joseph said. It was the first time he'd ever addressed her forcefully. "She is not common. She is an intelligent woman who works harder than any nurse we have, Louisa. When others need rest, she continues to work.

We cannot afford to lose any volunteer. What if Richmond sends us more of their wounded? What then?"

The only other person Joseph recalled having a posture as rigid as Louisa's was Jefferson Davis, the day he stood on the porch of the Chesnut home and spoke to an overflowing crowd. Like Davis also, Louisa was always certain of the rectitude of her judgment. She was silent for a few moments. When she spoke, her voice was calm, though the tone still harsh: "I will not dismiss her unless I have proof of scandalous behavior. But I will certainly discuss this with her."

Joseph nodded. "Just give her a chance to defend herself. That is all I ask."

He left the room shaking. He feared, had he stayed a moment longer, that he would have spoken more harshly to Louisa, which would have caused irreparable damage not only to their personal relationship but also to their professional one. The disruption would compromise their ability to lead the staff. In the supply room, he tried to settle himself with a survey of the inventory. The effort failed. As always, he was frustrated by the need of more supplies, more in fact than would be sent in one or two shipments. And as the need for supplies increased daily, so too did the workload for everyone administering to the needs of the wounded. Richmond had sent two hundred convalescents to Columbia, Charleston another seventy-five. This could not continue. Already rooms were overcrowded. The quality of care had diminished as too few nurses were assigned too many patients. The ordering and receiving of supplies were a losing battle, each transaction slower and the quantity less sufficient than the previous one.

It was after six o'clock when he left the supply room and returned to Rutledge. He entered the building, climbed to the second floor, and stopped in the hallway when he heard two voices behind a closed door.

"I would never do such a thing. And you have no right to accuse me."

"I have every right to accuse you if I think the reputation of my hospital is being threatened by immoral behavior."

"This is not *your* hospital. And you are not the only one concerned for its reputation, or for the care we provide our soldiers."

"Watch your tone with me, young woman."

"And you watch yours with me."

Joseph wondered whether to enter the room, then thought better of it. Any attempt to intervene might exacerbate the tension. He listened for a few more minutes. The tone of the exchange gradually became more conciliatory. Joseph judged that neither woman was willing to yield to the other, yet both sounded as if they genuinely cared about the work they were doing and the needs of their patients. At stake for both of them, he knew—indeed, for many women of the South—was the life of the Confederacy. It was the only life they knew.

If Louisa McCord and Meredith Simpson had no regard for each other, at least they cared enough about what they were fighting for to find a way to work together. If that required compromise between mutually antagonistic forces, so be it.

As he stepped away from the door and walked down the hallway, he wondered at the strangeness of his emotion. Perhaps there was nothing to it. Nothing more than that he wanted Meredith Simpson to get the better of Louisa in their argument because her doing so relieved him of the guilt of having called her character into question. Yes, that's it, he told himself. That must be it. Has to be it. He repeated the mantra to himself for much of the afternoon in the belief that doing so would calm his agitation.

| 24 |
The Dark Queen

Rachel lay in a depression she'd dug at the base of a tall oak near the bank of a river. She could not call the river by name. Nor did she know that she was twelve miles south of Newberry. All she understood was that she was cold and hungry, and her chest ached from a rattling cough she'd had for six days. The socks Isabella had given her long ago served merely as wraps around her blistered feet. She'd been certain that she would reach Columbia, but her confidence had wavered in the last few days. Two days ago, she considered crawling to the road when she heard people pass in a buggy. She was close enough to discern the voices of white people. They would turn her over to Patrollers. She would be whipped mercilessly, but eventually she would be given food. Then, she had a vision of Jim, his arms open to her. She would crawl to him if she had to. Die before she quit the journey.

The voices faded. She slept. At dawn, she crawled toward the river, surveyed either bank to make sure no one was there, then broke off a thin, lower branch of a scrawny pine tree, and gnawing at the bark, fashioned a prong. It took her nearly an hour, but finally she impaled a bream on the spear, and quickly scaled and gutted it. She thought once more of Bill, always a friend to her, a protector. He'd taught her years ago how to start a fire with stones and twigs. Soon she had cooked the fish, then scattered the embers and crawled nearly half a mile with the meal clenched in her right hand. When she finally settled to eat, she couldn't remember a meal so satisfying.

She slept again. Still she couldn't walk. That night, she slinked once more to the bank of the river and put her feet in the cold water. Her body shivered, but she knew the water would do her feet good. When the cold became too intense, she removed her feet, wrapped her hands around them, then moments later resubmerged them. After more than an hour, she crawled south for more than half a mile, reentered the woods, and once more laid her head on the ground.

When the first rays of dawn light splintered the sky, she woke. Her feet still ached, but not as severely as before. She wrapped the residue of socks around the balls and heels of her feet, and stood. The first step was excruciating. She leaned against a tree and looked through tear-filled eyes at her feet. Presently, she stood to the full measure of her height, refused to acknowledge any longer the pain, and walked, imagining herself a dark queen approaching her throne, the trees her people bowing before her, waving their spindly arms in honor of her strength and beauty.

| 25 |
Another Letter Home

Dear Mother:

See how this riting is difrunt from what you seen earlier. Mrs. Mukord is not here today. She is probly at her home cooking or sowing socks, for that is what she does. The man who rites these words is from Iowa. That sounds strang, don't it? That I wud have a Union man rite for me. But he is a fine Christun man. Remember the words of Skriptur how Jesus says bruther will turn against bruther and the father his sun in the last days. Well these are the last days, as you probly have figured. What you thawt was your enemy is your bruther and your bruther now your enemy. This man from Iowa his name is Tobias and he is my bruther.

What I said to you befor about the stuwerd is not true but I had to say it becaws Mrs. Mukord rote those words and she and him are frinds. Some say they are more than frinds but I do not know about that nor wuld I say because she is a Christun woman even if he is not. He is mean. I wish everbody loved the Lord as we do.

Is Lawra pregnunt? I hope she is well. Is Randal good to her or was he befor he joined up? Do you know is he still living?

Bles the Lord all my soul and all that is within me, as King David says. I will rite to you agin either in Tobias hand or Mrs. Mukord.

Your loving sun,
Georg

| 26 |
The Bark of the Woods

There was nothing lovely about the deep dark woods in which the three escapees sought shelter. They made less than two miles their first night. Hampered by Jim's diarrhea and loss of blood, they had little choice but to hide in a thicket of brambles near the Congaree River. Not long after they made shelter, rain began to fall. It continued throughout the night. They were cold. The river presented the safest means of avoiding detection, but passage seemed impossible. In the shallows lay slippery rocks that allowed no sure purchase by either thin-soled shoes or bare feet. Nor was the sandy bottom level; with one misstep, a wader could plunge to a depth of five feet or more. Against a strong current and frigid temperatures, even the strongest of swimmers stood little chance of crossing. If luck delivered one to the far shore, then there was the danger of hypothermia setting in.

Yet they had to move. The dogs would come, sniffing, leaping, snarling, rabid in their hunt. Those who held the leashes would not restrain them if they found their prey. What did soldiers care, anyway, at this stage of the war? Better to let loose the hounds than to chase on bruised feet one more escaped prisoner. And it would be Confederates recently come to the city— not the old men or young boys appointed to guard them at Camp Sorghum and later at the asylum—who would be sent to search. Veteran soldiers had long lost their enthusiasm for battle. What stirred the fanciful notions of young men four years earlier no longer served to motivate. Visions of valor and glory were dimmed by the ruin of slaughter and carnage. *Leave it to the dogs*, they said. *At least they still have an appetite for the hunt.*

Lorenzo roused the others two hours before dawn. "Come on, boys. We got to get going. If we don't move now, we'll hear a terrible baying soon enough."

Charles crawled out from beneath a pile of wet pine straw. Jim lay curled at the base of a thin pine, both arms around the trunk, knees pressed to the scaly bark. He tried to look over his shoulder but a jolt of pain arrested his movement. Into a small declivity of earth he spoke, sound issuing in a dull reverberant moan: "Head hurts."

"What about your bowels?" Lorenzo asked.

"I squirted through the night. They ain't nothing in me."

From a distance of several feet Lorenzo eyed the seat of Jim's breeches. The stain was darkest there, but the whole fabric was so soiled by mud that discoloration was ubiquitous.

"You got to wash yourself," Lorenzo said. "You and them breeches both. You don't wash, you not coming with us. Now get on down to the river."

Fear of being left to his own devices persuaded him to do as told. He was too weak to fight and too brittle at this point to survive alone. Someone needed to change his bandage. Someone needed to offer a shoulder when his legs got wobbly. And if he were to eat anything at all, it would come from the hands of those who could forage better than he.

"Help me up," he said, and raised his left arm.

"You heard him, Charles. Get to it."

The little man and Jim limped together down to the river. The hike was less than forty feet, but by the time they got there, Jim was exhausted. "Got to lay down," he said. "Die if I don't."

Charles helped Jim to a sitting position, and said, "Best not lay back. Might not get up if you do. Lorenzo means what he says. You best get them breeches washed. Yourself, too. He aims to get out of here quick."

Jim's mouth hung open and he stared at a sliver of moonlight dancing on the rippled water. After a few moments, he said, "Help me with my boots." He stretched out one leg, then the other, and Charles tugged at each boot until he removed it. Jim moved cautiously to remove the breeches and his shirt, crawled to the edge of the water, dipped and scrubbed the soiled clothing against a boulder. He wrung them out as best he could. He shivered and his teeth clicked. Pulling the wet clothes back on was more painful than removing them had been. "I ain't gone make it," he mumbled. "Everything's against me. Wished I was home. Had me a dry blanket every night. Good place to bed. Now look at me. Everything's against me."

"Hush your moping," Charles said. "We got to get back to Lorenzo. He means to go, I tell you. He won't wait."

Up the embankment they struggled. Lorenzo was doing what he could to cover their tracks. Straw they'd piled together he had separated and spread out as evenly as he could, in spite of the darkness. With a thin pine brush almost bare of needles he swept the ground clear of footprints. "Back down to the river," he said, and walked backward sweeping the brush side to side.

"We just come from down there," said Jim.

"Well, we're going to follow the river. Unless you know a better way. They'll send the dogs, you know."

Jim turned once more to the river with the aid of his diminutive crutch. It was impossible for them to keep up with Lorenzo. He stopped only twice in places that offered a navigable crossing, then changed his mind and went on. Finally, almost a mile downriver, he settled on a narrow channel and waited for the others to arrive. Moonlight offered a hazy glimpse of land less than forty feet across.

"This is our best chance," Lorenzo said. "It's not far to the other side. From the sound of the water on the rocks, I'm guessing it's shallow all the way. Watch your footing."

The walk had revived Jim. His stomach was settled. He was hungry. The breeze had done a fair job of drying the shirt and, to a lesser degree, the breeches. He removed his arm from Charles's shoulder.

"You think you can make it?" asked Charles.

"I reckon. I ain't gone let you pull me in when you topple."

"Suit yourself," said Charles, and he waded in behind Lorenzo.

Presently Jim heard thrashing. Lorenzo called out, "There's a drop," then the water swallowed him. Twice he broke to the surface; the second time he grabbed a low-hanging willow branch and hoisted himself up.

Jim knew better than to fight the current. He let it carry him several yards to the next swell of rocks. He crawled partway, then stood and walked four steps to the bank. In spite of the cold, his spirits revived quickly. He whistled a hymn his mother used to sing on the porch as she darned socks.

Lorenzo called: "Hey. Where you at?"

"Down here," said Jim.

"Well, come on, both of you. We got to move." He paused, then said, "Charles." After a few moments: "Charles?" The rush of water carried his voice away.

Lorenzo said nothing to Jim as they trudged through the tangle of shrubs and pines. Occasionally he sniffled.

Dawn slithered through the woods and finally burst above the tree line. Lorenzo quickened his pace. Jim kept up. Shortly after ten o'clock they heard the distant bay of hounds. Lorenzo turned and looked wild-eyed toward the river. His heart raced as he recalled the most horrifying scene of the war for him. It wasn't the bullets or sabers that frightened him as much as the dogs. He'd witnessed a pack of them chase down a Federal prisoner who attempted escape on the march from Charleston to Columbia.

Amid the scream of cannon and gunfire and his own war yells on various battlefields, he'd not heard so distinctly the cries of the fallen. Initially he did not hear the voice of the officer who ran from the dogs. What registered with Lorenzo was the way the man's body twisted toward the chorus of barks, the luminous fright in his eyes, the pallor of his complexion. The body seemed to contort fabulously, legs churning as the head turned in the opposite direction. Then a complete swivel to face his attackers. Arms uplifted to shield the face. And just before what would recur to Lorenzo's imagination for many nights as a choreography of leaping brown-spotted bodies, the eerie stillness of the world. No sound, not even of wind on leaves.

Then, out of the silence, the thud-thud-thud of dogs on human flesh. Sounds of which the human voice seemed incapable, as flesh came off in mouthfuls. Hungry growls and snuffling. Lorenzo never knew the man's name. But thereafter he knew something about him: He knew the man's eyes; he knew the scent of his fear.

"We got to run," said Lorenzo. He charged ahead and tripped over a bed of vines. With both hands he tore at the bonds. Thorns pricked his fingers. "Help," he said, not even glancing at Jim.

Jim laughed. "Got yourself in a mess, didn't you?"

Lorenzo didn't hear him. He freed himself and scrambled to his feet, began to run again. Now the baying seemed to come from ahead. He stopped and turned in a circle. He saw Jim, wondered at the crazy man's strange smile, but still did not hear his laughter.

At a distance of less than fifty yards a large burly man with a grizzled beard chased a pack of hounds, cracking a bullwhip behind them. The man shouted at the dogs, then laughed. He stopped running when he saw Lorenzo and Jim. Then, he opened his mouth in a wide, yellow-toothed grin, and picked up the pace again. Behind him came men with rifles.

Lorenzo turned to run again. He heard Jim behind him. In the next moment, Jim passed him, his wild laughter ringing through the woods. No animal would catch this creature, Lorenzo thought. Jim was more accustomed to the wild than ravenous barking hounds.

The crack of a rifle stopped Lorenzo. He turned and staggered. His eyes widened. He moved both hands to his chest. A plume of red appeared on his shirt, then spread outward. Lorenzo sank to his knees. All the world changed before his gaze. Sound had color. Trees swayed to an ethereal melody. And then the vision of flight: air-borne missiles, monstrous in their strength. Sparkles of sunlight on glistening white fangs.

| **27** |
Last Will and Testament

"Psst."

"Wha—?"

"Hey. Tobias. Wake up."

Tobias opened his eyes to darkness. He thought he'd dreamed. He rolled over and tried to go back to sleep. He felt a punch on the arm. "What the hell?" Tobias peered over his left shoulder. Now he could make out a human form, but no distinctive face. "Who is it?"

"It's me, George. I want you to write me a letter."

Tobias sat up. "What time is it?"

"Night."

"I know it's night. You think I'm blind? What time of night?"

"Don't rightly know."

Someone in a nearby bed said, "What's all the goddamn fuss? I need sleep."

"Be quiet, Wendell," said Tobias.

Wendell pulled the spread over his head.

Tobias got out of bed and pulled on his breeches. He followed George into the hallway and to the stairwell, where George handed him a quill pen and a piece of paper. "Just a line or two, not much," said George. "I got to write Laura."

"Laura? Who's Laura?"

"I done told you about her. Asked after her in that other letter you wrote for me. She was meant for me, but she up and married that no good Randall Craft."

Tobias sat on a step and ran his hand through hair that stood on end like a rooster's comb. "You got no business writing a man's wife. That's a bad thing. You might get killed that way."

"I ain't gone get killed by Randall Craft or no other man. I'm dying of my own accord." He shoved pen and paper toward Tobias.

Tobias looked up at George. "You're not dying, George. You've got no mind, that's for sure, but you're not dying."

"My time is come. Now I want you to write that letter. I'll pay you for it."

"With what? You got less money than I have, and what you got isn't worth spit. Hell with Confederate money."

"It'll get you another night down the way. Write that letter for me, then we'll go. I aim to see Becky."

"And writing another woman about loving her? Jesus God in heaven, what are you thinking?" Tobias shook his head, then picked up the pen and laid the paper on the step. He wrote as George dictated:

Dear Lawra,

I luv you. You must beleve that. I have always luved you. More than Randal ever did or cud or wud. That baby is mine. I'm as shur of it as you are. I will see both of you in hevun. I am dying. Georg.

After a few moments, Tobias looked up. "Is that it?"

George nodded. "That's it." He handed Tobias an envelope and told him to address it. Then he said, "Now get your boots and your coat. We going out."

"What about Stewart? He'll want to go."

"Forget Stewart. He's trouble."

A short while later they made their way across the college green. Tobias said, "Damn, I stepped in sheep shit. Hold on." He snapped a twig from a tree limb and cleaned his boot. When he finished, he said, "I want to walk by Market Square."

"That's out of our way," said George. "Besides, it's cold and it's liable to start raining again any minute."

"It always rains here. I'm used to it. I still say we go by Market Square and see that whipping post I've heard tell about."

"Yeah, I heard that son-of-a-bitch Crawford talk of it to Mrs. McCord yesterday. He seen a nigger get whipped good, and one behind him waiting to get his."

"What you reckon they did?" asked Tobias.

"Run away, I'd guess." George looked up at the dark sky and flared his nostrils. "No, that's not right. Crawford said it was on account of them niggers talked about Sherman. They think he's coming here."

Tobias stopped in his tracks and grabbed George's arm. "Really? He's on the way here?"

"How should I know? That's just nigger talk. You can't trust that. They so dumb they don't know who's going where. What's Sherman want with Columbia, anyway? Ain't nothing here but women and niggers."

"He'll want plenty in this city. This is where it all started, right? Down there at the Baptist Church, what I hear. All those big men voting to secede. Reckon if they'd knowed what they was in for, they'd have been so brave?" Tobias laughed.

George took a step back and balled his fists. "You got something to say, go on and say it."

Tobias sized him up. "George, you're not fit to fight, and all the fight that was in me when I signed up is spent. I didn't mean you no offense. What say we let it go?"

George backed up another step and eyed Tobias hard. Then he loosened his hands and said, "No harm, I reckon. But from here on out, keep your thoughts about Sherman to yourself."

They soon approached the whipping post. They stood before it like communicants preparing to receive the heavenly host. Tobias broke the silence: "A hundred lashes. That's what I heard. Imagine a whip striping your back a hundred times. Think you could stand it?"

"I could if I had to. But who you figure will put a whip on a white man? Hell, I'd shoot him."

They walked around the structure to get the full view, each of them remarking the heft and sturdiness of the lumber, then turned toward the river. Several minutes later they arrived at their destination. Neither George nor Tobias knew any men in the establishment, but judged by their attire that some of them were important people. Several smoked cigars and played cards at a table in the back parlor. Three skimpily clad women catered to their needs, bringing drinks when they were called for, otherwise keeping silent as the men concentrated on the game, wagering, raising, calling, folding, hauling in their winnings, or shaking their heads over the loss of a hand.

Becky sat next to a man dressed in a suit, a red cravat around his neck. She rubbed his thigh and kissed his cheek when he won a hand. George cleared his throat. She turned her head but gave no indication of recognizing him. From the doorway, George could see under the table. He watched Becky move her hand from the man's thigh to his crotch. Moments later, the gentleman folded and told his partners he would sit out a few rounds.

George backed out of the doorway as the man approached. Becky held his hand and walked a half step behind. George trailed the couple at a distance of several feet. When they reached the top of the stairs and turned right, George grabbed the handrail and started his ascent. Behind him a deep matronly voice sounded: "Hold on there, young fellow."

He turned to see a large woman, face heavily powdered, draped in a purple dress. The woman held something in her right hand. George couldn't be sure, but thought it was a derringer. "I come to see Becky," he said.

"Becky's occupied at the moment. Perhaps you'd like to see Charlotte or Bernice."

"No, ma'am. Becky's the one I aim to see."

The woman shook her massive head. "Well, you'll just have to wait your turn. Why don't you come on down here and rest up. She ought to be ready for you shortly."

George didn't like the woman's bossy tone. He looked at her hand again. She curled her fingers around the mysterious object. A tall, thick-chested Negro entered the room from a back door. "Any trouble, Miss Mary?"

"No, Israel. I think this young man has decided to wait for his true love."

George's face burned. He stepped off the stairwell and walked over to a couch on the far side of the room.

"Well," said Israel, "I best haul in some more wood. No telling when this rain's going to let up."

"Thank you, Israel," said the woman. "I'll holler if I need you."

George understood that she was speaking to him and not to Israel. He sat, folded his arms, and stared at the bottom step of the stairwell. The woman took her seat behind a table and began to sort through papers.

Twenty minutes later, the well-dressed man descended the stairs, tipped his hat at George, and returned to the poker lair.

"If it's Becky you're wanting, I think she's ready for you now," said the matron. "Knock before you enter her room. A lady likes to have time to present herself when a gentleman calls."

He bounded up the stairs. The thud of his boots resounded in his ears. He considered the difference between his movement and that of the gentleman, so elegant that his footfall hardly made a noise. George gathered himself before he knocked on Becky's door. He spat on his hand and slicked back his hair. His heart pounded. He was aware at once of wanting and not wanting the woman, of desiring her and hating her. He'd never felt this way with Laura. For her, he'd had only love. Now, something in him felt low and snarly, punitive and lethal. He rapped twice on the door.

"I thought you was going to play poker."

George spoke gruffly: "It's not him. It's me. I ain't got no mind for poker."

A moment later the door opened and Becky stood at the threshold and eyed him curiously. The dress she'd worn earlier was draped across a chair. She wore a loose-fitting robe that exposed her left breast. "Have you been here before?"

"I was here last week. You don't remember me?"

She smiled. "Oh, sure I do. I see you better now you're in the light."

A candle burned dimly on the bedside table. She pulled him into the room and closed the door. "You got money?" she asked.

"Hell yeah, I got money. I wouldn't of come if I didn't have money." He pulled a few bills from his pocket and threw them on the bed. Becky looked at the money. Her head bobbed as she silently counted the script. Then she said, "I reckon that'll get you about anything you want," and pulled him onto the bed. She doffed her robe and was working to remove his breeches when George grabbed her wrists and twisted hard.

Becky winced and tried to pull away. George let go her left wrist and yanked from his boot a dagger and pressed it to her throat. "Holler out, I'll cut you ear to ear."

"Don't," she whimpered. "Please don't. I'll do anything you say."

He pressed his face to the other side of her neck and breathed deeply. "You stink of a whore. I smell that other man on you. You think I'm low enough to follow him?"

"He's nothing to me. I like you."

"You lie, Laura."

"I'm not Laura."

"Lie again. Quick as I finish with you, Randall's next. He stole you from me."

Becky opened her mouth to scream, but the only sound that issued was a gurgle. A plume of blood spat from her opened neck and covered George's shirt and much of his face. Her body jerked a few times and then went limp. George laid her back on the bed and watched the life drain out of her. He'd never seen a soldier on a field of battle die so quickly, not even when a bullet entered his skull. There was always a death struggle, however brief, but not this time. *Must've been weaker than she looked*, he thought. *Serves her right. Whore stink on her.*

He removed his boots, tiptoed to the door, opened it, and peered out into the hallway. No one. He moved quietly. At the top of the stairs he bent low to see if the large woman was still at the desk. She wasn't.

Down the stairs, he stopped once on the fifth step when it creaked. Then again downward, he as light as air, body fluid like water in a creek bed. At the door separating the parlor from the poker room, he listened. One man laughed. Another cursed. "Damn your luck, Hyatt."

"I wish they'd fall for me like this every night."

George pushed open the door and launched himself toward his enemy. The man with the red cravat looked up. George made to plunge the knife into his eye. The man blocked the downward thrust with his arm. George didn't hear the gun go off, but felt a sharp pain in his belly and smelled smoke. He staggered. The knife bounced once on the floor and lay still. George dropped to his knees. He looked at his stomach and shook his head. "I fought at Manassas," he mumbled. Then he raised his head, looked at the man with the red cravat, said, "Randall," and fell over dead.

| 28 |
A Lonely Trek

Two days had passed since Jim lost his companions. "One to the river, one to the dogs," he repeated to himself, sometimes in a singsong voice, sometimes in a mournful chant. But it wasn't the deaths of Lorenzo and Charles that made him sad. He missed their voices, but not their company. The only person he missed was Rachel. He'd thought of her often at the asylum, but there he'd found so many other diversions to occupy him. Now, alone and surrounded by trees that reminded him of his abode at home, he could think only of Rachel. He missed the way she looked at him, her dark eyes softening every time she lifted the ladle to his mouth. He missed her smooth voice, the heat of her breath on his face, the tenderness of her touch. "I love you Rachel I love you Rachel I love you Rachel," he mumbled, as if the invocation of her name might make her materialize. When she didn't, he sat in the dirt and wept.

When he tired of weeping, he picked himself up and continued northward. He had no destination. Or rather, he had one, but it was not to a place or a time or even an ideal structure: an oak with moats on all sides, just like the one on his father's plantation. He certainly remembered the fortress he'd dug in the earth around that tree, but if he never saw it again, that was all right. He could find another tree, dig more holes, pile more leaves on top of himself. No, that was not his destination. His sole destination, the only longing of his heart, was Rachel.

How long would it take him to walk to his father's plantation? Could he find it on his own, or would he have to ask people how to get there? And if he asked, would someone try to handcuff him, take him back to his father and demand a reward for capturing a runaway? Even if he made it back on his own, would Rachel be there? Maybe his mean father had sold her as he had Big David. Maybe her new white owner had beaten her, the way Big David's beat him. Maybe he had hanged her, as he had Big David when he tried to return to his family.

Hanged? He crumpled to the ground again, this time wailing like a banshee. "Don't kill my Rachel don't kill Rachel don't kill my Rachel pretty throat bad rope pretty throat bad rope pretty throat." Eventually he fell into a deep sleep. Dreams tormented him: Rachel swinging from a tree; Rachel calling to him; Rachel's scar peeling away from her left shoulder, the whole of her body disappearing until only the scar itself remained. He trembled. He sweated. His gnashed his teeth. He jerked awake and felt his heart beating madly.

"Got to find her got to find her." He ran northward. Rage would sustain him for days. That and love, the deadliest of passions ever to haunt the human heart.

| 29 |
Dueling Duties

Sunday evening, February 12, Joseph stood in the parlor of the McCord home and warmed himself by the fire. He held a copy of Saturday's *The Tri-weekly South Carolinian*. He'd saved it to show Louisa the article which boasted that if Sherman had any intention of advancing on Columbia, he would be met with more Confederate resistance than he'd seen in his Georgia campaign. The writer said that a Confederate victory in Columbia would prove once and for all that God "has vouchsafed to South Carolina the proud privilege of closing as she began this war—in triumph."

Like any person in the city, Joseph wanted to believe the reporter. And yet everything he'd seen the day before and earlier that afternoon indicated that few, if any, people had confidence in the boast. Every street in Columbia teemed with people scurrying down to the depot for transport out of the city.

Joseph was of two minds. Duty to the hospital and to the Confederacy required that he discuss with the head nurse what would be done with the patients in the event that Sherman marched into Columbia. Duty to himself demanded discussion of a different order. He stared at the fire. A piece of wood splintered at the base.

He wondered at the reports that had circulated daily since Sherman's defeat of Johnston and the razing of Atlanta. Homes and barns reduced to smoldering cinders. Pigs, cattle, chickens, domestic animals burned alive. Property ransacked or destroyed, depending upon soldiers' predilections.

Worst of all, as some women in Columbia had suggested, the deranged general encouraged his troops to subject the women of the South to an agony more bitter than death. Now the rumor in Columbia was that Sherman's troops had left Orangeburg and were making more than ten miles a day by cutting timber and corduroying the swampland.

Joseph couldn't recall which newspaper—*The Charleston Mercury, Richmond Enquirer, The Tri-weekly South Carolinian, The Columbia*—reported that columns of smoke darkened the sky as Sherman entered cities and homes by day. By nightfall, the glares of fire lit the sky with an eerie glow made more horrendous by the rush of a ravening wind.

He turned toward the door as it opened.

"I'm sorry to have made you wait," said Louisa. Her voice bore the strain of fatigue. A strand of hair had escaped her bonnet and lay matted against her temple. She wore the black dress that she'd had on that morning at the hospital.

"Please, do not apologize. Have you stopped even for a moment today, Louisa?"

She shook her head and sat on the couch. "I've not eaten since breakfast. I'll have Harriet bring us something." She picked up a bell from a coffee table and rang it. Presently Harriet appeared and stood at the threshold. "Mr. Crawford and I will take some refreshment, Harriet."

"Yes, ma'am."

Joseph noticed a change in Harriet's appearance. The first time he'd visited the home, she was sullen, head bent downward, shoulders stooped. Now she stood straight. She didn't look directly at him or Louisa, but cast an expectant gaze at the window, as though anticipating a loved one's arrival. She also neglected to bow before closing the door behind her. He wondered if Louisa noticed.

He took the chair nearest the couch. "Are you prepared to leave Columbia, Louisa?"

"I am not. I've no intention of leaving."

"Sherman is in Orangeburg now. I'm sure he will come."

"Beauregard and Hampton say he will not."

"And you believe them?"

"Why shouldn't I believe our generals?" she asked.

"They speak as if they know Sherman's plans. I doubt that Grant himself knows what Sherman will do next."

"I will not abandon my duties here, Mr. Crawford."

The chill in her tone unsettled him. He wondered whether he had been too familiar with her. "I mean only to secure your safety."

"My safety is not your concern."

"The safety of all the hospital staff is my concern. Do you not understand that we may have to move the patients?"

"To where?" she asked. "And to what purpose? If Sherman comes here to kill our convalescing soldiers, will he not pursue them elsewhere? How many times do you expect wounded men to move? And what of his own men? Do you think Sherman will set fire to these grounds knowing that his soldiers are here?"

"He is a marauder. He aims to destroy everything in sight. If that includes his own men, he will say they died well and in the service of their country."

"I care not a whit about Sherman or his plans. Besides, General Hampton will not let him take Columbia."

Joseph tapped the rolled-up newspaper against his thigh. "And who will stand with Hampton? Do you dare to imagine that he commands half the number of soldiers Johnston had in Atlanta? Less than that. Not even a fourth. There is no one here to defend the city."

"If that is your fear, then perhaps you should leave."

"Louisa!" He stood and stepped toward her. She leaned forward and gripped the edge of the couch. In her face he saw not fear, but loathing. He felt lightheaded. He stepped back to his chair and laid a hand on it. In every possibility he had conceived for the evening, he had not imagined the conversation taking such a turn. What had he done to deserve her contempt?

The door opened again and Harriet entered with a tray of tea and sandwiches. She laid the tray on a table and waited for further instruction. To Joseph, her expression seemed more defiant than it had earlier.

"That will be all, Harriet," said Louisa. "We are sure to have many soldiers on the porch tomorrow morning. Attend to those duties."

Harriet left the room. Louisa went to the table and poured two cups of tea. She glanced over her shoulder at Joseph. Her manner invited him to help himself or leave, whichever he preferred. He remained by the chair. "I did not mean to offend you. I wish only to impress upon you that we are facing a grave danger."

"It has always been so. People speak as if this war began only four years ago. This war has been with us for more than three decades, ever since the days of nullification. If the country had listened to John Calhoun rather than to these vile abolitionists, we might have avoided all this bloodshed."

"It's not only the John Browns of this world who have caused the problem. Have you not seen the surly looks on the faces of your own slaves? Do you not hear their mumbling about freedom?"

"Oh please, Mr. Crawford I've heard nothing of the sort. What possible interest could my Harriet have in freedom when all her wants and needs are met here? Nor would any other slave who has ever served this family desire freedom. Where would they go? How would these ignorant creatures survive without our care?"

There was no reasoning with her. Joseph understood that if she could detect no change in Harriet, she would not notice it in any of the other slaves.

"Have you been to the railroad depots lately?" he asked. "Any of them?"

"Of course not. When have I had time to leave these grounds? It is all I can do to walk the hundred yards between my home and the hospital without being stopped by some crippled soldier asking me to write a letter for him." She held up her hands and curled them inward as if to suggest some deformity.

"People are beginning to leave the city. I've heard that Professor Rivers is packing up all the books in the library to send them somewhere for safe keeping. Professor LeConte is sending his chemical apparatus to Greensboro. And he surely doesn't want supplies at the Nitre and Mining Bureau falling into Sherman's hands."

"Then let them go. Let them all go. I will not."

Her gaze was as steady as her voice. Others might be confused about what to do—leave their homes to ensure survival or stay to protect their property—but not Louisa McCord. She would stay no matter what. Sherman's advance would only strengthen her resolve. Were they ever to meet, Joseph thought, the mad general would understand what a tough adversary she was.

She stepped aside when Joseph approached the table.

"I have made my position clear on the matter, Louisa. As steward of the hospital, it is my duty to see to the well-being of all employees."

"And as head nurse, I regard the care of patients as my preeminent duty."

There was no mistaking the point of her incriminating remark. Joseph wanted to defend himself, but he saw that it was useless. "I should go," he said. He tossed the newspaper into the fire and watched it crimple at the edges and then burst into flame. "It is late. We do not know what we may face tomorrow."

Louisa avoided his gaze when he stopped at the threshold. She said, "I will be at the hospital early tomorrow morning. If General Hampton or any other official orders that we evacuate the hospital, I will do as we are told, but I think exposing the men to the elements is unwise."

Everything Joseph had hoped to say to her now seemed grounded in the delusion of a child's fancy. "Goodbye, Louisa."

"Goodnight, Mr. Crawford."

He crossed the threshold and the door closed behind him.

| 30 |
Blistered

Even a queen's dignity can bear foot blisters only so long. She'd made remarkable progress. More than twenty miles in two days. Three times she'd approached near enough to the main road to overhear people talking to each other or to themselves or to the mules pulling their wagons. On the third foray, she peered out from behind a large pine tree and saw two large white men jostled side to side on a buckboard as the front left wheel bumbled over rough terrain.

"Goddamn pits," the older man said, and spit a stream of tobacco juice over his shoulder.

"You ain't looking where you going," said the other, a younger and more muscular version of the driver.

"Don't sass me, boy. I was steering a wagon long before the better part of you slid down your mama's leg."

"Well, you surefire missed that big hole. You blind? We won't make Columbia by nightfall way you drive."

Rachel had heard enough. If these men were aiming for Columbia before nightfall, she was close enough to crawl the rest of the way. There were less than two hours of daylight left. She turned back toward the river, but misstepped, and tripped over a fallen branch.

The driver said, "Whoa," and pulled the mules to a halt. He looked toward the woods. "You hear that?"

"Probably some critter," said the other. "Squirrel or something."

The older man looked at his son. "Damn if I didn't raise me a idiot. You ever heard a squirrel make such a racket?"

The young man said nothing, but looked toward the woods like his father.

"Get on down," said the driver. He kicked his son's shin. "See what's there. Here, take this with you." He reached into the wagon, pulled out a rifle, and handed it to his wide-eyed son.

Rachel held her breath. If she moved, he might shoot. She closed her eyes, prayed he wouldn't spot her, but heard his footsteps move closer and closer. When the sound of his movement ceased, she open her eyes and looked into the barrel of the rifle.

"Hot damn, look what I found," said the young man. His knees trembled with excitement. "She's a pretty one, too. This our lucky day, pa." He moved the barrel of the rifle toward her head. "Get your ass up. Right now, or I'll peel back your skull with one shot of this here rifle."

Rachel rose. She winced the moment her feet touched the ground.

The larger man scrambled down from the buckboard. He pulled from the wagon a rope, and started pulling a knot in one end as he approached. Rachel feared he would strike her. She offered no resistance, held out both wrists to him. Two minutes later, she was harnessed to the rear of the buckboard. Her feet ached with every step forward, but she knew that if she stopped, she would be jerked to the ground by the movement of the wagon, and dragged the rest of the way.

It wasn't long before the men got into another argument, this one more heated than the one she'd overheard from the woods. The younger man refused to back down, even when his father balled up his fist and struck him on the shoulder. His son struck back with more force, almost knocking his father off the buckboard. "Goddamnit, you want to fight it out, we'll go to it right here and now."

The man pulled on the reins and halted the mules. He rubbed his shoulder, and said, "All right, then, have it your way. But this can't go on too long. I mean to sell this woman, make me a profit."

"Sell her, hell," said the other. "They's better things you can do with one such as that."

Within minutes, the mules and wagon were harnessed to a tree by the side of the road, and Rachel was being dragged by the young man down toward the river, the older one lugging his big-bellied body behind them.

The force of the blow to her head was so great that she lost consciousness before she hit the ground. When she regained consciousness, the younger man was already in her, thrusting furiously, his face contorted by lust, which would turn to hatred the moment he spent himself in her. He'd no sooner finished and lifted himself from her body than the older man took his place. He was slower than his son, but just as rough. And he stank. She turned her head toward the river. Tears formed in the corners of her eyes, but did not drop. *So close*, she thought. *So close to my Jim, and here's where it ends.* She understood that when they finished with her, they would kill her.

| 31 |
The Logic of War

The morning of February 14 was eerily calm. Rain had fallen heavily through the night, but ceased a short while before dawn. A still gray sky hovered over the city. Before breakfast, Joseph checked supplies in the pharmacy. A shipment of opium had arrived the day before. He had enough to take him through the next week if no more soldiers were sent from Richmond or Augusta. After checking the rest of his list and filling out order forms, he conferred with Dr. Thompson.

"What do you hear of Sherman's advance?" asked Thompson. He sat humped over his desk, anchoring himself with his elbows. His head looked as if it might drop from his shoulders.

"Nothing since yesterday. He's left Orangeburg. Surely he's headed to Columbia, although no Confederate official confirms it."

"What do soldiers in the street say?"

"I haven't seen many of them lately. I've hardly been off the college grounds the last couple of days."

"I want you to walk to Market Square this morning, Joseph. See what news there is."

"Should we prepare for evacuation?"

Thompson raised his head and looked through bloodshot eyes at Joseph. "We might as well shoot half of the wounded this morning. Many of them are dying of typhoid or chronic diarrhea, and we can do nothing to help them. They'll not last a day on a march."

"What about the trains? Can't we board the men who can't walk?"

"Where would we send them? What hospital can take them? Even if we could find provision for them, they would have no way of boarding the trains. The depots are overcrowded as it is. People fight for position. Women and children cry to leave the city. Many discard what luggage they have in the muddy streets just to be able to scramble aboard."

Joseph winced as he recalled his conversation with Louisa two nights earlier. Thompson's logic was the same that Joseph had attempted with her, to no avail. If he'd exaggerated the severity of the problem in order to get her attention, the scene he'd fabricated had become reality in less than forty-eight hours. Forget LeConte's effort to save his chemical supplies and Rivers's attempt to protect the library's almost twenty thousand volumes. Forget people's concern for their precious commodities; now they were fleeing for their lives.

Although he understood their alarm, Joseph had no desire to leave. It wasn't bravery or devotion to the hospital or the Confederacy or any other noble enterprise that stirred him. In fact, he felt no stirring at all. Since Sunday night, he'd felt as he had in the months following the deaths of his wife and daughter. Although Louisa's spurning had not broken his heart as cruelly as had the loss of his family, it had nevertheless augmented the power of a cumulative despair caused by the war's terrible effects: unlucky survivors whose mutilation would forever hold in the forefront of their visions the gore of battle; a homeland devastated by destruction of property and the desecration of its holy places; the collapse of an economy that would leave people impoverished as their crops were destroyed and their homes burned and growing mountains of debt threatened to crush them.

"Answer me, Joseph."

"Sir?" Joseph pressed his fingers to his forehead.

"You look tired. Perhaps you shouldn't go to the Market. I'll send someone else."

"I'm fine. I'll go now, and return within the hour." He stood and donned his coat.

Sumter Street was vacant, except for Confederate soldiers moving cotton bales from homes and places of business out into the street. Troops were similarly engaged on every street. Joseph knew the procedure, for it had been enacted in most Southern cities in anticipation of Sherman's arrival. Cotton was to be burnt before Sherman could seize and turn it to profit to outfit his troops with more materiel.

Other than the soldiers, Joseph saw no one until he neared the Market. Even there activity was practically dormant. Two drunks in tattered clothes reeled down Assembly Street. From the opposite side of the street Robert Towns crossed and came toward him. Joseph hoped the man would not speak. Towns was filthy. His clothes appeared not to have been changed in weeks. His beard was encrusted with tobacco juice. There was a mean arrogance about the man that Joseph detested. Joseph understood the master's rationale for having rebellious slaves whipped in the center of town to discourage others from similar activity, but why hire the most brutal man in the city to administer the beating? Towns's enjoyment of the spectacle was worse than cruel; it was maniacal. The man liked to inflict pain. It was said around town that if he thought his dogs had not adequately mauled an escaped slave, he would use the whip on the beasts.

Towns stepped in front of him. "I seen you at the whipping post the other day."

"I was there. What of it?"

"I'll tell you the what of it. You looked all high and mighty when you turned away. You didn't want to see them niggers whipped. You one of them abolitioners?"

"Of course not. But I do not delight in barbarous displays of cruelty."

Towns jutted his thick head down toward Joseph. "You better watch the way you use words on me, mister. I'm liable to take a whip to you."

The man's acrid breath turned Joseph's stomach. Towns had a primitive, feral quality that inspired dread. His eyes threatened death. He stepped closer, bumped Joseph with his massive chest. Joseph felt the blood rush from his face. He spoke, and cringed at the breaking of his voice: "I meant you no harm, Mr. Towns."

Towns's face was impassive for several moments. Then, a slow and malicious grin spread, revealing a line of yellow teeth. He stepped back from Joseph, eyed him once more up and down, as if to measure his body and calculate the little effort required to break it. It seemed to Joseph that several minutes passed before Towns finally turned away and swaggered across the street. Thirty feet away, he shouted over his shoulder so that the two drunks could hear: "I see you again, I'll kill you," and kept walking.

Joseph clenched his fists. He couldn't be sure what enraged him more: hatred of Towns, or his own cowardice. He'd never felt so belittled, not even in the face of battle. Why couldn't he stand up to Towns the way he'd stood up to advancing Union soldiers at Manassas? It was the only skirmish he fought in which opposing armies broke through the lines of artillery and gunfire and fought with fists, swords, bayonets, stones. He grappled with a man in the dirt. Each pounded the other with his fists. Finally, they separated long enough to grab their discharged rifles and turn their bayonets on each other. Joseph reached his first. In the briefest of moments, less time than it took to draw a dust-filled breath, he allowed his enemy to pick up his own. Each looked into the eyes of the other. In the infinitesimal split of time that could neither be registered by a clock nor forgotten in a lifetime, between the men passed what no word could convey: a measure of respect akin to love. The strange and ethereal love shared only by men who demand each of the other his best in strength and valor. When he killed him with a plunge of the steel point into the throat, Joseph felt the exaltation of instantaneous relief. Soon, however, sadness wormed its way into his heart and lingered. For days, weeks—even now, the memory renewed—he could not dispel the nauseating thought that in the killing of his equal he had lost an essential and immutable part of himself.

As Towns receded from view, Joseph wished that he could exchange the life of the fallen brother for Towns. He understood this aberration in the order of things to be the cruel logic of war: that one's allies and enemies can never be identified by nationality or creed, but only by something deep and enduring in the core of one's being. A quality he could not name with precision, but that he intuited to encompass notions of honor, dignity, and that strange and indefinable essence that compels enemies of a certain stripe to love each other.

He crossed the street and entered the Market. No one was selling wares. He exited through the east portal and headed for the depot on Laurens Street. Along the way, he saw Mrs. Bryce and Mrs. Palmer standing next to their husbands on the side of the road, all of them looking forlornly at a rickety carriage they appeared resigned to board.

Joseph made his way toward them. As he approached, Reverend Palmer turned toward him. His face was drawn. He said something to Joseph, who, not understanding every word, leaned close to the minister's ear and raised his voice above the shouts of the passing crowd: "You and your wives are leaving, sir?"

Reverend Palmer cupped his ear and leaned closer to Joseph, who repeated the question. Palmer shook his head, looked through swollen eyes at Joseph, and said, "Our wives are insisting that we leave without them."

Confused by the elderly gentleman's response, Joseph turned to Mrs. Bryce. She stepped forward and laid a hand on Joseph's arm. "Sherman will kill our husbands if he finds them here. Mrs. Palmer and I have nothing to fear. We will be reunited with our husbands when the war is over."

Communication was nearly impossible amid the din of bustling traffic and shouting. Joseph looked at each of the four in turn. On the faces of the men he saw shame and indecision. Their wives were surely right, as everyone in Columbia knew. Palmer had been one of the most vocal secessionists to pound any Southern pulpit. Until his health failed, he'd been a chaplain in Beauregard's army. Campbell had served the Confederacy as first lieutenant for the Congaree Troop. He accompanied them to Virginia and served there until imperfect hearing and poor health forced his return home.

Mrs. Bryce pulled on Joseph's arm. He leaned toward her again. She said, "You must help us to persuade our husbands. Mrs. Palmer and I can stay to protect our homes and to help at the hospital. If they stay, we will lose everything."

"Are you certain that Sherman is coming to Columbia?" he asked.

"Have you not heard the cannons this morning?" she asked.

"No. I've heard nothing other than this loud roar." With a sweep of his arm he described the crowd.

"We saw Dr. Parker earlier this morning. He told us that a guard at the asylum overheard a Negro tell some prisoners that he'd heard Sherman's cannons in the distance."

"That hardly seems a reliable report," said Joseph. "Was the man not arraigned and punished?"

"Dr. Parker said the man appeared not to fear punishment. He'd been whipped two days earlier at Market Square for talking about Sherman's advance. At the asylum he shouted, 'They may kill this nigger, but they can't make him hate the Yankees.' Dr. Parker said some of the prisoners hurrahed him, then put their ears to the ground and moments later confirmed the report with shouts of victory."

Joseph winced as he recalled the empathy he'd felt for the man beaten at the whipping post. He saw once more the bound man's eyes. He shook his head. "Surely the guards put an end to that."

"How could they? The guards are old men and young boys. They are there because they have nothing else to do. The only security at the asylum is the wall."

The women took their husbands by the arms and led them forward. Joseph couldn't remember seeing two more miserable men in all the war. They must have felt, he thought, as he had since the moment Towns threatened him.

Joseph continued his march to the depot. There, he encountered a frightful scene. Women trudged along the platform, weighted down with layers of clothing. From the awkward sway of their bodies, it was obvious that they hid beneath their garments as many valuables as they could carry—gold watches, rings, bracelets, and other jewelry, no doubt. Many of the women, especially those with children in tow, clamored for spaces on the next train.

Fights broke out among several young men vying for position on the platform. One man, his wife and three small boys behind him, pulled a knife on another and said he would kill him if he shoved his wife or children another time. The other backed away, taunted by the shouts of others egging him on.

Sickened by the frenzy, Joseph left the station. On his way back to the college, he strained to hear cannon fire. He heard nothing but the rush of a cold wind through branches—some barren, the magnolias heavy with leaves—and the movement of soldiers who continued to haul cotton bales into the streets.

As he turned off Pendleton onto Sumter Street, he saw two men standing in front of the college gate. The smaller man, a gray-haired gentleman with his back to Joseph, gestured with his hands as if pleading for understanding. The poor man's whole body shook. As Joseph moved closer, he recognized Mayor Goodwyn. Always fidgety, he seemed more nervous than ever.

The man who faced the mayor wore a Confederate uniform. He was tall, and of a regal bearing and stalwart posture that made him appear as immovable as granite. Although Joseph had never formally been introduced to the man, he'd seen him in Columbia eighteen months earlier when the officer was home for a brief period of convalescence. There was no mistaking this towering figure. Anyone in Columbia would recognize General Wade Hampton.

| 32 |
Death Prayer

Three days earlier, Rachel had grieved the loss of Jim more than the imminent loss of her own life. Now she simply wanted to die. She could not suffer the pain of another beating. Her head hurt constantly. One eye was swollen shut. And worst of all, the repeated rapes. She couldn't count the number of times each man had taken her. Not that she wanted to remember any of it. The younger one—*Roberts*, he'd heard the father call him—had been on her at least four times the first day, more since then. The father less often, but it was worse with him. The stink of the man was awful. And his big belly pressing against her made her want to die.

At night they left her tied to the tree with only a dirty blanket and her torn clothes as shield against the chill wind. They returned each morning riding bareback on the mules. Draped over the back of the young man's mule was a sack filled with sweet potatoes, pone bread, beans, and hog meat, most of which the men ate, feeding her only enough to keep her alive.

Rain soaked her the first night. When the men returned in the morning, they didn't bother to dry her off or pull the leaves off her body. Robert was on her immediately. She was too weak and hungry to cry out. All she could do was whimper.

Now another night had passed. She was feverish and hungry on the third morning, even though Robert several times forced bits of sweet potato into her mouth until she gagged. Maybe today they would kill her after all. She'd heard the father tell Robert that they couldn't sell her, given what they'd done to her and the way she now looked. Robert wouldn't hear it. "I ain't had my fill of her."

"Hell, boy, you can't keep her tied up in the woods forever. She's 'bout dead as it is. We don't kill her, she'll be found soon enough by wild dogs. You reckon she'd rather the dogs get her or us? Ask her to pick." He laughed, as if amused by his clever wit.

Robert cursed his father, then took her again.

Please, God, make this be the last time. Let him kill me. Make him kill me. With what little strength she had left, she lifted her head as much as the rope allowed and tried to bite his face. She would make him kill her if God wouldn't. But Robert was too quick. He jerked his face away, arched upward, grabbed her hair with both hands, and slammed her head against the ground as he continued his wild thrusts. In the moment between the sharpness of pain and the loss of consciousness—a moment that felt like a slow fall from a high place—she had an eerie, pleasant sensation that she would never again wake.

| 33 |
The General

Joseph leaned against an elm tree half a block from the men and looked across the street. He contemplated whether to cross. Hampton did not know him, and Goodwyn's back was to him, but if he stood there long enough, the mayor might look his way and extend a welcome.

It was impossible to hear anything other than the rise and fall of the mayor's voice. No distinguishable words, nothing he could piece together. As he watched the men, Joseph marveled at Hampton's stature. He seemed powerful beyond measure. Easily six feet tall, thick-limbed, blue eyes that glimmered like sunlight on water, thick mane of brown hair, heavy mustache and beard.

Joseph recalled the stories of the general's battle prowess: wounded five times in the war, first when a bullet creased his head at the first Battle of Bull Run; shot in the foot at the Battle of Seven Pines, yet remained astride his horse, under fire, while a field surgeon treated him; led at Fredericksburg a number of cavalry raids behind enemy lines yet suffered no casualties.

His own post he never surrendered. Not even three saber wounds to the head at Gettysburg could remove him from the field. It took a piece of shrapnel in the hip to disable him. He and Hood rode in the same ambulance back to Virginia.

Wade Hampton, all of Columbia knew, was as zealous in battle as the God-sick Stonewall Jackson. No mortal could defeat him. Only the war itself could do that.

And did. His face soon scarred with the deep mark of sadness. It followed the downward curve of his mouth, shone in the hollow of his eyes. Marked ever after by the Battle of Burgess Mill that October of 1864.

His youngest, Preston, his father's aide-de-camp, had the general's flair and daring. Face of Apollo and figure of Hercules, if Mary Chesnut were to be believed. Wild for heroic deeds, he charged into the fray amid a hail of bullets. One struck him in the groin. He reeled in the saddle, right arm ascending and then falling backward, body following like the plunge of the sun beneath the rim of the world. Young Wade reached his brother first, only to be felled by enemy fire as he dismounted. With hand outstretched, he cupped and held his brother's head.

Then the father at full gallop, a jerk of the reins so powerful the horse reared high and twisted. Dismount with a leap. With his massive arms, he lifted his youngest, buried his bearded face in the boy's neck, and shook like a mountain riven by earthquake. When it appeared obvious there was no hope for the boy, he then saw to young Wade, who would survive his wound. The general ordered the attending surgeon to care for the living, then returned to his post and directed the fighting for the rest of the day.

Or did he return? Joseph wondered. Was it he—the man, the general, the bold leader—who returned that awful day to the field of battle? Or was it not rather some semblance of the man, a shadow of himself, the ghost of a life lost that inhabited the space once occupied by the living? Lichen attached to a gravestone.

Now the old general was home by order of Lee for the purpose of mounting the men of the state and placing them in the field. Yet where were those he hoped to gather? The leading voices of secession—Rhett, Magrath, Hayne, Gist, Pickens, Chesnut, Barnwell, Bryce—were at home, as most of them had been since the war's beginning, or safely ensconced in some civil office. No one really expected these men to surrender home and hearth for the field.

Joseph believed the general's homecoming signaled the final collapse of the Confederacy. Here, where secession began with shouts of defiance, a conflagrant end was at hand.

He could wait no longer. He pushed away from the tree and walked toward the men. The general nodded as Joseph approached, and made a slight movement with his hand. Abruptly the conversation ceased, and Goodwyn turned to face Joseph.

"Good morning, Mayor Goodwyn." Joseph bowed and stuck his hand out to the general. "General Hampton, we have not been introduced. I am Joseph Crawford, steward of the college hospital. I am honored to meet you, sir."

"The honor is mine, Mr. Crawford." The general's words did not match his expression. His gaze was stern and penetrating. The heavily bearded face did not offer the hint of a smile or a frown, but was enigmatic in its stillness. Joseph did not appreciate the man's size until he stood before him. If he was not larger than any man Joseph had ever seen, he certainly seemed so. His hand engulfed Joseph's. The calloused flesh portended enormous strength.

Unable to hold the general's gaze, Joseph turned to the mayor and said, "I have just returned from the depot. On the way down there I saw the Palmers and the Bryces. Mrs. Palmer and Mrs. Bryce are forcing their husbands to leave town. They say they have heard reports of cannon fire in the distance."

"Sherman is coming," said Goodwyn, his thin lips quivering.

Hampton cleared his throat and crossed his hands behind his back. The mayor paid no attention to the subtle rebuff.

"I wonder about such reports," said Joseph. "I've heard nothing today."

"Sherman is less than twenty miles from Columbia. They are making more than ten miles a day by corduroying marshes and washed out roads. If you've not heard cannon fire yet, you surely will by nightfall."

"Now, sir," interjected Hampton, "there is no need to alarm the citizenry. The city is well protected."

Joseph glanced at the general, wondering at both the disgust with Goodwyn that sounded in his voice and the preposterousness of his assurance. Surely Hampton understood that he could offer Sherman little resistance. If he could, wouldn't he be gathering forces to launch an attack outside the city? Was Hampton deluding himself as much as he was Goodwyn and the city? What could possibly make a man speak so assuredly when all the available evidence countered his every word?

"I'm afraid your confidence is lost on the citizenry, general," said Goodwyn. "They appear to be leaving the city in droves."

It was an awkward moment for all three of them. Joseph sensed the general's immediate distrust of him, and the mayor's desperate need for Joseph to side with him. He said nothing.

"I am prepared to surrender the city in the hope of avoiding complete destruction," said Goodwyn. "I have discussed this with the aldermen, and they are all in agreement."

Hampton's eyes flared. "You have no authority to surrender Columbia, Mr. Goodwyn. I am in charge here, and will remain so until General Beauregard countermands the order."

Goodwyn looked afraid, whether of Hampton or the possibility of Sherman's attack—or both—Joseph couldn't be sure. The mayor said nothing, but with a nod indicated deferral to Hampton's command. Hampton bade them farewell and turned away. Joseph and Goodwyn watched him until he turned left on Greene Street, then they took their leave of each other.

As Joseph made his way toward the campus, he was bothered by thoughts that seemed almost treasonous to him. Not about the Confederacy itself, or his devotion to it, but rather about his reaction to the general's exchange with the mayor. Hampton's fervid defense of his authority over the city disturbed Joseph. He did not want to entertain the question that invaded his psyche like an enemy storming a citadel: namely, whether prudence or ambition governed the general's thinking. Was Hampton's primary concern the city's preservation or his reputation? If the latter, how much would the general risk in order to make a show of his valor? And how great would be the cost to the city?

| 34 |
Grievances of War

Joseph found Dr. Thompson slumped over his office desk, head resting on his palms. "Sir?" Joseph tapped on the open door.

Thompson looked up. His face was ashen. "I have bad news, Joseph. Two men left the college grounds last night and wound up in one of the brothels near the river."

"McClinton," said Joseph. "I'd bet on it. We know he's in the early stages of syphilis. He's a scoundrel."

"You have the man, but the problem is far worse than that."

"More advanced?" asked Joseph.

Thompson shook his head. "Dead. Gunned down last night by a man he attacked. And that after killing a prostitute."

Joseph sat in the chair facing Thompson's desk. "We will be accused of not keeping order in the hospital."

"Everyone in the city knows it is impossible to keep the men within the gate. This is a hospital, not a prison. We barely have enough staff to run the place, much less keep watch over every soldier. Even so, the problem is complicated. McClinton had another man with him."

"Who?"

Thompson folded his hands behind his head and leaned back in his chair. He studied the ceiling as a man might pore over a ledger to track his business's debts and credits. He cleared his throat. "A Yankee."

Joseph tented his index fingers beneath his chin. "I see. Well, it can't get any worse than that."

"The man's name is Frederick."

"Tobias Frederick," said Joseph. "I know him. I'm surprised he and McClinton were together. They didn't seem likely companions."

"Perhaps," said Thompson. "But there's nothing strange about two men far from home encouraging each other to seek the favors of women. War and sickness aggravate the basest compulsions in men."

"Where is Frederick?"

"In the city jail. He's to be tried within the week. I've no doubt he'll be hanged."

"As an accomplice?"

"No charge that would stick in a fair court of law," said Thompson. "He was with another woman at the time of both slayings. But he'll be hanged because he's a Yankee, a convenient target for the many grievances of war our people have suffered."

What was the good of healing men who sought their own destruction? Joseph wondered. Even for soldiers who were compliant with the rules of the hospital—men who followed the ordered regimens of diet and gentle exercise, who took medicines prescribed, did all in their power to promote their health—of what ultimate benefit was healing to them when, their bodies sufficiently recuperated, they would be turned out once more to war?

Thompson stood. "We've work to do, Joseph. Have you done inventory today?"

"Early this morning."

"Our supplies are holding out?"

"For the rest of the week, unless we are expected to take in others from Richmond, Augusta, elsewhere."

Thompson rapped his desk with his fingers. "What did you learn at the depot?"

Joseph recounted the scene, relayed the conversation he'd had with the Bryces and Palmers. He told of citizens who claimed to have heard cannon fire in the distance. "On the way back, I came upon General Hampton and Mayor Goodwyn at the gate. Goodwyn says he is ready to surrender the city. Hampton says he has no authority to do so."

Thompson nodded. "Poor Thomas. He is a good man, but of delicate composition, especially in dire circumstances. I am sure, however, that most of our citizens feel likewise. If Sherman is coming, the panic you saw today will be as nothing to what we shall witness in the days ahead. The Confederacy is about to fold, Joseph. We are facing the end."

It was the first time Joseph had heard his friend speak so fatalistically. "Not the end," he said. "We shall recover. Not even emancipation can topple an agrarian culture. People have to eat. They need cotton for clothing. Men will always want their tobacco."

"Yes. And there will always be owners of land, and those who are forced either by enslavement or by economic necessity to work the land. That will not change." Thompson's voice shook with anger. "But the South will not rise again on the strength of its land and conscripted labor. This way of life is dying, I tell you. Perhaps it should. Men long before us have warned of the dangers of slavery. Jefferson himself noted its barbarisms, its threat to the ideals of justice and liberty."

Joseph knew that Thompson was right, yet much of what he said militated against the hopes that Joseph wanted to pursue. That slavery would end was as sure as the Confederacy's defeat. The notion pleased him. When Negroes were free, no more would barbarians like Robert Towns be able to entertain crowds of gawkers by scoring the backs of men with his whip. No longer would men like the one whose vision penetrated Joseph's heart be made to suffer the indignities of public humiliation. Nevertheless, there was much about the Southern way of life he coveted.

He'd come to envision himself as an owner of land. Not for the land itself, or even for its potential economic value, but for what it represented. If he had land, he could persuade Louisa to marry him. He would convince her that they did not need slaves to work their property. What they could not manage alone, they could hire others to do as the workload waxed and waned from season to season. Nor did they need hundreds of acres to thrive. All they needed was enough to make a good living. A decent parcel of land. A modest house. A small library in which he would build from the finest wood a case filled with books from floor to ceiling. Together they would rebuild the way of life that honored the cycles of nature, that saw to the proper nurturing of the land, tilling and planting and harvesting in their appointed times. It was the way of life Louisa held sacred. She believed it was the way God intended, for hadn't He given man dominion over the earth and the waters and the creatures of the world, and commanded him to tend the garden? No industrial power from the North, however strong and rapid its growth, would overthrow the order of creation. God would prevail, and with Him, the South. If Joseph could not fully subscribe to such a theological view of the order of land, work, and human fulfillment, he could nevertheless profit from it, if Louisa would have him.

He would have to patch up the wounds of their recent disagreement, but that could be done. She would come around. If Louisa McCord wanted anything more than to fulfill her duty to the hospital, it was to see the restoration of a way of life that reconnected her to the land, to the fecund soil from which life sprung. To achieve that dream in its fullness, she would need someone to help her manage the work. She would need a husband.

Thompson stepped ahead of him and out of the office, then held the door for him. "Check on Hospitals One and Two, Joseph. I don't yet know how many surgeries have been scheduled in either of them. We have none at present scheduled in Three. Let us hope the same is true of the others."

The men parted and Joseph turned once more to the college gate. He went first to Rutledge at the south end of campus. He marveled at how war had changed the entire campus, this part in particular. Joseph believed that buildings stored treasures of the past—not only those that were visible, but the numinous that could be sensed if one were attentive. He could easily imagine the learned debates that inspired students of earlier years. How many professors had enlivened the minds of young men in these halls over more than half a century? How many sermons had been preached in the chapel? How many discoveries made in the laboratories? In this building was a solidity of structure and of history that Joseph admired.

He made the rounds of Rutledge, then crossed the horseshoe to DeSaussure. In a room on the second floor he found Louisa writing a letter for a patient who had lost a leg to gangrene. She laid her pen on the tablet when Joseph entered.

"Good morning, Mrs. McCord. How are you, Mr. Hayden?"

Louisa returned the greeting. Basil Hayden appeared disgruntled at the interruption. In spite of the fact that the gangrene had set in before he arrived at the hospital—as was true of many wounded in battle and not adequately treated by the field surgeons before being carted off to a more sanitized facility—he faulted the surgeon and the chief steward, who had assisted with the amputation, for his loss. Joseph was accustomed to such blame. He was grateful, nonetheless, that Hayden treated the nurses courteously.

"I'm sorry to interrupt," said Joseph, "but at your earliest convenience, Mrs. McCord, I need to speak to you of an urgent matter regarding one of our patients."

"Can we finish this letter?" growled Hayden. "It's to my wife. She ain't heard from me in over a month."

"Of course," said Joseph. "I'll wait, Mrs. McCord. Good day to you, Mr. Hayden." He left the room, and spoke with a nurse on the ward. It was obvious they'd heard nothing yet the double slaying. Best to avoid discussion, he thought. It would only arouse the staff, jittery enough as it was with all the news of Sherman's advance.

Presently, Louisa came out of Hayden's room. Joseph ended his conversation with the nurse. He asked Louisa to walk out to the college green with him. "The subject is delicate," he said. "I don't want to risk being overheard."

They gathered their coats and left the building. When Joseph faced her, Louisa folded her arms together. Her posture was stiff.

"A tragic misfortune occurred last night," he said. "The repercussions may be injurious to us all."

"I have heard all I want to hear about Sherman," Louisa said. "If he comes, he comes. My mind has not changed."

"It's not Sherman. George McClinton killed a woman last night."

Louisa paled. "Oh, please. Not one of my nurses."

"A prostitute. He left the campus late. His absence was not detected until this morning. By then, Dr. Thompson had been informed of the murder."

"George McClinton? Are you sure? He seemed—"

"Not what he was. McClinton was a rough fellow, Louisa."

"But he was kind. The boy asked me several times to write his mother. Always he asked tenderly after a young woman, a cousin, I think, who married one of his companions. Where is he now?"

Joseph shook his head. "He attacked a man after killing the woman. The man shot him at close range. McClinton is dead."

Louisa looked at the ground. After a few moments, she said, "I must write his mother. What shall I say?"

"Perhaps it is not wise to divulge the whole story. I think I would say only that he quarreled with a man, and the altercation turned fatal before anyone could intervene."

"Yes," Louisa said. "I needn't say any more. I'll tell her how sorry we are. Will the body be transported to his home?"

"I don't have details. Perhaps I can inquire further into the matter today." He hesitated. "Louisa, there is one other matter. A young man was with McClinton. Tobias Frederick, from Iowa."

"Dead, too?"

"No. In jail. He was not an accomplice to the murder, but Dr. Thompson says that is inconsequential. Any jury selected from the citizenry of Columbia will demand that a Yankee hang."

"That is true. And I must confess that if I did not know him, I'm sure I would feel the same. In the eyes of a jury, they would not be pronouncing sentence on an individual, but on a nameless representative of the enemy. A scapegoat."

Joseph said, "Will you walk with me?"

They walked down the north side past DeSaussure, the college well, McCutchen, Harper, Elliott, and the library, until they reached the gate. Joseph told her of the conversation he'd witnessed between Hampton and Goodwyn. "I am not trying to dissuade you from your intent, Louisa. I know you are not going to leave Columbia. But you must understand that the days ahead will bring trouble. Who knows what effect Sherman's advance will have on our patients? We have been fortunate thus far to avoid conflict between the men. I fear that once news passes through the hospital, there will be considerable excitement from the Union forces and from our boys, and a possible outbreak of hostilities. We will have to prepare the entire staff for such disruption."

"Perhaps we should ask Hampton to station some of his men here," she said. "Not only to protect the hospital from Sherman, but to protect the convalescents from each other."

"I will carry your suggestion to Dr. Thompson. It is a reasonable request. But who knows how Hampton will respond? I don't pretend to know the mind of any general, much less one with whom I have only a passing acquaintance. I do know that he has ordered his troops to haul cotton bales into the city streets. He will destroy them before Sherman can turn them to profit."

"He will burn them," she said. "Let us pray the wind abates before the fires are started."

As adamantly as she'd defended Hampton two days earlier, Louisa now seemed to question his judgment, perhaps even his leadership. This was the lot of any military officer, Joseph thought. Hampton would be praised or condemned depending on the outcome of battle. The same was true of Joseph Johnston, former commander of the army of Tennessee, now residing in Columbia, offering to anyone who would listen his commentary on the mistakes made by Jefferson Davis, whom he despised, and his supreme commander, Lee, whom he envied. The same was true of General Lovell, whom Joseph had also seen in Columbia. The poor man was still being vilified for having lost New Orleans in 1862. Hampton would suffer similar reprobation if he could not defend Columbia. Perhaps Lee himself, idolized by soldiers, citizens, even Grant and Lincoln, would not finally escape the judgment of the fallen. Wasn't it true that more men had died under his command than under that of any other American general, including those who fought the Revolution? Gettysburg alone—the mad defenseless charge up a hill into the lion's maw of slaughter—would surely one day leave its terrible imprint on the legacy of the pious leader.

| 35 |
The Whole World Wet

Jim studied the body of the dead squirrel. It was attached to a six-inch prong that he'd fashioned out of a thin pine branch. He admired the sharpness of the point. He'd done a good job whittling away at the wood with a sharp stone. It had taken hours to get it just right. He was so pleased with the knife that he then broke off a bigger branch and whittled a spear nearly the length of his body. He hadn't heard the dogs in four days of travel. But if they came after him again, he'd be ready with the spear and the knife. *Like to get that fat man what was running the dogs,* he thought. *Seen him grinning at all the fun he was having. Reckon he'd grin when I stick him with this here spear.*

But no matter the strength of his weapons, he couldn't do anything with the squirrel. He'd tried to flint a fire, but it was no use. Too wet. Everything wet. The whole world wet. He wanted meat, but there'd be none without a fire. He had no more appetite for worms. He figured they'd turned on him, made a mess of his bowels that night he escaped with Lorenzo and Charles.

Well, better to walk and be hungry than just sit and be hungry. Stay close to the river. Might gig me a fish with this here spear. He studied the notion hard for a moment, then muttered, "Still can't cook it. Goddamn all this rain."

And on he walked.

| 36 |

Exodus

Joseph and Louisa turned back up the south side of campus. As they passed the building where the LeConte family resided, a Negro drove a mule and wagon through the gate, and the gray-haired professor opened the front door of the house. He carried down the steps a large box that concealed his body from waist to chin. Joseph marveled that such a slender frame could house so much strength. He'd heard from Dr. Thompson of LeConte's athletic prowess and boundless energy. He was said to be an expert swimmer and, if Joseph could believe the story, once did a chin-up with 120 pounds attached to his feet.

"You have more than any man can manage alone, Professor," said Joseph. "Please let me help you."

"Mr. Crawford. Yes, yes, I could use some assistance."

The driver leapt down from his seat and helped LeConte load the box on the wagon. LeConte turned once more to his house and motioned Joseph and the driver to follow.

Louisa said to Joseph, "Tell Mrs. LeConte that if she needs help of any kind, I am at her disposal. Send for me at DeSaussure. I will come as soon as I am able."

Joseph and Louisa heard commotion in the house. LeConte and his man were hauling a wooden crate through the front door. At a window to the right of the doorway stood Emma, her dark eyes fixed on her father. As Joseph had on the few occasions he'd taken the time to notice her, he marveled at the young woman's beauty. He couldn't decide, however, whether her serious demeanor augmented or diminished her elegance. In an older woman, the look would be considered refined. But in one so young—of marriageable age, to be sure, yet still on the cusp of womanhood—an unmistakable lack of gaiety, even in time of war, was unsettling. She seemed to brood.

"I will relay the message, Louisa." He grazed her arm with his hand. She did not pull away. For the first time in a while, he saw in her eyes a gentleness for which he longed. It lasted but a moment. She turned toward DeSaussure. Joseph followed the men into the house.

"Good morning, Miss Emma," he said as he stepped over the threshold.

She curtsied. The gesture accentuated the perfection of her lithe and graceful body. "Good morning, Mr. Crawford. Thank you for helping my father."

"What are you reading, Emma?" He pointed to a book she clutched in her left hand.

"Oh, this? It is nothing of merit. Only my scribblings."

"A writer, are you? I should have known. It is only fitting that from this household should come another generation of writers and scientists of great renown."

Emma blushed. In that moment her face softened. Yes, he thought, a woman of remarkable beauty.

"Up here, Mr. Crawford." Motionless, the professor's body nevertheless looked like a repository of combustible energy. Joseph could imagine him bounding through the woods, as indeed he had on a daring trip in early December, sometimes by train, sometimes on foot, to Liberty County, Georgia, to rescue his daughter, Sallie, his sister, and a niece threatened by the Union army's advance. When LeConte returned to Columbia, he regaled family and friends with his adventures of sleeping in the woods, shooting the rapids of a river, hiding in swamps, and avoiding detection by enemy soldiers until he reached his loved ones. Joseph was in one such audience of enchanted listeners, and recalled with what enthusiasm LeConte told them how agreeable he found life in the woods.

"Coming, Professor." Joseph climbed the stairs. He followed LeConte into a room that housed shelves of books floor to ceiling.

"I cannot take them all," LeConte said. "But each of us in the family has his favorites. I must do what I can to preserve those."

On one shelf Joseph saw illustrated tomes on archaeology and engraved plates of the works of Hesiod, Aeschylus, Sophocles, Shakespeare, and Goethe. All other shelves had been removed of books, packed in boxes lined up in rows on the floor. LeConte moved swiftly, but with care. He mumbled each time he grabbed a book, as if conversing with a friend. In less than five minutes, he laid, as would a mother her child in its bed, more than seventy-five volumes in five boxes. That number represented a small fraction of what already had been packed. LeConte surveyed the room a final time. Then he looked at Joseph, pointed to the smallest box, and said, "We must go now. Mr. Crawford, if you can hoist this load, Thomas and I can carry the others."

The Negro picked up the two largest boxes, LeConte two others. The professor led the way down the stairs and out to the wagon. As they passed through the hallway, Joseph glanced into the room where he'd earlier spoken to Emma. She was seated at a table, bent over a composition book, her pen-laden hand moving furiously over the page. Yes, he thought. More like it. Yet he wondered what fanciful notions might entertain a young woman's mind at such a frightful time. Well, no matter; better dreams of romance and adventure than morbid reflections on war and death. The advantage of youth.

The men made several returns up and down the stairs, and deposited their loads in the wagon. LeConte moved them carefully to a secure hold, draped two blankets over them, and thanked Joseph for his help. "Thomas and I are going to the bureau to pack up my instruments, Mr. Crawford. I wish I had occasion to return your kindness. Perhaps that time will come soon."

"I am happy to have been of assistance, Professor. If I do not see you again, I wish you and your family Godspeed in your journey."

They shook hands. Joseph detected in the gentleman's eyes a hint of concern, surely for his family and other loved ones, but also for home, college, the city. But that speck of worry vanished the moment LeConte bounded onto the carriage beside Thomas. Next to the bulky servant, LeConte looked like a boy, his wiry frame bouncing with the movement of the wagon.

Joseph walked across the college green to Harper. He'd not visited the ward since Sunday afternoon. His habit was to pass through every building at least once a day. When exigencies forced him out of the routine, he was nervous about what he might encounter the following day. Had a soldier taken a turn for the worse? How were medicines, bandages, other supplies holding out? Had there been enough rotation in the already depleted staff to ensure a modicum of rest for the overworked?

He flinched just before entering the building, for he heard distinctly for the first time, in the distance, what no one who had ever heard the sound could mistake: the echo of cannon fire.

| 37 |
Rock of Ages

He was weak from hunger, but with the spear in one hand, the knife in the other, Jim was not afraid. He saw smoke not too far distant. *Best go quiet. Sneak up on them, judge if they friendly or not. Might have food, coffee.*

He'd gone less than a quarter mile when he heard voices. Jim dropped to his knees and crawled forward. The voices grew more distinct. Two of them. Men. Sounded friendly enough. One of them said something, then laughed. Jim inched along, got close enough to the clearing to see the small fire and the two men sitting, each on a large rock that looked as old as the earth itself. The men stared into the flames.

A large fat man held a rope in both hands. He studied it with the care Jim had given to the carving of his weapons.

"I want to keep her, pa. Take her home with me."

"You not doing that. Think what your ma would have said to such."

The other shook his head. He spoke angrily. "Ma's been dead three years now. I don't care what she would have said then, nor what she might now. I'm a grown man. Do as I see fit."

"Shut your mouth, Robert. Watch how you speak of your dear departed mama."

Robert rose from his rock. "I know good and damn well Ma might still be here if it wasn't for you, way you drove her. She didn't get no favors from you when she was alive. Don't go talking like you reverence her now. Your talk's as good as dry spit."

The fat man kept his seat. He eyed the other meanly, but showed no inclination to fight. His shoulders sagged and he pointed toward the river. "She ain't gone make it through the night."

Jim crawled toward the river to see what the fat man was pointing at.

"Well, by God, she'll make it through one more turn," Robert said. He stood and started to walk away, then stopped, looked over his shoulder at the fat man, and held out a hand. "Toss me that rope. You was foolish to untie her in the first place."

The other gripped the rope tighter. "You don't need this to keep her down. She ain't got strength enough to move, much less fight you."

Jim came to a gap between two small shrubs and peered through. On the water, moonlight shimmered, allowing him poor sight of what lay on the ground twenty feet away. A heap of rags, it looked like. No movement beneath.

The young man dropped his pants to his ankles, then fell to his knees. Jim remembered seeing his father in that posture many years ago. Not with his pants around his ankles, but kneeling just like this man, knees pressed to the cold wood floor. This was before his father chained him to the tree. Jim used to live in the house. He remembered it. Remembered the wood floors. The staircase. The kitchen. His parents' bedroom. He wasn't allowed there, but he remembered passing by it quietly one night. The door was cracked. That was when he saw his father on his knees, hands folded together, mouth moving. He was praying. Jim recalled, too, that several times his father made him go to his knees and pray with him. And then after praying, his father took the belt to him. Whipping always followed prayer.

Praying with your pants down. Jim shook his head. *Never thought to see such.*

The young man raised his fist and brought it down on the heap. "Wake up, Goddamn ye. Wake up."

A dark arm rose slowly from the heap. The man grabbed at something and pulled. Jim saw it: a face, one side swollen so that flesh covered the entire eye socket. The man pulled harder. He had a hank of hair. The head turned.

Jim thought he'd seen a vision. His eyes flared. He rubbed them with his knuckles, looked again. The man on his knees raised his fist again. Before he could bring it down, Jim sprang.

His fist still above his head, the man turned his torso toward the rush of sound. He said, "Wha—" and then grabbed at his throat where the spear entered. A trickle of blood started at the right corner of his mouth, then gushed out as the man tried to make sound. His eyes, wide with fright only a moment before, already had begun to dim. His body was contorted by the first turn of his shoulder toward the sound behind him. The awkward attempt to clutch the spear made him topple backward, toward the river.

The fat man, having scrambled to his feet the moment he saw the wild creature leap from the bushes, now had his hands on the rifle. He might have had a chance at getting off a shot if Jim had not been so fast. He plunged the knife into the great round belly. Before the fat man could stagger backward, Jim had both hands around the rock on which the man earlier sat, raised it above his head, and brought it down on the man's forehead. The man stumbled against a tree, then fell forward. Jim saw his father, the open Bible in his hands, his voice reciting Scripture as the foreman whipped Rachel. Jim leapt, straddled the large back, raised and lowered the rock again and again and again. His eyes rolled. He gnashed his teeth. His face was as red as the wood at the bottom of the flame.

Presently, the touch of a hand on Jim's thigh arrested the furious movement of his arms. He was confused. He looked at the hand on his thigh, moved his eyes from the hand to the arm, from the arm to the body, and settled on the face so disfigured and swollen that it seemed no part of the neck and shoulders beneath it. Then he looked at the pool of blood and bone fragments and gooey matter between his knees. He tossed the stone, crawled off the dead man's back, and cradled Rachel in his arms.

| 38 |
LeConte's Arsenal

Thompson's prediction was correct: By the morning of the 15th, the city had turned to mayhem. Joseph went early to the depot to investigate. What he'd witnessed the day before was as nothing compared to the present bedlam.

He didn't attempt to jostle his way through the crowd to the far side of the loading platform. It would have been useless; or worse, he'd have had to fight any number of men and women who thought he was trying to board ahead of them.

Children—some of them clinging to their mothers, others who seemed to have lost theirs—wailed. In the press of the crowd, the smallest ones were seamed in on all sides. If one fell, he risked being trampled.

Tree branches on either side of the depot drooped under the weight of clinging sleet. In the mud lay broken furniture, heirlooms abandoned by people more desperate to fight their way onto the train than to protect their goods. Joseph heard two men's angry voices rise above the din of tumult. One man struck the other in the face. The victim fell back against a ring of people, then regained his balance and charged his assailant, but was held back by several others. The assailant cursed and shook his fists, but he too was subdued by a group of men. As quickly as the fight began, it ended.

Joseph tried to pick out of the mass some people he knew, but faces and apparel blended together. He started to turn away when he heard above the commotion a shrill voice: "Keep your distance. This is dangerous material."

At least a foot above the tallest man in the crowd stood Professor LeConte—elevated by some apparatus that Joseph could not see—waving his arms, bobbing on his knees as if preparing to launch himself from his perch. Beside him were three rows of crates stacked level with his head.

My God, Joseph thought, he's attempting to move explosives. The whole depot could blow.

There was no telling how much nitrous powder was in the crates. Joseph understood the need to move ordnance out of reach of Sherman's army, but this was not the way to do it. Too many lives were endangered.

Cries of the children echoed in his ears. His vision blurred. The swarm of people moved like an ocean wave hurled against the shore by torrential winds. The platform swayed, then the depot itself.

He thought of Hampton, the man's rigid posture, stern gaze. He'd silenced the mayor and claimed sole authority to dictate terms of engagement or surrender in the face of Sherman's advance. If only he were here to bring order to this confusion. People would listen to the general. Without such force of command to corral them, little could be done to avert disaster.

But there was no time to search for Hampton. Whether Joseph wanted to or not, he would have to make his way over to LeConte. Someone had to help him keep people away from the explosives.

He descended five steps and edged along the embankment at the back of the station. If he were lucky, he might find easier passage here than through the press of people. Twice he slipped and fell to a knee. His coat and the legs of his breeches were heavy with water and mud. When he finally made it to the far side of the depot, he saw Thomas on the other side of the crates opposite LeConte, arms extended to hold the crowd at bay.

Only a few people stood between Joseph and his destination. They struggled to move forward. Joseph decided they'd probably been at the front of the line, but had been displaced by the slow-moving swell. They were pushing back to reclaim what had been lost. They looked like a herd of cows trying to squeeze through a narrow gate to get to their fodder. If at any point the fence broke and one were to charge through, a stampede would follow.

He looked for a way through the line. There—a woman with a passel of children on either side of her. Joseph would speak kindly to her, offer help with the children if she let him through. She was large enough that no one man could budge her as long as she maintained her balance. Nor did any try. If any person other than one of the children bumped her, she gouged the antagonist with an elbow. Before Joseph reached her, she bent a thin man double with a vicious blow to his side. She kept a wide stance—in part because of the girth of her thighs, the form of which was discernible even beneath her billowing dress, but also because she appeared to know how to use her body to its greatest advantage. Her head tilted forward on a bulbous neck, a portion of white flesh visible between the frill of her dress and bonnet. She leaned her heft into the juggernaut before her.

Joseph walked up behind the woman and said, "Let me help you, ma'am."

Her head swiveled. Joseph stepped back when she snarled, teeth bared, stubble shading her chin and jawline. Joseph had seen older women with a few dark hairs protruding from the chin and upper lip, but never one so prickly.

"Get the hell away from me," she said.

The voice gave him away. Dress and bonnet made a clever disguise, but he should have shaved more closely. Even so, the crowd would have been no more sympathetic to an old woman than to this behemoth of a man.

Joseph regained his composure, stepped forward, and said: "Listen to me. We are in danger. That man shouting at the crowd is standing next to explosives. If I don't get over there to help him keep people away, this whole place will blow."

The pink bonnet fell forward on the man's brow as his neck jerked. He'd nearly lost his balance. He dropped one hand below his waist as if to gird his loins, then exerted himself with a mighty forward push. What strength, Joseph marveled. The mass actually advanced, no more than an inch or two, but it was a noticeable change in direction and force of movement.

"Damn well better worm your way through," said the man. "I can't hold off this army much longer. My back's about give out."

Joseph did exactly as the giant said: He squiggled through the labyrinth, ducked beneath arms and elbows, sucked in his breath to worm through the narrowest portal. Fortunately, he had to pass through only four rows of bodies.

By means of LeConte's frantic gestures and shrill voice, and Thomas's strength, the men had managed to keep a narrow wedge between the crates and the swarm. It surely wouldn't hold, however, when the next train pulled into the station. Then, everyone would shove more frantically against his neighbor in the struggle to board. If a fight broke out, it was likely that one or more antagonists would topple into the explosives.

Joseph said, "Professor!"

LeConte looked down from his perch, an empty, upturned crate the size of the others that were full. He waved at Joseph and smiled. Joseph noted the incongruity between the severity of the situation and the professor's friendly greeting. But then, once more alerted to the danger by a cry from someone in the crowd, LeConte turned his attention back to the problem.

"We must tell the people what's in these crates," Joseph said. LeConte cupped a hand to his right ear. Joseph repeated the statement and added, "It will alarm them, but if we can get them to be still for a moment, we can clear a path and get all this loaded when the train docks."

"I've told them already," LeConte said. "They don't care."

"Don't care that they will die? That's absurd. Surely they didn't understand you." Again he had to repeat himself.

LeConte leaned over and said loudly: "Glass may cut them, but they'd spill a little blood for a place on the train."

"Glass?" Joseph called.

"Beakers. Mainly that. A few other supplies. All glass."

Joseph said, "But I thought—" then stopped. If I could reach him, he thought, I'd wrap my hands around his thin neck and shake him. "You've shipped the books already, I presume."

"Eh?" LeConte cupped a hand to his ear.

"The books we packed in your wagon yesterday. Two days ago. I can't remember when. You've sent them somewhere?"

LeConte smiled. His shoulders jiggled. "Thomas and I got all the way to the depot, then I decided I couldn't bear to part with my books. We returned them to the house. Thomas has reshelved them all. I think they're safer at the house than they would be elsewhere. What need would Union soldiers have of my books?"

Joseph's mouth hung open and he stared at the tireless man in disbelief. LeConte turned back to the crowd, waved them away from the crates. He looked like a rooster strutting in a small circle. After a moment, Joseph shook his head and turned back. Egress was easier than entry. People were happy to allow him passage out in the hope of moving an inch or two forward.

He managed a little better on the embankment for a while. Then, one leg sank and got wedged in the mire. Sludge oozed over the top of his boot and down into his sock. By the time he worked his foot loose, his toes were numb.

When he reached Laurel Street, he removed the boot and cleaned out the muck as best he could. The exposed foot ached. He pulled the dirty sock on again, tugged at the boot until it settled into place, and walked against the flow of traffic. A stream of people continued to flow toward the depot, but the congestion was nothing like what he'd left. He weaved through with ease.

When he turned onto Sumter Street, he heard three cannon blasts in succession. That distinctive pitch of sound meant two things. First, Sherman was so confident in his army's superior power and vast supplies that he was now using ordnance to knock down trees to corduroy the swampland. The more immediate concern, if Joseph could still trust his ears, was that Sherman's troops would be in Columbia by tomorrow.

| 39 |
A Healing Touch

"Good thing about a fire, once it's going, all you got to do is keep throwing kindling to it. Ain't that right, Rachel?"

Rachel squinted through the one good eye and nodded. She couldn't talk above a whisper. She couldn't remember whether it was Robert or the father who choked her in a fit of anger, but her vocal chords still hurt. She mouthed at Jim, *How long?*

"Been two days, Rachel. You getting stronger. I'm gone have you walking before sunset. Then I'll have you on one of them mules." He pointed at the two mules tethered to a nearby tree. "Quiet as kittens, they are. Good thing, too. If they went to braying, I'd have to kill them. They keep on acting right, we'll ride to Columbia soon enough." He smiled at her.

She tried to smile back, but winced at the pain of movement, and closed her eyes.

The truth, she told herself, is that she hurt now more than she had the night Jim killed the men. Then, she'd willed her body to go numb. She'd wanted to die. She'd asked her spirit to leave her.

But it didn't leave, and now that Jim was here, her spirit yearned to live. It had been satisfying to see him dig a deep hole with the spear, dump the dead bodies in, and cover them again. He told her he had to do that to keep the crows away. Not that he cared what the birds would do to the bodies; he just didn't want those scavengers pecking at their food when they slept. Rachel reasoned the rain had been a good thing, though she'd hated it earlier when it spat at them through the night. But it softened the ground and made the grave-digging easier for Jim.

She admired his good judgment, too; it was a smart thing he'd done stripping the men of their clothes and boots. She sat on the bank of the river while Jim washed out the clothes and listened to him tell her they would dry fast by the fire. Then he would wrap her feet enough times with the men's shirts that she would have both a cushion and a snug fit for her feet when he helped her pull on the boots. She said, "You a smart man, Jim Wells."

He stopped scrubbing and looked at her curiously for a few moments. Then he shrugged his shoulders and smiled, as if pleased at the novelty of the compliment.

Yes, she told herself, she was getting stronger. Jim was right. But with the return of strength came acute awareness of pain. Healing hurt.

Most painful was the task of eating. Her face hurt every time she moved her mouth. Her throat hurt every time she swallowed. But at least she wasn't hungry. Jim coaxed her to eat. In addition to the remains of the dead men's sweet potatoes and beans, Jim fed her morsels of fish that he speared with his weapon. They'd eaten a lot of fish.

What most satisfied her, though—more than any food—was the sound of Jim's voice. He talked to her throughout the day. He told her of the place where he'd lived in Columbia. He talked of Dr. Parker, and of some fat woman who always ate pound cake. He spoke of a man he hated and had tried to lay by for, but he couldn't recall the man's name. He told of his sickness the night he escaped with Charles and Lorenzo, and of how Charles drowned in the river, and of how Lorenzo was mauled by the dogs, and of the ugly man who ran the dogs, and of how he'd missed only her from the day he left the plantation to now. When he told her that, she smiled inside herself.

"My heart's smiling," she whispered.

He had to lean close to her mouth. "What'd you say?"

She said it again, and this time he heard.

"Mine, too," he said. "Soon as you get better, we'll go to Columbia. It's lot of things to see there."

When the sun reached its zenith, Jim carried her to the river and sat her on the bank. "I know it's gone be cold," he said, "but washing up'll do you more good than anything else. Make the swelling go down."

She wasn't sure she could stand the cold water, but she made no protest as he bathed her legs and arms and the rest of her body. He moved his hands quickly across her skin, and with enough pressure to provide warmth without causing too much pain. What felt wonderful was the way he bathed her feet, dribbling water over the blisters, then cupping his hand around the flesh and gently stroking the toes and ankles and the tops of her feet.

He nestled his hands around her feet until they were dry, then wrapped them in the shirts made warm by the fire. "Want to try them boots now?" he asked her. She nodded. He pulled them on gently and, placing his arms under her shoulders, helped her slowly to her feet. She held on to him for a few moments, then said she would try it alone and see how she felt. He released her and took a step backward.

"Feel all right?" he asked.

She looked out over the water as if to divert her attention from the strain she was about to put on her body. Her expression was grim as she jiggled her knees, but not once did she frown. She tilted her head leftward and looked Jim in the eye. "You not gone believe it," she said. "I don't feel nothing."

"You can't feel your feet?"

"'Course I feel my feet. It's the pain I don't feel. You done healed me, Jim Wells."

His eyes bulged. "You pulling my leg."

She shook her head. "'Twas you pulled mine."

He looked confused for a few moments, then he grinned, and they both laughed.

Yes, she told herself, she was healing. She hadn't been completely honest with Jim. She did feel some pain, but it wasn't crippling. It was the pain of healing, and that sensation, in comparison to what she'd felt for a long time, was altogether pleasing. She was ready for them to mount the mules and make their way toward Columbia. After weeks of searching for it—or rather, for Jim in it—she wanted to see the city, especially since Jim had told her about it.

She thought it strange that she was getting better so quickly after wanting only days earlier to be dead. Strangest of all, after all the suffering she'd endured, was that for the first time in her life that she could remember, she felt safe. And happy.

| 40 |
Buried Treasure

Louisa was fast losing patience with all of her servants, particularly Harriet. The woman moved indolently from one task to the next. Her mind was anywhere but on the discharge of her duties. Louisa thought to whip her, but had neither the time nor the energy to give to the effort.

Besides, the others were just as bad. The boys—Tom and Jonah—worked with shovels in the backyard as if they were sick. "You boys get this work done," Louisa called from the stoop of the back porch. "Time is precious. We've not a minute to waste." She had ordered them to bury silver, jewels, and other valuables in various spots in the backyard in the hope that Sherman's troops would not discover them. "Tom, get with it. If you take no more care than that to cover the hole, you might as well put up a stake so the thieves will know where to look."

Tom dropped to his knees and made a show of packing the dirt back into the hole and replacing the upturned sod. As soon as Mrs. McCord turned back into the house, he kicked at the spot.

Upstairs, the girls gathered their valuables. The secret to the ploy, their mother told them, was to leave enough worthless pieces around the house to make the enemy believe they'd been successful in their plunder. Hannah separated her good jewelry from hair pins and other bric-a-brac. Lou was frantic about securing everything that belonged to her.

"Hurry, Lou," Hannah said, as her sister fondled each item. "You must decide what you're willing to part with."

"I don't want to part with any of it," said Lou. The girl was in tears. She fingered the beads of a necklace she'd placed on her bed, then moved to another object and another, gazing adoringly at each.

"Oh, for heaven's sake." Hannah snatched up the necklace and feigned a toss toward the window.

"No!" Lou grabbed her sister's arm.

Hannah returned the ornament, and said, "Unless you decide quickly, I'll choose for you. And if Mother sees you dawdling, she may throw everything away."

Lou's expression was sullen, but she picked up her pace. Soon, both women had several small boxes of goods, which they carried downstairs and out the kitchen door to hand over to Tom and Jonah for burial.

"How are the boys doing out there?" Louisa asked when the girls returned to the front room. She glanced at them over her shoulder, then resumed her work of rifling through papers she'd taken from the drawers of her dead husband's desk.

"They are too slow," said Hannah.

"They'd better be careful with my things," said Lou.

Henry, the oldest slave in the McCord family, shuffled into the front room. As always, he was looking for his daughter, Harriet.

"I put her to work in the cellar," Louisa said. "Don't interrupt her, Henry. Do you understand what we are up against?"

Henry smiled. He had lost his mind not long after his wife died. Were it not for Harriet's devotion to her father—and Louisa's knowing that the daughter would have grieved so when he was gone, and therefore been useless to her—she would have sold him years ago. He turned and shuffled back out of the room, bumped the wall after a few steps, and nearly fell before Hannah reached to help him regain his balance.

Louisa had to restrain herself from shouting at the old man. What is the use? she told herself, and buried her face once more in the pile of papers.

| 41 |

Panther on the Loose

A few minutes before 5:00 A.M., Joseph gave up the effort to sleep, rose from his bed, and stepped outside in his nightclothes.

The morning of the 16th was temperate, so unlike other days of the previous two months that Joseph sensed in the weather itself an omen of change in the affairs of the world. He was accustomed to rain, fierce winds, skies dark and swirling with clouds that moved like soldiers under fire.

He turned back into the building. The thought of food repelled him, but he needed sustenance. A piece of stale bread would suffice. He was to meet Thompson at 6:15 to decide what to do with the soldiers in their care.

At 6:00 he left his room. In every window of the LeContes' residence, candles burned. Joseph was careful of his step. The path used by pedestrians, horses, mules, and wagons looked more like a bog than a passageway. Wheel tracks were so deep that Joseph wondered how a wagon could make it through. How many times had LeConte moved goods to the depot? Would he ever return to this place of learning? Would Sherman leave the college intact, or reduce it to ash?

Joseph passed through the college gate and turned onto Sumter Street. He sensed he'd entered a different world. Long lines of people trudged past the college wall. Many of them hauled provisions in shoulder sacks.

Children carrying small parcels in one hand clutched their mothers' dresses or an elder sibling's hand with the other. Except for an occasional word of encouragement or rebuke from a parent to a child, the only sound was the squirt and suck of shoes in mud.

A burst of cannon fire quickened the pace of the walkers. A child cried. Her mother hushed her. On the woman's face, Joseph observed something more terrible than fear: rage. Demonic in its intensity. Indiscriminate. She was not the only one whose fury smoldered. He saw it in people's eyes, veins bulging from their necks, balled fists, the mean hunch of their shoulders. Who would suffer the brunt of all that anger? he wondered.

Before Joseph took his seat in Thompson's office, the surgeon spoke: "We must proceed with haste, Joseph. Those who are fit to travel are to be released. We are responsible only for our intent."

"And what of the outcome?"

"We leave that to God," he said bitterly. Thompson glared at his desk for a few moments, then looked at Joseph. "He destroyed the world once. Who is to say that His good pleasure is not to destroy it again?"

"Where shall we send them?" Joseph asked.

"Each must choose his own direction."

"The depot is more disordered than a battlefield. They will have to fight their way aboard."

"Most of them will take to the woods, I suspect," said Thompson. "They are more comfortable there than among a mad crowd."

"Are we to release Confederate and Union men alike?"

"Our men only. If anything will stay Sherman's hand, it will be the derision he would suffer in the North for burning his own wounded."

The strategy was sound. Hampton and Beauregard had no men or supplies to offer a line of defense. Reports had come into the city from outlying scouts that from Orangeburg to Columbia the only difficulties Sherman encountered came from occasional snipers singly prowling the woods, many of them seeking vengeance for a slain father or brother or friend. Some of them were so habituated to killing that they'd come to feed on it, vultures devouring carrion.

Thompson said, "Have Mrs. McCord instruct her nurses to inform each able patient of the opportunity to leave. No, the *need* to leave. That must be impressed upon them." Thompson sat back, closed his eyes, and pinched the bridge of his nose between thumb and forefinger. He said, "We must do this with caution, Joseph. We cannot incite alarm. There is enough of that without our adding to it."

"I will speak to Mrs. McCord immediately." Joseph left the room and retraced his steps toward the campus gate. In the few minutes he'd spent with Thompson, the crowd had thickened. What earlier had been a single line of walkers was now a throng separated into several flanks on either side of the great swell. As the number grew, so too did the intensity of their movement. People jostled for position. A boy fell when a large man shoved him. The man continued to press forward until three others turned on him and told him to slow down. He pushed two of the men away and struck the third wildly. A plume of blood burst from the victim's nose. Joseph heard a shout but could not determine whether the voice was male or female. A space around the four men opened and closed again, like one wave rushing forward as another receded. Joseph had not seen the man with the broken nose pull the pistol, but there it was, pressed against the right temple of the assailant. Joseph was sure the man would discharge the weapon. A current of anger rushed through the mass of people. Joseph felt it in his gut, a conduit of congregational rage. Killing the bull-necked man would have felt right, would have satisfied in that moment a communal need for vengeance.

But the weapon did not fire. Either it malfunctioned or the owner resisted; Joseph could not tell which. What was certain was the coward's flinching. He begged the other not to kill him. Tears dripped from his eyes. A stream of mucus slimed from his bulbous nose. He blubbered.

"Kill him," someone shouted. "He knocked my boy down, would have killed him if he'd had his way."

A murmur of assent rose from the crowd. A child no more than seven or eight years of age squirmed through the onlookers and kicked the man in the groin. He buckled. Several people laughed, cheered on the brave boy. Joseph knew as he felt the urge to assent to the dehumanized spectacle that passion had overtaken them all. Even so, he could not resist the attraction of vengeance. Madness reigned, and with it, a visceral delight.

The man who wielded the pistol lowered it and backed away from his captive. Joseph could not hear him, but whatever the man said seemed to mollify the people.

Head lowered, the humiliated bully wiped his nose and eyes with the back of his hand and slinked leftward until he made his way to the far side of the crowd.

On the other flank, nearest Joseph, a group of Negroes advanced, striding confidently. They did not turn their faces away or look down when any white person looked at them. Joseph thought he recognized one of the men. He stepped forward. The man who appeared to be in the lead of the roiling, serpentine black body turned instantly, as though ready for attack. He stared at Joseph. If the first time they locked eyes Joseph hardly had been able to bear the intensity of this man's gaze, now he welcomed it. For as surely as the man had seen into Joseph's soul days earlier, Joseph now saw into his. The sensation he had was so strange that it made him dizzy. He was certain in that moment that in the depths of that man's soul lay the better part of himself: the man Joseph wanted to be, courageous in the face of defeat, true to himself in the face of all that persuaded a man to betray his last vestige of honor. This was more unsettling than that moment in battle when he'd recognized in the face of his dying enemy his brother. At least they were of the same race. That, he could understand. This was incomprehensible.

He took two more steps, then stopped abruptly, waited for the other to make a move, some gesture of recognition or of attack; it made no difference. Joseph would have welcomed either. All that mattered was that he either break this mad spell or make sense of it.

The other's dark eyes danced. He moved with languid confidence, a panther toward his prey. He hunched his shoulders. Joseph imagined the welts on the man's back rising, tearing through the fabric of his loose-fitting, ragged cloak. And then, so subtle that no one in his group would have seen it, the man bent his wrist upward, arm still at his side, and nodded. Joseph lifted his hand to his shoulder and opened his palm in salute until the man passed.

Joseph reeled toward the college gate. What was happening to him? Was he losing his mind? He was desperate to return to his duties in the hospital. Here was order. Here, the wounded lay docile in their beds, the dead made ready for transport to their tombs. Here, the passage from life to death made sense. Beyond the confines of this sanctuary, however, was danger. Chaos reigned when a black man looked into the eyes of a white man and made him see visions of one world dying, another more violent yet to be born.

| 42 |
Till Death Do Us Part

Joseph found Louisa on the second floor of Rutledge a few minutes before 8:00 A.M. He told her to assemble the staff. She sent to each building a nurse to tell people to gather in the chapel.

As they filtered in, Joseph looked into each tired and rigid face. He knew most of them by name, had worked alongside them, including some who had come to the hospital as volunteers as recently as October, in the days following Jefferson Davis's speech from the front porch of the Chesnut home.

When all were seated, he took his place behind the lectern. With his sleeve he brushed a bead of sweat from his brow. He gripped either side of the dais, steadied himself, and spoke: "We know what we are facing. If any of us acts alarmed, all will suffer. Our responsibility is to ensure by every measure possible that we care for our patients." He paused and scanned the room. Every face registered understanding. Nothing more needed to be said.

By 10:00 A.M. forty-seven Confederate soldiers had left the hospital. Those who were too sick to move, yet alert enough to question the activity, were told that more sick and wounded would be sent from Richmond, and that those who were well enough to travel had been sent home.

"That's a Goddamn lie," a legless soldier said to one nurse.

"I'm sure it is not, sir," she replied without looking at him directly.

"Some of 'em's going back to the field," he said. "They'll fight till the day of judgment, or till Lee tells 'em it's over, one or the other."

"Yes, sir. They are courageous men, all."

"It's got nothing to do with courage," he said.

She finished dressing his wounds and hurried to attend the men in the next room.

After distributing to each departing soldier his various goods—a change of clothes, a blanket, scant provisions of hard tack and bread—Joseph set off once more toward College Hall to report to Thompson. As he approached the gate, he recalled the swell of people moving toward the depot earlier in the morning, and his salute to the man at the head of the band of Negroes. As the black face appeared to his memory, Joseph was disturbed again by conflicting emotions. It seemed to him that he and the black man had communicated—that words of understanding had been spoken and that a bridge that the sound of voices alone could construct had been erected between them. But that was nonsense. No word had passed between them. Joseph had not heard the man speak, not even on that day when the lash of Robert Towns's whip across his back should have forced the expulsion of curses. Instead, one shrill and defiant cry, not a plea for mercy, but a protest to the Almighty.

Joseph looked again for the man, but he was nowhere in sight. Perhaps he'd left the city, was making his way north, toward freedom. Other Negroes passed by, but all of them appeared to be under the watch of their masters or mistresses, for the men bore on their backs trundles larger and heavier than any white man would have willingly carried. And of course the women and children presented no threat. In spite of their ignorance, they appeared to act as if they were safer with their owners than they would be on their own. Louisa would say they had no ability to care for themselves. Perhaps that was true of those who walked behind their masters and mistresses. It surely was not of the man who occupied Joseph's thoughts.

Outside the gate, he picked up his pace. The toe of his boot caught a tree root and he stumbled. Behind him a horse whinnied. He turned and saw the general astride his stallion, back rigid, thick white beard and cold eyes accentuating the enormity of the man. Wade Hampton could have ridden alone against Sherman's troops, Joseph thought, and his demeanor would not have changed. The man was stoic. No; more than that, he looked incapable of emotion, any emotion, including fear or love. Death held as little threat to such a man as indigestion.

Hampton nodded at Joseph, halted the horse, and rested his left hand upon the pommel of the saddle. When he spoke, the people slowed down and looked up at him. He told them there would be no fighting in the streets. They might have understood him to mean that the Confederates would not engage Sherman's army, or they might have heard a command: There would be no fighting among the citizens as they went to the depot and scrambled there for position on the trains. Perhaps he meant both.

Hampton turned his horse toward Gervais Street. He dug his boots once into the animal's flanks. The horse raced down Sumter Street, muck flying from his hooves. A clump of sludge splattered the side of a man's face. His lifeless expression did not change. With a lethargic sweep of his hand he removed most of the mass, the residue smeared from temple to jaw. He did not break stride.

At College Hall, Joseph reported the morning's procedures to Thompson.

"How are the nurses holding up?" Thompson asked.

"Well. They seem to have adopted Mrs. McCord's resolve."

"Joseph." Thompson locked his hands together and placed them on his desk. He spoke haltingly: "I do not mean to offend. Or intrude. Perhaps this is none of my business." He stopped, waited.

Joseph welcomed the intimacy of the address, yet it also disturbed him. He felt he was standing before the idealization he'd had since youth of a father, his own having shattered the boy's desperate conception too many times with a leather strap and harsh denouncement of Joseph's frailty. He was always a sickly child, at once awed by and fearful of his father's angry strength.

"You're not interfering, sir."

"It's about Mrs. McCord."

"Yes?"

"I understand your regard for her. I am concerned."

"We are guilty of no misconduct, sir. I assure you. We work together. We discuss the needs of the staff and our patients. Our behavior, publicly and privately, is beyond reproach. If rumors are spreading about us, they are nothing more than vile hearsay."

"I know that. I am not making an accusation, Joseph. I know you both to be good and noble people." He stopped again, a struggle revealed in the fix of his brow.

"Then what, sir? Please, speak your mind."

"I don't want to see you hurt. The war has caused us enough pain. How much more can the heart bear?"

Thompson's face, more than his words, gave Joseph to understand what he meant. Still, he needed to hear the words, needed a declaration of the matter, a bringing into immediate focus what speech alone could provide. Thus, the provocation of a lie: "I do not understand."

And its rebuttal: "I suspect that you do. Mrs. McCord is a married woman."

"She is a widow."

"Bereft of a husband, yes. But do not think that she is not married." Thompson turned in his seat and pointed out the window. "She is married to this, Joseph, as are many women who have lost husbands, fathers, and sons to the war. These women are bound to the Confederacy in a way that we men, even our soldiers, are not. Their allegiance has little to do with ideology. It has to do with what they have suffered and lost. What hope do they have of rebuilding their lives? Imagine what it will be like for them to oversee the duties of their homes, their farms, attend to the needs of their remaining children, with no husbands, no elder sons, to help."

"But I am here to help. I *want* to help. That is what I want her to understand."

"She cannot. She will not. It is beyond her capacity."

"You speak as if she is ignorant."

"It has nothing to do with ignorance. Louisa McCord is as intelligent as any person I've ever known. More intelligent than most. What I am telling you is that her world has been destroyed. You can no more give her that world back than you can change the outcome of this war. She *cannot* love you, Joseph. It has nothing to do with you. You're the finest man I know. If I had a daughter, I would want her to be your wife. Mrs. McCord is no man's wife. She is wife and widow both, and in equal measure, to the Confederacy. She will mourn its death and tend its grave as long as she lives."

Joseph did not trust himself to respond. Thompson had spoken the truth in all its decayed murk. As much as Joseph hated that truth, he knew he had to bear it.

He nodded to Thompson and left his office. Outside, he squinted against the sun. The great disk seemed a stranger to these parts after weeks and weeks of dark clouds and heavy rains. He walked once more toward the college gate, slowly this time, pensive and sad, but strangely renewed. If he was not to be a husband ever again, not to share a woman's bed, make a life with her, settle into old age together, he'd nevertheless received a measure of consolation.

He was, in the view of another he loved, a son.

| 43 |

Sacking the City

The Congaree Bridge was burning. From the second story of Rutledge, Joseph saw flames arc into the pale blue sky and bend toward the heart of the city. Sherman was destroying any means of movement in and out of Columbia. His aim was obvious: to keep Confederate troops from entering and citizens from escaping. The depot would burn next, Joseph thought.

He overheard, from an adjacent room, a young soldier ask Louisa Mc-Cord in a tremulous voice what was happening outside. Joseph recalled the boy's bravery when, a week earlier, Thompson told him he would have to remove his gangrenous left arm at the elbow. In the days following the amputation, a thick wrap, through which turgid yellow pus oozed, shielded the cavity. Not once had the boy complained.

"The devil from the north has arrived," said Louisa.

"He means to kill us all," the boy said.

"Hush that talk. He won't do anything to you or to anyone else in this hospital."

The shrill of her reprimand subdued him. Moments later, Louisa's footfall sounded in the hallway. Cannon fire echoed throughout the city.

Joseph walked into the room where the boy lay still in his bed, eyes wide with fright. Louisa reentered the room. The boy propped himself up on his elbows and looked at her. Joseph motioned her back into the hallway and followed.

He said, "They are firing on the capitol."

"How can you be sure?"

"I know the sound of a cannon ball when it strikes concrete. I can also judge the distance."

"Of the shot?"

"Of the impact. Its distance from us. I must go now, see what I can do in the city."

"It's not safe," she said. "Are not your services more needed here?"

"Nothing is safe. You yourself have said as much. What more can we do here than to move soldiers? The staff is seeing to that now." He turned and marched down the hallway, the sharp thud of his boots resounding against the wood floor.

Outside, two Union convalescents—one monstrously large, the other slight of build—cradled their crutches as they gazed at the inferno. A crier raced down Sumter on his stallion proclaiming the enemy's arrival and warning people to flee. The big soldier hurled his crutch high into the air and shouted, "Uncle Billy's here!" Eyes ablaze, he pivoted on his leg, faced his comrade, and grabbed his thin shoulders at the very moment that he slipped on a small mound of sheep dung. He was saved from falling face-first onto the cold mushy ground by his diminutive friend, whose spiny back absorbed the impact.

"Get off me, Goddamn ye. They's sheep shit in my mouth." The little man fought terrifically. His left leg, which looked to Joseph like a replacement for the other's missing right one, shot upward. A bony thigh struck the prone man's groin. The victim quivered, then deflated like a pricked balloon. His tremendous shoulders encased the other's body and sank into the muck. Beneath the large man's bulk the other squirmed like a lover in the heat of passion. His airborne leg jerked right and left. It took him, by Joseph's reckoning, a full two minutes to extricate himself from the mountain of flesh. Then, holding both hands to his throat, he slumped against an elm tree and gazed stupidly at the hazy world.

Joseph shook his head and resumed his trek. He was less than a block from the capitol when he heard a cannon volley and saw smoke rise from the building. My God, he thought, they're going to destroy it. He wondered whether Sherman would also burn the old wooden structure at the corner of Senate and Richardson. The building had served as the statehouse for more than half a century before construction began on the new one more than a decade ago. He remembered Thompson's telling him that the value of the new capitol, according to its architect, exceeded a million dollars. All of it soon to be gone. The entire city. The business district. Market Square. Houses filled with furniture, artwork, books, food, wine, whiskey. Streets lined with orange and magnolia trees. Gardens teeming with jasmine, oleander, damascene roses. Sidney Park, where walkers strolled, lovers held hands, children played, their joyous shouts reverberant.

He ran down Sumter. Between Senate and Gervais he veered left and cut across the statehouse grounds. At the sound of another cannon blast, he fell and covered his head with both hands. A ball resounded against concrete. He looked up and saw an impression on the west face of the building. He counted four other indentations in the wall. A voice called. Though the sound was muffled, he thought he heard his name.

Again he heard his name, but could not locate the source. He turned his face and saw hundreds of people, but no one he recognized, no one coming toward him. Then he felt a tug at his left shoulder, gentle at first, then strong, urgent. Like a baby being jostled in its crib, he felt himself lifted, turned, the back of his head laid gently on the ground.

"Joseph! Answer me. Are you hit?"

No, sir, he wanted to say, but words would not come. The ringing in his ears slithered throughout his entire body: inside his mouth first, then outward to the head, nose, lips, jaw, and from there downward until he felt the sensation in his toes. He was not having a seizure; of that he was certain. He knew what a seizure was like. Or rather, knew it was so unlike any shock to the system that when it came, the mind ceased to work. At Bull Run, the evening after his first fit, a fellow soldier sat beside him and described to Joseph the way his body shook, the purpling of his face, the foaming at the mouth. Joseph could recall none of that. Had his mind ceased to function during the seizure, refused to assimilate the body's wild trembling into the consciousness of memory? Or maybe it was the horror of Bull Run itself that robbed him of understanding. This was different. He had complete comprehension of the frenzy of activity around him. He recognized Thompson. He was aware of his own fear. Hearing and speech would return, he reasoned, when the echo of cannon fire ceased.

Thompson placed his hands on either side of Joseph's head. "Can you hear me?"

Joseph nodded, opened his mouth, closed it, and nodded again. He was more concerned about his friend's pallor than his own loss of speech. Perhaps the run across the capitol lawn had exhausted the doctor, finally depleted him of the last vestige of vitality that endless hours of work at the hospital had not already stolen from him.

"We must get out of here. Come. I'll help you." Thompson pulled Joseph to his feet, draped the younger man's left arm across his shoulder. Another cannon ball roared over the landscape and struck the building. Thompson faltered at the crash, regained his balance, wheezed with the effort, and pulled Joseph along.

Swarms of people blocked their movement. Thompson pointed ahead to Richardson Street. He stumbled twice, would have fallen had Joseph not anchored him. With each step ahead, Joseph regained his legs. By the time they reached Richardson Street, he was able to move of his own volition.

What the two men saw horrified them. Marauders—some dressed in Confederate uniforms, others in overalls and loose-fitting cloaks, mostly whites but some blacks too, oblivious to each other, mindful only of provisions they sought—were breaking into stores in the business district. Solomon Marvin's Bakery had been pilfered of every item, and broken glass lay everywhere. Only the shell remained of what had been Mrs. Gebenrath's Boarding House. Books—some still intact, others with pages torn out—lay on the street in front of Townsend & North Booksellers and in front of Peter Blass's store. Boots, shoes, hats, clothes, china, glass, and other household items littered the street.

The men moved ahead. Thompson turned right on Sumter, Joseph a step behind. The closer they moved toward the college, the greater the swell of people they faced. All of them moved with mad determination toward the depot. Joseph motioned left at Gervais. Fewer people coming from this direction. Among those, fewer still moving away from the blasts. Instead, they hauled cotton bales from their homes out into the center of the street. Better to burn it than to let Sherman seize it and turn it to profit.

They were less than a hundred feet from Mayor Goodwyn's house when a cannon ball whistled through the air and shattered the front porch. Wood splinters rose high and then drifted downward like snowflake. Thompson covered his head with both arms and limped forward. He was halfway across the yard when the battered front door swung open loosely on its hinges, and a black woman called, "Everybody inside all right. Mr. Goodwyn not here. Gone to town."

The woman appeared to Joseph to be strangely calm. He'd seen people in shock in the moments following a horrible occurrence. The mind simply shut down, unable to assimilate the catastrophe.

Thompson backed away from the debris. The men continued toward Henderson, from there to Pendleton, and up toward the backside of the campus. When Joseph caught sight of the McCord house, his voice returned. "Stop!"

Thompson wheeled around. "She's not there."

"The others," Joseph said. He was thinking of Harriet, the woman who had served him and Louisa when he was last there. He would tell her to send for him if she saw Union soldiers advance toward the house.

Joseph passed Thompson and turned into the McCord yard. He climbed the porch steps and yanked the door open. "Who's here?" He entered the dark hallway and called again: "Hello. Who's here? I demand to know who is in this house."

An old white-haired slave shuffled into the hallway. He teetered and rubbed his eyes like a man roused from sleep. Joseph recognized him as a McCord slave, but couldn't call him by name. He might have been Harriet's father or uncle. Or perhaps no relation. It didn't matter; he would know her whereabouts. He would know where they all were hiding, or whether they were stealing Louisa's goods, or simply shirking their duties.

"Where is everyone?" Joseph asked.

The man shook his head, gazed at the floor.

Joseph took three steps forward and slapped the dark face. "Answer me. Is Harriet here? The others who serve this house, where are they?"

The old man raised his head, opened his toothless mouth, and grinned. "Most of them gone," he muttered. "To the river."

To Sherman, Joseph told himself. He slapped the old man again. This time the man stumbled, tripped over his feet, and struck his head against the wall. The blow drew blood from the left side of his head. Horrified at what he'd done, Joseph knelt by the man's side. He placed a hand on the man's chest. "Are you all right? I didn't mean to hurt you, but you must help me. This house is in danger."

The man grinned again, but said nothing. Joseph then stood and turned his back on the man, flung open the door, and raced down the steps. Across the street Thompson walked toward the college green. Joseph caught up with him on the back side of DeSaussure. "They've left Louisa," he said.

"Of course they have. What did you expect?"

"They're fools. They've abandoned the only woman who cares anything about them. Sherman has nothing for them. They'll find out soon enough the mistake they've made. He will turn them away just as he has others before them." Joseph knew Sherman wouldn't slow his troops down for old people and women and children who couldn't keep up. One look at the old man who lay on Louisa's floor would be enough to convince the deranged general of the idiocy of his mission. Then it would be too late. What would the North do with such people? Their celebration of victory would be short-lived, for they would understand that the fall of the Confederacy portended their own moral collapse. This fiery apocalypse would destroy both nations.

"Fools or not, they are gone," said Thompson. He wheezed again. He pressed a hand to his coat and pulled it tight under his chin.

Joseph reached for him. "Let me help you to College Hall."

"What? And hide? To what purpose?" rasped Thompson.

"Not to hide. To rest. You have pushed yourself too hard."

"Don't mollify me, Joseph." Thompson faced him. He cleared his throat and spoke again through fits of coughing and wheezing and struggling to catch his breath. "This city will be destroyed by evening. We've work to do. Return to Rutledge. Proceed from there to all the buildings. Ask the nurses what they need. In two hours, report to me."

Before Joseph could respond, Thompson turned away and, shoulders curled forward, walked across the green toward College Hall.

Above the din of noise made by people running down Sumter, mothers calling to scattering children, came once more the sear of cannon fire. A rumble, as of wood collapsing. The sky to the west alight with the sickening hue of flame and char. A chorus of wails rising like prayer to the impotent Baals of Babylon.

| 44 |
Preparing for Surrender

Joseph returned to College Hall an hour before sunset. He found Thompson crumpled in his chair, snoring gently. Joseph sat facing the desk and bowed his head. Within a few minutes he too dropped off to sleep. Presently, a cough awakened him. He adjusted his eyes to the evening light creeping aslant through the window. Thompson shuffled papers at his desk.

"I have exceeded the limits of my endurance," Thompson said, shoulders stooped in resignation. "Surely you know how terrible a confession this is for a surgeon to make."

"Yes, sir."

"Next year marks the fortieth anniversary of my medical practice. I remember the day I graduated medical school. I made a public pledge to do all in my power to care for the sick, to promote the health of every human being who came to me for help."

"The Hippocratic oath," said Joseph.

"It is a sacred charge, taken seriously by every doctor whose love of medicine and concern for mankind hold equal sway in his heart." Thompson paused, cleared his throat, and continued: "I hope I do not sound arrogant."

"No, sir."

"You will understand, then, my feeling at this moment. This is a bitter day."

Joseph nodded. He did not know what to say. Thompson's admission sounded like a confession, and Joseph was no priest. He searched his memory for words of Scripture that might offer comfort. All he could call to mind was the twenty-third Psalm. He'd heard it recited countless times over the graves of the battle-slain. Once, at an evening mass burial, he questioned the integrity of the psalm. That afternoon a man who fought beside Joseph in a trench had risen to make a charge. It was an act of madness, the man's fear having turned, as it did for many soldiers under fire, into uncontrollable rage. From his mouth came a scream that Joseph thought no human voice could make. The man stood, leapt out of the trench, and before he could take another step, the cannon ball struck, taking both legs cleanly at the hip. He fell back into the hollowed earth. His body jerked. His mouth gaped, but no sound issued. Eyes wide with fear seemed to plead for help. Moments later he was dead, the blood beneath his contorted shape seeping into Joseph's pants.

That evening, when his friend was buried with all the other fallen, Joseph wondered whether he would walk again in the afterlife. *Yea, though I walk. . . .* Are bodies restored beyond the grave? he wondered. The risen Jesus, marks of his wounds still visible. Joseph's friend, raised to squirm, all valleys beyond time dark before him.

"I saw Thomas an hour ago," said Thompson.

"Sir?"

"Mayor Goodwyn. He came to tell me that Generals Hampton and Beauregard are soon to meet at Hunt's Hotel to plan the departure of their forces from the city."

"We are doomed," said Joseph.

"Thomas is waiting to hear from the generals. He thinks it his duty as mayor to surrender the city, but he can do nothing without a military order."

"And what is Hampton doing? Preparing his troops for retreat? Where are the high and mighty who spoke so convincingly of the Confederacy's cause?"

Thompson leaned back and shook his head. "What would you have them do? Imagine the chaos of battle on the streets of the city. Is that what you want?"

Joseph closed his eyes and saw once more the gore at Bull Run. His friend falling legless into the trench; his own blood-soaked pants and the blood of other wounded and dying soldiers oozing along the ground and seeping into pockets of earth; human flesh ripening for consumption by maggots; the horizon dark with smoke and apocalyptic cloud cover.

Thompson said, "The city will burn. How much of it, we do not know. Thomas is going to ask Sherman to spare the hospital and the library. I am confident he will not risk the lives of his own soldiers, so these grounds should be safe. Still, if the wind is high, we must be alert to danger. Make sure we have plenty of buckets. We may be scooping water for hours."

Joseph returned to his room in Pinckney. He wanted to lie down, close his eyes. Not sleep, but remove himself from the noise of cannon fire, the grating voices of people, the nausea of caring for the sick. Before his head hit the pillow, another cannon blast sounded. He heard in the distance inarticulate cries of desolation. Or perhaps he imagined rather than heard them. Either way, the sounds of war surrounded him.

He pulled himself to a sitting position on the edge of the bed and looked at himself in the dingy mirror above the lavatory. Wrinkles he'd not noticed before. Hair gray and thinning. Slackness in the neck. He'd detested that turkey-neck look on his father when the old man, having turned sixty that autumn, lay on his death bed. Joseph couldn't decide what was uglier: the translucence of the flesh or its wrinkled pits. He hated the stern man, was prepared to feel no remorse when he died. What a painful surprise it was for him when, a week after the burial, Joseph fell to the floor of his father's barn and wept for his loss.

Look as bad as he did, Joseph told himself, and pulled taught the skin beneath his chin. No time for rest, he muttered. Must get back to Rutledge, check on the staff. Louisa. Make sure she's eaten. Not likely. Either forgets or simply refuses when there's too much work to do. Hard woman. Unyielding.

He rose, put on his coat, shuffled outside. In the distance, near the river, he saw firelight rise moonward, smoke spread in every direction. Sign of the coming holocaust.

| 45 |

Fiery Dawn

The night brought little rest. Joseph stuffed his ears with cotton, but to no effect. What he did not hear distinctly, he nevertheless felt in the tremors of earth every time a cannon ball landed near campus. Shots were sporadic, but well-timed. Pandemonium in the streets. As the threat moved closer, people continued to loot stores and scavenge for everything they could carry away.

A forty-minute gap between the roar of one cannon and the next seemed only a few seconds to Joseph, who finally fell into a restive sleep sometime after 2:00 A.M. only to be fully awakened minutes later by a blast. When he got out of bed at 5:45 and put on the same clothes he'd worn the day before, he convinced himself that he must have gotten some sleep, for he wasn't as weak as he'd felt before.

Outside he heard a bustle. He stepped onto the lawn and heard distinctly the slap of feet on the ground outside the gate. People moved in a steady stream past the college, some of them heading for the depot, others afoot for Winnsboro and Alston. Fierce winds howled about them. Two boys and a girl walking side by side were knocked to the ground at one point by the force of the gale. The youngest boy cried. His mother turned to the children and ordered them to stand. The two oldest scrambled to their feet. Each of them grabbed an arm of their flustered brother, pulled him up, and held on to him as they resumed their trek behind their mother's billowing skirt.

Joseph fought the wind as he trudged up the walkway to Rutledge for the first leg of his rounds. He was halfway down the hallway on the second floor when Miss Simpson walked out of a room carrying in both hands two blood-soaked towels. Her face was ashen, dark circles under her eyes.

"Is there trouble, Miss Simpson?" Joseph asked.

"Johnston," she said, and motioned back toward the room with her head. "He stole a razor from someone else's room and cut himself."

"How bad is it?"

She held the towels up. "We've stanched the flow. He'll need quite a bit of stitching. Mrs. McCord is with him now. She has sent for Dr. Thompson." She moved at a rapid clip down the hallway. Joseph watched her until she turned the corner, then he stepped into the room.

Louisa sat by the soldier's bed. She glanced at Joseph, then turned her gaze back to Johnston, a boy not yet twenty, whose mind had been warped by the sight of too much bloodshed. Joseph remembered reading the report from the hospital in Richmond. *Prone to self-mutilation. Speaks of father and two brothers killed at Shiloh, but recounting of events changes from one telling to next. Seems to present no danger to others. Given to contrition, often in form of tears and inarticulate moans.*

The boy refused to open his eyes when Joseph spoke his name. Louisa held up a hand. She glanced over her shoulder at Joseph and shook her head.

Presently, Thompson arrived. Joseph administered the morphine. Within minutes Thompson sutured the laceration with twenty-one stitches.

An hour later, Joseph and Louisa met each other coming down the hallway from opposite directions. She said, "Hampton has left the city."

"They are gone already?"

"Most of the troops left last night. Beauregard told Mayor Goodwyn to surrender the city this morning."

"What's left to surrender? Most people have fled. Shall we open these vacant homes to Sherman and tell him to take what he pleases? Perhaps we should prepare a feast, send the Union troops to the brothels for a bath and an afternoon siesta. We surely want to be hospitable."

"What good is your bitterness, Joseph? Do you think our generals are forsaking us because they are frightened? They have fought against insuperable odds for four years. Staying to put up a defense will only ensure the complete destruction of the city. Our only hope is to surrender and plead for mercy."

"Of all people in this world, you are the one I least expected to say that. You plead for mercy?"

"Not I. That shame falls to the mayor." She walked past him and did not turn her head when he called her name.

He wished he could hate her. Only once had his heart burned with more emotion. Nothing could compare to the loss of his wife and daughter, but her persistent rejection wounded him deeply. The heat of battle could not compare. Fear, yes. Rage. Bloodlust. But what he felt now made those passions seem childish, the fleeting playthings of effete boys. Here today, gone tomorrow. This, however, was lasting. An ardor that time could not diminish. What fool gave voice to the silly notion that time heals all wounds? As though time itself were a healing agent, or the universe that stretched from the remotest dawn to never-ending night solicitous of its momentary inhabitants. He knew better. There was no balm for the broken heart—his own, that of the boy so deranged by war that he'd taken to carving his own flesh, those of soldiers dead and those of soldiers who killed them. No redemption but the end of history, the following dawn barren of life.

A few minutes after 9:00 A.M. Joseph completed his rounds. The moment he walked out of Harper he saw in the sky a funnel of smoke above what he knew to be the depot. Sherman must have burned everything—building, loading platform, perhaps even the last train attempting departure. By now railroad ties would be disfigured, twisted like gnarly wisteria roots. The only means of escape now were the woods and the river, the one infested with Union troops blocking the way, the other cold and raging from two months of rain.

What most frightened Joseph was the raging of the wind. If it continued unabated, one spark might set the whole city ablaze.

He'd intended to go to College Hall to confer with Thompson. But outside the gate, he was overwhelmed by a compulsion to head toward Market Square. How much damage would the stores on Richardson Street have suffered by now? And the capitol? Joseph could see a portion of the south side of the building from where he stood. It hadn't collapsed, but that was no guarantee that beneath it remained anything other than the shell of a structure. Lured by the wonder of decimation, he turned toward the heart of the city, lowered his shoulders into the wind, and stumbled forward.

Cotton bales lay everywhere. Most of them were split like a cadaver prepared for examination. The wind seized wisps of white gossamer and swirled them about until they were snatched out of the air by the wild, waving arms of thrashing trees or by the broken brick and splintered wood of buildings.

At the corner of Gervais and Richardson, Joseph looked to his right. A landau advanced. Beside the driver was a long pole and attached to it a white sheet billowing so wildly that it looked as if at any moment the wind might rip it to shreds. Joseph recognized the mayor's carriage. As it passed, he saw Mayor Goodwyn and three aldermen inside. Heads bent downward, their bodies shifted lifelessly with the rickety motion of the vehicle. It looked to Joseph like a hearse leading a funeral procession, its somber occupants dreading the sight of the maw of earth that would house the dead.

Joseph wondered how Sherman would receive the diminutive mayor. He'd heard, as had every Confederate soldier, of Sherman's agitated behavior. Some said he didn't sleep, but turned his devilish mind in the wee hours of morning to battle tactics, surprise maneuvers that Grant himself knew nothing of until after the fact. Others said he didn't eat. His diet, they said, was cigars, which he chewed more than smoked. Those who said they'd actually seen him—and more than a few Confederates made the claim, as if it conferred upon them the status of prophet or the visionary authority of the blind Tiresias—said he didn't walk like a man, but rather strutted like a bantam rooster, his body jerking with anger and foul calculation. Would this devil incarnate see in the nervous Goodwyn an older image of himself? Would the mayor snap out of his moribund posture at sight of the general, and would the general receive him graciously? Two men fully aware of what each side had suffered, more burdened with the war's communal costs than those who had the luxury of attending only to personal loss.

The coach turned right on Richardson. Joseph watched for a few moments, mumbled "Godspeed, Thomas Goodwyn," then turned to view the imposing capitol, which appeared to be intact. He walked forward a few steps, then stopped as his eyes settled on the large sculpture of General Washington, a solemn figure whose regal bearing had always seemed to Joseph to possess an aura of invincibility. The general's walking stick had suffered damage, the bottom half broken off. Joseph wondered whether it had been taken by a cannon ball or by some crazed, drunken marauders wielding clubs and hammers. Who of either army would do such a thing to this revered figure? Ransacking a church of its holy relics would be no less a sacrilege. He was so shaken that he stumbled at the foot of the statue.

He moved ahead, circled to the west side of the building. He surveyed the wall and counted five indentations. No more defacement than he'd witnessed the day before. He circled the building and found no more evidence of damage. At the sound of gunfire coming from down near the river, he jumped. Is this the end? he asked himself. Where would the final desecration begin? The river's edge offered an assortment of enticements: ramshackle houses that would ignite like paper; brothel houses that would serve the twin appetites of debauchery and destruction; the Saluda Factory, where women turned cloth into soldiers' uniforms; the spacious brick building, Evans and Cogswell Company, where Confederate currency was printed; the Confederate Armory. *My God, they'll burn everything in sight*, he thought. *Pillage, rape, murder. There'll be no end to it.*

He thought of Louisa, whose harsh tongue would incur the wrath of some violent soldier. Joseph raced ahead to the college.

| 46 |
Revenge

By nightfall the entire city was ablaze. Homes, offices, government build-ings, stores, fences, trees burned. The pop and splinter of wood sounded on every street. Wind carried burning cinders to every nook and cranny of the city. Ravaged women shrieked. Hordes of people gazed upon incalculable loss. A pig squealed, churning its squat legs in a vain effort to outrun the flames that engulfed its body. It did not race far down Senate Street before it crumpled, the bone of a rear leg snapping like a twig. There it let out a final scream, spasmed a few times, and lay still, martyr to the consuming power of fire. Above it all, cotton wisps rose and fell, some still white, as if making a last attempt at escape, only to give in to its indomitable foe and fall like dew on the blistered ground.

Joseph felt imprisoned within the walls of the college yard. Many towns-people had gathered there after fleeing their homes in search of rescue. If word around the city were true—that Sherman had promised Mayor Good-wyn that the college would not be destroyed—then no place offered greater security. Joseph helped many people carry their meager provisions and settle inside the gate. Then he walked into the city. He couldn't help himself. The draw of destruction was irresistible. He kept his head down and his mouth shut to avoid confrontation. Mercantile stores, women, drink, and the frenzy of theft were enough to keep enemy soldiers occupied.

He walked past the old capitol, a dilapidated wooden structure that looked like an abandoned shed. In the front yard, John C. Calhoun's statue, formerly draped with the toga of a Roman senator, had been reduced to a puddle of quicklime. Joseph continued toward the new capitol. Fires from cotton bales, trees, and nearby buildings silhouetted the state house in a ghostly haze.

Along a three-block stretch of Richardson Street, the city's main thor-oughfare, Joseph surveyed each building. Broken windows everywhere. Doors caved in, torn from their hinges. Inside, shelves once laden with goods were empty. Clothes, blankets, furniture, tools, food, registers—all signs of commerce gone.

People moved past him in either direction like scarecrows, voiceless, jostled by the breeze. Most of them were Negroes. The few whites he saw wore looks of long-suffering deprivation. They scavenged among the debris of stores and offices. Joseph was about to step over the rubble of wood and shattered glass to enter the ruins of the State Ordnance Warehouse when shouts erupted behind him. He turned and saw the crowd break apart, leaving two men in the center of a widening circle.

"I'll carve you like a pig, nigger!" The crouched man held in his right hand a long knife. He moved slowly to his right. Joseph saw only the man's back, but knew, the moment he heard the growling voice, its owner: Robert Towns.

The other man said nothing. His eyes were darker than the bowels of a cave, pitiless. In his large black hand he clenched a thick piece of wood two feet long. With the other hand he pulled up the sleeve of his tattered coat past the elbow so as to allow free range of motion. His forearm was thick with the twisted cord of muscle. Joseph started when he recognized the man: the one whom Towns had whipped at Market Square; the same man who had passed by him a day earlier at the college gate. Joseph's stomach roiled. He felt a surge of guilt. No matter how much he detested Towns, he was more sickened by the thought that he was becoming a traitor to his people, his race. Yet he could not help himself. He admired the way the black man faced Towns.

Towns continued to circle. The other held his ground, merely turning his head to follow Towns's movement.

From the inner circle of the crowd a small Negro crept behind Towns. Eyes on the white man's knife, arms outspread, he was about to pounce when the quiet but commanding call of his name—*Josiah*—arrested him. Josiah looked up, nodded once at the club-wielding speaker, and melted into the circle. Towns glanced over his shoulder, seemed to consider the possibility of flight, but the group of black bodies tightened immediately. He jerked his head back and stared at the impassive face of his adversary, who'd made no attempt to take advantage of Towns's distraction.

Towns moved to his right again. Joseph now saw the brute's face. The same disfigured, ugly scowl he'd seen when Towns stood on the scaffold, whip in hand, and then later the next day when, near the Market, he threatened Joseph. He was even uglier now. An ogre transmogrified by fear.

Joseph wasn't sure who moved first, Towns or the other, but in the next instant, the knife and Towns both lay on the ground. Someone leapt from the crowd and grabbed the weapon, squirreled it away in his pocket, and disappeared back into the mass. The large black man straddled Towns's body. His forearm was striated like the neck of a stallion at full gallop. He lifted the wood above his head, held it there for a moment, then tossed it.

Towns stirred. His left leg juddered. His eyes opened onto the stolid face above him. He scuttled like a crab on hands and feet. The black man leaned down, grabbed Towns by the collar of his coat, and jerked him up. He slapped the grizzled face twice. Sound echoed in the chamber of the human circle.

A woman—one of the few whites trapped by the mass of onlookers—gasped. A rumble of maniacal laughter rose from the dark faces around her. Joseph knew he must do something. He had no compulsion to protect Towns. The man was worthless. He did not matter. Principle, however, did. Joseph could not stand by while black men took advantage of a white woman. No self-respecting man could allow such barbarous behavior. But he was afraid. For the first time in his life, he knew the terror of being imperiled for no reason other than the color of his skin.

He called out, "Help her," and as soon as the plea erupted from him, he knew to whom it was directed. As on two previous occasions, their eyes locked again. This time, Joseph was sure, the other recognized him. The man raised the arm which gripped the club. The crowd fell silent. Joseph pointed toward the spot where he'd earlier seen the woman. She had disappeared from his view. The black man turned his gaze toward the place and waved the club once, left to right. A moment later, Joseph saw the woman emerge from the outermost part of the circle. She backed away several steps, then spun around and ran toward the highest blaze.

The disruption lasted but a moment, then the crowd lurched forward. Someone bumped Joseph. He tripped, reached instinctively for ballast, gripped an arm, but it jerked away. He managed to right himself and stumble ahead. There was no way to turn back against the swell. All he could do was to let it take him. The very light of the world seemed to have been extinguished. Something—a fist, an elbow, the barrel of a gun—jabbed him in the back. He coughed, drew his arms tight against his ribs. Right and left he glanced, desperate for the assurance that a white face alone could provide. Where was the woman he'd helped? Had she found safety? Would she seek out white men to come to his aid or to Towns's? Joseph hated the realization that his own safety was tied to Towns's. And if rescuers did come, it would not be because the woman had named either of them, or, had she been able, given a report of either man's character. They would come only because they had been told that two white men were surrounded by a wild group of savages.

As the crowd pushed ahead, their angry clamor grew. They wanted blood. The blood of a white man. Perhaps Joseph's, too. If moments earlier he'd been assured by the look of the mob's leader, his confidence was now gone. He was afraid. He thought to cry out in the hope that a few Union soldiers would come to their senses long enough to put a stop to this madness. Where were they? He heard their yells, their shouts of bravado from nearby streets, but as yet he'd not encountered one blue coat. Perhaps by now they were too drunk to care about imposing martial order on a band of hostile Negroes. And if he did call out, what might this murderous mob do to him before help came?

Within minutes, amid the din of angry voices and the stench of smoke swirling from the river's edge, the rabid pack arrived at the whipping post on the other side of Market Square. Towns screamed, fought, cursed, his wails at once pathetic and inhuman.

His captor hauled him up the steps of the platform as if he were pulling some recalcitrant child. Towns struggled. The black giant slapped him. A stream of blood spewed from Towns's mouth.

As if seeing the whipping post for the first time, Joseph was struck by the enormity of the structure. Previously, he'd merely glanced at the platform. Towns had demanded Joseph's exclusive attention—and everyone else's—with his arrogant, swaggering boasts. Now, pinned between the edge of the platform and the pressing phalanx of chanting Negroes, Joseph faced the size and rigidity of the crossbeam, the spectacular construction of torture. The floor was made of thick pine. It could have held seventy-five people easily. The crossbeam was made of oak so hard and unyielding that it would not bend under the weight of the heaviest man. Its inflexible strength served to augment the sting of the whip, reverberant off a body that, shackled, gave little sway.

A guttural voice called from the crowd: "Jeremiah. Son. Let him go."

The giant turned, a shock of recognition on his face. Joseph was startled by the transformation. What had been passive, frighteningly stoic was now alive. Nervous. Agitated.

An old gray-haired Negro hoisted himself with difficulty onto the platform. On wobbly legs he teetered forward, arms outstretched. "Jeremiah. Let him go. This is not the Lord's way, son. Sherman will hang you himself."

"Sherman be damned!" Jeremiah said, and stomped his foot. "Every white demon from Adam to now be damned."

Towns tried to break Jeremiah's hold of his collar. Jeremiah wheeled and struck him with a fist hardened by a history of rage. Towns's head snapped back like a thin willow branch bent to the apex of its yield and suddenly released. His body slumped.

Two men grabbed Towns by either arm and held him up. Jeremiah looped a rope around his captive's wrists and cinched it and tossed the other end over the crossbeam. A boy Joseph judged to be no more than twelve scrambled to pick up the loose end and hand it to Jeremiah, who then passed it to a friend who pulled hard until the white man's listless body was stretched to its full length. The two who held Towns by his armpits bore the full of his weight while the other man knotted the rope three times.

"No, son." The old man moved like a shadow, thin arms undulant in the breeze.

Jeremiah looked into the man's pleading eyes. He seemed to Joseph to waver. But only for a moment. In the next instant his gaze turned stony again. Like a young man who has discovered his father in a gambit of treachery and deceit that imperils the family, he shook his head imperiously. Honor and principle, his demeanor seemed to say, outweighed allegiance to his father. He leaned close to the wizened man and said something. The old man's head bowed. His shoulders drooped. He backed away. Two women on the ground helped him down the steps.

A man on the platform yanked the rope. Towns's body swayed forward and back again. Another standing next to Jeremiah soaked a rag in a pail of water and wrapped it around Towns's face. Presently, the head jerked upward, then shook violently. Jeremiah unwound the shroud. When it fell from Towns's face, he gasped and coughed. Jeremiah seized a tuft of hair at the crown of Towns's head and pulled upward until their faces were almost touching. In a loud voice he said, "You know me?"

Towns said nothing.

"What you need to remind you?"

From the crowd came a murmur and rustle of feet.

"This?" Jeremiah flung off his shabby coat, ripped his shirt chest to navel, yanked it off his shoulders, and turned his striped back to Towns.

An explosion of jeers shot from the crowd. Someone yelled, "Give him the same."

Another: "Make him bleed."

Joseph could neither bear to watch nor look away. He felt trapped, bound, yet void of the desire of escape.

On the far side of the platform a white face came into view. It was the first one Joseph had seen since fixing his eyes on the frightened woman on Richardson Street. But there was something strange about this face. Brutal. Primitive. Preternaturally dirty. The face of a man accustomed to darkness. There was in his eyes an unsettling gleam of excitement, feral in intensity. His hair was like the fur of a wild animal. His clothes appeared not so much fitted to his body as attached, adhered to the skin. Garment, dirt, body—all one. The man, small and compact, moved sideways, eyes glued to the spectacle on the platform.

Jeremiah pulled the torn shirt back over his shoulders. From the crowd came a chorus of shouts. A meteor of fire driven by strong wind darted from the topmost branch of one tree to another nearby. Gunfire not two blocks distant. Someone dashed to the edge of the platform, leaned down to take an object from a spectator on the ground, and brought it to Jeremiah. A whip, long and tasseled, sight of which brought a collective sigh from the congregants, and in the next breath a low murmuring chant.

His thick muscled arm alight by the fire's apocalyptic glow, Jeremiah unfurled the whip. His eyes burned with lust.

He took several measured steps backward, let the reptilian cord hang listless by his side, then raised the handle, and brought the lash down on the wood beside his right foot. The sound was dull. A thud rather than a bristling crack. He looked quizzically at the leather, as if questioning its worth. Then, with his left hand he pulled the thong up and wound it—thong, fall, and cracker—until he had a thick bundle of concentric circles.

Jeremiah unfurled the whip with a deft movement of the arm and wrist. This time, the cracker whistled and snapped in the fiery air. Towns's body stiffened. Joseph looked at the white, meaty flesh, now stripped of clothing, bare to the elements.

"Whip him," someone cheered.

"Cut that white skin!"

Jeremiah, sure of his arm, lashed the simian back. Towns sucked air through his teeth. Another lash. Joseph could not see the beaten man's eyes, but imagined their bulge, the distension of the orbits, the intensification of vision followed immediately by blurring.

At fall of the second lash, the grunts of assailant and victim were eerily harmonic. Exertion and pain were fraternal. But with the third and fourth lashes, Towns cried out. His flesh quivered. Even his breeches moved with the tremor of his legs. He would soon soil himself, Joseph thought, the bowels releasing under pain of torture.

Joseph lost count of the number of times the whip whistled through the fire-lit air, the crack of leather on skin. Smoke, lacerated flesh, and the odor of excitement filled his nostrils. A metallic taste, not unlike that he'd noticed preceding seizures, lingered on his tongue. The nerve endings in his arms and neck sparked each time the whip's cracker scored the bulbous back. Gunshot, distant screams, the rush of fire and collapse of buildings echoed in his ears. Yet rising with gentle but sure insistence, like some mystical incantation that suffused the cacophony of all other discordant sounds, was the melodious prayerful chant of those gathered. Joseph looked up to the swirl and wonder of the smoke-filled sky. Star-gleam skittered through intermittently, as if the light of the heavens were playing a game of hide-and-seek with earth-bound creatures.

"Uggh." The expostulation was involuntary. Joseph jerked his head when a piece of flesh struck him beneath the left eye. He swiped at it, but not with enough force to dislodge the bloody particle. With thumb and forefinger he peeled it from his face, sniffed it. It stank. His anger arced. The rage fell not to mad people around him, but upon the scored pulp from which flesh had been torn. If he'd had the whip in hand, he'd have turned it on Towns more viciously, dared him to release another piece of rank skin into the air.

Towns cried out again. Soon the timbre of his voice would descend to a groaning whimper before he lost consciousness. Joseph studied the men on the stage. How dissimilar they were. Jeremiah's cries, he remembered, were gut-wrenching. But they were not craven. As if, no matter the severity of injury, he would not permit his body to admit of its brokenness at the hands of the white man. He might die—he would be willing to die—but he would never plead for abeyance from his tormenter. His cries aimed higher. A protest against the timeless duration of injustice. A defiant shaking of the fist at the universe, and the unanswerable curse of a challenge issued to God alone: *Why?*

The cries issuing from Towns's ragged throat were different. They were abject, pitiful, like those of a child incredulous that something mean and brutal could be done to him. They were the wails of a man not questioning God, but complaining that God had abandoned him, discarded him to the degradation of barbarous treatment at the hands of filthy heathens not worthy of the Almighty's attention.

Towns's back ribboned under the scoring of the whip. Joseph glimpsed slivers of fatty tissue, white as bone, and within seconds the suffusion of blood that rose from the gaps, spread over flesh and body hair, and spilled onto the platform. The initial seepage, like water from a tilted pail, turned into a steady stream, as when the pail is overturned. Joseph closed his eyes and saw once more the white fatty tissue and then the blood that dripped from Jeremiah's body when he was whipped. How strangely similar were these two bodies under duress of torture. And how disturbing, how unscientific, for the journals of medicine he had studied over the last three years made much of the difference between white skin and black hide. And of course everyone understood that because black hide was callous, unlike the smooth and velvety quality of white skin, the brutal treatment of whipping was not only justified, but redemptive. Indeed, every slave owner had to sting the bodies of their property with particular ferocity in order to drive home the lessons of humility and godliness.

Yet here, before his eyes, the excellent wisdom of medical practitioners Joseph admired unraveled like the skin off Towns's back. Or rather, the skin from both men's backs. Joseph remembered. He saw clearly, as if together, this very moment, both Jeremiah and Towns being whipped, one with every even lash, the other with every odd. The flesh opened simultaneously. Tissue and bone alike in hue and depth. Blood to blood.

His reverie of thought was shattered by the catapulting onto the stage of a white man, the diminutive dirt clod Joseph had noticed earlier. He seemed not merely to leap but to take flight, air-borne longer than was humanly possible. He landed lightly, his feet causing no more than a susurrus of sound, like a skimming of the hand over dry sand.

Jeremiah, as shocked as anyone, paused from his work. The fellow obviously presented no challenge to him. Intended none. Nor did any of the others on the platform move to corral him.

Like some elfin jester, he hopped on one foot across the platform to the crossbeam, where he settled in front of the bound figure. He cupped Towns's chin with a hand and lifted it so that they were face to face, the one animated, the other unconscious. The sprightly one waggled his head, grinned maniacally, then barked out at a stunning clip a speech that seemed, in its effortlessness, rehearsed: "Slaves be obedient to them that are your masters according to the flesh with fear and trembling in singleness of your heart as unto Christ not with eye service as men-pleasers but as slaves of Christ doing the will of God from the heart."

He executed a dramatic sweep of his hand and a bow from the waist, kissed the head of the victim, reached his arm back as far as it would go, and with a roundhouse swing, slapped the grizzled face. Then he released the head and let it drop.

Like a crack of thunder, the shock of the gesture frizzled the air and held the audience in suspense for a few moments. Then, someone in the crowd laughed. Cheers erupted. The sprite danced away, took flight once more, and seemed to be running before his feet hit ground.

Jeremiah dropped the whip at his side. Now that Towns was unconscious, Jeremiah seemed to have lost interest. Others scrambled to take up the whip. The boy who earlier had picked up the end of the rope when Jeremiah tossed it over the crossbeam was the first to lay hands on the snaky cord. He struck the mutilated flesh a few times, but was dissatisfied with the effect. He didn't have the strength or agility of Jeremiah, and now crept away, ashamed of his puny effort. A few more took their turns, but the crowd's interest waned as Jeremiah departed, and with little provocation from onlookers, whippers could not generate enthusiasm for the exercise.

As Jeremiah walked down the steps, his broad shoulders and thick arms dripping with sweat, he was met by admirers on all sides. Joseph understood their adoration. He, too, had experienced a perverse enjoyment of the spectacle. It was wrong to delight in the punishment of a white man by a Negro. If others knew of his attitude, he would be scorned, ostracized. And if they knew he'd done nothing to prevent the humiliation, he might suffer far worse than public rejection. Nevertheless, his contempt for Towns was so great that he could not help himself.

With everyone gathering around Jeremiah to touch him, whisper to him, now make room for him as a woman draped a garment over his shoulders, Joseph managed to slink away. At first he simply stood his ground and let people pass by. The communal movement soon opened a gap large enough for him to turn and escape with ease. When he reached the edge of a shadow cast by a tall magnolia not yet burned, he thought to run. But then he saw, athwart the trunk of the tree, Jeremiah's father. Etched in the crevices of his face was the deep mark of sadness. Sadness that only a parent could know. Joseph felt the press of that inimitable ache as if he were that moment laying his daughter into the earth. He looked once more over his shoulder at the crowd, the whipping post, Towns's lacerated body, then limped away beneath the conflagration of ruin.

| 47 |
More Hell than War

Joseph returned to the campus, but stayed only a short while. He could do nothing there. Every minute the green was filling with people from town. If the place provided shelter, overcrowding created yet another peril. If one of the buildings caught fire, or flames leapt over the wall and danced from tree to tree, those in the hospital would have to be moved outside. Already there was no space for them. Joseph gave a thought to consulting with Thompson, but decided against it. Better to act now than to delay and risk catastrophe. He would go at once to the Insane Asylum and ask Dr. Parker what accommodations he might make for others seeking refuge.

Instead of retracing his accustomed path to Gervais, he turned on Pendleton. He would pass by the McCord home once more. There he would follow Bull Street to the asylum. He couldn't let himself hope to find Louisa at her house. Nothing would compel her to leave the hospital. She would stay there, defiant until the terror passed, not with any hope of avoiding it, but rather to face it head-on. It was not courage alone that motivated her; of that he was certain. Nor was sympathy for her patients and her workers the sole principle that guided her. Louisa McCord held in the cavern of her soul a rage that flowed like lava.

Joseph faced the gate of her home from the other side of the street. Hidden in darkness, he saw figures moving about on the porch and talking excitedly. He could tell by their speech that all were Negroes. He tried to discern the hollow voice of the man he'd slapped hours earlier, but too many spoke at once. He managed, however, to make out the theme of their discussion: Some escaped slaves who had left their masters' homes days earlier had hidden out in swamps where they greeted Federal soldiers marching toward town. Joseph strained to hear every word. He learned that slaves had provided Union troops with descriptions of the city, locating their masters' houses and places of business. He wondered whether Harriet had been among the traitors. Perhaps she'd made no attempt to escape at all, but had left with every intention of returning to see Louisa's home destroyed.

He balled his fists, wished he could muster the courage to approach the house and plead with those on the porch not to betray Louisa. Yet he dare not approach them. Perhaps some of them had just returned from the whipping post and had been encouraged by what they witnessed. They might turn on him, make him their next victim. He remained hidden in darkness as he crept down toward Pickens Street, then, certain he could not be seen from Louisa's porch, cut a horizontal path to Bull and reached its intersection with Gervais.

Two blocks from his destination he saw flames climb from LeConte's Niter Bureau Office. He recalled seeing the professor and his man Thomas at the depot two days earlier. How many supplies had they removed? Where had LeConte sent them? Had Union forces overtaken the train and set fire to it? The explosions would be heard miles around. Bodies burned to cinder. He quickened his pace, tried to dispel the frightful image.

At the asylum he found the gates wide open. In the yard women, children, and elderly men milled about. From within the building came the cries of infants. There were not as many people here as had gathered on the college green, but their number was growing. There was more open land here than at the college.

He found Parker at the entrance of the building.

"Joseph, how is it at the college?" Parker asked. His face was creased with worry, dark bags under his eyes.

"The green is full, sir. How many can you accommodate here?"

Parker pointed toward the fence on the far side of the field. As many as will come, I hope. Until a few hours ago, the place held more than twelve hundred Federal officers here."

"Escaped?"

Parker shook his head. "Released. Sherman himself was here."

"You spoke with him?"

"No. I spoke with a Colonel Stone."

Joseph recalled the cold morning in December when prisoners were led from Camp Sorghum down near the river through the city on their way to the asylum. Citizens lined the streets and jeered at the prisoners. Some threw trash at them. Some spat on them. A woman screamed, "Hang them all! They killed my boy. Eye for an eye!"

Many others supported her. A boy broke free of his mother's grasp and ran toward the line of marching prisoners brandishing a stick. He would have struck wildly and indiscriminately had not one of the guards caught him and taken the weapon from him.

Would the prisoners remember the faces of those who taunted them? Would they seek those people out now, return the insults, and worse?

"Stone demanded release of the prisoners," Parker said. "I had no choice but to open the gate. Had I resisted, I am sure this building would no longer be here."

"Did he say that Sherman would not burn the asylum?"

"He did."

"He said the same about the college," Joseph said. "Let us hope he keeps his word."

"I have no doubt that Stone's word is reliable," said Parker. "He impresses me as a man of honor. It is obvious the moment you meet him. But who can say what Sherman will decide? And the winds." Parker raised a hand to the sky. "We are at the mercy of the weather."

Joseph looked out across the dark expanse of land. He could make out human figures moving into the compound, could distinguish the shape of a dress from that of men's clothing, the form of a child from that of an adult. But beyond that his vision offered nothing. And yet, there, in the distance, was a figure neither childlike nor fully grown, head bobbing, legs churning, body darting in and out of the growing assembly. By his side hobbled a woman in a torn dress, and wearing what appeared to be men's boots. Periodically, the man stopped moving, turned to the woman as if to confer with her, then, assured by a nod of her head, they continued to weave their way through the crowd. No, Joseph thought, surely not. The man wouldn't have come from the whipping post to the asylum. What could be of possible interest to a crazed little man in this place? And yet, Joseph decided, this is where the deranged creature ought to be, if not of his own volition, then by force.

"Will you return to the hospital now?" Parker asked.

"Not immediately. I need to speak to a Federal officer who will listen to reason."

"Reason? This is war. We are in no position to negotiate terms of surrender. Sherman will do with us whatever he chooses, assurances to the contrary notwithstanding."

Joseph told Parker of the scene he'd witnessed at the whipping post. Parker flinched when Joseph described the flaying of flesh. Otherwise, his expression was impassive. Joseph finished the account and said, "Not even Sherman will allow anarchy to reign. Left to their own devices, these devils may do more damage to the city than all the Union troops together."

Parker made no reply. His attention was directed to the gathering throng, as people two or three abreast now entered the gate.

Joseph had difficulty leaving the compound. It seemed to him that he'd spent much of the past week moving against the crush of people—from the depot back to the heart of the city, from the college green to Thompson's office, from the black mass advancing toward the whipping post to any place free of dark, menacing faces. Now, as he twisted through the moil of people to return to the city, he felt once more the turgor that had gripped his intestines too many times over the past few days. Inertia would have been a healthy alternative to counter-movement. At least people might avoid him, as they would a rabid mongrel, rather than push against him, gouge his ribs with their elbows, and look threateningly at him, as though suspicious that his opposing direction indicated something malevolent about his intent.

Finally, he squeezed past a woman with three children. Outside the gate, he undertook once more to find a Federal officer, if not the general himself. What the army provided was order. It did not matter which army, Confederate or Union. In the face of mass confusion, they might even work together. After all, officers on both sides had been to school together. They'd trained together. Opposing generals had once been close friends. He'd heard that Longstreet, his former commanding officer, was best man at Grant's wedding. All these men shared a fraternity—a common respect and civility—that civilians could never understand. And they were as skilled at securing order as they were at killing.

As he hastened toward the inferno, he began to question whether to trust that Sherman or any of his officers would give him a hearing. Would they listen to reason? Perhaps Parker was right. What reason? This was war. Tired, homesick, hungry, cold, ill—these soldiers were surely more eager to put a bloody end to this drudgery than they were to corral a pack of marauding Negroes and impose martial order on them. What did they care if vengeful slaves whipped a white dog runner whom no other white man would bother to defend?

When he turned onto Laurel Street, everything he saw bore witness to the futility of his earlier hope. Soldiers in tattered blue coats ransacked homes and businesses with raucous glee. There were others not dressed in uniform, people Joseph had seen in the streets of Columbia from time to time, though he could not name any of them. Soldier and lawless citizen alike ran from building to building, destroying and plundering. Some held in either hand a bottle of spirits, swigging alternately between crazed yells. How many cellars had they broken into and torn apart? In the middle of the street, less than fifty feet from a burning building, was a piano. One drunk soldier banged away at the keys while another hacked at the instrument with an ax.

Joseph heard a shriek behind him. He turned and saw a woman holding her head with her hands and crying hysterically. Her dress had been ripped from the left shoulder, exposing her undergarment. She might have been a prostitute from one of the brothels down at the river, or a lady from a family of means. Her present condition gave no definitive clue to her person. In front of her whirled a bearded man in a blue dress. He was bedecked in jewelry that hung from his neck and both arms. His antics attracted the attention of others. A companion offered the man a bottle and he turned it up. Joseph saw his Adam's apple bob several times. When he'd had his fill, the man jerked the bottle from his lips, hurled it into the sky, and bayed at the moon. His companions cheered him on.

Renegades. Where were their superiors? No decent officer would allow such behavior.

Joseph backed away, careful to remain undiscovered. In the shadows of an alley, he scanned the street for the woman with the torn dress. She had disappeared. Had she run? He hadn't heard her scream since the first time. Had some man—or several men—taken her into an alley and raped her? Killed her? If her, how many others?

He ran. Wildly at first, with no direction, his only aim to get away from the madness. Moments later, breathless from his pace and from the smoke-congested air that burned his lungs, he stopped, placed his hands on his knees, and heaved. He was afraid he would faint if he did not settle his heart. He covered his mouth and nose with both hands in an attempt to breathe in something other than heat and cinder. Several minutes passed before his head cleared. He tried to think, piece together a sensible plan.

Richardson Street, he told himself. Jeremiah's band would not return there. They would disperse, infiltrate every dark corner they could find. For now, flames rising higher in the center of the city than elsewhere, every sinister act would be discovered. As much as he craved the darkness of the night, Joseph needed the light of those flames. He could bear the heat as long as he had light. Light enough to see, to gather his wits, to distinguish between the wicked and the just.

He stumbled ahead. His head pounded with the cacophony of shrill laughter, screams, pistol and rifle shot, the roar of fire, splinter and crackle of wood. He'd heard these sounds on fields of battle. But this was different. No matter how brutal warfare became—and what he'd seen was plenty brutal—every moment of it was real. Immediate. You never mistook the enemy. Even if he was the object of your rage, he might also gain your admiration—a subtle and mysterious form of love—in the brief duration of mortal encounter.

Not so here. No one to trust. Your throat could as easily be slit by a rebellious slave or a white rebel as by an unruly Union soldier bent on the annihilation of the South. This was not war. No rules of engagement. No understanding of who was the enemy, who the ally. This was worse than war. This was hell.

At the intersection of Richardson and Gervais he saw a sentry in a blue uniform, rifle perched on his shoulder. People were gathered about. Some women pleaded with him to send guards to their homes. "My daughter is nine months gone with child," one woman cried. "She may deliver tonight. You must send someone to watch our house."

The soldier's deep frown did not disguise the sympathy in his eyes. One of the good ones, Joseph thought. He'd seen them on both sides. Bad ones, too. Some in his own camp at Bull Run.

Joseph stepped forward. An explosion shook the ground. In the distance, a funnel of fire raced starward. At an apex of more than one hundred feet, it arced like a graceful dancer at the height of his jump, then billowed out in a great umbrella and fell in showers of cinder. The depot. Knowing that it contained a stockpile of gunpowder and ammunition combined to register in his bowels a sickening certainty. He anticipated the odor of burnt flesh. He'd smelled it more than once in battle. There was nothing like that stench. It was worse than the stink of rain on charred wood. He hoped the deaths were instantaneous, that the explosions severed heads, limbs, tore into organs, consumed in that very moment every human body in its torrid path. If any survived, their fate would be worse than death. The pain of movement would be enough to kill them if the fire hadn't. He once saw two men come to the aid of a friend whose body, engulfed in flames, writhed like a serpent on the ground. The men tried to smother the fire with their coats. The screams of the burning man were horrendous. By the time the rescuers got the fire out, it was too late. The man was fortunate to die quickly. Later, when his friends tried to move the corpse to a grave, the body came apart; first an arm that pulled away like the wing of a cooked chicken, then a leg. He was an assortment of blackened pieces when they finally got his body onto a blanket and lowered it into the earth.

Two women standing beside the sentry lost their balance and fell. Others stood, but crouched like scared animals and stared at the burning sky. Only the sentry stood firm, and that because the crowd pressed so heavily against him that he could barely move.

"I'll speak to Colonel Stone," the sentry said in a splintered voice.

Stone. Joseph had heard the name once that night. Parker, he remembered. Parker said he was an honorable man. That was all Joseph had to go on. He must find Stone.

He approached the circle of people and waved a hand at the sentry. "Stone? Where is he? I must speak with him. I am the chief steward of the hospital. If any more people come onto the grounds of the college, we are doomed."

The soldier looked at Joseph and nodded, but his eyes conveyed the impossibility of their situation.

As he turned back toward the campus, Joseph saw another inferno climb the ladder of the sky east of the city. The general's home, he thought. If the Union army itched to burn anyone's property—and with it all his prized possessions—it would be Wade Hampton's. Better than his property, the man himself, if he could be found.

| 48 |

The One-Armed Gentleman

From the backyard of the McCord home came the sounds of coarse laughter and cursing. Louisa looked through the kitchen window and saw men stab the ground with their bayonets. One man stumbled into another. They punched each other playfully.

"I'll plug your sister," yelled one, and raised a bottle above his head.

"It'll be my brother you're plugging," said the other. "I got no sister."

"Your mother'll do." He pulled the bottle to his mouth and turned it up.

"My mother? You bastard." He shoved his mate, who tripped and crashed to the ground.

"Oh, Robbie," the fallen man moaned drunkenly, head lolling side to side. "You cracked my ass bone."

"Defile my mother again with your filthy mouth, and I'll be cracking your head."

Louisa stepped away from the window. She turned to Lou and Hannah behind her and ordered them upstairs.

"But, Mother," Lou said.

"Now, Lou!"

Lou jumped at her mother's command and raced up the steps. Hannah followed. Before they entered their room, they heard two rifle shots in quick succession and the sound of wood breaking.

"The storage rooms," Hannah said. "They'll take everything. Murdering thieves."

"Oh, Hannah, I'm afraid," Lou said.

Hannah gave her sister a look as fierce as the one her mother had just turned on her. "Don't be a child. If those men enter our home, we'll have to defend ourselves."

"We must hide."

"Where? And leave Mother to fend for herself? Hush your whining."

Hannah moved to the bedroom window and looked out on a copper sky. Flames swirled in every direction. How long before fire scorched their property? What then? The worst place to be was on the second story. Should she defy her mother's orders and return to the kitchen? At least there they had a chance at escape. The fire might distract the men.

Another sound of wood splintering. This one directly beneath them. The kitchen door, Hannah thought. She ran back to the stairwell. At the bottom of the steps stood her mother, her glare unyielding. "I will not tell you again," she said.

"And I will not leave you alone." It was the first time in her life that Hannah stood up to her mother. Youthful defiance had never been a match for her mother's indomitable will. This was different. Hannah felt the raw and dangerous strength of rage fueled by fear. *Is this courage?* she wondered. *Is this what soldiers feel in battle?*

They held each other's stare even as the door creaked on loosened hinges and collapsed. Louisa's face blanched and softened. She whispered, "Please, Hannah. I beg you. Watch your sister. I cannot bear another—" Her voice broke.

Hannah saw in her mother's face the renewal of the grief that nearly killed her two years earlier when Cheves died. In that moment, she understood what she must do as clearly as if her dead brother himself were telling her. If Hannah and her sister were fated to die, they could not allow their mother to be witness to their mutilation. She hurried to the bedroom, closed and locked the door, and ordered her sister to help her move a chest of drawers in front of it.

"If only we still had the outside stairwell," Lou whispered, her voice quavering.

"Don't be foolish," Hannah snapped. "Those men would have used it. They would be in this room now. Here, help me."

Hannah pulled a sheet from the bottom drawer. The sisters tore it into three strips of equal width, tied them together at the ends, and secured one end to the bedpost. Hannah lifted the window and laid the cotton rope on the ledge. "It may be our only chance," she said.

They heard commotion downstairs: glass breaking, furniture being overturned, shouts and curses. Hannah knew that her mother would make no effort to stop the marauders from destroying her property; she knew as well that her mother would sacrifice her life to bar access to the second story. It would take more than one man to remove her from the stairwell.

The noise ceased. An eerie stillness, more frightening than the bedlam, suggested one of two possibilities: either a quick exodus after having taken what they wanted, or the contemplation of more destruction.

Downstairs, a gravelly voice spoke. Neither of the girls could make out what the man said, but he must have addressed their mother, for her reply was clear: "There is nothing of interest up there. An old woman's clothes, nothing else."

Now the man's voice was distinct: "I'll decide what's interesting. Move away from those steps."

"You have either broken or taken the only things I have of value. I'll ask you to leave my house now."

"You're in no position to ask anything, old woman. Out of my way."

Hannah heard a struggle. She imagined her mother grappling with the man. She looked at Lou and pointed to the window. Lou's eyes widened. Hannah nodded, motioned her forward. But before Lou moved, they heard another uproar below. A different male voice. Deep and stern. "Remove your hands at once, sergeant. I'll have you court-martialed for such insolence."

"Begging your pardon, General Howard. I meant no offense. The lady has a smart mouth, she does."

"If I were she, I'd shoot you for the offense. I might do it myself. You boys clean up this mess."

A few moments later, Louisa called upstairs in a croaky voice. Hannah and Lou moved the bureau away from the door and stepped into the hallway.

"Mother?" Hannah said.

"It's all right. You and Lou come down."

From the top of the stairs, Hannah's eyes settled on the empty right sleeve that dangled at the side of the officer nearest her mother. Was this the man whose voice moments earlier had made her shiver? She'd imagined that the voice belonged to a towering, grizzle-faced creature with mean eyes. Battle-hungry and pitiless. He was nothing of the sort. Of medium height, thick-chested but not heavy, he appeared, in spite of his disfigurement, ready to charge into any fray. Yet his dark eyes exuded a gentleness that drew Hannah into its depths. The paradox unsettled her. Even more disturbing was the impulse to reach out to him, to lay a reassuring hand on the shoulder below which hung the truncated stump.

She was almost to the bottom step when Hannah averted her eyes from the general and looked at her mother. Louisa held a hand to her neck. Hannah gently pulled the hand away and examined the imprint of fingers on her mother's flesh. "You're hurt."

Louisa shook her head. "I'm fine," she rasped. "I just need water."

"Harriet," Hannah called. No one answered. Then, "Tom?" Again, no answer. Hannah nodded at the general and went to the kitchen.

Lou stood by her mother. She wanted to cry, but knew that her mother and her older sister would chastise her for any show of weakness.

Hannah returned with the glass of water and handed it to Louisa, who took small sips, wincing between each one.

The general took a step forward and bowed. "I am sorry for your discomfort, Mrs. McCord."

Hannah glanced once more at the empty sleeve. It reminded her of her favorite male cousin, John Haskell, who three years earlier lost an arm in a battle in Virginia. She remembered what a shadow of a man John was after that loss, and how it hurt her when she saw the flesh around the bone fragment folded together like a poorly sewn garment.

Yet there was more than the ghost of a resemblance that drew her to the general. Her thoughts passed from her cousin to her father, who died when Hannah was twelve. There was the greater likeness. Was it the men's ages? Her father was fifty-seven when he died. General Howard looked to be about that age. Perhaps that was it. Or perhaps it was the combination of authority and courtesy, a noble consanguinity, that lived on in her idealization of her dead father and now presented itself in living, disfigured flesh.

"I hope it was a Confederate bullet that took that arm," said Louisa.

"Mother!" said Hannah. The women faced each other with gazes equally fierce and uncompromising. Hannah knew that if her mother slapped her for being impudent, she would return the blow. And that, too, would be a gesture of love. Love that the eldest daughter alone held for the mother whose strength she finally understood.

She read in her mother's eyes hatred for every man in her home. Particularly for the one-armed general, whose attempt at civility only stoked the fire of her rage. If the general's bow impressed Hannah, it infuriated her mother. When the sleeve of his coat flapped with his movement, she interpreted a crude gesture meant only to unnerve her.

Louisa said, "Perhaps I could offer you a tour of our hospital and introduce you to young men who have suffered worse. Just moments ago I left the room of a nineteen-year-old boy who lost both legs to one of your cannons."

"Surely not one of mine," the general said. "I've no one in my company in possession of such skill."

Two soldiers behind him laughed. He looked over his shoulder at them. The effect was so immediate—and the quiet that followed so profound—that Hannah wondered whether she had imagined their laughter. The men's faces reddened.

General Howard turned back to her mother. "Mrs. McCord, I must request the privacy of a room where I may meet with my officers."

"You and your men have taken my home, General Howard. Do you mean to request a room or to seize it?"

He said nothing but looked at her with calm detachment. They might have remained in that posture indefinitely had not Louisa started when the front window shattered. A fiery ball of turpentine rolled across the floor. The general walked over to the burning mass, stepped on it, and ground out the flame with no more effort or concern than a man might have given to a cigarette butt. His mouth hinted at a smile as he said, "It is remarkable how the wind blows these cinders about, is it not? And now, Mrs. McCord, if you would be so kind as to have one of your servants direct me to the room of your choosing."

Hannah said, "I will show you to the parlor, sir," and walked past her mother.

Louisa tried to call her daughter's name, but her voice broke. Hannah did not look back, but moved ahead, the general behind her, into the hallway. She was certain that Howard knew, as did his two attendants and the six other soldiers who were now smoking on the porch, that the McCord slaves had deserted the family. Only Henry remained, and he was too addled to do anything. No wonder her mother seethed. Hannah saw the matter differently. General Howard had saved her home from certain destruction. Moreover, he had saved her mother, her sister, and herself from the vicious lust of his men. The general, like every soldier in both armies, was merely an instrument of war, not its cause. Hannah would later tell her mother that nothing the general did was calculated to humiliate her. He had no personal quarrel with her, or with any other Confederate. This was war. How fortunate they were to have been overtaken by a gentleman whose conduct was above reproach.

After she escorted the general and his men to the parlor, Hannah walked into the kitchen, where she found her mother leaning against the sink, arms twined. In the corner of the room Henry was propped on a stool. He held a bloody rag to his head.

"What happened?" Hannah looked from Henry to her mother.

Louisa shook her head contemptuously at the old man. "He's mad. All of this has undone him." She described a circle with her hand to indicate the house, the trespassers, the burning city. "He says a doctor from the hospital did this to him."

Louisa's demeanor gave Hannah to know what she was thinking. Any time Henry exasperated her, the thought renewed itself. She'd often chided herself—several times in her children's presence—for not selling him years ago, when she first saw signs of mental deterioration. She had kept him only out of devotion to Harriet. He'd become worthless after the death of his wife.

How many times had she heard her mother complain to her father that Henry's grief over the loss of his wife was unnatural in a Negro? Hannah remembered how, two weeks after the burial, her father had whipped Henry for his unseemly weeping in the field. It was an affectation, her father had said, the purpose of which was to avoid work. *Laziness in a nigger*, he said, *must be punished at once, so as to discourage shiftlessness in others.*

Hannah respected her father's authority. He was a wise and godly man. On those rare occasions when he had to be severe with slaves like Henry, the children understood that it was for their own good. She'd even learned to close her ears to their howling when they were whipped, and to pray throughout the duration of their punishment for the salvation of their dark souls.

Now, as her mother stared with loathing at Henry, Hannah knew that she was berating herself for letting him and other slaves take advantage of her. She would castigate herself for keeping Henry only to appease Harriet. If anything, his presence had only encouraged in Harriet a stubborn devotion to the shiftless man. And Louisa had allowed it. It was, she often told herself, her great failing as a mistress, this soft-heartedness that persuaded her to be too lenient. How many times had she and her late husband discussed the matter and agreed that indulging these creatures encouraged insolent behavior? And how had these ingrates repaid her Christian charity? By abusing every privilege she afforded them.

Hannah wanted to comfort her mother, but now was not the time. They had to hold up as best they could, not give in to hysteria. But it was too much. Too much for all of them: her mother's abuse at the hands of the sergeant, the overtaking of the house, the now certain collapse of the Confederacy, and all of it together bringing to the forefront of their consciousness every loss they had sustained over the past three years. Her brother, Cheves, wounded in the head, leg, and foot at Second Manassas in August of 1862. His too brief convalescence at home, and his mad insistence to return to his company against doctor's orders. That January his head wound ruptured. A stroke followed. By nightfall, he was dead.

Hannah recalled the awful words her mother wrote to her friend Mary Chesnut as Hannah stood behind her, both hands on the back of the chair. Her eyes welled with tears as the black ink inscribed her mother's grief, and her own more complicated pain: "The light of my life is gone, my hope fled, and my pride laid low. My son was my greatest gift to the world. Now he is gone."

That would not be their only loss that year. Seven months later, Louisa's nephew William Haskell fell at Gettysburg. His older brother Charles would die at Battery Wagner, shot through the head in an assault by black Union troops.

And now the enemy had taken over their home. So yes, it made sense that her mother's rage would fall on Henry's bloody head, but only because he happened to be sitting there. Hannah had to take charge of the situation before her mother did something she might regret.

"Come, Mother, let us go to my room. Lou is already there. She needs us."

To Hannah's touch, her mother's arm felt like an appendage on a ragdoll. She seemed to follow Hannah mindlessly. The usual clomp of her feet on the wood was replaced with a shuffle.

Before Hannah crossed the threshold, she said, "Don't just sit there, Henry. Clean yourself up. You are not the only one who has been hurt in this affray."

The old man moved his feet from under the chair, leaned forward as if to stand, then eased back in the chair when the women left the room.

Upstairs, Hannah led her mother to the bed and sat her down beside Lou, who moved closer and wrapped an arm around Louisa's shoulder.

"Rest, Mother," said Hannah. "We are safe now."

Louisa said, "We are not safe. No one in this city is safe. The devil himself is in our parlor, and the fires of hell billow about us."

Hannah stepped to the window and looked out at the ghoulish sky, thick with fire and smoke. In the street below soldiers bearing torches stood at attention as a man dressed in a civilian suit and a dirty dickey passed by them. "Dreadful," she said.

"What?" Louisa stood and approached the window, Lou behind her.

"That." As Hannah pointed at the man, he turned his back to the line of soldiers and looked toward the roof of the house, as if he'd heard her. Startled by his movement, Lou stepped back toward the bed. Hannah kept her place. Louisa moved closer.

"Can hair be that red, or does the glow of fire create an illusion?" said Hannah. "Those fierce eyes and stubby beard. No, Mother, I am sure the devil is not in our parlor. One of his minions, perhaps. But there is Lucifer himself."

Although Louisa had never laid eyes on the man, she was as certain of his identity as that of the daughter who stood beside her. It was as if all the news reports she'd read and the tales that had circulated throughout the South as the Union army made its way to the sea had finally conjured the man himself. Word made flesh.

Mother and daughter stood side by side at the window and looked out at what each understood, but neither dared say, might be the last night of the world. And there beneath them, strutting like a rooster past the line of soldiers, was the devil incarnate.

Louisa tightened her grip on Hannah's arm and whispered, "Sherman."

| 49 |
Gutting the Pig

Hannah found another reason to admire the one-armed general. He had left the McCord home and met Sherman in the street. She imagined that General Howard had suggested they not enter the home. Given her mother's reaction to Howard, he surely understood that Sherman's presence would further enrage her.

Besides, Sherman would have established his own quarters by now. Better for all his officers to come to him as a group than that he move from house to house for individual consultation.

Howard returned to the house. From the bottom of the steps, he called, "Mrs. McCord?"

Hannah and her mother descended the steps while Lou remained in the room.

The general held his hat with both hands. He bent slightly at the waist and said, "May I ask for the favor of your man's attendance? I am to meet the other officers at the home of Mrs. Simons, where my commanding general is quartered."

"The only man I have here at present is Henry. He will be of no help to you."

Whether Howard took her response as an honest appraisal of Henry's abilities or an outright refusal to aid him, his demeanor did not change. "Perhaps you can offer other means of assistance," he said.

"I cannot imagine how I can be of help to you, Mr. Howard."

Her mother's refusal to acknowledge the dignity of the man's rank embarrassed Hannah. There was no reason to impugn a man who was making every effort to remain civil. Even opposing generals, if they were men of honor, would accord each other respect. She stepped around her mother, and said, "I will draw you a map, General Howard. The house is nearby. You will have no difficulty finding it."

"Unless of course your men have burned it, too," said Louisa.

"Mrs. McCord, were the danger not so great, I would encourage you to walk the streets of your city to see who is starting these fires. You might be surprised to discover that not every Union soldier is to blame for this conflagration. I have passed by many brave soldiers who, at risk of their own safety, are doing all in their power to extinguish the flames before they destroy homes. Surely you know that General Hampton commanded his own soldiers to move cotton bales into the streets. Every Confederate general who has guarded a city has done the same."

Hannah saw that the general's patience was wearing thin. She knew also that her mother would do nothing to mollify the tension. She took Howard by the arm and led him into the parlor. There she drew the map she'd promised him. She handed him the drawing and said, "I do not have a good hand, sir, but I have marked every street between here and Mrs. Simons's home, so the path at least is clear."

"I am grateful, Miss McCord. Thank you for your kindness." His dark eyes conveyed tenderness and a lingering melancholy. She'd seen the look in her father's eyes, particularly in the last three years of his life. Perhaps it had always been there, but Hannah began to notice it at the age of nine. She'd asked her mother about it, and Louisa had said that her father loved the wonder of life and mourned its brutality. And so with this man, Hannah thought.

"General Howard, I wish to apologize for my mother's behavior. She is normally a gracious person."

"Your mother is an extraordinary woman, Miss McCord. This war has taken much from us all, and particularly from women. I understand that she lost a son, you a brother."

"Two nephews, as well," Hannah said.

"I am sorry for her and your loss. I think it must be impossible for a mother to recover from the death of a child."

"It takes time, sir. A long time."

"I wonder whether all the time in the world can outlast a mother's grief."

Hannah smiled. It was the sort of thing she could imagine her father saying. "What will happen, sir, when all of this is over?"

"We shall try as best we can to rebuild our lives. By that, I mean we shall try to reconceive the nation. If we can—and the effort will be monumental—then America will survive. If we cannot—well, I think you can imagine the outcome."

Hannah nodded. They were silent for a few moments. The general stood with his hand behind his back and waited for Hannah to move toward the door. He turned and opened it for her, then followed her into the front room, where he commanded two soldiers to make ready the horses.

"Sergeant," he said gruffly. Hannah started at the voice, so different from the one he used to speak to her. She'd almost forgotten having heard the strident tone when he first entered the house and she listened from behind the closed door. "You will guard this house as if it were your own. Better yet, guard as if it were mine, and the inhabitants my family. Upon my return, if I hear any damaging report from Miss McCord"—he nodded toward Hannah—"her mother or her sister, I shall hang you at dawn."

The pale-faced soldier saluted the general and kept his eyes riveted to the far wall. Except for the movement of a tremulous arm, he looked to Hannah like a statue. It was the first time in her life that she felt raw hatred for a human being. The emotion moved like an upsurge of bile from her stomach to the back of her throat. Fear she understood, and could accept, even pity, in any creature, human being or animal. What she could not abide—and what stoked the burn of her contempt—was cowardice.

She went to the kitchen. If the soldier were foolish enough to disobey General Howard's orders, she would save him the trouble of a hanging. She'd seen it done often enough on her mother's plantation in Abbeville. Old Henry had been the first to demonstrate the technique. It was a lesson her father insisted that Cheves learn when he was twelve. Every man needs to know the procedure, her father had said. The principle is the same here on the farm as in the woods. The same for the deer and the bear as for the pig. Hannah hid in the loft of the barn that day, knowing that her father would not have allowed her to accompany the men to the ritual. The whole procedure fascinated her. The way Henry and Lawrence and Moses bound the pig's feet and splayed them. The pink-brown chest tilted slightly so that the slant of sunlight through the barn door glistened on the fine particles of hair. "Oh, stop talking about it, Henry," she murmured to herself, hidden in a bed of hay, lifting her head just enough to get a view of the men below. "Stop goading him, Father. Get on with it."

When he finally got on with it, Henry said, as he opened the cavity with a sharp plunge and an upward pull of his arm, "It's called *guttin' the pig*."

The flow of blood was so copious and eerily beautiful that Hannah swooned. And now, as she recalled the event, she was glad that she'd been lying in the hay. Had she been standing, her knees might have buckled. She might have fallen from the loft.

In the kitchen she opened a drawer, made a selection, lifted her dress to her knee, and slid the carving knife through her garter.

| 50 |
Fire on the Roof

Joseph wept as he witnessed the magnitude of destruction. He passed six banks, all of them burning wildly. Confederate currency was so devalued as to represent no great loss. What could never be recovered were the jewels, title deeds, silver services, and heirlooms stored in vaults. Columbians were not the only people to suffer the decimation of their personal effects; many people from Charleston and other low-country areas had moved their valuables to one of Columbia's seventeen banks under the impression, given by Beauregard and Hampton, that the capital city would remain safe. Joseph had heard—perhaps from Thompson, though he could not recall—that a manuscript of Edgar Allen Poe, owned by the Confederacy's leading poet, Paul Hamilton Hayne, was stored in one of the banks. All was lost.

He came to First Baptist Church, remarkably intact. On the other side of the street were the charred ribs of Dr. Gibbes's house. Joseph wondered why the Union army would bother with a solitary home and neglect the very place where secession began. He remembered what Dr. Perry told him and Thompson on their way to the Chesnuts' dinner party several weeks earlier. No value could be put on the contents of Gibbes's home. All the volumes of science, history, literature, art. Eighteenth-century manuscripts that documented the state's involvement in the Revolution. Thousands of fossils and other specimens. Paintings by Allston, Sully, Inman. His collection of ancient coins. All of it burned, melted. Joseph hoped the great doctor was not in his house when the soldiers came with their torches.

He passed by the remains of other buildings. In the front yard of the mayor's residence stood Mrs. Goodwyn and several women, their faces illuminated by the blue-orange glow of the blaze consuming the house. He did not see the Union soldier on the other side of the gathering until Mrs. Goodwyn stepped to her right and shook her fist at the man. She railed, "I sent six sons into the army of the Confederacy. Two have died. I wish I had six more to send."

"Sure you do," said the young soldier as he retreated. "Damn you women, you are the ones keeping up the war."

An explosion shook the earth. Joseph turned and saw flames rise from the direction of the depot. Hadn't it blown already? Or was this the second depot to go up in fire? He envisioned people trying to run or crawl through the flames, finally collapsing, their bones snapping like twigs. He recalled the pig he'd seen hours earlier on Senate Street, the pierce of its squeals, the final cry before its fat body jerked a few times, then lay still and roasted as if on a spit.

On he ran. He turned onto Heyward Street, at the far end of which a mass of black bodies moved forward. He ducked into an alley, crept forward into the smoky darkness. He stumbled on something. A pile of trash? Discarded clothes? He kicked at it, felt the give of human flesh. On the street, the black mass rolled forward, voices rising with excitement. He lay on the ground, his face within inches of the lifeless form. Then he saw it: the naked, ravaged body of a Negro woman. Blood covered her head, deformed by the blow of some blunt instrument. How many men had raped her? he wondered. And who? Union soldiers? Confederate renegades? How many more like her?

He reached for the woman's hand, folded it into his own. His compulsion to crawl toward the lifeless body met with an equal force of resistance: fear of being overheard by the men advancing up the street. If they found him with the dead woman, surely they would kill him. They would blame him for the mutilation of her body, and enact a terrible vengeance on his. What had happened to Robert Towns would be nothing in comparison to what these savages would do to him. What if she were the wife of one of these men? Or the daughter?

His mind raced. Wife. Daughter. On the street, the men's voices grew closer. The backs of his hands were now wet with the woman's blood. He was certain the dark red liquid was soaking into the arms of his coat. Life draining out of her. No longer herself, or the self she was, as death robbed every person of more than a body; its cruelest theft was that portion of a human being that might be called unique: personal identity. That piece that made any woman herself, any man his own person. He remembered how, on the day he buried his wife and daughter, it seemed to him that they were not the people he had known. And maybe, too, he was not the person he'd been. Something had to account for the disturbance of mind that made their bodies seem alien to him, a sensation that simultaneously augmented his grief and enabled him to lay the bodies in the earth.

Now, all these years later, he saw their faces clearly. It was as if they stood before him, each beckoning to him with a gesture. His wife's smile. The way she brushed her fingers across his arm as she stepped around him toward the kettle hanging over the burning logs. His daughter's lithe movements as she played in the field below their house and turned to wave at him as he stood in the doorway. Joseph could not restrain himself. He pulled himself to his knees, crawled to the woman, cradled her bloody head in his lap. What came from his lungs was a sound he'd never made, neither at the gravesite of his loved ones nor on the field of battle. A sound not human. Primitive and feral in its anguish. The accumulation of years of grief that finally burst forth in a storm of emotion beyond his power to subdue.

"What?" came a voice from the street.

"From in there," said another.

"Don't you go in there, Lucius. Not alone."

A pause, and then a deep voice: "You come out. Come out, or we're coming in."

Joseph pulled the body into his arms and stood. He stepped forward, knowing he would be dead before his eyes adjusted to the light of the raging fire. He would not be able to make out the faces of his killers. He didn't care. They could do no worse to him than life already had.

And he was right: He could not distinguish one face from another. Emergence from the dark alleyway into the smoke-filled sky nearly blinded him. But he felt them: hands at his throat, so violent a yanking of his hair that he thought it would tear away from his head. His ears filled with the shrill terror of murderous voices. The woman's body was taken from him. He struggled to make sure she was not dropped, but offered no final resistance to the taking. He was lifted off his feet and hurled against the brick wall. His head struck first. He was on the verge of blacking out when other hands grabbed him and held him up. A fist struck him in the mouth, another between the eyes. A tooth loosened. He spat blood. He was no longer afraid. *Time to die*, he told himself. He could not tell whether he was laughing or weeping. Nor did it matter to him. He was ready.

"Stop!" Above the din of their racket the voice thundered. Out of the haze stepped a large man. The moment he placed his hands on Joseph's shoulders, the other hands fell away.

"Kill him, Jeremiah! Kill the son-of-a-bitch. Look what he did to Ruth."

"He didn't do it."

Jeremiah pulled from a pocket of his torn coat a rag and pressed it to Joseph's mouth. "You're going to feel this one for a while," he said. "What's your name?"

Already his lips had begun to swell, so that the sounding of his name was muffled. Joseph repeated it, turned his head away from Jeremiah, and spat blood again. His legs felt wobbly, but Jeremiah's grip was firm. He would not let Joseph fall. Joseph shook his head and sputtered, "Why'd you stop them?"

"I did for you what you wanted to do for me the day I was whipped."

"I don't understand. I did nothing."

"You kept me alive, Mr. Joseph."

"Joseph. That's all. Joseph. What do you mean?"

"I wanted one of two things that day at the whipping post: Either to kill every white man I could lay a hand to, or die myself. But when the whip jerked my head up, I saw you. What I saw in your eyes made me want to live, Joseph."

Joseph shook his head. Nothing made sense. He might have thought he was dreaming if not for the growing pain in his mouth and head. "I didn't do anything. I was—" he stopped, met Jeremiah's eyes with his own, shook his head again—"I was a coward."

"If you had tried to stop that beating, it would have been worse for me in the end. Might have gotten you, too. You don't interfere with a man who pays to have his slave whipped."

"What did you see?" Joseph asked. "In my eyes. What?"

"Sorrow. And a mighty anger at the world."

Joseph frowned and winced at the pain. "I don't see how that would make a man want to live. Justice, maybe. Love. Not sorrow. Not anger."

"Aren't they all the same?" Jeremiah turned his face toward the man who held the woman's dead body. "Why do you think they wanted to kill you? For love of that woman. That's why. For love of our people. There's many have had the same done to them. We loved them all, and are saddened by their loss. I'd kill every white man ever laid a hand on a black woman, if I could. Might yet. I've killed some tonight, Joseph. I aim to kill more. Every bastard I know, and I know a few. Lot of anger in me, built up over more years than I've had life. Anger at what's been done to people I love. Anger at what's been done to me, what's been taken from me. Anger for want of justice."

"Anger's as deadly to the avenger as to the victim." He spat blood again. "You can't kill everyone, Jeremiah. Not even the ones who deserve killing. There'll be no end to it."

Jeremiah chuckled. "You sound like my daddy."

Joseph remembered the frail, sad man who pleaded with Jeremiah not to whip Towns. "I saw him that night. He begged you not to whip Towns. Told you it wasn't the Lord's way."

"I don't know what the Lord's way is. He hasn't revealed it to me. But if it's waiting around to see my people beaten down to nothing, then the Lord can keep his way. I have my own."

Joseph wanted to argue with him. Not to prove a point—there was none to prove. Everything Jeremiah said made sense. Some kind of sense. If not rational sense, at least the sense of what *felt* right. He knew from his own experience that anger in war did not always rule out love of an enemy in the pitch of battle. He remembered Manassas. That anguished, piercing love he felt for the soldier he killed. The anger he felt at all the armies of the world and all the men who called others to battle. Anger at the injustice of warfare. Anger at the injustice of the greed and the puniness of men. It was futile to separate the anger from the love, the outrage at injustice from the passion that drives people to terrible deeds provoked by love. The division would not hold.

He crossed an arm over his chest and placed his hand over Jeremiah's, atop his shoulder. "You aim to kill more."

"One more. After that, my killing is done until I see the need again."

Joseph looked inquisitively at him. He knew he had no right to ask.

"Towns," said Jeremiah. "I've had some satisfaction from him. I'll pay him one more visit."

Joseph nodded. "He has dogs. I'm told they have torn men to pieces in minutes."

Jeremiah moved his head slowly, side to side. "The dogs are gone." He pulled his hand from beneath Joseph's and patted a long sheath that extended from his right hip halfway down his thigh. Joseph saw, through blurred vision, the handle of a long knife. "What I did to them was a warning. He knows I'm coming. That's what I want. Let the dread set."

Jeremiah stepped away. Joseph's mouth and head now throbbed, but he had balance. He could move. They looked one last time into each other's eyes. "Be careful," Joseph said.

"You do the same," said Jeremiah. He turned and, with his men behind him, walked away into the smoke.

Joseph staggered down Heyward to Pendleton, turned right, and continued until he reached the back of the campus. There he stopped, bent over, and clutched his knees until he regained his breath. He wanted to find the quickest route to a supply room so that he could bandage his mouth enough to stop the bleeding. When he stood and resumed his trek, he decided that movement had done him some good. At least he could walk more briskly now in spite of the pain.

From the back of the buildings that faced the campus green, he heard the rustle of people everywhere. He walked to the back door of DeSaussure and pulled at it. He cursed when he found it bolted, and then realized that barricading all the back entrances to the buildings made sense. If it didn't keep Union troops from storming the buildings from Pendleton on the one side and Greene on the other, at least it prevented easy entry.

He walked around to the front of the building and saw people pressed together from one end of the green to the other. Nothing to do but to fight his way inside. He hugged the face of DeSaussure and squeezed past people. "Pardon me," he said, when a large woman tripped over one of his feet.

"Watch where you're going," a man said, and shoved him. "Push my wife again, I'll kill you."

"I'm sorry. I have to get into the building. I'm the hospital steward."

The man snarled and balled up a fist. Joseph pressed his back against the brick surface and continued to inch toward the door. Finally, he reached the stoop, hoisted himself over the wrought iron banister, and entered the building. He dropped his coat on the floor, entered a small room, and with a piece of cloth dabbed at the wound to his mouth. A line of dried blood had crusted over the wound. He swiped at the residue of blood around his chin, but that did little good, so he gave up the effort. As he exited the building, he spied a woman leaning over the well, drawing water. Behind her were others with pails in hand. When she stood, he recognized her, and called from the stoop, "Miss Simpson."

The tall blond woman spun on her heels and looked at him. Above the noise of the crowd and the fierce wind, she shouted, "There is no time, Mr. Crawford. The men need our help." She pointed across the green to Rutledge. Flames danced on the roof. Men fought the fire with pails of water.

Joseph squeezed past people. He trailed Meredith Simpson, the crowd parting as she and the other carriers made their way toward the president's house. On the backside of the house no people were congregated. The carriers moved freely.

The cold air cut into his flesh. Behind Rutledge he followed other men to the ladder and climbed. His hands burned. Each rung was hotter than the previous one. He could hardly bear to grip them. At last he reached the roof. Someone bumped him, said, "Take it," and shoved a pail toward him. He did as he was told, then received another pail, and another, and another, until he lost count. Eventually, the flames were extinguished. All that remained was the acrid odor of smoky dampness.

"We need men on every roof," someone called hoarsely. "This wind, anything can happen." The speaker moved along the slick roof toward the ladder. When he came into view, Joseph could hardly believe his eyes. The last person he'd expected to see was Thompson. His face was as sooty as that of the dead woman Joseph had carried out of the alleyway.

"Joseph." Thompson's voice caught. He coughed, spat dark phlegm. "Didn't see you come up."

"I got here a few moments ago."

"Where have you been? What happened to your lip?"

Joseph hesitated. "I fell earlier, coming from the asylum. I spoke with Dr. Parker, asked him whether he could accommodate our overflow."

"We can't move the patients who are still here," said Thompson. His eyes watered. "They are too weak. Attempting to transport them is dangerous." He pointed to the roof. "This was started by burning cotton blowing from Greene Street. This wind carries the flames everywhere."

"I wasn't thinking of the soldiers. These are the people we need to send to the asylum." He pointed to the throng on the ground.

Thompson shook his head. "They won't move, no matter who gives the order. They're scared, and they believe this is the safest place in the city."

"But it isn't," said Joseph.

"Whether it is or not is of no consequence to them. They're afraid and cold and beyond the capacity to reason. They won't leave this place unless the fire jumps from one of the buildings to the trees on the green. Even then, they may not go. Come. We've work to do."

Thompson walked to the ladder. Joseph noticed that he did not flinch when he grabbed the rails. Perhaps his hands were accustomed to the heat by now, or so cold from the water that they were numb. Joseph followed down the ladder, using the sleeves of his shirt to protect his flesh from the hot wood.

Halfway to the ground, he felt faint. His legs trembled. He tried to wrap his arms around the ladder, but it was too late. He crumpled, felt the bump of a rung against his chin, and lost consciousness before falling the last ten feet. He had no awareness of his body's crashing into Thompson's, but the collision broke his fall and saved him from landing on the back of his head.

The elder man landed on his back, his right arm twisted behind him. Meredith Simpson, at whose feet he lay, heard the bone snap. "God forbid," she said as she dropped to a knee and nestled Thompson's head in her lap.

"Find Mrs. McCord," Thompson muttered through clenched teeth. "She will know—" His head slumped against Meredith Simpson's stomach. She understood. No one could bring order to this madness more quickly than Louisa McCord.

| 51 |
Duty Calls

"Who needs my mother?" Hannah McCord approached the front door where the sergeant cursed and threatened to shoot a boy if he did not get off the porch.

The sergeant's head swiveled. He shot Hannah a lascivious look.

Hannah curled her upper lip and said, "Move." Their eyes locked. After a moment, he looked away.

"Aren't you the lucky one," he said, then winked at one of his fellows standing with his back to the fireplace. "General's taken a shine to her, he has. Gives a woman confidence. Makes her saucy with the gents. Wonder how smart she'll be if the general fails to return."

Hannah smiled, stepped closer to him, and said in a syrupy voice, "We never had the pleasure of an introduction, sergeant. What is your name?"

"Baird," he said haughtily. "*Sergeant* Baird to my men."

Her smile dropped from her face like a vase toppled from a mantle. She barely moved her lips, but the man at the fireplace heard every gritty word: "Well, Sergeant Baird, insult me again in my house, and I assure you that you will never see the general again, whether he returns or not. I'll make sure the men give their Sergeant Baird a proper burial."

The man by the fireplace laughed. The sergeant backed way. He'd seen something that his friend had not: in the woman's stony gaze, an instinct more savage than any man could summon. It was not the instinct to kill—common enough to soldiers—but something more powerful, almost more than human, either demonic or holy in its implications. What he saw in Hannah McCord's eyes was the instinct to protect, to shield, to preserve that which she regarded as sacred—and which made the capacity to kill no more than an afterthought, a meaningless consequence not worth the calculation of cost.

Standing on the porch was a thin, brown-haired boy Hannah recognized, although she could not call him by name. She'd seen him around the campus often enough to guess that he might be the child either of a professor or of a doctor who served the hospital. "You're not Mrs. McCord," he said.

"I am her daughter. What need do you have of my mother?"

"Dr. Thompson fell off the roof of Rutledge and broke his neck. Another man fell, too, but he just jerked around and foamed at the mouth like a wild dog. Dr. Thompson needs help. He sent for Mrs. McCord."

"Wait, son. You say he broke his neck, and then sent for my mother? How can that be possible? Did you see Dr. Thompson?"

"I didn't see him, but I was there when it happened. My cousin's a nurse. She sent me for Mrs. McCord. All I know is the doctor broke something big: a neck or a leg or his brain or something."

Hannah could see that the boy's excitement over having been appointed a grand errand was of greater moment than the accuracy of his report. Nevertheless, she knew her mother would want to hear of anything that concerned Dr. Thompson. She went upstairs and found Louisa sitting by the window where she'd first spied Sherman. "There's been an accident at the hospital, Mother. Dr. Thompson has been injured. I don't know how serious it is, but he—or someone on his behalf—sent for you."

Louisa stood. She seemed ready to depart, but then looked to the bed where Lou lay curled in a fetal position. "I can't leave you alone with these men," she said, and then looked at Hannah.

"We are not alone, Mother. We have each other. You will return when you can. General Howard will also return shortly. He has issued stiff orders that the men are to keep watch over the house as if it belonged to him.

You must go at once. I am certain you are needed more there than at the house."

Louisa hesitated, then threw a thick wrap over her shoulders and followed the errand boy across her yard. Hannah watched from the front porch until the child and her mother disappeared in the smoke.

| 52 |
Nursing Their Own

Louisa questioned the boy's path around the backside of the college green. He motioned for her to follow him to the edge of the lawn, from which vantage point she could see the swell of people on the horseshoe. Then she trusted him to lead her on the quickest route.

When they approached the back of Rutledge, the boy stopped and said, "My cousin said we have to knock and tell her who we are before she'll let us in. The doors to all the buildings are bolted, but she'll let us pass."

"Who is your cousin, son?"

"Meredith Simpson."

"Yes. Well, you're a good boy to help your cousin."

"I'm obliged to help her. She took me in when Pa died."

"What happened to your mother?"

"Don't know," he said, and shrugged. "Never met her."

Louisa felt the tremor of loss that afflicted her for weeks after her son's death. Then, her body shook uncontrollably, and although the disturbance lasted only for minutes at a time, her bones ached for hours afterward, her body the repository of guilt. She blamed herself. She never should have allowed Cheves to return to his company after the head injury. The torture of self-incrimination was enervating. A weakness worse than any physical ailment she'd ever suffered. She felt it now as she stood before the child whose name she could not recall. Like a soldier shocked by the self-recognition he glimpses in the eyes of his dying enemy, Louisa saw in the boy's defenseless posture her own naked stupidity. How could she not have seen, present before her every day, the strength of the boy's aunt, the courage of her own daughter? How many others had she misjudged? How severe would be the Lord's judgment of her wickedness on the last day?

The boy walked up to the door. She followed, stopped at the foot of the steps, and, using as her guide the glare of the fires climbing the sky along Greene Street, surveyed the damage to the roofline of Rutledge. The upper part of the façade was black. The cornices looked like gristle that might drip to the ground at any moment. She wondered if any of the patients had choked to death on the thick smoke. Had any jumped from the building to their deaths?

The boy banged on the door and called, "It's me, Meredith. I've brung the woman."

The door opened and Meredith Simpson pulled the boy into the folds of her skirt. "Are you all right, Jimmy? Did anyone bother you?"

"A Yank is living in Mrs. McCord's house. He pointed his gun at me."

Meredith looked accusingly at Louisa. Blocking the doorway, pressing Jimmy's small body against her, she was imposing. A good four inches taller than Louisa, wider in the shoulders, Meredith had a powerful body.

Louisa said, "I was upstairs when Jimmy arrived. He was met at the door by a Union soldier. Our house has been commandeered by General Howard."

"The soldier threatened my nephew?"

"My daughter was there also. If the sergeant made any advance toward Jimmy, she would have intervened."

Meredith cupped Jimmy's chin with both hands and tilted his face upward. "You're my brave boy. But I won't tolerate lies. Do you understand?"

He pulled his head away in protest. Meredith reached a hand to his chin again and made him look her in the eye. A moment later, his body seemed to deflate as he said, "Yes, ma'am."

"All right." Her frown dissolved and she squinted one eye at him. "I just hope you didn't scare that Yank too much."

Jimmy perked up. Meredith looked again at Louisa. "Dr. Thompson is on the second floor. He was on the roof with others fighting the fire. He fell coming down the ladder. Broke his arm. We found Dr. Trezevant in Harper. He set the bone."

"How bad is the break?" Louisa asked.

"Not as bad as it might have been. Dr. Trezevant says he'll be fine."

Louisa, who had come to the hospital every morning with a list of duties she had written up for herself and her nurses, now found herself at a loss. She had never asked any nurse what needed to be done. To do so would have diminished her authority, made her seem unequipped for the hard work of tending the patients and administering the duties of the nursing staff. Age, too, was a factor. Louisa was old enough to be mother to any nurse she supervised. She could not seek the counsel of these young women without appearing to be weak, unprepared. Now, however, she knew neither what was needed of her nor whether she had the energy to give what might be asked. She stepped closer to Meredith, touched her arm, and whispered, "What must we do?"

Meredith answered, "As you tell us, Mrs. McCord. Dr. Thompson wanted you here not for himself, I think, but for the patients and—" she hesitated.

"What is it, dear?"

"Mr. Crawford. I believe that Dr. Thompson wanted you to be aware of what happened to him."

"Yes?"

"He had a seizure and toppled from the ladder. He fell on Dr. Thompson, which caused the arm to break. It likely saved Mr. Crawford, though. He is in the room with Dr. Thompson."

"How is he?"

Meredith shook her head and frowned. Her concern for Joseph was obvious. So, too, was her resentment at turning the duty of his care over to Louisa. "He's not conscious. Dr. Thompson is more concerned about Mr. Crawford than about his own condition. I heard him tell Dr. Trezevant that he fears the seizure may have done irreparable damage."

Louisa leaned against the door jamb. "I see," she muttered. "Well, let us check on the men, do what we can."

"Mrs. McCord, there is another reason the doctor called for you. Some of the patients left the building when it caught fire. They went out to the green and sat on the ground. They are too sick to endure the cold, but more afraid of burning than of freezing to death."

"God help us." As if the utterance itself clarified what needed to be done and stiffened her resolve, she said to Meredith, "Come," and marched ahead.

Upstairs, Louisa glanced first at Joseph. She was relieved not to see the body contorted, twisted in the vice of a grand seizure. She turned to Dr. Thompson, looked at the bandaged arm, and said, "I am sorry for your distress."

Thompson forced a weak smile. "This will heal." He nodded toward Joseph. "Miss Simpson has taken good care of him. I suggest you assign her to attend him through the night."

He knew she would not receive the recommendation well, and knew as well that she had no desire to see to the care of Joseph herself. Louisa McCord simply did not want anyone, including the doctor, telling her how to supervise her nurses. Thompson ignored her disapproving glare, and said, "How is he?"

Louisa moved to the side of Joseph's bed. As she looked down at him, she remembered laying eyes for the first time on her wounded son the day she went to Richmond to bring him home. Cheves was too much with her this night. The awful swelling around his head. Not even thick gauze could mask it. Discolored flesh around his eyes, disfiguration of the nose, purple lips. She'd wept that day, and was angry at herself for allowing her son to see her distress.

Joseph's skin was of a different hue. Streaks of smoke along either side of the jaw reminded Louisa of late summer evenings when Cheves, a child of eight or ten years of age, would come in from a day of play in the fields, clothes and flesh caked with dust. The difference between her son's face and Joseph's was that beneath the smoky film was not the ruddy complexion of a healthy child, but the translucence of a cadaver. Only the lips—their color a sickening bruise of blue and pink—held the hint of life.

"His convulsions were severe," said Thompson.

Louisa returned to the doctor's bedside. "He will recover," she said.

"His color?"

"Not good."

Thompson nodded ruefully. He grimaced as he used his good arm to leverage his body to a more comfortable position. Beads of perspiration covered his forehead. Meredith moved from the doorway around the foot of the bed, pulled from a bedside drawer a towel, dipped one end of it in a bowl of water, and cleaned his brow.

"Thank you," he said. His face pantomimed an appreciation more sincere than his weak voice conveyed.

She leaned toward him, whispered, "No, thank you," and with her elbow made a subtle gesture toward Joseph. Thompson understood her meaning. Meredith folded the towel and placed it on the table.

Louisa noticed something remarkable in the exchange between the nurse and the doctor.

Pain and relief had distinctive physical articulations words alone could not express. Just as the body's awful contortions bespoke the intensity of torment, so the face—the laxity of the jaw, the wrinkle of skin around the eyes and mouth, the eerie look of wonder in the dark center of the iris—expressed a depth of gratitude otherwise incommunicable. Deep in the heart of that gratitude swirled the mystery of human connection: that the smallest act of tenderness was, more often than not, the last and only means of grace that bridged the chasm between one human being and another.

She'd seen it often enough in the past three years. A cup of water held to the mouth of an armless soldier had the miraculous effect of staying, if only for a short while, his agony. Turning a boy in his bed so as to alleviate pain on one side or the other evoked a teary expression of gratitude. A hand on a shoulder or the brush of an irritating lock of hair from a man's brow drew from his face a beatific look of relief. The closest approximation to the image of God in any creature was surely the delicate, transformative sensuality of human touch. She found solace in its regenerative power during periods of oppressive physical strain and soul-killing despair. Hard experience had taught her that no amount of chloroform, opium, or any other palliative held the restorative wonder of human contact. It lay at the heart of all healing.

Meredith took up the towel again, dipped it in the bowl of water, walked to Joseph's bedside, and treated his brow.

Thompson turned his gaze to the sloe-eyed boy standing in the doorway. Jimmy stepped forward and pressed the back of his head into the folds of his cousin's dress.

"Is this the brave young man who went for Mrs. McCord?" Thompson asked.

Jimmy said nothing.

"Not so brave that he has learned to speak up for himself," said Meredith. She pulled the bed sheet up to Joseph's neck, then walked over to Jimmy and rested a hand on his shoulder.

"You did us all a great service," said Thompson.

"What do you say to Dr. Thompson?" asked Meredith, her voice at once gentle and admonitory.

"Thank you, sir."

"No, Jimmy. It is I who owe you thanks."

"Well, then, you're welcome, sir." Jimmy hesitated, then stepped forward cautiously. He pointed at the thickly bandaged arm, and said, "Does it hurt awful?"

"It hurts, but not awfully. I have felt worse."

"That's something I've always wanted to know about doctors. Do they hurt like regular people?"

Thompson smiled. "Am I not a regular person? How many eyes do I have?"

Jimmy waggled his head, eyed his questioner with apprehension. "You never looked in a mirror?"

"Why, don't you have two ears?" asked Thompson.

Jimmy's hands shot to his ear lobes. He tugged them. "You might as well not have any eyes if you can't see no better than that."

Thompson laughed, and winced at the movement of his arm.

"Whew," Jimmy muttered admiringly. "I reckon you do hurt."

"Same as regular people," Thompson said, supporting the broken arm with his other hand. He closed his eyes, opened them again, and said, "Jimmy, I wonder if I may ask another favor of you. This is a tall order for a young man."

Jimmy moved closer to the edge of the bed. He whispered, "You want me to go back to Mrs. McCord's and kill them Yanks?"

"No. Something more valorous than that."

"More what?"

"Braver. What I'm asking now requires great courage and attentiveness." He arched one eyebrow. The boy rested an elbow on the bedside. Thompson leaned closer. "Will you do everything your cousin and Mrs. McCord ask you to do to take care of our wounded men?"

"I'm a Confederate, ain't I?"

"The best I've seen," said Thompson. "And will you stay close by Miss Simpson and Mrs. McCord the whole night?"

Jimmy nodded soberly. Thompson stuck out his good hand, and he and Jimmy shook.

"Come, Jimmy," said Meredith. "Help me tend to some matters while Dr. Thompson and Mrs. McCord talk."

They left the room. At Thompson's request, Louisa sat in a chair near the bed. He explained, as Meredith already had, what the soldiers did when the roof caught fire. He acknowledged the difficulty of rounding them up and moving them back into the building. "But we must do what we can, or what we face tomorrow in providing for their care may exceed our capacity."

"How many men left the building?" asked Louisa.

"I do not have a precise count."

"I suspect Miss Simpson is seeing to that now," said Louisa.

"I neglected to ask her to do it."

Louisa pointed at the arm. "I would not term it negligence."

"I'm sure I saw some fifteen or twenty leave the building when we were on the roof. But that is no more than a guess. In all the chaos, it was hard to think clearly, much less get an accurate count. I may have counted some more than once. I may have missed others. They were a poor sight, though, some of them on crutches, others nearly crawling. They can't have gone far."

"I will gather the nurses that are here. We shall do all we can."

"It would be wise to appoint some men to guard the other buildings." He pointed to the ceiling. "I fear this will not be the only fire we have to contend with tonight."

"You should rest now. Your labored breathing is of more concern to me than your arm."

"The smoke was so thick up there I felt I was swallowing whole cinders. And my feet feel as if they have walked the desert of Arabia."

Both feet were exposed. Louisa saw that a salve had been applied to the blisters. He should not walk on them for a couple of days, at least, unless his own stubbornness prevailed over reason.

She promised to check on him and Joseph later in the evening, then left the room in search of Meredith Simpson. She needed someone to confide in, to coordinate a strategy to rescue those who had wandered out into the cold night. And working as a team offered another advantage: Should any disaster befall either of them, the other would know how to proceed alone.

| 53 |

Gather at the River

General Howard returned late in the evening to the McCord home. Sergeant Baird met him on the porch and nervously informed him of Mrs.

McCord's departure. "I didn't want to let her go, you see, but that daughter is a fearsome quarreler. She'd've provoked a fight with all of us if I had've refused to let her mother pass."

Howard heard footfall in the front room and looked inside to see Hannah emerge from the kitchen. He dismissed the sergeant, entered the house, and bowed to Hannah. "I hope you are well, Miss McCord. I trust that none of my soldiers has embarrassed me."

"None has given offense, General Howard. As you have heard, my mother has gone to the hospital. One of our doctors fell from the roof of a building as he was working with others to put out a fire. I do not know the extent of his injuries, but Mother felt it necessary to attend to him."

"Mrs. McCord performs surgery?" he asked incredulously.

"Oh, no. She has certainly assisted the doctors in surgery, but she has no skill in that department. Mother coordinates the staff. The nurses report to her. From the little that I was able to piece together from the messenger—a young boy overwhelmed with excitement—it seems that the doctor who was injured wanted Mother to organize the workers and to restore order."

"I see," said Howard, and rubbed his chin for a moment before snapping, "Sergeant. At once."

The door swung open and the scruffy man appeared. He saluted the general. He avoided Hannah's glare.

Howard said, "I left Colonel Stone a few minutes ago at the home of Mrs. Simons. He will be somewhere between the capitol and the college. Take McCallum and Turner with you. Be quick about it. Take the horses we requisitioned in Orangeburg. Find the colonel and tell him I want guards stationed at the college immediately. His men are to be on the lookout for fire coming from any direction. Secure the buildings and the grounds. Should anyone threaten to set fire to the college, that person is to be arrested on sight. If he resists, shoot him. You will discharge this duty at once and report back to me within the hour."

"Yes, sir." The sergeant saluted again and raced down the porch and barked out orders to McCallum and Turner.

The younger men did not share the sergeant's eagerness. They were comfortable at the McCord property. Each of them had dug up silver and other valuables from the backyard. They'd hidden the treasure in their pants, coats, shoes, then covered the holes they had dug with their bayonets and hands, and took care not to let the trinkets jingle as they walked like men anxious of diarrhea. The sergeant's call to action challenged their concern for discretion; it did, however, get them out from under the nose of the general, who seemed to have taken such a liking to the McCord women that he would surely punish them if he discovered their thievery.

The privates brought three horses around to the front. Sergeant Baird was the first to mount. McCallum and Turner glanced at each other, silently communicated the hatching of a design planned long ago. They mounted and rode behind the sergeant into the heart of the city.

Turner said to his friend, "Fancy us riding steeds. All that goddamn marching we done through swamps, this here suits me."

"Damn sight better than foot soldiering," said McCallum. "I don't care for marching again long as I live."

The farther they advanced, the more they saw of the plunder and destruction that were bringing the city to ruin. They saw stately homes being reduced to charred and crumbling skeletons. More would burn before the night was over. Old black men danced in the streets. As Union troops moved past them, the old men doffed their hats and bowed. They sang. They laughed. One man approached Sergeant Baird's horse waving his hands and shouting, "Thank the Almighty God! We prayed for Sherman to come, and he came to set us free! The Lord Jesus heard our prayers!" As he made to touch the horse's neck, Baird kicked him in the face. The man crumpled, unconscious, to the ground. Baird and the others rode on.

They came to Richardson Street. A large fire burned near City Hall. A block away and to the north, they saw the office of Southern Express Company going up in flames. Turner looked to his right and spied a wooden sign with the inscription *A.R. Phillips, General Merchandise* on the walkway in front of a burning structure.

They turned the horses back toward the capitol. Union soldiers combed the street. Some of them clutched bottles of liquor in both hands. Others held rifles at the ready.

"Private!" Sergeant Baird barked.

A small man, just over five feet tall, looked up. He looked as though he had not eaten in months. His eyes were recessed in a cavernous skull. He said in a brittle voice, "Yes, sir."

"Where is Colonel Stone?"

The diminutive man pointed toward the capitol grounds. "He topped that hill on his horse not three minutes ago."

Baird turned his horse and spurred him. Behind him rode McCallum and Turner. The moment they crested the hill, they saw Stone circle his horse and direct men to various points throughout the city. When Baird and the others approached, Stone pulled on his reins. The horse stood still. "What is it, sergeant?" Stone asked.

"Sir, General Howard sent us. His orders are to post men at the college to guard against fire. He suspected you may be short of men, so ordered me and McCallum and Turner"—he waved a hand behind him to introduce the men—"to join with yours at the college."

"Very well," said Stone. He raised himself on his stirrups and called, "Johnson, Burns: Take these three men and a dozen others to the college grounds."

"Where, sir?"

"The hospital. We just passed it. Where the crowd is gathered behind the wall."

"Right, sir."

"If you need more men, send word. At the moment, this is all I can spare."

The soldier saluted his lieutenant and immediately named the dozen who would follow him. Baird trotted his horse up to the leader and said, "Sergeant, me and my boys will take the building at the east end. We just come from there."

Turner leaned toward McCallum and said, "His *boys*. Hell with him. We'll see what his boys got in store for him tonight."

"Yeah," said McCallum.

The other sergeant nodded at Baird, who then waved McCallum and Turner forward. Just as the two privates suspected, Baird veered away from the college the moment they were out of sight of the others. They rode again along Richardson Street. Baird stopped his horse and turned to the men. "I got to carry a message to the general. You boys wait here till I get back. We gone make sport tonight." He galloped away.

"Wonder if General Howard will try to catch him in his lie," Turner said.

"General'll be glad to be rid of him," said McCallum. "He don't hold truck with Baird no more than the rest of us do. What's that son-of-a-bitch ever done for us?"

"Not a damn thing."

The men began to discuss the particulars of their plot.

Baird soon returned, all smiles and self-praise. "That one-armed coot's dumber than a mule. We finish this war, me and him's gone have it out once and for all."

Turner said, "I don't believe I'd take it on with the general. I've seen that man do more with one arm than most men can do with two and a little bit of help."

"You shut your mouth," Baird said. "You'll talk when you're spoke to."

"Sure, sergeant. I just figured you to be speaking to the two of us direct, you see. But I misfigured. You must have took a notion somebody else was listening."

Baird's face was a jigsaw of confusion. He looked askance at Turner, muttered something indecipherable, then spurred his horse, and said, "Come on, you loggerheads. I seen some enticements yonder way a while back."

They rode several blocks. McCallum and Turner had guessed right: The sergeant was headed toward the brothel district down by the river. But surely no one was there now. The whole area had been set afire hours ago when the Union army crossed the Congaree and began their trek toward the capitol.

They were wrong. Shanties were no more than piles of cinder by now, but many people who earlier had run from the fires now sat near ash heaps clinging to what few possessions they had. Men and women passed bottles of liquor back and forth. A few smut-faced children sat in the laps of whores whose painted faces looked ghoulish against the low light of still-burning timbers.

Baird dismounted and joined a group of five portly women and two wizened men. He intercepted the pass of a bottle, took a deep drink, and sent it along. When the bottle made its second pass around the circle, he drank deeper, draining the contents, and then cursed the depletion.

"No cause for worry," said one of the old men. He pulled from his coat another bottle. "Plenty more where that'n come from."

McCallum and Turner sat away from the group, eyeing the sergeant, and whispering to each other. Within the hour, they had pulled three large women aside and passed some of their McCord treasure into their hands. The women laughed. One of them pulled at Turner's belt between swigs on a bottle. After a few moments of consultation, the five of them came to an agreement. The women moved toward the river and soon disappeared in the darkness.

By the time the group had finished the second bottle, McCallum muttered to Turner, "I'd say he's had enough. What you think?"

"He's ripe."

McCallum stood, walked over to where the sergeant sat, knelt, and said something to him. The sergeant's head jerked. He peered into the darkness downriver. "Where?" he mumbled.

McCallum waved toward the river.

"How many?" Baird asked.

"It was three of them. They made eyes at me and Turner for near 'bout an hour. Tried to get your attention, too, but you was too busy."

"Jesus Christ, what we waiting for? Mount up." The sergeant struggled to his feet with some assistance from McCallum and lurched toward his horse. He missed the stirrup on the first go. McCallum helped him place his foot and hoisted him into the saddle. By that time, Turner had untied the other two horses. He handed the reins of one to his accomplice. The three men moved toward the river, following the path traced earlier by the women.

Conversation was sporadic in the camp. When it came, it came in spurts of invective, incoherent mumblings, whimpering curses. A sharp cry carried over the water from downstream. A man sitting perilously close to a smoldering timber jerked his head upward and squinted at the stars. "Sounds like Betsy got hold of some man, made him happy. Cain't no woman do it better than her."

"No, sir," said another. "That wasn't none of Betsy's doing. That was the sound of a pig squealing."

"What?"

"Gutted."

The man dropped his head again, and gave himself to the darkness.

| 54 |
Revelation

Dreams reveal nothing to a man that he does not already know. Joseph was so convinced of this truth that he often repeated it to wounded soldiers who spent restless nights in the grip of nightmares: enemies running them through with swords; limbs hacked away piece by piece; eyes gouged out by bayonets; entrails slipping through their blood-soaked fingers as they tried to stuff the viscera back through gaping flesh.

You have seen all this, Joseph would tell them. You know what sword, knife, bayonet, and bullet do to the body. Dreams do not foretell the day and time of your death. They merely reinforce what you know to be true: that death is the end of war.

So he told himself of his own intermittent dreams throughout the long hours of Saturday, February 18th, and the following morning. He had visions of human flesh burning, of a black woman being raped by white men, of drunk men cursing and fighting in the streets of the city, of the leather tassels of a bull whip clawing the skin from a man's back. He saw soldiers enter homes and steal food, clothing, guns, watches, silver, jewelry, wine, liquor. Any man or woman who dared interfere was threatened at gunpoint, beaten, struck with any hard implement the assailant could put his hands on.

He saw trees bend like twigs under powerful winds. Fire danced along treetops, leapt from one to another like gruesome sprites. Bodies burnt beyond recognition were pulled from the debris of homes and stores and government buildings.

Yes, he told himself, all of this I have seen. Dreams the reenactments of what has occurred.

But he heard, also, as people filtered in and out of the room throughout the late night and early morning. Somewhere between sleep and waking, he felt the voices waft over him like a gentle breeze. Words mumbled, at first disjointed, soon cohered, created images of all that was reported: Union soldiers carving their names and those of their companies and regiments on city landmarks; a soldier walking out of the old state house building with the clock, thermometer, and state surveying instruments; flames arcing more than a hundred feet in the sky and falling to earth to form cords of fire that moved like primeval creatures from street to street. He had seen enough to know that the reports, visions, dreams—whatever they were, however they came to him—were true. Nothing revealed that he did not already know.

And above every mumbled word, every disjointed utterance, a voice, low and soft, repeating into his ear a mantra: "You're going to be fine, Joseph. You're going to be fine. I will take care of you. I won't let go of you." The voice was disembodied but no less real to him. He was certain he could not have imagined it, could not have dreamed the countless repetitions of that gentle insistence that he survive, endure, go on. He knew, too, that the impulse of that demand to live was love. Love of him. And like a voice divine, it renewed his spirit. He did want to live, and he welcomed the desire after having been ready only two days earlier to die.

Perhaps, he thought, I am a fool to allow myself to hope again.

No matter, he resolved. Love makes fools of us all.

So he allowed himself to hope that the source of that disembodied voice was Louisa. Who else but she would have attended him through the night? Who but she would have sat by his bed, prayed over him, promised not to let him go?

He was bothered, nonetheless, by his inability to attach her person to the voice. Disembodied though it was, the voice gave shape to a woman, and though her face and neck and shoulders and chest and limbs were hidden, as though behind a veil, the shape was distinct and lovely. He berated himself for his lack of ardor when he whispered Louisa's name. There was a time not distant when the very thought of her name was intoxicating. Must be my condition, he thought. So weak. Addled. Still, mustn't lose hope. When I see her, my strength will be renewed.

He was disappointed by his apathy when less than an hour later, Louisa entered his room. He willed himself to remember the hope inspired by his dream, the power infused in his veins when the voice spoke. He would force himself to speak candidly to her. Surely then the strength of his conviction would return.

Seeing that he was awake, she smiled. "Feeling better, I trust," she said, and moved closer to his bed.

"Much better, thanks to you." He lifted the hand nearest to her, waited for her to grab it. She seemed puzzled, so disturbed by his movement that she took a step back. He lowered his hand.

"You have had excellent care, Mr. Crawford. I can attest to that." No gentleness in her voice now. In the few moments in his room, her demeanor changed from that of a caring friend to that of a hospital administrator. He was not the only one in need of attention. There were others—many others—as needy and deserving.

Two days ago, her manner would have disheartened him. Now, given all he had seen of the city's ruin and the waste of life, he could not muster the energy to give a care to her demeanor. He had resolved to make and to seek full disclosure and he'd best get to it. He struggled to sit up in bed. She watched him warily. He breathed deeply, tried to exhale the pain caused by movement. Then he gazed intently at her and spoke: "Louisa, I have reason to believe you spoke freely to me last night. I was in and out of dreams, to be sure, but the voice I heard was not that of a dream. The words were too distinct, too forceful." His forthrightness and the deep timbre of his voice made him bold: "It is time for us to stop these silly games, this annoying miscommunication that has stifled us. I have tried time and again to make obvious my affection for you. Apparently, I have failed. Now I shall be clear: I love you. You have been through these difficult months a faithful friend and confidante. I daresay that the good we have accomplished here together, neither of us could have done alone. We make a good team. If you will have me, Louisa McCord, I will be a good husband to you. I will treat your daughters as though they were my own. I ask you now to give serious consideration to this proposal."

No sooner had he made his declaration than he cursed himself silently for his indifference. *Goddamn this epilepsy. It takes everything, even emotion. It has made me less than a man.*

He shook his head as if to dislodge these impotent thoughts. Joseph couldn't judge now which emotion held greater sway over him: relief or exhaustion. Certainly the dream had encouraged him, but more than the substance of a dream had inspired him to speak. He had been clear in his declaration, revealing both his intent and his vulnerability, and though his heart was for the moment cold, the disclosure felt good.

Dizzy from the rush of his speech, he did not notice immediately its effect on Louisa. The sway of her body brought him out of his reverie. She reached for his bedside chair. Her knuckles turned white as she steeled her grip.

Joseph said, "Sit."

She did, and then folded her hands in her lap and looked beyond the bed to the window hazed with smoke. Joseph waited. Several moments passed. When Louisa lowered her head and looked at her open palms as if they held the contents of a mystery that only a sorceress could read, Joseph almost told her that he understood and that there was no need for words. But he decided against it. He had been honest with her. He deserved as much in return.

"I am flattered by your proposal, sir." She spoke slowly and with effort, as though each word were a stone she struggled to extract from the earth.

"And I do admire you. What you have done for these soldiers, for this staff, these doctors . . . I do not know another man who could have done so much or so well. But the chasm between admiration and love is vast. Vast indeed. I cannot—" she shook her head wearily—"I cannot accept your proposal, Mr. Crawford. I am sorry, I cannot."

She raised her head. Joseph saw in her eyes an unfathomable emptiness— a void, he decided—that moved him to neither remorse nor pity. He had spent too much of both emotions on this woman. Although still attractive, she looked beleaguered, almost haggard. Joseph recalled what Thompson had said days earlier: that Louisa was in equal measure wife and widow to the Confederacy. The old doctor was right. Joseph saw now that he had no future with her. She was married to a past that was dead. Her husband's name, like that of the Confederacy, would go with her to the grave. He knew in that moment that those who longed for the past were doomed to inherit misery, to become ghosts haunting the world with ragged cries against all the cruelties that stole their happiness and good fortune. The death of the Confederacy would fill more graves than the war itself.

She stood and forced a weak smile through pursed lips. He nodded, un-sure whether she would receive the gesture as a sign of forgiveness, affirma-tion, regret, or farewell. Nor could he read her expression as she returned the nod and left the room.

He lay in bed for the next hour or so wondering why he felt relieved rather than sad. Was he too exhausted to bear the weight of gloom? Would he suffer the pangs of rejection when he regained his strength, when his body was better equipped to endure emotional upheaval? Or had the disem-bodied voice of his dream yet retained something—a quality, a substance, a vitality—that Louisa's living voice had not eclipsed? It was as if the words of the dream rang with more vibrancy in spite of her inability to speak them in his waking presence. They were not her words. They did not belong to her, yet they still lived in him. He heard the measure of their cadence. He felt, like a breeze blowing over his body, the breath that animated their utterance, and they gave him comfort.

He went to sleep in search once more of the dream.

| 55 |

Rapprochement

Two hours later Joseph awoke and adjusted his eyes to a face he had not seen in weeks. There was no mistaking the ponderous jaw, dark eyes, mat of black hair. Joseph offered his hand. Matthew LaBorde wrapped a firm grip around it.

"You have passed a rough night, Mr. Crawford. I am glad to see you on the mend."

"How is it out there?" Joseph turned his head toward the window.

"A poor sight. The college, at least, has been spared. The city is laid waste."

"What of those who left the hospital? Have they returned?"

LaBorde frowned. "Nineteen men died last night from exposure to the cold. They were too weak to move. I am sorry, Mr. Crawford. We did all we could."

"How are the staff holding up?"

"As well as can be expected. Exhausted, to be sure. Too little sleep, too many duties to attend to."

Joseph was almost grateful for his ailment; at least it masked a more injurious truth. He was in league with a runaway slave who had spent the night slitting the throats of white men. How many, Joseph could not guess. But the number did not matter. What mattered was that Joseph had made a decision: Nothing would compel him to report Jeremiah to the proper authorities. *I am no better than an accomplice to murder,* he told himself. Even worse, he was pleased to know that by now, Robert Towns would be dead. And worst of all—insofar as the notion caused him shame and discomfort that he was sure would last the rest of his life—he had, by some awful calculation that argued against every parcel of religious and moral instruction he had ever received, justified to his own flawed reckoning Jeremiah's vengeful acts.

A man can bear only so much shame, he thought. One more ounce of it would crush him. He had failed himself, his people, his heritage. As he looked up at LaBorde, he thought, *I have failed you, professor, and all of our kind.*

"Mrs. McCord has the staff in order now," said LaBorde. "She is back and forth between the hospital and her home."

"Is she all right? And her daughters?"

"They are fine. I have spoken with them. Hannah assures me that General Howard has treated them with utmost respect."

"I would be surprised to hear such a kind word from her mother."

LaBorde nodded. "Her view is different from her daughter's. She does report—with some sense of vindication, I might add—the apparent ruin of one of the occupiers. A Sergeant Baird, if I recall. General Howard sent them to the college last night to help secure the area. The sergeant neglected his duties, however, and encouraged the privates to do the same. They followed him to the river in search of unsavory activity. Once there, the young men repented their foolishness and returned to the college. The sergeant's body was found on the bank of the river this morning. The soldiers report that he was waving his pistol and threatening men and women alike when they left him."

"I have known the type," Joseph said. "Men for whom war is recreation. They cannot get enough violence on the battlefield, so they seek it elsewhere."

"Hannah says the general is relieved to be rid of the fellow."

Joseph kneaded the back of his neck. He ached all over, but he'd known worse. He recalled other fits that left him dumb with pain and nausea for two or three days. Once, in the grip of seizure on the battlefield, he'd nearly bitten off his tongue, and might have had a soldier not pressed a piece of bark into his mouth.

"I hope you will recover quickly," said LaBorde. "The hospital needs you."

Joseph might have recoiled at the insinuation that his illness imposed a burden on others, but he could see in LaBorde's expression that he intended no insult. The man wanted to make amends, to settle differences that neither of them fully understood. Why, after all, should brothers of the Confederacy be at odds? If there was to be any accord, any unity of spirit among men of the South, it must hold together now. Joseph understood that LaBorde wanted as much. What the professor could not possibly comprehend was that Joseph could resolve to lie, deceive, do whatever he must to guard a black renegade's secret, and that such a decision negated forever the possibility of an honest union with his own people.

Joseph said, "I seem to remember that Dr. Thompson was here last night. Am I right?"

"You are, sir. We could not keep him in bed. I am afraid our excellent doctor is not a good patient. He insisted early this morning on attending to his duties. Mrs. McCord says it is obvious he's in pain when he looks contemptuously at his bandaged arm, as if to accuse the appendage of insubordination."

"That is like him," said Joseph. "Do you know what he is doing at the moment?"

"Preparing for a meeting with General Sherman. Mayor Goodwyn came by this morning to tell Dr. Thompson that, if he is able, his presence in a delegation of town leaders would be most welcome."

"Death would not keep him from such a meeting," said Joseph. "Where is Sherman?"

"In the Simons's home."

"What is happening in the city?"

"The morning has been quiet. Who knows what the rest of today holds?"

"Sherman has the city," said Joseph. "What more does he want?"

LaBorde looked out the window. "Revenge. Perhaps he wants to send a message to Jefferson Davis. What better place to send it from than the cradle of secession?"

"What word do you hear of Sherman's treatment of citizens?"

LaBorde frowned. "Sherman himself seems to wish no further ill on the people than the burning of their homes. Some of his soldiers, however, are bent on revenge. I spoke with Reverend Shand this morning. He told me that five Union soldiers took the sacred vessels of Trinity from him last night at gunpoint. When the reverend pleaded with them, one of them cursed him and swore to burn the church and the whole city to the ground. Mrs. Bryce led a group of women to a conference with the general this morning. She begged for guards for their homes. Sherman asked for the whereabouts of the women's husbands and sons. 'Why are they not here to protect you?' he asked. If Mrs. Bryce responded, I do not know what she said."

"I saw Mrs. Bryce and Mrs. Palmer several days ago. They were forcing their husbands to leave town."

"Yes," said LaBorde. "I think the women were wise to send their husbands away."

"How many others have had audience with Sherman?"

"I do not know. All I can tell you is that those who have spoken with him have been disheartened. Reverend Porter went to him early this morning and asked that the college library be spared."

"Reverend Porter? I should think William Rivers would speak for the library."

"He is gone. He and his family left yesterday."

"How did Sherman respond to the request?" Joseph asked.

"The reverend said that Sherman sneered and said that if he could, he would send more books to the South. He repudiates our cause by saying we are ignorant, and that if there had been a few more books in this part of the world, there would not have been all this difficulty.'"

The men said nothing for a few moments. Between them settled the stillness that comes with acknowledgment of defeat, an understanding of the futility of having fought so desperately to uphold what the will of heaven seemed ready to crush. All the prayers of the pious in all the holy places of the South had not moved God to defend them. The inscrutable ways of Providence had allowed the destruction of their land, their homes, their institutions, their army—in short, all that they held sacred. All that they revered. All that they consecrated to the name and glory of God.

Joseph looked up. The professor's eyes were closed and he swayed on his feet. How long since he slept? Joseph wondered. How long before he would collapse? Joseph cleared his throat. "Dr. LaBorde."

LaBorde's head jerked. He opened his glazed eyes and struggled to bring Joseph into focus.

"You are exhausted," said Joseph. "You must rest."

"No more than any other person in the city. I fear that if any of us should lie down, we might awaken to flames all around us."

Joseph offered his hand to LaBorde and the men shook and held each other's gaze in such a way as to affirm whatever tenuous connection might bind men together in time of loss.

| 56 |
Beneath the Light of the Moon

Late Sunday afternoon, Joseph stood, gripped the bedpost, and judged the distance between the bed and the chair over which his clothes were draped. If this day should be his last, he would not be lying down when the end came.

"Mr. Crawford, you should not be on your feet."

He looked up and saw Meredith Simpson in the doorway holding a tray of surgical tools.

"I have to get out of here. What's going on in the city?"

"Sir, you need rest."

"Your concern is appreciated, Miss Simpson." He looked at her. Despite the fatigue evident on her drawn face, she was still beautiful. He regretted having insinuated to Louisa that the soldiers' lewd talk might have been provoked by this woman. "You are a fine nurse, Miss Simpson. The hospital has profited greatly by your services."

"Thank you, Mr. Crawford. But really, you should be mindful of your health. You had a hard fall."

"I understand that Dr. Thompson put up similar resistance."

"There is a great difference between a broken arm and what you suffered."

"Please," he said, and reached out an arm. "Help me to the chair. I wish to dress myself and move about."

"I object to this, Mr. Crawford. Will you at least allow me to get a cane for you?"

"Yes. And I promise to use it. Thank you."

She helped him to the chair, then stepped out of the room, and closed the door. Joseph dressed slowly, each movement requiring deliberation. His joints ached. His head felt swollen. He hated to see himself in a mirror, but wanted to make certain his features were not as distorted as he imagined. He did not trust himself, however, to rise from the chair without assistance.

"I am dressed," he said when he heard a rap on the door.

Meredith Simpson entered with the cane. "I still object. There is no reason for you to be out of bed now. Rest is what you need. Rest, and nothing more."

Had her concern not been so alluring, he might have been annoyed. "Meredith Simpson, I have not been so mothered since I was a child. I believe you intend to spoil me."

"I intend to see you come to your senses, sir."

"Ah, first you mother me, then you address me as *sir*. I think I'm being insulted."

"Oh, no, I—" She stopped talking the moment she looked at him and saw that he was teasing her. Her eyes softened, and this time she spoke with no alarm in her voice: "Well, if a man does not have the good sense to see to his health, perhaps he needs mothering."

He laughed, gripped the armrests, and leaned forward: "If you do not help me out of this chair, I may topple and hit the floor face first."

She stepped toward him. "I will help you. I won't let go of you."

The words jolted him. He looked up at her. With her help, he stood. He was dizzy at first. It took him a few moments to feel settled. He got a good grip on the cane, released her hand, and shuffled toward the door. There, he looked over his shoulder at her and said, "I do not know how to thank you for the care you have given me, Meredith. I am a fortunate man to have such an excellent nurse."

She smiled, and with a finger brushed a lock of hair behind her ear.

He admired her beauty for a moment, then shook his head and told himself he was a fool. He'd been a fool earlier in the day when he proposed to Louisa, and now he was on the verge of proving himself a greater one. How could a man who has been reserved all his life, he asked himself, turn profligate with his affection in an afternoon? There was no making sense of the matter. Perhaps the fall had done his head greater injury than he imagined. The difference in their ages alone was enough to create scandal. He guessed eighteen or twenty years. Best to leave and go about your business, old man, he thought.

Against the better grain of judgment, he thought again. *I know those words. As surely as I live and breathe, I heard them last night again and again, and I hear them in her speaking. The gentle insistence. The plea. The cadence. The breath. Embodiment of the voice.*

He told himself to forget caution. What good had it ever done him? He could as easily die on the spot as take his next breath, and what would he have to show for his life? He cocked his head to one side, and said, "Meredith

Simpson, if I were not so old and you not so young, I would make a nuisance of myself calling on you."

She blushed but held his gaze. "You are not so old as you claim, nor I so young as you appraise me. I'm not sure what is worse: exaggerated humility or false flattery."

"False flattery?" His eyes flared. "There is neither flattery nor falsehood in what I said. You are barely out of your teens. Twenty-two at the most."

She suppressed a smile by clenching her jaw. She put one hand on her hip and raised the other and pointed toward the ceiling with her index finger.

He turned fully toward her and shook his head. "Now who is being false?" She punched the finger upward. He whispered, "Twenty-five?" She continued to point. He laughed and said, "Oh, come on, we have twenty years between us if a day." He mocked her by imitating her stance and waving a finger at her. "You would do well to respect your elders, young lady. At least be honest with them."

"Gladly, if only my elders learned to speak more wisely. The one who addresses me presently has little wisdom and less self-understanding."

"Really? And on what preposterous grounds do you base such a judgment?"

"Why, on the grounds of your claiming what you would make of yourself. The claim is senseless, impossible, and without any evidence that proof requires."

Now Joseph was puzzled. He couldn't recall making any claim, other than that he was older than she. He grinned and shrugged. "I'm sorry. I don't know what claim you're referring to. Did I make one?" He held his hands in a questioning posture.

"You did," she said, and took a step toward him. He scratched his head trying to remember everything he'd said. "That outrageous claim," she continued as she advanced another step, "of making a nuisance of yourself by calling on me. Impossible, Joseph Crawford. Impossible. And, if I may be so bold, rude of you to suggest it."

They reached for each other, gave themselves fully to the ecstasy of the embrace. Two bodies cleaving together out of need, want, longing, despair, suffering, the hardship of war and death and loss and loving and hating and praying against belief for an end that would justify the agony of all they had endured. When he moved his hand to her face and bent to kiss her, he saw all of that in her eyes and, shimmering through their wetness, the hope and promise of daring to live together in a new world that was coming to be.

He placed his hands on her shoulders and they faced each other. "I must go to see Dr. Thompson now, Meredith."

"Now? Joseph, you cannot walk all the way to College Hall. You are hardly out of bed."

"Oh, I can walk now. On the wings of angels, I can do more than walk. Besides, shouldn't he be the first one we tell?" Before she could respond, he was out the door.

Joseph negotiated the stairs carefully, then rested at the bottom a few moments before stepping outside. The slant of evening sunlight hurt his eyes. He'd grown accustomed over the past two months to dark skies and rain.

As he hobbled toward the gate, he nearly castigated himself for his glee. How could he feel so giddy as he traversed the college green where only two nights earlier lay the bodies of dead soldiers entrusted to his care? How long had it taken to remove them? The place was now a ghost land. Smoke drifted upward from trees and the roofs of buildings.

At the gate he stopped and looked toward the capitol. How great was the destruction there?

He shuffled toward College Hall. Twice he had to stop and lean against a tree. When finally he arrived at the building, he had to rest before he climbed the stairs to the second floor, and then again at the top he rested. He knocked on Thompson's door, heard the command to enter, and did so.

Across the room Thompson stood at the window. A white wrap held the broken arm in place. He did not turn to see who had entered, but asked, "How long has it been since we have seen clear skies?"

"Two months. Perhaps longer. It seems years."

Thompson turned. "Joseph! What are you doing out of bed?"

"I could not rest."

Thompson nodded. "Nor could I. I was up before dawn yesterday. I stood by your bedside and prayed for your recovery." Thompson paused, cleared his throat. "I have not been given much to prayer these last few months. I say that with shame. I was a pious man in my youth, Joseph. Would it surprise you to learn that I once gave thought to the study of divinity?"

Joseph hesitated. "I suppose it should not," he said.

"But it does."

"Yes, sir."

Thompson turned again toward the window and looked somberly at the burned landscape. "I wanted to help people, to do what little I could to relieve others of pain and sorrow. I realize now it was because I'd known so much of both in my youth. I was eight when my mother died two months after giving birth. The child died also. Her name was Esther. My parents chose it early on. A good biblical name, they said. My two younger brothers and I would call her name at the dinner table even before she was born. My father sought God's blessing on Esther and on all his children every time he prayed at table. I remember whispering her name at night. I had long wanted a little sister. My brothers and I fought, as brothers do. I imagined that my sister and I would not. I would be her caretaker. I had a boy's wild fancy of being his sister's hero." He shook his head and chuckled derisively under his breath.

"I had the same fancy about my daughter," said Joseph. "I hoped that she would see her father as a great man."

Thompson turned and looked at Joseph. "I'm sure she did."

Joseph shrugged, swiped the back of his hand across his mouth.

Thompson turned back to the window and mumbled, "Oh, ye hypocrites, ye can discern the face of the sky; but can ye not discern the signs of the times?"

"Sir?"

"From Matthew's gospel, Joseph. The scribes and Pharisees ask Jesus for a sign from heaven that will reveal his authority. He condemns them for their blindness."

"Oh, yes."

"And what of this generation?" asked Thompson. "Does it not seem curious that in the last two days we have had, with the exception of high winds, temperate weather? It's as if heaven is smiling on Sherman's advance."

"Is this how you discern the face of the sky?" asked Joseph.

Thompson stepped away from the window and sat in his chair. He rubbed his chin contemplatively. "I said that in my youth I was a pious man. I have lost much of that in the past forty years. Disease, war, and death offer a stern challenge to a man's faith."

"Do you no longer believe?"

"No, I believe. But do I believe as I once did? That God determines every action of man? That there is a divinity that shapes not only our ends, but every human event from the dawn of history to the apocalypse? That God takes a child's life because doing so suits some grand purpose, or one soldier rather than another on the field of battle for the same reason, or one part of a country rather than another because the one is more faithful to God than the other? No. That I do not believe."

"Then what, sir? If I may be so bold, what do you believe?"

"Don't you see, Joseph, that precision is the problem? The older I get, the more certain I am of what I do not believe, the less about what I do."

"Do you see the hand of God in this war?"

"I see the stubbornness and blindness of men in this war. Our theology is informed by our desires, not vice-versa. If we decide to fight for land and money and a way of life, then we implore the Almighty to sanctify our decision. Soon enough we begin to say that God has called us to a defense of what we have chosen. If we hold to that line of reasoning, and if we are honest, then we must admit that our defeat is the surest sign of God's judgment on what we have chosen. But can you imagine the Reverends Shand or Palmer or Martin or any of their congregants admitting that their view of God's blessing of the Confederacy was wrong? That they had misunderstood God, or misread Scripture? We are more likely to see them engaged in theological trickery that prophesies our eventual holy triumph and the consequent destruction of the godless North."

"So our theology is little more than tricks and games."

"Well," said Thompson, "that is the view of an old man who has seen too much death. Perhaps I am a dotard, too foolish to be listened to."

"Yours is the only reasonable voice I have heard on the matter," said Joseph.

"Reasonable? I suspect that many would charge me with heresy."

Joseph waited a few moments, then asked, "What have you learned this morning about the fate of the city?"

Thompson's brow furrowed. "Mayor Goodwyn was kind enough to invite me to go with him and several others to meet with Sherman. The general received us kindly, then proceeded to ridicule us."

"How so?"

"He told us we ought to be in church on a Sunday. 'Do not you good Southerners fear the Lord?' he asked, looking directly at Reverend Shand."

"'Our churches have been burned and vandalized,' said the reverend. 'And our people have fled.' Then Sherman turned serious. He told us we had only ourselves to blame for what has happened. We were foolish to have fought against the nation, he said. He railed against the evils of plantation slavery, yet said he himself favored domestic help. I could sense that some in our group wanted to argue that we treat our slaves better than Northerners treat their domestic workers, but they held their tongues."

"What did he say about burning the city?"

"He blamed that on us as well, saying there was too much liquor in our town, and we alone bore the responsibility for the destruction that ensued when his soldiers began to consume. He even accused our citizens of distributing the liquor to his soldiers."

"Good God," said Joseph. "What a preposterous charge."

"What charge in war is not?" asked Thompson.

"So the delegation received no concessions?"

"Some. Sherman agreed to leave five hundred cattle, medicine, arms and ammunition, wire for a ferry across the Congaree. He then sent Mayor Goodwyn to General Howard for the securing of provisions, and assured him that Howard would treat him better than Beauregard, Hampton, or any other Confederate general would. He had no kind word for any of our generals, including Lee. Beauregard received the harshest criticism. Sherman said his poor maneuvering left the state defenseless."

Joseph massaged the ache in his neck. "I have long grown weary of this war. I am relieved to see it coming to an end."

"I, too." Thompson drummed his fingers on the desk. Consternation shone through pursed lips and fretted brow. "What will you do, Joseph, when the war is over?"

"Is it not already?"

"There will be more fighting. We may receive more transfers in the coming weeks. We still have work to do. But you—" Thompson paused.

Joseph leaned forward, interlaced his fingers. "I don't know. I've no home to return to. Nothing I can call home, that is." He wanted to speak of Meredith, to tell his friend of his joy, but now questioned himself. Would Thompson think him as flippant as a schoolboy whose delirium over the attention of one girl enabled him to forget his devotion to another without hesitation?

"There is a place for you here."

"In this hospital? These halls will soon enough be empty of soldiers."

"I do not mean the hospital. The college. I have spoken to Professor LaBorde. He is quite impressed with you."

Joseph recalled the number of times he had silently reviled LaBorde for the man's aggravated concern for the college to the neglect, Joseph thought, of the hospital's soldiers and staff. He had been wrong. His conversation with LaBorde earlier in the month, as they passed from the college green to College Hall, had forced him to see the professor in a new light. Even so, LaBorde had sensed Joseph's ill feelings. He would have had to, Joseph told himself. How many times had he scowled at LaBorde, refused to offer a kind word when he had the chance? Yet LaBorde saw something good in him. Hard to believe, as the last few days had rendered Joseph incapable of seeing much good in himself.

"I have no credentials that would allow me to teach," said Joseph.

"The college needs more than teachers. You are an exceptional administrator. You are good with figures, with budgeting, with supervision of the staff. You have much to offer the college."

"I am flattered, both by LaBorde's estimation of me and by your endorsement."

"You seem hesitant. Are you sick of this place?"

"It's not that. I am rather overwhelmed. I've never considered myself worthy of a position at a college."

"I would ask you to give it serious consideration. You would be a great asset to this place. And not only to the college, but to the city itself. We will have much to do in the months and years ahead. Who knows whether we can rebuild this place after so much destruction?"

"I will consider it," said Joseph. "I will talk to Professor LaBorde to understand what role he wishes me to play at the college."

"Can you stay in Columbia, knowing what the immediate future holds?"

Joseph understood that he was talking about Louisa. He was more nervous than he had been when he entered.

Thompson said, "I have been so bold as to intrude on your personal affairs once, Joseph. I apologize."

"No, sir. You were right on two counts. Right in your assessment of the matter, and right to have offered sound advice. I am grateful."

"Perhaps you will forgive me, then, for intruding again." His right eyebrow arched.

"Sir?"

"I believe I am not the only person in this city who hopes you will stay. There are others. I have spoken to them. One in particular has a special interest in your remaining. Perhaps you know of whom I speak."

Joseph feigned ignorance.

Thompson said, "Meredith Simpson. She is a lovely woman, Joseph. Kind and smart. I have never seen a woman more solicitous of a man's well-being than she was of yours after your fall."

Joseph pulled a hand to his mouth to cover his grin. He gathered himself and nodded. "You do not have to plead her case. I am flattered, believe me. She is, as you say, beautiful and kind and smart. But she is also quite young. I would guess the difference between our ages to be twenty years or more."

"You have guessed wrong. She will be thirty in four months."

"Impossible." Although Meredith had challenged his reckoning of her age, he still could not believe what he was hearing.

"The more accurate term is *improbable*. I know she does not look her age, but I am not deceiving you."

Joseph could no longer suppress a smile. He chuckled and scratched his head. "How is it you know so much about Meredith Simpson? Surely you did not ask her how old she is."

"She volunteered the information. And since we are disclosing everything, I might as well tell you that the subject of her age was in reference to our discussion about you."

"About me? Of what interest could I—"

"Open your eyes, young man! Must I spell it out for you?"

Joseph laughed. He felt silly. "Dr. Thompson, you are a matchmaker. And all this time I mistook you for a surgeon. Your truest skill is not with surgical tools, but with Cupid's arrow."

Thompson smiled, looked Joseph in the eye, and said earnestly, "One may be as good as the other, Joseph. You must know that Meredith Simpson has a child. Not her own. The boy is her nephew. He is twelve years old. She took him in when his father died. I like the boy. He loves his aunt, and she him. You would make him a fine father." He paused, then continued: "I want you to stay, son. And I want you to be happy."

Joseph turned his gaze downward. He felt like a mischievous son playing a joke on his father. He could not control the shaking of his shoulders.

"I did not mean to upset you, Joseph. Once more, I have overstepped the bounds of decency."

Joseph shook his head vehemently. When he looked up, he could hardly see his friend for his clouded vision. "I have come to tell you," he said in a tremulous voice. "To tell you of my good news. Meredith Simpson and I have spoken. We have an understanding, and it is most agreeable."

Thompson's eyes flared. He came around the desk and with his good arm grabbed Joseph's shoulder and shook him gently. "You have played me, son. Played me to the hilt. Swear that you are not teasing me."

His excitement made Joseph shaky. He placed a hand on Thompson's arms and lowered himself to the chair in front of the desk. It took him a few minutes to tell his friend of the encounters he'd had with both women. To his own ears, his attempt to explain his relief at Louisa's rejection sounded lame, a childish boast to say he did not care that he had been rejected. But if his own words were not convincing, Thompson assured him: "I knew she was not the woman for you. Did I not tell you? Did I not? But Meredith Simpson. Now there is the woman for you, young man. The very one, I tell you."

The men laughed together. Thompson's delight was as real to Joseph as his own, a blessing he cherished.

They regained their composure after a while. Thompson leaned against his desk and spoke in a steady voice: "And now, to a matter of more pressing concern."

Joseph looked up.

"You need rest."

"As do you, sir." Joseph nodded toward the broken arm. "You'll be performing no surgery for a while."

"That is true. But I can direct others to that task. You, meanwhile, are to return to the room you left." Thompson scribbled a note on a pad, tore off the sheet of paper, and handed it to Joseph. "This is to go immediately to Miss Simpson. It provides instruction for your care for the next three days."

"I do not need—"

"This is not a request, Joseph. It is an order. Shall I accompany you back to Rutledge?"

Joseph saw that objection was futile. He shook his head. "I wish to be alone for a few minutes."

"I have your word that you will return at once to Rutledge?"

"You have my word."

Joseph left the office and made his way slowly down the stairs. Outside, the sky was ablaze with the red glow of the sun's descent. He watched it sink beneath the rim of the world, and marveled at the calm majesty of nature, oblivious to human designs of war and pillage.

It took him nearly half an hour to make the trek to Rutledge, and then he was exhausted. The college green was empty. Heat from the fires and three successive days of temperate weather had left the ground dry, if barren of grass. Joseph sat at the base of a large elm and nestled his back against the trunk. He thought of Meredith. And of her nephew. Would the boy welcome Joseph into their lives, or resent him? Could Meredith really love him? Had Thompson exaggerated her regard for him? Was she merely desperate for a man, any man? Had Joseph himself exaggerated the care in the voice he'd heard two nights earlier? But she had spoken. He'd heard her only an hour ago. Her words. Her passion. Could he trust his heart?

He tried to imagine himself as an employee of the college. Would Meredith be content with such a life? She was smart, to be sure, but would she be happy in such a place? Did she love books, ideas, learning? They would have the library at their disposal. Much rebuilding to do there. How many volumes had William Rivers boxed and sent away for safe keeping? Would they be returned? Or had they suffered the fate of Dr. Gibbes's books, maps, illustrations, fossils? The thought of helping to rebuild this place had some appeal. Excitement, even. Was there not some reciprocity between the resurrection of a place of learning and the resurrection of one's life? Was that not the purpose of learning? To better one's worst self? To improve one's mind, one's soul, one's being? Wouldn't that be good for the boy? For her? For all three of them? What better place for them all than the college?

These questions occupied him until he fell into a deep slumber at the base of the tree.

Two hours later, he was awakened by the hoot of an owl. He sat up, stretched his back, and listened to the sounds of the night. He passed the next few minutes in peaceful contemplation until he heard some disturbance at the wall. Movement. Laughter. Surely the soldiers had not returned. Or worse, deserters looking for more loot.

Fifty feet from where he sat, two figures entered the gate. Joseph leaned forward and squinted. The couple moved forward into a sliver of moonlight. Joseph could not make out their faces, but judged by their apparel that they were a man and a woman of indeterminate age. They held hands and appeared, by the movement of their heads, to be whispering to each other. The woman laughed. A strange, high-pitched laugh, not altogether human.

The man raised his arm. Joseph started. *Don't shoot,* he was about to cry. *I'm not armed.* But the man lifted his arm higher, as though tracing the measure of the tree, its height, its width, its grandeur. The movement seemed to Joseph a gesture of adoration.

"Like the one back home," said the woman. A Negro. Joseph was sure of it. The lilt of her voice gave her away.

"We not going home, Rachel," said the man. His head jerked and he dropped his arm.

No, Joseph thought. It can't be. He was not afraid, so much as mesmerized by the man's feral posture. His shoulders sloped downward and his head jutted forward and his knees were bent, as though he was prepared to pounce on some wild prey. And then, with the lupine quickness and ease Joseph had witnessed when the man leapt from the whipping post two nights earlier, he was off, pulling his mate with him through the gate and out into the darkness beyond. Their laughter rumbled like the echo of thunder through the charnels of the smoldering city. Joseph closed his eyes and imagined the two mad creatures on a romp, viewing the desecration as though it were a burnt offering, a sacrifice appointed for their glee.

ABOUT THE AUTHOR

JOHN MARK SIBLEY-JONES teaches English at the South Carolina Governor's School for the Arts and Humanities in Greenville. Prior to moving to Greenville, he taught English literature for fifteen years at the University of South Carolina, where he won several teaching awards, including the Michael A. Hill Outstanding Honors Faculty Award. Sibley-Jones has published more than fifty academic and professional articles and two short stories. He has been a finalist in several national fiction competitions. This is his first novel.